WHIRLWIND

EDGE OF EXTINCTION
BOOK 3

KENNY SOWARD
MIKE KRAUS

WHIRLWIND
Edge of Extinction Series
Book 3

By
Kenny Soward
Mike Kraus

© 2023 Muonic Press Inc
www.muonic.com

---

www.kennysoward.com
kenny@kennysoward.com

---

www.MikeKrausBooks.com
hello@mikeKrausBooks.com
www.facebook.com/MikeKrausBooks

No part of this book may be reproduced in any form, or by any electronic, mechanical or other means, without the permission in writing from the author.

WANT MORE AWESOME BOOKS?

Find more fantastic tales right here, at books.to/readmorepa.

If you're new to reading Mike Kraus, consider visiting his website and signing up for his free newsletter. You'll receive several free books and a sample of his audiobooks, too, just for signing up, you can unsubscribe at any time and you will receive absolutely *no* spam.

You can also stay updated on Kenny Soward's books by visiting his website at kennysoward.com.

SPECIAL THANKS

Special thanks to my awesome beta team, without whom this book wouldn't be nearly as great.

Thank you!

READ THE NEXT BOOK IN THE SERIES

Edge of Extinction Book 4

Available Here

books.to/thcoy

LAST TIME IN EDGE OF EXTINCTION

With the Alaskan Rift pouring hydrocarbons into the air and sending the world into a hyper-inflated global catastrophe, weather patterns worldwide shifted in a dangerous imbalance. Hurricane Jane tore up the East Coast, leaving millions dead and entire cities destroyed and locked in a deep freeze. At a Navajo reservation in Chinle, Arizona, an old man saved his family from sudden flooding in Canyon de Chelly. Outside San Francisco, weather reporter Jennifer Hughes spotted three cyclones coming in from the ocean that devastated several beaches and Camino Del Mar before taking her helicopter down in a deadly crash.

In Washington, DC, the President showed up in front of the Alaskan Rift special committee, dripping with ice and snow after Hurricane Jane had left the city deadlocked. While Craig, Stephanie, and Colonel Davies did everything they could to come up with answers to the rift, they weren't making much headway. FEMA struggled to establish camps in such harsh conditions, and the country's fate hung by a thread.

Taking a leap of faith, Craig suggested they drive to Alaska to discover what was happening, though he had doubts the US military had the equipment to get them there. The President was keen on the idea and assured Craig they had some prototype amphibious armored personnel carriers that could take them. Frightened but eager for answers, Craig volunteered to go and joined a group of Marines who would get him to Fairbanks as soon as possible. Craig and Stephanie, although divorced, had a tender moment before he got in a Humvee and drove away.

Zach Christensen was on his way home after dropping off the survivors of Deadhorse, Alaska. With just a snowmobile and a few supplies, he camped on an Alaskan hillside, sheltering from the firestorms ravaging the sky. While figuring out his next steps, fiery winds and cinders set the surrounding forest on fire, forcing him to take cover beneath his shelter as his provisions and snowmobile slipped down the hill. Although singed, and his vehicle slightly damaged, Zach gathered what supplies he could and drove hard south to flee the severe storms.

He pulled into Wiseman, Alaska to find the town still intact but with workers and citizens looting the stores and homes in the area before packing up trucks and moving south. Stumbling upon an assault in progress in someone's front yard, Zach used his sledgehammer to beat off the attackers and save the homeowner, Gina Morosov. Gina invited Zach inside where she made him food while trading information. Her husband Hank had gone north with the rescue workers, but Zach was sad to report he hadn't seen him. Gina owned the store on the other side of the building, and Zach helped her defend it from looters and dissuade more attackers before settling to sleep. While dreaming on Gina's couch, Zach had a flashback to when he worked for the NYPD. A failed hostage situation led to the deaths of several people, and Zach's guilt over his delayed action haunted him. He started awake, and realized he was at Gina's and needed to get back on the road.

After saying goodbye, Zach drove his snowmobile south with a few supplies, moving fast across the wintry tundra as a firestorm threatened to overrun him. Just before he was caught by the grasping winds, he hunkered down, digging deep into the snow next to some deadfall, chaining it onto his snowmobile and burying himself as the fiery winds melted everything around him and burned parts of his

snowmobile's seat. When he thought he was done for, the storm passed, allowing the dripping water to refreeze as shrieking gales swept in. The warring weather continued chasing him south, where he rescued a man from freezing in a lake after being left by his so-called friends. Zach warmed the man next to a fire and set off again, finally reaching Fairbanks to get the man some medical help. They met groups of soldiers guarding the road, Zach accepting their aid and giving up his beat-up snowmobile and rifle, grateful to have his life.

Fairbanks bustled with activity as military personnel confiscated all the vehicles and forced citizens onto buses to limit traffic and ensure an orderly evacuation. It didn't stop people from trying to escape on their own, including Zach. After grabbing something to eat and speaking to a local man, Zach talked his way out of camp, but was caught by soldiers while stealing a vehicle. They took him to Colonel Red Hawk, who gave him the option to join a special mission north to shut down the source of the hydrocarbon leak. Zach declined before meeting Craig Sutton, who convinced him to go on the condition that Craig would radio Washington to have troops check on Wendy and the kids. After agreeing to go on the mission, Zach was reunited with Grizzly, a former driver for the Russian military, who Red Hawk had recruited to drive one of the ultra-secret P-10 AAVs north to the Alaskan Rift.

When the briefing was over, Zach, Grizzly, Craig, and a contingent of Marines drove north with Craig using advanced navigational equipment called Navpax to help them avoid firestorms on the way. Once they reached the rift, they rendezvoused with their Russian counterparts and met the overbearing Commander Andrei Orlov who was at odds with Colonel Red Hawk right away.

After meeting with the Russian scientist, Liza Kovaleva, the joint US-Russian team drove north in their amphibious vehicles, pushing through battering winds and a frothing sea to reach their destination via a series of ice tunnels formed by the hydrocarbon flood and freezing waters. With tactical gear, the joint teams entered the caves, reached the seafloor where they found the rift, and placed ordnance to blow it up. From the onset, the Russians were up to something, their plans becoming apparent when they killed two Marines and attempted to leave Red Hawk's unit behind. With Zack's help, the Marine contingent survived the attacks and an armored assault. Packed into the three remaining P-10s, they watched from a distance as the Russians blew up the rift in a massive explosion that sent small tidal waves in every direction. When the P-10s reached the command station, they found out Orlov had destroyed it, though several scientists, including Liza, had escaped. She explained that Russia was going through major political strife and Orlov was part of it. With the Alaskan Rift partially shut down, the Marines took the Russian scientists on board and traveled south to get word to Washington.

Back in Stamford, Wendy and the kids emerged from their basement to discover their neighborhood in the Arctic grip. Everything was destroyed, and part of their home hung precariously above them, threatening to fall. Their neighborhood had numerous fires as well as signs of life, yet their first task was to pull down the dangerous second floor. Using ropes, and with help from the Myers, they pulled down the dangerous remnant, leaving a pile of wood to use for campfires. When Sue Myer invited them to a town meeting, Wendy balked but eventually agreed, later explaining to her kids they needed to keep an eye on the neighbors and couldn't seem standoffish. Before going into their basement shelter, Charlie found a freezing dog beneath a porch and persuaded Wendy to adopt him as a guard dog. Though unconvinced a gray Labrador would be ferocious enough to protect them, Wendy allowed it, and Charlie named him Clyde.

At the neighborhood meeting, they ate, and Wendy agreed to go on a mission to the hospital in the southwest part of town. She didn't want to go, however she agreed for the sake of being helpful and scouting for rescue workers in surrounding blocks, hoping to locate anything they could use on the way. Her only caveat was that she leave David and Charlie to protect their supplies.

The following day, they trekked across the ruined city of Stamford where Hurricane Jane had done her worst. Buildings were torn to pieces, rubble and debris everywhere, with survivors huddled around fires and in makeshift hovels. No vehicles would run, and they stumbled upon several frozen bodies on their way through town. At the hospital, a group who'd gotten there first and taken the building over attacked them. Wendy and her neighbors fought back, and Wendy shot a few of them as her friends beat off the rest. Wendy still didn't like two guys in her group, although she'd become close with Fred and Roderigo and was thankful she'd gone to help them. They returned to the neighborhood with supplies, and everyone celebrated their victory. Before Wendy could get too comfortable, she spotted some figures at her house. Sprinting over, she discovered they were the teachers from the school, Mr. Turley, Mrs. Cheney, and the gym instructor, Mr. Lionel. They pressed Wendy to get inside her shelter under the guise of friendship and helping her neighbors, and when she refused, they demanded she give them some supplies. Outnumbered and outgunned, Wendy was still ready to fight when Fred, Roderigo, and the rest of her neighbors intervened and drove off the teachers.

Two days later, the weather broke, and an unseasonable warmth passed over the neighborhood despite the dark skies. The temperatures rose from minus twenty to forty-three degrees, melting the snow and ice and bringing giant mud puddles and water dripping on their heads. Wendy found the neighbors celebrating and throwing their coats into the fire, proclaiming winter was over. Not trusting the sudden weather shift, Wendy kept her jacket on and the heaters ready.

In the meantime, the neighbors wanted Wendy to come with them on another trek through town, hoping the break in the temperature would make a difference and bring out the friendliness in people. Wendy refused to accompany them and stayed home with her kids.

In less than forty-eight hours, the weather changed yet again, refreezing everything in a brutal death grip. Soggy wood and pavement cracked and broke, and Wendy stepped outside to find frozen neighbors who'd given up their coats a few days before. The teachers returned and attacked, pinning Wendy and her kids in their shelter and exchanging gunfire. Wendy used traps in her basement to take out several intruders in brutal fashion, forcing them to back off and

5

give the family some room. Mr. Turley and Coach Lionel tried to burn Wendy and the kids out, though everything was so wet and icy they couldn't get a fire started. Wendy slipped through a side passage and surprised the teachers, shooting a few before she was driven back. Huddled behind a car, she tried drawing the attackers away to give her kids a chance to escape when Zach's father, Morten, and his sister, Alma, arrived with their wagons and guns. Together, they broke up the assault and killed most of the teachers. Abandoning their Stamford home, they left a message for Zach in Dutch, directing him south to another Amish community to seek shelter.

And now, Edge of Extinction, book 3...

CHAPTER ONE

Zach Christensen, Fairbanks, Alaska

The P10 armored amphibious vessel trudged south on Dalton Highway, armor scorched and dented, tearing up ice and snow, the lead vehicle in a three-truck convoy heading toward Fairbanks with the survivors of the Alaskan Rift mission almost home after their harrowing journey. Normally flying along at a maximum speed of forty-three miles per hour, the line periodically stopped and waited as a twisting cyclone of fire and smoke burned a path across the tundra.

Inside the cramped cabin, Zach relaxed and listened to the turbine engine wind up and down depending on the terrain, hearing knocks and pings in the suspension that would require maintenance soon. Thankfully, they were just a few miles outside Fairbanks, barreling by the charred ruins of the towns Fox and Coldstream. No cars or people were on the roads, though his view was obscured inside the AAV with only the external cameras to give them an idea of what was happening.

Images flickered as the damaged equipment spasmed with white noise despite Craig's best efforts to fine-tune the picture. With a frustrated grunt, the scientist turned away from his control panel and

CHAPTER ONE

glanced at Zach before shifting to Liza and her technician, Nikolay, where they were strapped into seats on Zach's right.

"I can't get these images to come in at all," he said.

"I can try." Nikolay spoke for the first time all trip. He was a typical Russian technician with a buzz cut and bright, gray eyes, quiet and dedicated to Liza, always by her side, whispering to her when he had questions or didn't understand some English.

Craig gave the man a once over and gestured at his console. "This is in English. Can you even read any of this?"

"I read English well enough," he said with a hesitant glance at Liza.

"Nikolay is self-conscious about his English," Liza explained, sweeping a lock of short black hair behind her ear. "He doesn't want to look foolish."

"Don't be self-conscious, Nikolay." Craig stood, gripping the armrests of his chair so the P-10's bumping and jostling didn't throw him off balance. "Come on. Switch seats with me. The video controls are up here. Don't touch anything on the left-hand side. That's the Navpax stuff."

"Very well," Nikolay agreed, switching positions with Craig, who fell heavily into the seat next to Liza, all of them now practiced at adjusting to the armored vehicle's movements. The Russian technician focused on the topmost screens and experimentally flicked a few switches.

Craig leaned across Liza. "I tried to send a message to Washington, but it was no good. Still too much static, plus some communication equipment was damaged."

"Is it the weather?" Zach asked with a soft breath of air, his body sore but relaxed as the salve the medic had put on the stab wounds around his neck numbed some of his pain.

Craig shrugged. "Either the weather or the Russian guns, I don't know. Let's just hope Nikolay can fine-tune those images and help us get something sent. It might not matter much since we're almost to Fairbanks. We should be able to get the message and data out to Washington from there."

"I will be happy to get out of this stuffy truck," Liza's Russian

CHAPTER ONE

accent was thicker in her frustration. "While I appreciate the ride, it is claustrophobic."

"I agree," Zach replied, nodding at Craig. "And I'm curious to know what those soldiers found at my house."

Doubt flashed in Craig's eyes before his expression cleared. "Once we're done briefing Washington, I'll talk to Stephanie and see what they found. I'm sure she got someone out there, though I can't pretend to know what they found."

The grim implications weren't lost on Zach, and he gave the scientist a thankful nod. "I know things might be hard on them right now, but I just want to know they're alive."

"No matter what," Craig added, "we did the world a big favor by partially shutting down that rift. It's at least a fifty percent cut in emissions, maybe more. That has to influence things. We have to have given our people a chance."

While he was tired and burned out from the trip north, Zach nodded. "I hope so, and we can all agree that getting as far south as we can right now is our next best bet."

"Yes, absolutely," Craig agreed, "though I wouldn't put it past them to make another attempt on the rift and seal it once and for all. I just know..." He glanced at Liza with a nervous smile. "I want to get home, too. I want to see my kids and..." He laughed. "I guess I want to see Stephanie, too. Just to know that she's okay and doing fine. What divorced person ever says that?"

Liza caught the humor in his voice and patted his hand.

Zach only nodded. "Oh, I'm sure there are a lot of friendly divorces."

"Well, mine wasn't one of them, but I'm glad things worked out the way they did. Stephanie is a great lady and brought the kids up right."

Lieutenant Colonel Stillman left his seat up front, spun, and kneeled behind Nikolay. He gave Craig a wide grin. "We just contacted Fairbanks, and they're happy to have us back. I went ahead and sent that data package you put together. Fairbanks will relay it to Washington once they receive it all."

CHAPTER ONE

Craig clapped and bent forward, resting his elbows on his knees and his face in his hands. "That's amazing. Thank you, Colonel."

"Thanks to all of *you*." Stillman glanced across the lot of them, even the handful of Marines sitting in the back compartment where they sat wounded and scraped up, scowling in anger about losing their friends. "Thank all of you."

Grizzly called from the driver's chair. "We are coming up on Fairbanks now. It is not looking good."

"Have you made any progress on those screens, Nikolay?" Zach asked.

"Actually, yes," he replied, his fingers flipping down a pair of switches before pointing at the top-middle display. "I patched into Grizzly's feed, and the far-right camera angles toward the sky. Like so. See?"

Zach scanned the images, looking at the road ahead with its wispy clouds drifting across the P-10's nose and whipping around the tracks, making it almost impossible to see. Still, through the near whiteout, he made out the dark shapes of buildings, white flakes lashing across charred frames, cars and trucks on the roadside. Some were simply stalled out, while others had become victims of the flaming winds that had swept over them when the military convoy headed north days ago. Like most of the Alaskan landscape, it was a half-melted countryside of burned trees and buildings, charred corpses bumping beneath their tracks as they entered the downtown streets through clouds of sweeping smoke. In the sky, the same dark gloom and yellow-green winds swept over them, lightning cracking to ignite magnificent explosions that billowed and pushed the sky downward. Many of the corpses weren't burned at all but lay on the ground with bloated faces, clutching their throats after suffocating on currents of poisonous fumes. Icicles hung from their frozen coats, and their lips and noses were frosted with the last breaths they'd ever taken.

Something made Zach lean forward in his chair, squinting at the screen as small shapes flitted and danced in the vicious storms. "Are those jets?"

Stillman's gaze shifted to the display, pausing in disbelief before fleeing to the front and grabbing the communication officer. Liza nodded while Nikolay tapped his finger on the screen.

"I would say, yes." The technician put his face close to the screen and tuned a knob. The image sharpened, and Zach made out winged shapes zipping through the sky. "Definitely jets. Helicopters, too."

"Russians?" Craig asked.

Nikolay continued to improve the image, spreading it across three screens for an even wider view. Jets swooped back and forth, spurts of tracer fire cutting through the sky, missiles zipping toward each other, missing or hitting in fatal explosions, though they couldn't say which were American and which were Russian. Beneath the boiling skies the planes fought, at least two engulfed by tails of lightning that ignited into fingers of flame around the fuselages. The billowing conflagration spread downward from the black clouds to fry the jets and plummet them to the earth like comets. Grizzly took them east, cutting through the charred Fairbanks streets, Fort Wainwright coming into view where more of the fiery battles were taking shape above them. The radio chatter from the other P-10s grew heated, and Stillman grabbed Grizzly's shoulder and called for evasive action.

Zach hung on as the armored vehicle swung south, the turbine whine ratcheting up so high it shook his boots. A screeching jet cut through the wind and grew louder, followed by a staccato rip of sound — *pa, pap... ka ka ka* — cutting across their hull, rocking the P-10 and causing Liza to cry out and grab both Zach and Craig until the jet zipped overhead in a whoop of sound that quickly faded.

"I told you, this is good machine," Grizzly said from his driver's seat. "Direct hit by puny Russian jet didn't make a dent."

Stillman patted Grizzly's shoulder. "Cut east again, man! Turn into our support teams so they can cover us."

The sounds of anti-aircraft battery, small arms, and big guns reached them through the speakers in a terrifying symphony of battle noise. After several turns and more rough driving, Grizzly sat back in his chair and slapped his palms on the U-shaped wheel.

"We are now on concourse. The command center is very close now."

CHAPTER ONE

Stillman eased back and held a headset to one ear, glancing at his tactical displays, finally nodding and giving the Russian driver a friendly pat on the arm. "We're out of hot water for now." He turned to everyone in the truck's rear. "We disembark in three minutes. We're to head straight into the command center for debriefing."

Zach unbuckled and reached for his gear, his scratch step helmet, pack, and carbine, leaning forward as the P-10 ground across the icy pavement, into the hangar motor pool where they'd started. They came to a screeching halt, the back hatch clicked open and slowly lowered until it banged down, and the Marines disembarked with quick, confident strides, followed by Craig, Liza, and Nikolay.

When Zach stood, he winced and slouched to avoid banging his head on the metal ceiling. His shoulders and neck ached, the trapezius muscles at the base of his neck lancing with pain. His skin burned from the stitches, and his shoulders and knees were sore from climbing the sheer ice walls back in the caves. The sounds of jets and distant repercussions of anti-aircraft missiles ripping into the sky were cut off when the bay doors shut, leaving wind rocking the hangar so the metal walls groaned and creaked.

A contingent of military personnel met the depleted Marinesin the middle of the hangar, shouting and pumping their fists, cheers echoing through the building. Red Hawk gestured to Craig and Liza to follow, and the entire group marched across the hangar and down the concrete stairs into the subfloors. From the markings on the walls, Zach realized they'd entered the actual command center bunker. Branching corridors and short passages were flooded with military personnel. Two staffers grabbed Colonel Red Hawk and Stillman and directed the group off to the right with Zach, Grizzly, and Nikolay lagging behind. The corridors grew more cramped with each turn until the officers and Marines passed through a thick steel doorway.

A female staffer stopped Zach, Grizzly, and Nikolay and gestured toward a passage to their left. "We just need officials in the debriefing room."

She guided them into a large mess area with coffee urns and plates of military snacks and danishes spread out on a counter. As soldiers

CHAPTER ONE

walked by, they grabbed shots of coffee or an apple from a basket before heading back to their posts to support the fight waged outside.

"If you could wait in here, gentlemen," the woman said, gesturing to a well-used table with a couple of dried-up spills and crumbs on the surface. "Someone from the officer corps will be with you shortly."

"No problem," Zach said. "Thanks."

The staffer vanished, leaving the trio alone. Nikolay looked around warily before sitting, while Grizzly went to the counter to check out the options. Zach fell into a green metal chair, its joints creaking under his weight, expression pained as he tried to settle into a comfortable position, though no matter how he sat, his body replied with a new, agonizing ache.

Craig was breathless with exhaustion despite having tried to sleep on the return trip, sitting for hours on end in his cramped chair in the ever-lurching, jostling armored vehicle, every bump and divot in the ice painful to his back and legs. Out of everyone, he'd suffered the least and had survived relatively unscathed. He couldn't imagine how Zach must feel after climbing the sheer walls, fighting the Russians, and getting stabbed in the neck and shoulders. And there was Liza and Nikolay, too, betrayed by Orlov and left to die on the Alaskan tundra before being picked up by Red Hawk and the Marines. She was under the scrutiny of the US military, likely not easily trusted, despite her joining their side.

"Don't worry, I've got your back," he said to her as they walked through the corridors and into the underground command center.

The pretty Russian smiled at him and nodded. "Thank you, Craig. I would be terrified if not for you. I have heard so many things about American commanders. They told me death would be preferable to being captured by the Americans because they would torture me for information."

CHAPTER ONE

Craig leaned in. "That won't happen here. Colonel Red Hawk is a good man. I would never let them do anything like that to you."

She huffed. "You would not have to torture me, anyway. After what Orlov did to us, I will gladly tell your commanders anything they want to know. But I am not military, so I know nothing about troop positions or secret weapons."

"All the better," Craig replied. "Ah, here we are."

After moving through a series of tight passages, they entered a heavily guarded doorway and tactical command room with vertical glass panes above a central desk. The largest pane displayed light-based terrain markings and troop positions in digital color, varied squares and triangles superimposed on those as they moved in real-time. Red Hawk and Stillman were talking to another Marine commander and several younger officers. The room was small and stuffy, the walls steel and reinforced with beams that ran the entire length and stretched into the surrounding chambers. Ducts and vents were fitted alongside the beams, circulating the smell of electronics in the ventilated air. The aromas of stale coffee and sweat drifted from the communication technicians who'd been at their stations for days, working consoles and murmuring messages into microphones. In some sections, pods of military personnel were operating radar systems or joysticks, controlling drones in the sky, while others directed tactical information for the live fighter pilots.

Craig and Liza stood to the side, hands clasped in front of them as they waited to be called. Numbers flashed on the vertical displays, and new blips appeared or went out seemingly at will. Red Hawk used a stick to point at a formation moving across the screen, turning to say something to Stillman and the other commanders, then giving brisk orders to the tactical folks. Alaska's West Coast was lightly drawn on the display, and the American forces were mostly white and black triangles while the Russians were red or orange, though he couldn't say what types of military equipment they represented. Just as Craig's legs started to ache from standing, Red Hawk put down the wooden pointer and turned to gesture for he and Liza to follow.

Craig flashed the Russian scientist a comforting smile and gently guided her ahead of him and behind the officers, who flowed through

CHAPTER ONE

the bustling room into a side chamber. It was a small meeting space with a videoconferencing kiosk against the far wall and several chairs situated around it. The Colonel gestured to the seats on the right, which Craig and Liza took, leaving the ones on the left to Stillman and Red Hawk.

"They're patching us in to Washington now," Red Hawk said. "How are you two doing?"

Craig had been situating himself in his tactical gear, wondering if Stephanie would think it looked silly or manly when he met the Colonel's gaze. "I'm doing okay," he replied, "Liza?"

"Nervous but fine." The scientist spoke through pursed lips, gaze shifting across Stillman and Red Hawk before settling on the wide monitor right in front of them. "Craig told me I would meet the American President."

"That's correct," Red Hawk replied. "You'll speak to President Eric Holland face-to-face with us."

Liza rubbed her knuckles on her legs and shrugged, holding the pose girlishly. "Yes, I am very nervous. I have never even met the Russian Prime Minister."

"Don't worry, President Holland is a good man. You're not in trouble, and nothing bad will happen to you." Red Hawk leaned forward, and for the first time, Craig noticed some abrasions on his cheeks and a bulge beneath his tactical gear with the edges of the bandage clinging to the base of his neck. Part of the white dressing was stained with blood. "We are indebted to you, and if the President doesn't do so himself, I want to give you my thanks."

"I as well," Stillman said, sitting stiffly on Red Hawk's other side with his eyes pinned to the monitor and looking about as nervous as Liza.

Craig raised a finger. "Me, too."

They sat in comfortable silence for another few minutes before a speaker on the wall came to life. "Hello, Colonel Red Hawk. I'm just working on the feed now. Please hold."

Red Hawk nodded, and Craig shifted in his uncomfortable gear, wishing for a shower with his skin well beyond itchy. But after being

CHAPTER ONE

strafed by a Russian jet, he wanted out of the area as soon as possible, so a shower would have to wait.

"Almost there, sir," came the cryptic voice from the wall, and the ordinarily patient Colonel shook his head but stayed still.

The screen in front of them hitched with static, the image of the command center in Washington flashing before going out. It came back, wavered, and held steady. President Eric Holland stood at the head of the conference table with his hard hazel eyes staring into the camera, his tactical outfit changed to a white button-up shirt with a loose tie around the collar, his thick shoulders stretching the material where his arms were crossed. To his right sat Colonel Davies, fair-haired with light eyes, his uniform cinched tight at the cuffs and neck. Just behind him sat Lauren Tracey, the senator leaning back in her chair, long legs crossed in her black slacks. Her pixie haircut was slightly tousled, and her eyes were sharp but also betrayed a weariness he could relate to. Across from her, Stephanie, looked confident as usual, her dark hair falling over a red blouse and her hands resting comfortably on the arms of her chair. Three laptops were spread around her with paper booklets and disaster plans she'd be coordinating with Genevieve Clark. While she was staring into the screen, he caught a corner of her mouth turn up in a smile, but he didn't know if it was because he looked silly in his uniform or if she was genuinely happy to see him.

"Good afternoon, Colonel Red Hawk," Holland said in a stiff greeting. "We're all delighted and impressed to have received your report. Glad you made it home."

"Thank you, Mr. President. Not all of us made it."

"I've seen the casualty list, and I'm sorry you lost so many good Marines. It was for a good cause. The people of the United States are grateful."

"Thank you, sir. "

"I've read the report about the trouble up north with the Russians, and I've got a pretty good idea of what's happening up there now. Can you give me an update in your words? What are your thoughts?"

"It's a Russian incursion, sir. You're probably aware of the betrayal at the Alaskan Rift where the Russians tried to take us out." The Colonel went into the details about the events leading up to them entering the caves, the fight down in the ice-vent system running from the sea bottom to the surface, briefly touching on Zach Christensen's contribution to them escaping with their lives. Next came the battle on the ice, where they lost most of their men and equipment, and the explosion when the Russians set off the bombs. "Based on what Dr. Kovaleva told us, and the maneuvering by the Russians off the Alaskan West Coast, it's safe to assume they're looking to secure areas where we've sampled oil or have critical refineries. They may try to take the pipeline and the oilfields in the Beaufort Sea for their own, blocking any joint US-Russian ventures."

"It's fairly common knowledge the Russians never wanted to enter that deal in the first place with those mega-rigs," Holland nodded. "It doesn't surprise me they'd take advantage of this situation."

Shaking his head, Craig said what he was thinking. "Do you think they did it on purpose, sir? What I mean is, did they create a situation where the fields in the Beaufort Sea would be rendered vulnerable?"

"Believe me, Dr. Sutton, those theories have been making the rounds here in Washington, but maybe Dr. Kovaleva can give us more insight." The President's gaze shifted slightly in the camera. "Dr. Kovaleva, go ahead."

Liza cleared her throat and sat up straight. "Yes, Mr. President. It is good to meet you. I hope things are well in Washington."

"That remains to be seen. Go ahead. Tell us what you think might be happening with the Russian government."

"I am no political expert," she chuckled nervously, "but it is no secret that two groups in the Russian parliament have been at each other's throats for many years. The hardliners are an older group who are very much for military action before negotiations."

"War Hawks," Craig muttered, then winced and hoped the digital microphones hadn't picked that up.

Liza went on as if he hadn't said a word. "I know this mostly because members of the scientific community are often pitted

CHAPTER ONE

against one another for research funding, and we have never gotten support from the hardliners."

"I understand," Holland replied. "What can you tell us about Andrei Orlov's position? He's in charge of the incursion into our territory and responsible for the betrayal at the Alaskan Rift."

"Orlov is in the hardliner's pockets, as you American's say." She gave a firm nod. "He will do whatever they want, even sacrificing other Russians for their goals."

"That's very insightful, Dr. Kovaleva. Thank you." Holland's gaze shifted to Colonel Red Hawk. "Do you think this is a full-scale invasion?"

"I don't think so, sir. As you already know, NORTHCOM hasn't reported any other Russian activity along the West Coast. It's all in Alaska and relatively confined. They just want those resources, though I can't pretend to understand the political ramifications. To me, this is just another fight."

"A fight I expect you to win," the President said. "We're sending a carrier strike force and shipping more equipment your way. We've already tried sending by air and lost soldiers and supplies. I'm afraid it will have to be by train and truck, so you'll have to hang tight and hunker down until we can resupply you."

"Our pilots are holding up and already turned the Russians back several times." Red Hawk's expression grew grim. "We expect troops on the ground anytime, so we're preparing to fight them on land. I believe they'll try to create a buffer zone around the National Petroleum Reserve and may even move into Anchorage."

"Crazy Russians," Stillman murmured as he looked away.

"What about nukes?" Holland asked with the first hint of nervousness in his eyes. "The second all this started, I demanded a meeting with President Alexeev, but he's not returning our calls. Neither are the Chinese."

"My commanders and I talked about it, sir, and while we can't prove it, it seems the Russians are intent on keeping this localized. With the hydrocarbons continuing to flood across the Northern Hemisphere, global targeting systems would be spotty. The Russians couldn't guarantee they wouldn't drop nukes on their own territory."

"That's the assumption *we* made as well, though we've got plenty of places to strike from if need be." President Holland's jaw shifted. "Alexeev must know that, and I'm sure he wants to avoid a bigger war if possible. We see this as a Ukraine situation where he's going for a cheap land grab. One that he'll certainly regret once we engage our full diplomatic powers. We'll have the entire world turning on him within a week."

"Make no mistake, President Holland." Liza raised her hand almost painfully to get his attention. "I know Commander Orlov well enough to say he will try to turn this into something bigger. I cannot be certain that he would stop if he were called off. He commands a great number of our forces, and most of the soldiers and commanders would be on his side."

"We'll take that under advisement, Dr. Kovaleva. By the way, I'm assuming you won't be going back to Russia."

"No, sir. I will not be going back to my homeland. I have no family there, and..." She made a helpless gesture. "I have no way to go if I wanted to. No, Craig and Colonel Red Hawk have been very gracious to me, and I can speak for all of my science team when I say we are glad to be here."

"Good. Would you be willing to come to Washington and give us more in-person information?"

"Yes."

"Great. We'll transport you to Washington with Dr. Sutton." Holland shifted his gaze slightly. "I'd like to put the question to both of you. I read enough of your report to know that the Alaskan Rift was only partially closed. Is there any chance we could finish the job?"

"What we did worked well, sir," Craig replied. "But with the explosions detonated by the Russians, there's no way to know how the environment has changed. At the very least, we need more P-10s and possibly some submersibles to get the job done, and we'd probably be getting bombed by the Russians the entire time."

Holland scoffed and shook his head, looking disappointed. "We'll continue to use diplomatic and military means to change their minds, and there may be another chance at closing the rift, but it's clear we

CHAPTER ONE

need to get our most valuable scientific personnel safe before another attempt can be made. I'd like you and Dr. Kovaleva to get south as soon as possible, back to DC if we can swing it. I imagine with the skies the way they are up there, and with Russian jets prowling around, it'll have to be by ground transport until we can get you safely away on a helicopter or plane. How does that suit you?"

"Sounds good, sir. Thank you."

"Good, Colonel Red Hawk, see it done."

"Yes, sir. We'll provision them to go south with a driver and some protection."

"I know just the men who can take us," Craig said. "I'm thinking Grizzly and Zach Christensen."

"You read my mind, Dr. Sutton," Red Hawk replied. "Take it offline with them as soon as we finish our meetings."

"Would it be too much trouble if I brought my primary technician with me?" Liza asked. "His name is Nikolay, and he would be valuable to your science teams in Washington."

Holland gave a brisk nod. "I'm fine with the idea as long as the Colonel agrees."

"I'll authorize the equipment and the orders," Red Hawk replied.

"That's all I need from you, Dr. Sutton and Dr. Kovaleva. You're both excused for now."

"Thank you, President Holland." Craig nodded respectfully and stood, gesturing for Liza to do the same.

Liza rose beside him and bowed to the President and his staff. "Thank you so much, Mr. President. Good fortune for all your efforts."

Craig guided Liza from the room. Finding themselves unguarded, they turned right into a short hall and proceeded to another room similar to theirs. He pushed the steel door open and motioned Liza in, stepping to a kiosk terminal and punching in a long code followed by the number he wanted to reach.

"What are you doing, Craig?"

"I'm making a side call. I've got the authorization to do it." He frowned. "Not sure we'll have the network bandwidth. Going to try it anyway. She'll be waiting."

CHAPTER ONE

They sat and watched as the screen burst with static and flashes. The display cleared up, and the camera angle shifted, putting Stephanie's smiling face on the screen where she sat in a quiet room.

"Stephanie, good to see you."

While Craig had expected her to be happy to see him, her teary eyes and flushed cheeks inspired emotions he'd briefly felt in Washington when they were saying goodbye. Stephanie gasped and clutched her chest. "Hi, Craig. I'm so glad you made it. What you did was amazing. You actually closed the rift."

"Not all of it."

"No, but the reports you sent me are very promising. We could see an end to this soon."

"I hope so, because I don't think my blood pressure can take it much longer." Seeing Stephanie chuckle and wipe a tear from her eye, Craig's heart leaped, but a flush of embarrassment rose to his face. He quickly gestured at Liza. "Stephanie, I'd like you to meet Dr. Liza Kovaleva. I met her when we arrived at Station Yanovskya, and she was critical in helping us identify where to place the ordnance along the rift. She's brilliant."

Liza grinned and shook her head, addressing Stephanie with bright eyes. "I could not go near the place, but your husband was so brave and went with the Marines. He is the reason we could pull it off."

Stephanie smiled primly. "It turns out my *ex-husband's* full of surprises. I'm so glad you two made it out okay. Good work."

"Tell me about the Christensen's. Were you able to get a team out there to check on them?"

Stephanie's smile faded. "I sent a team of soldiers to check on them, but they were gone. The house was torn down, destroyed by Hurricane Jane. The details will be in the official report."

Craig deflated. "That's not good."

"It's not entirely bad, either."

"What do you mean?"

"While the family wasn't there, there was a message on the wall written in Dutch. I had someone translate it, and it says for Zach to

CHAPTER ONE

meet the family at a settlement in Pearisburg, Virginia. Sound familiar?"

"No, but it probably will to Zach. That's in the report, too?"

"Yes."

"Great. I'm sure he'll be pleased."

"How are you going to get home now?" Stephanie asked.

"I still have to talk to Grizzly and Zach, but I'm pretty sure I'll be driving home under their guard with Liza and Nikolay." Craig finished forwarding the message and put it in his pocket, then fixed her with a concerned look, trying to see into her dark eyes over the miles. The spotty digital connection gave the conversation a lifeless feeling. "How about you? How's it going there, and how are the kids?"

Stephanie looked off camera a second before returning to Craig with a flush of pink in her cheeks and a nervous smile. "The kids are fine. Larkin and Amanda are holding down the fort back home, though they mentioned the neighborhood is getting a little weird."

"Weird?"

"Something about strangers walking the streets and nosing around, but the kids are working with some neighbors, so they'll be safe. As for here, that's another thing."

"What do you mean?" Craig asked, sitting more rigidly.

"It's getting pretty tense around the Pentagon. They've been keeping people off the grounds with just troops and armored trucks, but now they're putting up fences and concrete barricades. And there're tanks outside, too."

"Tanks?" Craig's stomach churned slowly with discomfort, and he glanced at Liza. "What in the world would they need tanks for?"

"Craig, there are millions of civilians out there, desperate and angry. And the FEMA camps are struggling badly. I've been working with Genevieve and her team across the country, trying to warn them of the changing wind patterns and shifting pressure systems."

"Is it helping?"

"Yes, especially with the civilian and military drivers. We can direct them to calmer highways and back roads where the weather isn't as bad. The problem is we can't keep up with the requests, and some are getting caught in bad situations."

"How is the military handling it?"

"The President is circling the wagons, I guess. Marine units guard the facility, but it's hard to do when they can't keep anything in the air."

Craig recalled the jet battle as they were pulling into Fairbanks, helicopters and planes consumed by ordnance and the hungry sky. "Yeah, we've seen some similar problems up here, that's why we're driving."

"You be safe getting home, do you hear me?"

"I will. You be safe there, too. And keep checking up on the kids. If you have to get some soldiers out there to help them—"

"I'll do whatever it takes. I've even been thinking about…" A soft gasp escaped Stephanie's lips. She leaned back and glanced to the side.

"What is it? What have you been thinking about?"

"Nothing important. Just be safe and get home soon."

"I will. Bye, Stephanie." Craig clicked a button on the conferencing console and rested back in his chair.

After a moment, Liza said, "She is beautiful, Craig. And smart, too."

With pursed lips, Craig gave a half smile and nodded. "She's a good person."

"A good person?" Liza scoffed. "That is the mother of your children."

"Yes, I know. That's all I heard when they were dragging me through the courts." Seeing a dark shadow pass over Liza's features, Craig added, "But I can't claim all the pain. We went through some tough times through the divorce, especially the kids. No, there's plenty of blame to go around. And despite having ironed some emotions out back in Washington, it's still hard…"

Liza patted him on the back, her expression filled with genuine concern. "I cannot imagine what that must be like. I have not been married because my work always took priority."

CHAPTER ONE

"Same here, but we had kids anyway. I guess I'll always wish I'd done better."

"No matter what, we all wish that of ourselves. But we cannot be too hard on ourselves when we fall short sometimes."

Craig crossed his arms, letting the woman's words sink in. "That's good advice to live by. Let's go get Grizzly and Zach and talk about getting home."

"You injured badly in fighting?" Nikolay asked in his thick Russian accent from across the table.

Zach glanced at the sterile concrete walls and metal pillars that ran from floor to ceiling. "I'll live," he murmured. "I just need to get back on the road as soon as possible."

"You want to get home, right?"

"That's right. I haven't seen my wife and kids in months, and part of me still thinks the trip north was a waste of time. But Craig seems to think it made a difference."

Nikolay nodded and squirmed in his chair, unable to get comfortable. But not because of physical pain. A staffer had brought them cold-weather fatigues, which were more flexible than their tactical gear, and they'd used a bathroom to change and get washed up. While Zach's were a bit snug around the shoulders, he appreciated the clean garments and winter boots, which were better than those he'd had working north of Dead Horse.

"What about you?" Zach asked. "You seem nervous."

"I am far from home and family. I do not know if I will ever see them again or if they are safe."

With a sheepish nod, Zach checked his anxious attitude. "I'm sorry to hear that. At least I have a chance to see my family again. I can't imagine it would be easy to return to Russia now after leaving it behind."

"Abandoned," Nikolay corrected him. "Orlov abandoned us. For that, I do not wish to go back. Still, I would like to see my family again."

"We will leave soon," Grizzly said from his seat on Zack's right as he finished a pastry and licked the icing off his fingers with loud smacks. He had crumbs all down the front of his cold-weather fatigues. "Is possible we can ask American government for help reaching your family, though we may need to wait. With Orlov attacking our American friends, I do not see them taking time to help a wayward Russian. But do not worry, friend. Grizzly will guard you until we make things right."

Nikolay looked the big man over and laughed softly, saying something in Russian. Grizzly puffed his chest out in mock offense and shook his fist at the younger man. "He teases me." Grizzly explained. "Says I must make better appearance. No more crumbs on shirt."

Zach laughed wholeheartedly, then sucked air through his teeth at the sting in his neck and shoulders. He reached up to rub the area but drew back, realizing that would be a bad idea, and he looked around for someone from the medical staff to give him some pain meds. The hallway door opened, and he turned to face Liza and Craig. The bald scientist looked less awkward in his tactical gear and produced a broad smile that sent thrills through Zach.

"Did you hear something about my family?"

Craig replied with an almost smug expression eclipsed by genuine happiness. "Yes, I did. Stephanie came through for us and got some soldiers out to their place, courtesy of Marine Colonel Davies and his contact on the Army side." He waved a folder in the air. "I just got the official report. Wendy and the kids are alive but not at home."

Zach was caught between smiling and frowning as he shook his head in confusion. "What do you mean?"

"According to the report, when the soldiers arrived, they found the entire neighborhood demolished by Hurricane Jane. She did tremendous damage... entire houses ripped from their foundations, roofs caved in, and debris—"

Liza squeezed his arm and gave him a pointed look.

"Sorry," Craig said. "Your house was not in good shape when they arrived, and they found evidence of a firefight and some dead bodies in the basement."

Zach's expression darkened as tears welled in his eyes. "So far, none of this is good news."

Craig raised his palms and laughed. "Sorry, I probably should have

CHAPTER ONE

started with that. Your family is fine. Wendy, Charlie, David, and Clyde."

"Clyde?"

"You don't know that person?"

"He's new to me, but maybe they took in someone from the neighborhood. Anyway..."

"Your family evacuated the place with all their supplies and left with someone from your family..." Craig spread open the report and read off a page." People named Morten and Alma?"

Zach slouched, his body suddenly weak, breath coming in shallow gasps. Grizzly leaped from his chair in a heartbeat, rushing to Zach and putting one hand on his arm and the other around his waist.

"Are you okay, my friend?"

"I'm great." Zach's heart was thumping happily in his chest, relief flooding through him until he released a deep and thankful sigh. Seeing everyone's confusion, he explained. "Morten is my father. He's always supported me, even when I left the settlement. He loves Wendy and the kids... I should have known he'd check on them."

Craig handed over the report. "The exact message from the wall is on page two. It's Dutch or something."

Zach scanned the words, tears overflowing and streaming into his charred beard. "It's Dutch. It's been a while since I've used it, but it's what we spoke in the Amish community. It must've been my father's idea to write it that way so I would know they were safe with him."

Liza stepped over to Zach, gripped his wrist, and lifted the hand that held the message. "What does it say, Zach?"

Zach unfolded it and read it out loud in stilted English. "We are safe... we are all safe... we are going to Pearisburg with Morten and Alma. Please come soon. Wendy, Charlie, David, and Clyde."

"Where's Pearisburg?" Liza asked.

"It's down in Virginia. We've got connections down there... something must have happened in Fort Plain for them to have left, but I'm glad they did." Zach laughed and waved the message before fixing Craig with a firm but brotherly stare. "Thank you, Craig. Whatever you did, it worked. They're safe, and I know where they are going.

This makes things much easier, and I'm grateful to know they're alive."

"You're welcome," Craig replied. "And you can thank Stephanie when we return to the States."

"Any word about how we'll do that with all this fighting?" Though his spirits were high, a lingering sense of dread plagued him. "We're practically in a war zone."

"That's where I come in." Lieutenant Colonel Stillman stepped through the hall door and into the room, pushing past Liza and holding his hand out for Zach. "Excellent work out there, Zach. I had doubts when the Colonel suggested bringing you on, but you proved yourself out there."

Zach accepted the handshake. "Thank you, sir. I just wanted to pull my weight."

"You more than pulled your weight, son. You saved our butts more than once and helped stop those Russians from burying us in the Beaufort Sea."

"You're welcome, Colonel Stillman. About getting home..."

"At Dr. Sutton's behest, I've approved a vehicle and equipment for you and Grizzly to drive our science experts south into the US. We'll find an operating air force base to fly you back to the East Coast from there. We want Grizzly to drive and you on guard duty if that sits well with you."

Zach winced. "No offense to anyone, but I was hoping to go it alone. I'd be faster moving by myself, and I'm sure you could find a better-armed unit to get your scientists home."

"We need every military unit we can find for fighting the Russians." Stillman rested his hands on his hips, his expression firm but not overbearing. The Lieutenant Colonel had changed out of his tactical gear, though he still had smudges on his face and neck, and his hair was slicked back and sweaty. "The President sees Dr. Sutton and Dr. Kovaleva as high-priority and wants to ensure we've got the best men on the job. You and Grizzly were brought up as candidates. The President approved the mission, and we'll give you all the gear you can carry. Dr. Sutton will carry the United States military credentials to get you through any Canadian and American checkpoints on

CHAPTER ONE

the way there. That should speed things up for you. It's vitally important we get these two home."

"And my assistant, Nikolay," Liza said, gesturing to the young man sitting at the table.

"And Nikolay, too," Stillman agreed.

Zach scratched his head, feeling the weight of authoritative pressure. "The President wants me to guard three of his most valuable assets on a long journey like that?"

"Dr. Sutton asked specifically for you by name, and Colonel Red Hawk and I agreed."

Craig leaned in with a cocked eyebrow. "You heard the Lieutenant Colonel. We'll be maxed out with gear, and there should be a base to fly from once we cross into the lower forty-eight. That alone should be enough reason to want to do this."

Zach wavered, taking a deep breath and secretly wishing they'd give him a snowmobile and credentials to get through all the checkpoints. While he wanted to help, he continued to see one barrier after another blocking his way home to his family, the responsibilities piling up with the world falling to pieces around them.

Grizzly stepped past Zach to face the Lieutenant Colonel. "I cannot speak for my friend, but it would honor me to drive these excellent doctors, and Nikolay, to the United States."

Stillman held out his hand. "Good to have you on board, Grizzly." The Lieutenant Colonel shifted back to Zach and waited.

Craig stepped closer, soft-spoken and sincere. "I'm the last person to tell you what to do, Zach. But I can tell you I felt comfortable driving north with you on my side, and I'd love to travel with you a few more miles. I'd want no one else on this trip with us."

Liza backed him up. "I do not know you well, Zach, but Craig has spoken highly of you all the way home from the Beaufort Sea. I just know that with you and Grizzly helping us, we'll make it to the United States safely."

Grizzly started to pat him hard on the shoulder but drew back from his wounds, still grinning gruffly. "Come on, Zach. This is an important mission, plus Nikolay wants to see Disneyland someday."

CHAPTER ONE

Nikolay quipped something in Russian as Grizzly turned to the young tech and laughed.

Zach nodded, saying, "All right. I'll do it. We've got a good team here, but I want everyone armed with at least a pistol, and I'll take a carbine with some ammunition. I've still got my M18 right here." He patted the gun holstered at his side.

"That won't be necessary, Zach," Craig said. "The three of us aren't soldiers. We won't need pistols."

"I am not a soldier," Liza replied, "but I will take a weapon. I learned to shoot in Russian Academy when I was a teenager."

"Maybe Liza will show tree hugger how to shoot," Grizzly quipped gruffly.

Craig frowned and shook his head, saying in a singsong way, "That won't be necessary."

Stillman smiled. "It won't be a problem. It would be helpful for everyone to be armed in case of a close encounter." He clapped his hands once and turned to a young woman in Army fatigues with her hair pinned back and hands clasped at her waist. "Go with Private Danforth here. She'll take you up to the Humvee and make sure you get your T's crossed and your I's dotted."

"Great, Colonel. Thank you."

Stillman ducked into the hallway and left them with Danforth, who paused to wait for Grizzly to finish his plate by stuffing his half-eaten pastries into his mouth with both hands. Then they followed the Private upward to the surface, pounding up grated steel stairwells and through hard concrete core doors with Marines coming down in groups and nodding respectfully at the soldiers they passed.

They reached the ground level, where tremendous concussions rocked the sky. Wind rattled the hangar and washed gouts of fire across the windows and along its sides. Vibrations shook the concrete and ran up through Zach's hips, the continued sounds of jets taking off and landing filling the space with turbine shrieks. In the motor pool, some Marines they'd been in combat with up north waved and shook hands. Private Danforth guided them past the three beat-up P-10s and over to the far side of the building where a selec-

29

CHAPTER ONE

tion of Humvees stood with their doors open and Army staffers preparing canisters of ammunition and bins of other supplies.

"I'd like to get out of this tactical gear," Craig said. "I won't be needing it where we're going."

"Over here, Dr. Sutton." Danforth gestured for him to follow her to a series of rooms with the corridor passing down the center. "We'll find you some cold-weather fatigues."

"Nikolay and I will need some, too!" Liza proclaimed as the two Russian techs jumped in behind them.

Craig waved and went off with the Private to get situated, leaving Zach with the others where they gathered at the back of the Humvee and looked over what they were getting. Lifting the tops off several bins, they found ration packs that would last them for a couple of weeks and giant canisters of bullets and magazines.

"I don't recognize this ammunition." Zach tilted a box that read *6.8 by 51 mm*. "I'd like to see the rifle for this ammo."

Grizzly lifted the top off another canister, saying, "Looks like about a thousand rounds of 9mm here. Likely to fit our M18s."

"This is great," Zach admitted. "There's enough food and weaponry to get us pretty far. I guess a few Javelin firing solutions would be out of the question."

Grizzly raised his hand as if remembering where he'd put his keys. "I will go into the parts area and bring back some things we might need. Hard to know what we'll run into when we get on the road."

"Couldn't agree more," Zach nodded as Grizzly shuffled off to the rear of the motor pool.

A Marine approached with a soldier, each with rifles hanging from their shoulders and fully fitted with tactical gear. They walked with the boisterous and confident strides of military personnel ready to hit the field, a mixture of bravado and facade as they psyched themselves up for battle. Zach greeted them with firm handshakes before stepping back and crossing his arms.

"I see you guys are about to head out." He nodded at their heavy gear.

"That's right," the light-haired Marine said. "Just got back, and Stillman's sending us off again. This time, it's a joint operation with the Army guys." He elbowed his buddy. "Didn't even have time to shower or shave."

"I doubt they'll care where you're going." Zach grinned wryly. "Good luck."

"We came to give you this," the soldier on the left said, a burly black man with an amiable smile. He handed Zach the second rifle he carried, a beige-tinted weapon he'd never seen before. "It's an XM5. The Sig *Spear*. It's what us Army grunts are using now."

"What's the difference between this and an M4?"

"It's a great battlefield weapon for open terrain and against armored opponents. It doesn't have a high volume of fire because of the twenty-round magazines, but it's a heavier round that's fired with higher pressure. A real hot bullet."

The Marine whistled low. "You can put one through body armor at five hundred yards. Kind of wish we were using them."

"And with your size," the soldier said, "you won't have any problems with the weight. The suppressor on this is great as well. You're going to love it."

"All right." Zach picked up the rifle and tested its weight. "Show me the features and how to maintain it."

CHAPTER TWO

Wendy Christensen, New York, New York

Wendy and David walked on the left side of the wagons as they hugged the right-hand shoulder of I-87. The wind blew and sleet struck them from all sides, sweeping down from high to clatter on the pavement before whipping against them again, pinning their ponchos to their bodies and sending chill gusts across Wendy's neck. She shivered and shook off the goosebumps that raced over her shoulders and upper arms beneath her double-layers of long underwear. Her black and flannel-lined coat warded off the chill but was light enough to remove should the weather break into a warm spell as it had over the past two days.

David wore jeans, boots, and a black leather jacket covering his Springfield 1911. Charlie rode in the wagon with Alma and Clyde, though she sometimes came out to walk and talk with them, keeping them company whenever the weather wasn't battering them to death.

They drove the wagons along the right-hand shoulders of I-87 with abandoned cars scattered everywhere, dead from the double deep freeze. The roadside was crowded on both sides by waving trees with stripped-off branches, trunks bent and twisted by Hurricane

CHAPTER TWO

Jane's wrath. Deadfall spread out across the pavement, and Morten guided them adeptly around it. When there was too much, Wendy, David, Samuel, and Uri moved out front to clear it, sometimes by hand and other times with ropes that made it easier to drag things. Then they'd take their rifles and shotguns off their shoulders and hop in the wagon again.

Up front, it was Morten, Alma, Wendy, David, Charlie, and Clyde. The second was Samuel's family, his wife Lavinia, and their two girls, Esther and Lena. The last wagon was the largest of all and held most of their supplies along with Uri's family, his wife Miriam and their two teenaged children, Mara and Noah. David and Charlie were closer in age to Samuel's kids, though they hadn't said two words to them the entire trip. When he wasn't patrolling, Samuel stayed in the back of their wagon, tending to equipment and guarding the rear until it was time to get out and walk or move debris from the road. Uri always wore a broad smile above his short, scruffy beard and wide-brimmed hat, and Miriam was a kind woman who never failed to offer them food or drink whenever they finished clearing a tough spot on the road.

The New Jersey highways were frightening except for the narrowest back roads where people weren't fighting, stealing, or beating one another. Whenever they passed through a small township or city, everyone got out and walked beside the wagons with their guns on display. Samuel had wanted to drive fast past everything, though Morten preached caution and warned them that going too quickly through the streets could cause damage to the wagon wheels or wound the horses. Unless it was a clear strip of road, they moved slow and steady as the world screamed bloody murder around them.

Groups of people trudged through the blustery landscape, shadows in the trees and rushing along the roadside, almost everyone Wendy saw like a storybook character, dragging their luggage and bags of clothes behind them. Hands clung to hands as families bent against the winds. The ones she worried about lurked between crashed cars and watched the wagons with hungry eyes; hooded figures huddled in the cold, some breaking from their camps and following them for a while before giving up.

They came across a vehicle wrecked against the center median, the engine running but barely perceptible above the wind, a family packed inside to stay warm as the father poured siphoned gas into the tank. She noticed the right front wheel was bent with a broken axle, obviously stranding them there for good. Wendy nodded as they went by, though he only stared at her, wearing a jacket far too thin for such weather. The man wasn't smart enough to find a poncho or a garbage bag to stay dry.

Wendy closed her eyes against the screaming winds, glancing back to see Uri and Samuel walking with Lavinia and Miriam driving their two wagons, respectively. Uri was friendly while Samuel mostly scowled, looking more like Zach than himself. Nodding to the brothers, Wendy faced forward, using David's tall form to shield herself from the wind. She held her M&P 15 sport rifle tightly to her chest as if it could keep her warm, and her Hellcat was on her hip. They'd put all the guns and ammunition in the first wagon, within reach if needed. The middle wagon had supplies and was used as a rolling medical facility to take care of any bumps and bruises, with jars full of Amish poultices and leaves, crushed plants and roots, and other homeopathic remedies Wendy knew nothing about.

She'd stopped counting the number of desperate people on the road, though most of them avoided the interstate and kept to the underpasses and fought over buildings that Hurricane Jane had decimated. They were windswept and torn, scattered rubble in the shape of the sweeping winds, with bricks, vinyl siding, and garbage swirling out into the road in the form of Jane's carved arms. Warehouses and homes were smashed to pieces like piñatas, their bellies ripped open with bits spread out where yards used to be, endless piles of debris. A township's corner gas station burned in a spinning, curling tower of fire, the surrounding buildings devoured by cinder-filled winds, set aflame by the station and burning high and hot as their ashes floated into the wintry sky.

"Debris field!" Morten called, standing in his seat and peering around the wagon.

CHAPTER TWO

Wendy and the men raced ahead and spread out across the interstate, coming to a shattered tree with cracked limbs and a break running down the middle. Holding her right arm up to shield her face, Wendy gazed into the wavering forests along the roadside.

"It must've been carried out of the woods by Jane!" she shouted at Uri, who stood to her right, gaping at the massive pile of deadfall where it lay in a scattering of whipping leaves and garbage.

"We are going to need the ropes!" Uri called, jerking his thumb toward the main wagon. He moved to the rear where Alma handed them down. Uri ran them out to David and Wendy, each taking a coil while the Christensen brothers took the other. They circled the twisted shape with broad strips of bark peeled back to show the flat brown of rotting wood. They grabbed limbs and pushed at it, looking for a lighter spot where they could haul it around and make room for the wagons. Wendy took hold of an offshoot that ended in a half hook shape. She grasped it and shoved the massive log back and forth.

"This end is lightest!" She showed them how easy it was to move and stumbled forward a step when the wind sent a sudden gust up her back.

"Tie yours off at that end," Uri shouted, "and we'll put ours around the middle."

Wendy nodded and gave David the end of the rope, gesturing where he could slip it beneath the trunk, bring it up, and tie it tight. Once they had their knot set, Wendy grabbed her end and waited until Uri and Sam were ready. With David anchoring their position behind her, they gave a count of three and pulled, swinging the lighter piece around in a scraping of wood across the pavement, branches and leaves cracking off beneath their feet, turned brittle in the frosty air. The trunk came to rest with a groan, though Samuel slipped and went down on his backside, cursing. He shook his head and brushed off Uri's attempt to help him up. With the lane open, Morten drove through with tugs on the reins or low whistles that pierced the stormy winds. Lavinia and Miriam came behind him, and Wendy shook Uri's hand before running to catch up with David.

Morten pointed toward a bend that wrapped westward where the trees thinned out and disappeared. Hills loomed in the distance over the wide-open space, barely obscured by the dark storm clouds that clung to the lower atmosphere like a fungus.

"We are heading around that bend to the bridge!" The Amish leader called. "From there, we'll take it across to New Jersey and get away from these crowded towns!"

"God willing, we won't see much more of the rabble plaguing us!" Samuel snickered loud enough for Wendy to hear as he turned and marched to his usual position between the wagons. "I'm tired of seeing them!"

Wendy frowned at David. "Is he talking about us?"

"No, Mom. He's talking about the thousands of others running around homeless and desperate." David made a face as if second-guessing himself, then he leaned in. "You might be right. He probably means us."

"At least Uri likes us," she said, glancing at the friendly young Amish man who seemed wholly different from his brother, cautious and even a little curious as he walked toward the center of the road and inspected some debris.

"For now," David said. "Until he finally turns them against us. Makes me wonder why they came in the first place."

"Because Morten is a good man," Wendy replied. "He appreciates family no matter where it comes from."

"I know Grandpa is cool, but I'm worried about the rest of them."

With a deep sigh, Wendy dropped back beside Morten's wagon and watched as the curve swung them around. She couldn't name the bridge they'd come across, though she supposed it didn't matter as long as it got them to New Jersey. They paused before the start of the span, staring past its gleaming white girders that glowed in the dimness. Eight lanes stretched across the Hudson River, which carried chunks of ice and hull-stricken boats floating on their sides with bobbing corpses turning slowly in the brackish swill.

David stared at the eight-lane-wide span. "How long do you think it is?"

CHAPTER TWO

"At least a couple of miles!" Wendy shouted. "Do you see anything out there?"

David leaned forward and squinted, then shook his head. "Nada." Morten stood, peering across with his beard whipping and his poncho and coat gusting against his legs.

Uri and Samuel came up, and Uri turned to his father. "It looks safe to me. I say we cross now."

"Is everyone in agreement?"

Wendy glanced at the empty bridge where she knew wrecks were hidden in the blinding snow and shrugged. "If it gets us away from the city, I'm all for it. The longer we stay around New York, the more trouble will find us."

"I agree with them, Father," Uri said. "It is only two or three miles. If we run into trouble, we'll turn around. I believe the bridge is clear. Look..." Stretching his arm past David, he made swirling motions with his finger. "The winds are powerful out there. No one could withstand them for very long."

"It may be the perfect opportunity to charge through," Samuel added with gusto in his eyes.

Morten studied the situation with one eye squeezed shut, glaring defiantly into the shrieking gales as they pushed him hard enough to sway him on his perch. With a final nod, he sat heavily and waved them ahead. "We'll walk most of the way out, but when the wind gets bad, you all jump in the wagon, and we'll charge through. Assuming the wind has blown off most of the debris or stuck it along the sides, we should have a clear path across, and it would be good to have more weight inside the wagons."

With that, they set out to cross the bridge, Morten pushing the horses faster so they walked swiftly to keep pace. David and his long legs jogged beside Wendy, easily able to outdistance her, though he held back so she could stay close.

By the time they'd gotten a quarter of the way across, the bridge faintly shuddered to the storm's rhythm, groaning sounds emanating from the cable and steel beams, the pavement vibrating beneath their feet. The horses tossed their heads in their harnesses and shook their necks as their muscled bodies strained. Wendy ventured a look south,

CHAPTER TWO

way too far to see the New York skyline, but the low-hanging clouds gathered in that direction as if the city had turned into a giant smudge across the horizon. A sharp gust of wind caused her to wobble, and David caught her before she went down.

"Pay attention, Mom!" Smiling, shuffling, staggering, he let her go and raced ahead, his hood blowing back and his longish hair waving behind him, most of it black except where it was growing in blonde around the roots, his natural color like Charlie's.

With a soft chuckle, Wendy ran to catch up, her boots pounding on the pavement next to the clopping horses. Ahead, cyclones owned the bridge, their shapes visible by the clutter they threw up, pieces of dirt and gravel and an occasional plastic car part or shredded seat. The wrecks were dark squares twisted at odd angles, with the vivid outlines of their engines and frames pressed against the medians. Just when Wendy thought she couldn't run without falling, Morten gave the signal, and they all rushed to the wagons. Charlie and Alma stretched their hands to help Wendy and David into the warm and glowing lantern light.

Morten drove them into the whipping storm, the horses with their heads down and their manes flying in the wind. The driver hunkered in his seat, flicking the reins and calling into the gale like a madman, his grayish-white hair caught in the gusts. The carriage quaked and squealed, wooden walls groaning as tools and supplies hanging from hooks shook and fell onto the wagon floor. Alma picked them up and put them in a tight space to be reorganized later. Wendy and the kids took seats on crates, clinging to each other and to whatever would hold them, Charlie gripping Clyde's harness as the dog sat between her legs and stared through the whipping rear flaps dripping with moisture and stinging sleet.

Debris struck them, thumping the sides and striking the floorboards with an incessant clattering. David sat stiffly, his entire body spread out to keep his balance, and Charlie curled up, her eyes as wide as the dog's. The maelstrom obscured the two wagons behind them, hiding them in swirling mists; yet, they came into view now and then, with Lavinia looking as fierce as Morten, her skirt clinging wetly to her legs, coat threatening to pull her out of the seat, bonnet

CHAPTER TWO

fastened to her head as her blonde hair clung to her cheeks and wrapped beneath her chin. Wendy's stomach fluttered as concentrated gusts shoved them across the lanes, the rear end whipping to the left and taking the horses with them. Morten never stopped, rising to shout as loud as the storm, snapping the reins, and pumping his fist into the sky as if battling nature itself.

Charlie closed her eyes tight, and tears squeezed out. "Are we going into the river?"

"No!" Wendy let go of the side and wrapped her arm around her daughter, pulling her against her and wondering if what Charlie said might just happen.

Then the winds stopped, tapering to almost nothing, the rear wagon flaps settling into place and dripping water onto the floor. Alma climbed over to secure the bottoms with leather straps, leaving just a little space for them to see out. The second wagon had caught up, the horses slowing to a canter as they snorted and neighed proudly, and Samuel stepped into the seat to wrap his arm around his wife, waving at Alma that they were okay.

"That was close," Charlie said with a quivering sigh. "I thought we were dead."

"Not with Grandpa driving." David got up and climbed between the crates to sit with Morten up front, the older man greeting his grandson with a bellow.

Smiling, Wendy and Charlie helped Alma get things cleaned up in the back, using towels to wipe up the moisture that had gotten in and replacing items on their hooks. She squeezed Alma's shoulder. "I must admit; I thought this wagon would fall apart. Thank goodness for Amish quality."

Alma scoffed pleasantly. "My father made these with one of his friends back at the settlement. He wanted something bigger and sturdier. Many laughed at him and preferred the smaller, lightweight buggies you're used to seeing, but he insisted we Christensen's were tall and needed the legroom."

Wendy grinned and nodded, following David's footsteps to the front where she leaned through the wet flaps to hang onto the back of the seat. "Nice driving, Dad."

CHAPTER TWO

"Thank you, Wendy. I never doubted we'd make it, though I worried about Samuel's lighter wagon. I see they're right behind us."

"It seems everyone's okay," Wendy agreed. "Your horses are incredible... not that I know much about them."

"Marley and Fitzpatrick are the best horses I've ever raised. Tough and fearless."

"Like you, Grandpa," David said with a pat on the man's back.

Swift, wispy-dark cloud banks rolled overhead, sweeping from north to south even as the rest of the upper atmosphere shifted in the other direction.

Morten glanced up. "It seems the warring weather has reached a truce for now. We'll stay in the wagons and drive hard until we reach Nyack, which should be just up the road."

Wendy settled onto a crate and watched their progress as they rolled north past signs for Nyack and Spring Valley. The hills of Blauvelt State Park fell behind as nature gave way to more subdivisions and boxy streets, the intrastate junction up ahead with its pretzel turns and branches looming above and below. Morten guided them through clusters of debris and chunks of every kind of rubble. Mostly it was pieces of the forest to the southwest, big bushy branches thrown onto the highway and on top of stranded cars, poking through shattered windows at figures splayed across the dashboard, and seats stained with blood. Corpses in the roadway announced themselves with a sickening reek.

"Ew," Charlie said, holding her nose. "Something smells awful."

Wendy caught the pungent aroma, and she leaned forward to see bloated forms lined up on the shoulders with children's wagons and luggage carts parked against the median, their colorless skin marbled with dark veins and bruised spots where blood had pooled. Others sprawled in the center lanes like they'd been tossed there by Hurricane Jane's vengeful winds, their arms and legs at awkward angles, broken bones poking through.

"Pretty gross," David agreed.

Wendy was about to tell him to get in the back so he didn't have to see it, but there was no return. The kids had been exposed to terrible scenes, an ugliness no parent ever wanted their child to see.

CHAPTER TWO

And while she couldn't protect them whenever they passed a dead body or witnessed the actions of cruel people, she could continue to teach them about being human.

"That's a lot of bodies," Wendy agreed. "Just remember..."

"They were people once," David said, kicking his heels up on the floor runner. "I know, Mom, and sometimes if I see someone lying there, I make up stories about them so I remember it could be me."

Drawing a slow but surprised breath, Wendy pursed her lips and nodded, holding back tears as she rested her hand on David's back and rubbed between his shoulder blades. By then, they'd passed the junction, and the highway angled them down into town, where roads and exits branched north and south. Blown open warehouses lay scattered around them along with flattened neighborhoods and rain-soaked streets, the hills on the left-hand side of the highway filled with flood waters overwhelming drainage ditches and moving as fast as rivers. They navigated through more clusters of junk, and Morten slowed to a stop and stepped down.

Samuel and Uri met them by the wagons, and Morten pointed west. "I think we start walking again. Rest the horses and focus on clearing the roads."

"How long until we come to more back roads?" Samuel asked.

"Won't find much rural space here, son. Not until Suffern, anyway. Your sister has some maps back there, and she'll be directing us through the worst of it, and I trust her decisions. Uri and Samuel, you'll be upfront with me on this stretch, and Wendy and David can take the rear. Alma, you're with them."

"Okay, Father," Alma said, slipping a poncho over her head and grabbing a shotgun from a crate.

They took positions, with David striding on the right-hand shoulder and Wendy and Alma on the left. As Wendy proceeded, she glanced into the back of Samuel's and Lavinia's wagon. Mara and Noah poked their heads out with disdainful looks she was sure her parents were influencing. Resisting the urge to stick her tongue out, she waved to David on the other side and received a sharp salute in return.

Gazing across the ruined landscape of New York, she scanned the surrounding woods bathed in sheets of mist clinging to the sky and skittish movements of survivors sheltering in buildings. Farther north, looters picked a string of department stores clean, more like scavengers on corpses than human beings. Somewhere out there, a child cried, a man shouted, and a woman shrieked an angry reply, voices bouncing around in fractured echoes.

"How are the kids holding up?" Alma stepped close with her long strides, towering over Wendy and swinging her rifle in front of her with the barrel pointed toward the pavement.

"It's tough to tell," Wendy replied as she glanced south. "David seems to be handling it pretty well, but Charlie has been upset a lot."

"She's a strong girl," Alma said, "but I can't imagine how hard this must be for her. After all, we are all frightened of what's happening."

"The worst part about it is not knowing where we are going or if we'll have a home there."

"You'll always have a home with us."

Wendy smiled. "When I think of you and Dad and Uri, I feel nothing but warmth. But Samuel doesn't like us, Alma."

"He doesn't like many people, not even inside the Amish community. He and Zach always competed when they were younger, and Samuel almost always lost no matter the competition. Zach always came out on top, whether it was schoolwork, worship, or physical games. And it wasn't because he was bigger and stronger than the others. There is a quiet intensity about my brother that allows him to, um..." Alma shook her head, unable to find the words.

"He absorbs his surroundings. Takes things in and learns. He's one of the most observant people I've ever met, it's why I fell in love with him."

"That's a good way of putting it." The tall woman nodded as she shielded Wendy from some of the rain. Alma's ash blonde hair clung to her cheeks and neck as moisture had saturated everything. "That probably explains why he took to things so quickly. He could pick up a sport or class subject and expand upon it in his own simple way."

"Now you're making me miss him."

"I'm so sorry, Wendy. I didn't mean to bring your heart grief."

CHAPTER TWO

"It's okay," Wendy smiled warmly. "Having you here is as close as I could ever get to Zach. I know you were close when you were young."

"That's right. We always seemed to have a link between us. Mother said we could have been twins."

Wendy clicked her tongue. "I wish Elvesta was still with us. I wish I'd known her longer."

"My mother was a good woman and taught me how to be strong in tough times and navigate a world full of brothers who were mostly bigger and stronger than me."

Wendy smiled, thinking back on the green-eyed lady Zach had introduced her to so many years ago. "She was so understanding about Zach and me. She disagreed with it, yet she gave me the benefit of the doubt."

"Mother loved you very much. How often did I hear her talk about how you complimented Zach perfectly? Whenever another mother challenged her about marrying someone outside the community, she countered with something about us learning something new and branching out, absorbing the good things of modern society while still holding on to our traditional ways." Alma blew a low exhale. "It was a fine line to walk, but Father grew convinced over time and reached out to others outside the community to grow our business. That forward-thinking attitude enabled us to prosper far more than anyone else."

Wendy shrugged innocently. "It's not the side effect I was going for, but I'm glad —"

A low whistle drew their gazes, and Morten leaned forward, pointing to his eyes, and then ahead. Alma nodded and waved at Samuel behind her.

"David!" Wendy called, keeping her voice below a shout and getting her son's attention. Mirroring Morten, she pointed at her eyes and forward. He nodded and jogged ahead a few yards with his hand on his pistol while scanning the road.

Wendy searched the shadows along the roadsides, looking for who was coming and what weapons they had. They'd be easy to run off if they held bats or knives. Guns were another story; while they hadn't seen many of them, they were prepared for the worst. Still, she felt small and unprotected in the open, a sitting duck for anyone to take out. It wasn't long before a cluster of whistles and answering calls echoed in the streets, setting off shadows that slid through the din. Uri shouted from behind them, and Wendy turned in a slow circle to sweep the road to the south as she watched Samuel and Alma run to the last wagon, raise their weapons, and fire almost simultaneously. The three loud booms blasted her ears compared to the natural wind and rain they'd heard all day.

Uri, Samuel, and Alma scooted closer to the wagons and grabbed some flaps Morten had fastened to the sides with hinges. They flipped them open toward the back to protect themselves from incoming fire. Wood chips flew as small arms rounds pelted them. Alma swung her shield around the rear corner of the third wagon and shot off to her left with another massive shotgun boom and flash of light. The gunfire picked up, the sounds of ricochets bouncing in every direction, lead slapping wood. Wendy mentally went over the plan they'd laid out in the event of an attack. Resisting the urge to join the fight at the back, she stayed with the middle wagon and jogged alongside it to guard their south flank. She couldn't see David, though she was sure he was on the opposite side, returning fire with the other men, judging by the flashes of light above the wagon.

Someone screamed over the pops, and Wendy craned her neck to see if it was one of theirs, resisting the urge to help. Morten whistled two sharp bursts that cut through the cacophony and they switched direction. Samuel and Uri ran from the rear to the front as they reloaded, taking David with them. They joined the Amish leader at the first wagon. Morten was crouching above his seat with his rifle in hand, neck craned forward as he searched the highway. He nodded and jumped off the right side and darted out of sight.

A cluster of dark figures closed in from the front, creeping up the cluttered lanes, shadows carrying weapons and using abandoned vehicles for cover. This wasn't Wendy's fight, and she cut between the second and third wagons and jogged to the back of the train opposite Alma on the left side. Glancing right, she saw the top of Miriam's head and her rifle barrel jutting from the rear wagon flaps. Wendy settled behind the wooden shield, noting divots where the incoming

CHAPTER TWO

fire had punched through and splintered the wood. Gulping, she grabbed the edge and rested her M&P 15 on it as she scanned the darkness.

"They're faking," Miriam said. "Pretending like they were feigning a rear attack while hitting us in the front."

Wendy nodded and swallowed another nervous lump, her insides curling in fear for David.

"Are you okay, Wendy?" Alma called from the other side.

"I think so," Wendy sputtered as she searched the wrecks to the east, watching figures retreat and sprint north through the fog where a string of dead strip malls gave them plenty of rubble to hide in. On a whim, she grabbed the M&P 15 with both hands and tracked one lone assailant who made a massive target in the darkness, firing three times across fifty yards to hit him with the touch of death. The man spun and disappeared behind a pile of bricks.

"I'm okay now!" Wendy shouted.

Miriam grinned and picked out a target, taking a shot and charging the rifle with a clack. Bright flashes lit the gloom like fireflies, and Wendy ducked behind the shield, wincing every time a bullet struck it, expecting one to punch through and pierce her at any moment. Gritting her teeth, she rose and fired three shots into the window sections of a car frame that hit a figure on the other side with a glass-shattering punctuation mark. Miraculously, the horses stood calmly throughout the exchange, even when a rupture of gunfire broke out in the west where Morten, Uri, Samuel, and David fought the bigger battle. Glancing back, she couldn't see much farther past the lead wagon. Morten and the others charged into the gloom.

"They're coming this way!" Miriam shouted before she fired another round, reloaded, and fired again, the rifle's repercussions blowing strands of hair across her cheeks.

Wendy had it easier, peeping over her shield and dispersing shots at some figures ahead, then at another pair charging from her left. One of them clutched their chest and went down with a gurgling cry while the other kept running at her.

She hadn't been counting the number of bullets remaining in her magazine, figuring she had just a few more. Stepping away from the shield, aiming calmly, she fired twice into the other charging shape. A round took him in the gut, stopping him in his tracks as he gripped his stomach, pale face lifted, gaping at Wendy as he staggered to his knees. Wendy fired down her sights, and the man's head whipped back before he toppled like a wet rag. A cluster of shots flashed behind him, a bullet zipping past Wendy's left ear like a fat bug and striking the wagon with a splintering whack. The children inside squealed and shouted.

A dark shape swept up next to her, Lavinia with a large revolver in her skinny hands. She shouldered past Wendy, resting her arms on the wooden shield, and fired at more encroaching shapes. The woman's eyes were filled with tears, her cheeks red and lips trembling as she cocked the weapon and kept firing steadily, grunting each time.

"How dare they shoot at my children!" She scowled through clenched teeth. "These are our *children*! Cowards! You're nothing but cowards!"

Wendy nudged her with her elbow and gestured to the roadside. Lavinia turned her scowl on her, then followed her gaze and understood. They stepped from behind the wooden barrier to track three people running parallel to the wagon where buildings stood in ruined clusters. The assailants sprinted from vehicle to vehicle and fired on the second wagon where Lavinia's children were sheltered. Wendy and Lavinia caught them in between coverage and delivered four or five rounds that struck their legs, hips, and shoulders, buckling two of the three while the last attempted to limp away but collapsed behind a slumping sedan.

Men shouted from the east in what Wendy took as a signal to retreat, and Morten's brisk three-burst whistle ordered everyone back to the wagons. Wendy closed the bullet-ridden barrier and rushed with Lavinia to the second wagon as Morten and the others returned with Uri stretched between David and Samuel, bleeding from a wound in his middle, gasping and grunting in anguish.

"Oh, blessed be!" Lavinia exclaimed, stopping by the wagon stair and watching as they approached. "What happened?"

"We beat those bastards off!" Morten strode up, arms away from

CHAPTER TWO

his sides and his rifle gripped in one hand. "One of them got in behind us and shot Uri. My son! They shot my son!"

Wendy followed the men as they circled to the back and attempted to lift Uri into the wagon. Lavinia entered from the front and took his shoulders, straining to hold him up as Samuel climbed in to assist her. Once they had him inside, Samuel turned and pushed David back so the tall boy had to grab the tailgate to avoid falling. Wendy climbed in to see they'd placed Uri on a makeshift pallet made of straw bedding and foam.

"Let me help!" She squeezed in next to Samuel as they stretched Uri's legs out and tried to make him comfortable. "I've got some first-aid training —"

Samuel's elbow flew in, connecting with Wendy's side and forcing her off her seat with a pained yelp. The Amish man's nostrils flared, and he shouted, "Be gone! We'll take care of our own. If it had not been for you, this wouldn't have happened. I told Father it would, but he wouldn't listen to me."

"What are you talking about?" Wendy replied, her brow scrunching in confusion and hurt. "We fought back and —"

"I said be gone!" Samuel pointed at the rear of the wagon, angry eyes blinking from a blood-splattered face. "Leave now before I throw you out myself."

Wendy slowly backed off, shouldering her rifle and jumping out with Alma's help, who flashed Wendy an apologetic look before climbing up in her place. They tore off Uri's shirt, ripping it to shreds and tossing it to the side. Lavinia was there, falling to her knees with handfuls of gauze to dab at the bleeding wound. Alma stepped around Samuel and kneeled by Uri's head, comforting her brother as Lavinia inspected the injury, pressing with her fingers and inspecting the entry of the round where it had struck Uri just below the rib cage on his right side.

With tight lips, she used a suction device to clear the wound of blood and peer inside it with a penlight. "It's not gone in far. Just an inch or two."

"Can you get it out?" Samuel asked.

CHAPTER TWO

Lavinia nodded briskly, though her face was ashen as she turned and looked for instruments.

"Come, Wendy," Morten said, guiding her and David toward the first wagon. "We need to be on guard while they remove the bullet. Can you get Charlie to help?"

With a weak nod, Wendy turned and jerked her head at David, and he followed her to where Charlie waited in the back of the wagon.

"What happened, Mom?"

"Uri was shot in the side, and they're going to get the bullet out. We need to guard the wagons while they do it."

Charlie put down the wagon's tailgate and patted her leg, and Clyde barked and leaped to the pavement where he flipped his tail and looked around curiously.

"Charlie, you stay on this side, and David and I will take the other side. Let's walk down the line and meet in the back. Then David will join you and we'll walk to the front."

Charlie nodded and pulled her .380 from its holster, holding Clyde's leash and waiting for Wendy and David to get in position. Moving to the other side, they scanned their surroundings for any signs of a threat, catching movement out in the distance but nothing came their direction. She turned and nodded to Charlie, and they strolled back the other way on full alert, Uri's scream drawing her pained glance as they passed. They met Charlie at the end of the wagon train where Miriam peeked between the flaps with her shotgun.

"Is my brother okay?" she asked through tear-streaked eyes.

"He's been shot in the side," Wendy replied hoarsely. "Lavinia is trying to get the bullet out."

Miriam nodded, and David crossed over to join Charlie. Together, they walked west, weapons on display as they passed the middle wagon. Uri's screams rose to a sustained shriek that finally trailed off and fell silent, leaving just the pattering rain to keep them company. Meeting at the front of the wagon train, they stood looking into the gloom, Wendy with her head bowed and tears blurring her vision. A

CHAPTER TWO

large hand covered her shoulder, and she turned to see Morten standing there.

"Is he...?"

"He's stable for now." He nodded with relief. "We need to get moving. I want you seated beside me as I drive. Two sets of eyes on the road will be better."

Wendy strode to the front of the wagon and climbed into the seat on Morten's left. With robotic movements, she checked her magazine. One bullet remained, so she ejected it and loaded a fresh one into the well. Shaking and shellshocked from the firefight, Wendy rested the weapon across her lap with her left toe tapping nervously on the floor. Her emotions were scrambled, and her ears rang from the constant firing. Her heart hurt from the accusation in Samuel's eyes. Morten made sharp kissing sounds and flicked the reins to get the horses moving, and the wagon pulled away with the other two rumbling behind them.

"Wendy?"

"Yes?"

"Watch the road for threats. Shoot first and ask questions later."

Wendy nodded and leaned out, pushing the barrel forward and searching the slowly drifting mist for their enemies.

Morten drove them five more miles through the wind and the rain, but no one else accosted them from the rubble-filled streets. People moved in long lines north of them, heading west away from the populated areas, groups of refugees squatting atop piles of bricks and building materials while the skies cracked with lightning and the throaty growls of thunder.

The wagon rocked beneath them, Wendy's backside aching where her tailbone rested at the crook of the padded seat and rigid backing, understanding why Morten slouched after so many miles. They rode in silence except when Morten spotted something in the gloom, pointing it out to her before returning to his driving. The horses' heads hung low, and their pace had slowed to a crawl. Everyone on board kept alert, watching from the backs of the wagons or through wooden side windows they'd flipped down.

When an overpass appeared out of the thick mist, Morten flicked the reins and told Wendy, "We'll rest here."

She sighed with relief when they stopped, the concrete structure blocking all the rain and most of the gales, though the center lanes were like a wind tunnel, forcing them to stay to the right-hand shoulder. Wendy hopped out, holding her rifle in one hand, stretching tall and thrusting her hips forward to relieve some ache. Charlie and David climbed out with Clyde, and the three joined them at the front of the first wagon. Morten checked on the horses, running his big hands across their flanks, and wrapped his arm around Marley's neck, whispering encouragement and praise to the animal before doing the same with Fitzpatrick. Standing between them, he stroked their long snouts and stepped back.

"The horses are exhausted," he said.

"Can't we rest here, Grandpa?" Charlie asked. "It seems pretty safe."

Smiling sadly, he brushed a lock of Charlie's hair back and patted her face. "We need to keep driving ahead, though we'll rest here for a brief while. I want to check on Uri."

Wendy nodded and watched the tall man stride off with long legs and arms swinging tiredly. Before climbing inside, he spoke to Lavinia, who was driving the second wagon.

"I hope Uri is okay," Charlie said, tugging on Clyde's leash to bring him to the horses. The gray Labrador stared at the larger animals with big eyes and his tail sweeping back and forth in a puddle.

"Me, too," Wendy said. "It was a pretty nasty wound."

"He hasn't screamed in a while," David commented as he joined Charlie by the horses and rested his hand on Marley's neck. The horse knickered tiredly and nudged him with her nose.

"That could be good or bad," Wendy replied. "I'll assume it's good because Lavinia hasn't tried to kill me yet."

Charlie dipped under Fitzpatrick's neck and stepped out with her

CHAPTER TWO

hand lingering on the horse's bridle. "They don't seem to like us very much, Mom, do they?"

"Miriam and Uri do, but Samuel and Lavinia have something against us. I don't think they wanted to swing by and help us."

"But we're family," Charlie countered.

"We're not Amish, though. Stay here, guys. Keep an eye on things while I see what's happening."

Wendy strode to the rear of Lavinia's wagon, nodding to Miriam, where she sat in her driver's seat, knees together and shivering. She set the reins beside her and went back in with the kids right before Wendy got there. Inside the second wagon, Morten and Alma crouched on either side of Uri with Lavinia kneeling by Uri's head. Samuel squatted by the tailgate, half holding open the flaps as water dripped from the overpass although not at the same rate as the falling rain. He glared at Wendy, the flat distaste of accusation in his eyes. Wendy arched her eyebrows and sighed, turning away from the wagon and walking a short distance away. A part of her ached with guilt for the bullet Uri had taken, yet when she thought of where they'd be without Morten's family, her regret vanished. Yes, Uri had gotten shot, a terrible result of traveling dangerous paths, yet the kids standing over by Marley and Fitzpatrick were worth every bit of the grueling journey.

David and Charlie were gently slapping at each other, David's longer arms getting the best of the play fight until Marley put his snout between them and knocked him back. A smile lit Wendy's face, and her chest filled with warmth. No, she wouldn't feel guilty about surviving, and they'd done everything they could to protect themselves. Injuries were a part of life; her left shoulder still ached from the bullet wound she'd received fighting Turley and the teachers.

Her pleasant thoughts were broken when the voices in the wagon raised heatedly, Lavinia and Samuel arguing with Morten until he bellowed in anger and suddenly appeared at the back. He climbed over the tailgate and jumped down, landing on the pavement and reaching for Miriam's horses, patting their heads and whispering to them as Samuel and Lavinia hopped out.

"We should never have done it, Father," Samuel said, standing behind Morten with his hands on his hips and his reddish beard gusting in the overpass winds.

"We've been through this, Samuel," Morten replied. "We've selected our travel companions and are in this together."

Lavinia was on Samuel's left with her arms crossed and a stern expression, her stare boring into her father-in-law's back. "You selected our travel companions, Father. We had no choice."

"Love and loyalty to our family dictated our actions," Morten replied, still stroking the horses' snouts.

"A trivial fact." Samuel glanced at Wendy. Knowing she was watching and listening, he raised his voice. "They're *not* us. They're not part of our community."

"I am the one who owns these wagons and horses, and a good deal of the supplies." Morten stood as tall as the horses as he hugged one's neck. "You did not bring your own, yet my loyalty to you and your siblings and extended family took precedence."

"Our barns were blown over," Samuel complained with a gesture. "Our horses ran off during the devastation."

Morten spread his hands. "A trivial fact."

As the Amish leader started to walk away, Samuel grabbed his arm and turned him. "Father, you must listen to me!"

Morten reeled on them, his left fist coming up and pounding on the side of the wagon, causing Samuel to reverse course, running into Lavinia and retreating two paces. "What would you have me do? Leave your brother's family here? And what do you think Zach would do to you when he found out you were the one who pushed the issue?"

Samuel paled, yet a glance at Wendy strengthened his resolve. "Zach isn't here, and he hasn't been part of our community for years. He has no say in community decisions, especially for our *own* families." Morten glowered at him as he added, "God is punishing us for sheltering these outsiders, Father, I'm sure of it. He's cursed us with ill luck and hard lessons we could have avoided if we'd traveled with everyone else to Pearisburg."

Morten's face turned dark, his thickset eyebrows furrowing and

CHAPTER TWO

narrowing over his hard eyes. "Do you profess to know the word of God now, Samuel?"

Taken aback slightly, he replied, "No, I don't speak for God, but I know his scriptures, and I follow them wholeheartedly. Lavinia does, and so does our family. I don't believe he would have wanted us —"

"Hold your tongue, Samuel," Morten warned. "You do not have the authority in this family or our community to wield such words. I have ordered you to act faithfully in protecting Zach's wife and children." He gestured to Wendy, almost offering her a chance to speak, though her lips remained firmly pressed, the M&P 15 gripped in her hands. Morten continued, "Know this, Son. Keep defying me on this, and you'll feel my wrath. That is no trivial fact."

The tall Amish man turned and walked away with long, heavy strides, his scowl changing to a wide grin as he came up to David and Charlie. He reached down to pat Clyde on the head, the dog accepting the affection fearfully, since Morten's hand wrapped nearly around his skull. A crooked smile crept onto Wendy's face, and she glanced over to see Samuel staring at his father's back while Lavinia fixed her with an icy glare.

Wendy took two steps forward, letting the barrel of her M&P 15 drift toward the ground. "So, here we are. We can either get along or —"

Samuel cut her off. "We're down a guard. Charlie will have to quit slacking in the wagon and take responsibility. She and her dog can pull their weight."

"You can't order us around," Wendy countered. "You're not my boss, and we're not enemies. We fought together, and we won. Thanks to Lavinia, Uri will make it through this." The unexpected compliment softened Lavinia's features before they hardened when Samuel stepped out and clasped his hands at his waist.

"Post her as a guard, or not," Samuel said, leaning in with a stoic expression. "But if we're not properly protected because of your negligence, the next injury will be on your hands, not ours." With that, he gestured for Lavinia to join him in the back of the second wagon, and the pair climbed up and disappeared.

While they'd been talking, Charlie came up with Clyde's leash in hand, glancing uncertainly toward the wagons. "I overheard that, Mom. Do you guys need me to walk by the wagons now? I can do it. It's not a problem."

"I know you can, honey." Wendy stared after Samuel and Lavinia before turning to Charlie with a smile. "You'll be out here in this glorious weather with us now."

A gust of wind almost took Charlie's hat off, strands of her sun-shaded hair drifting in the breeze. The girl brushed them back and pulled her hood firmly in place and re-tied it. "I don't like Samuel. He scares me."

"There's nothing to fear. They're still family, no matter how much they hate us."

"What if he convinces Grandpa to leave us? What if he convinces them they'll move faster without us?"

"No way. Grandpa would never do that. Morten is a good man, and he loves Zach. Us, too." She wrapped her arm around Charlie's shoulders and squeezed. "We can't please everyone all the time, but that doesn't mean we can't be kind to them despite their resentment of us. Samuel and Lavinia will just have to deal with it until we make it to Pearisburg. From there, we'll find a place to live away from them."

Charlie smiled. "Okay, Mom."

"Why don't you get an extra magazine for your gun and meet me back out here? Morten wants to get started soon."

"Okay. Be right back."

Wendy watched Charlie jog off and petted the second wagon's horses before climbing into the back of their own to get ammunition out of her backpack.

CHAPTER THREE

Stephanie Lancaster, Washington, DC

Stephanie had been moved four seats to the left, replaced by more of Colonel Davies' military officers and others closely watching the defense of the Pentagon. She had three laptops open, each showing a different location where Genevieve Clark's rescue teams were spread out across the Northeast, one facility just north of Washington, DC, likely where the civilians standing outside the Pentagon and White House had come from.

Colonel Davies and the President stood in front of the flashing monitors, watching the various camera feeds around the building where barricades were being dragged into place by Humvees and tanks. The sweeping military presence formed a buffer zone three hundred yards in every direction, armored police and guardsmen with shields pushing back the crowds into the streets so they could erect more solid defenses. Stephanie had been tracking the weather patterns with great success. After helping a convoy get through Kansas City and avoiding a tornado that could have destroyed them, she found herself more frightened than ever as bottles and bricks were hurled at the military forces protecting them.

CHAPTER THREE

"Are you there, Stephanie?" Genevieve spoke into her earpiece, forcing her to take her attention off the battles being waged around them to help Genevieve with her problems.

"I'm here, Genevieve. Sorry..." Stephanie cleared her voice of any quivering notes with a cough. "Things are getting hectic here."

"What's happening?" Genevieve was at the site close to Baltimore, her brown hair windblown, eyes worried and tired. "Are you okay?"

It was directed at Stephanie, though she sensed an underlying question. She straightened in her chair and smiled firmly. "We're fine here, Genevieve. Yes, even the President. I've got that convoy of semis heading your way. ETA, thirty-five minutes." Stephanie switched to her left-hand screen, tracking the convoy along I-70 where they'd be getting off near the Turf Valley resort with its expansive golf course and open park areas. Civilians by the thousands were gathered amid blocks of tents and temporary structures directed by FEMA, Army resources, and National Guardsmen. The parameters were flexible, forcing military personnel to make snap decisions on who could be let in and who'd stay out, allowing families first while guessing which groups were using children that weren't theirs to get inside.

Every time she talked to Genevieve, gunshots went off in the distance. Not just small arms fire but machine guns and occasional tracers lighting up the gloom. Cloudy skies loomed everywhere, bringing more rain than she'd ever seen. The lack of sunlight and shifting air currents sweeping in from the north were screwing up jet streams, causing an atmospheric war that conjured massive tornadoes and hurricane-like winds where they shouldn't have been. Flash thunderstorms brought torrential rains that wiped out entire hillsides across Pennsylvania and Maryland, washing thousands of homes into the valleys in debris-cluttered rivers. Radar facilities atop high ridgelines took massive damage, cramping her ability to collect data, especially with the satellites unable to penetrate the thick, foamy cloud spread. Still, she could piece together what they fed her intuitively, using Craig's modeling systems to issue warnings to those in the trenches.

CHAPTER THREE

With the click of a button, she communicated with the lead trucker headed toward Baltimore. "Hello, um, Razzle Dazzle? This is DC Weather Control letting you know you've got quite a squall a quarter mile ahead of you. Be advised to take it slow and give the weather about forty-five minutes to pass."

A woman's husky voice replied, her twang reminding Stephanie of the Alabama Hills. "Roger that, DC Weather Control. We'll take that under advisement."

Another trucker piped up in a surly voice elongated with a Boston accent. "Yeah. At the current rate of speed, we're going to arrive in Baltimore sometime next year."

"Hey, Ice Man?" Razzle Dazzle responded. "Why don't you do what the lady asks and take it easy for about forty-five minutes?"

"With all due respect, DC Weather Control, it's dark out here, and we've got hungry people gathering on the roadside, and they are getting less and less afraid of the military boys."

A frown touched Stephanie's lips. "Roger that, Ice Man and Razzle Dazzle. All the same, let's follow protocol and give time for the storm to pass, unless you want to find yourself tossed a couple of miles into the sky."

"Get there a lot faster that way," Ice Man replied, followed by some laughter and snickers of truck drivers behind him. When Stephanie didn't respond right away, the trucker sobered up. "Roger that, DC Weather Control. We'll hang tight."

Stephanie turned to the middle screen where the camera person following Genevieve was jogging to keep up with the bustling leader. "Genevieve, are you still there?"

The wind gusted over the microphone as Genevieve gave unintelligible orders to someone off camera before turning back. "I'm here, Stephanie. Go ahead."

"That convoy is going to be delayed by forty-five minutes. Hang tight."

"Gotcha."

"You have enough security there?"

Genevieve laughed over the howling winds as a cluster of garbage and debris swirled overhead. "I've got military personnel

CHAPTER THREE

crawling up my backside. We're okay, but everything's rough around the edges."

"I understand."

A military guard had escorted her from site to site as she bolstered camps all around the Northeast, most of them surrounded by thousands of guardsmen or soldiers. When they were lucky enough to have local police forces still intact, they used those, too. It was a paltry effort against the tens of thousands of hungry, angry people, destitute after Hurricane Jane had ripped through their towns and left them without necessities. With the demand for goods far outweighing what was available, the existing supplies were shrinking. Bandits and angry weather were hindering their momentum, and only a spattering of deliveries were getting where they needed to go. Meanwhile, there were isolated warehouses filled with product all over the country, guarded by loyal troops and city officers, though many of those critical storage facilities had been looted and were on fire.

President Holland slammed his fist into his palm. "Colonel Davies. Your men need to get the situation around this building under control!"

"Yes, sir." Davies turned and barked commands into a radio. The commotion shocked Stephanie out of her thoughts, and she glanced over to see multiple screens filled with people rushing through weak spots in the perimeter where the barriers hadn't yet been put in place. Soldiers usually chased them down, bound them up, and dragged them back to the crowds. More egregious offenders were hauled off to cells on the subfloors.

As Stephanie watched, a group of outnumbered soldiers fought for their lives against raiders with pistols and crowbars. The high-definition footage showed civilians trying to wrest carbines from the soldiers until one soldier turned his weapon on them and fired, a full clip of ammunition emptied into a handful of people, the high-powered rounds ripping them to shreds and spraying blood across the Pentagon grounds. The room went quiet, the civilian leaders in attendance gasping and staring at the screen with glassy eyes and forlorn expressions.

CHAPTER THREE

"Colonel, let's roll out a few more hard bodies and see what they say!"

Davies stepped away and spoke into a microphone, his voice a growl as tanks and Humvees were deployed from the bowels of the Pentagon and onto the concrete walkways and grassy lawns, their fifty-caliber machine guns sweeping out across the crowds. What surprised Stephanie the most wasn't the bloodshed or the massive equipment being brought to bear. It was the civilians with their fingers gripping the chain-link fencing, faces screaming at the soldiers, unafraid of the armored vehicles and powerful machine guns. Either they didn't know what kind of damage those weapons could do or were beyond caring. With the perimeter secured, the President turned to the assembled group, where a pair of generals and several high-level commanders had joined them from another room. Stephanie understood that their responsibilities were communicating with NORTHCOM and the other United States command centers worldwide.

With a nod to everyone, Holland took on a more regal demeanor, looking like the President she was used to seeing on TV. "The news from our Fairbanks mission team is good. We partially shut down the hydrocarbon flood, but we're not out of trouble yet. As you all know, the Russians have started an incursion into Alaska, trying to secure the remaining oilfields and whatever's left of the reserves in the Beaufort Sea." He mumbled, "I can't imagine what kind of spillage is happening out there, and until we can get that carrier strike force into position, we have no way of knowing."

Stephanie had been ignoring calls from her company all day. They wanted to know the status of the oilfields they owned in the Alaskan region, though she'd replied to the company officers by email, explaining the situation with the Russians and that they should not count on recovering any of those facilities and crews unless the military could turn things around. And then she'd blocked them for the time being, tired of being hounded by their petty concerns for something out of their control.

"I'm starting to think like Craig," she whispered with bemusement.

CHAPTER THREE

General Adkins, a dark-haired man with a calm demeanor, stood. "Mr. President, it is our collective feeling that the Russians are creating a buffer zone by driving deep into Alaska and Canada, thinking we are more vulnerable than ever."

Holland poked his finger hard at the desk. "I want a full-scale retaliation short of nukes. And I want President Alexeev on the phone right now."

"We're trying, sir!" someone called.

"Well, try harder!" Holland glared across the table, his eyes freezing Stephanie where she sat, then he turned and looked at the displays. "Put Secretary of State on the screen."

A moment later, a wide-eyed woman in her sixties appeared on the display, her robust complexion and high cheekbones accentuated by silken hair wrapped in an efficient bun. "Yes, Mr. President. I'm here."

"Secretary Langmore, any headway with England and France?"

"Because of the friction in the atmosphere, we've resorted to ship-to-ship communication, and while it's slow, it works. Regarding the Russians, our biggest allies are on board with your condemnation of the Russian incursion. However, they express deep reservations about approving any military retaliation because of the catastrophes unfolding in their own countries."

"I understand everyone is struggling, but if the Russians are successful in this grab, they'll have the world by the throat, energy-wise. Do they understand what that means?"

"I'm sure they do, sir."

"This could shift the balance of world power in a terrible way."

"General Atkins, I want the Russians running into a brick wall on this. It's time we showed everyone what the best-trained military force in the world can do. Do you hear me, General?"

"Yes, sir," Atkins replied.

"There's something else, sir."

Holland squeezed his eyes shut and turned to Colonel Davies with a nod. "What is it, Colonel? Something happening on the perimeter?"

"No, sir. Well, in a way, sir." Davies shook his head, stumbling over his words.

"Be plain, Colonel." Holland faced the man and widened his stance as if preparing to accept another blow. "Can't be worse than a Russian incursion."

"It's just that…" Davies cleared his throat. "We're getting reports of key personnel going missing."

The President's brow creased, and he stared hard at Davies. "Missing? Are you telling me some of our bases are falling to civilians?"

"No, sir. Individuals are simply leaving. Several members of Congress were ferried to Raven Rock Mountain by Marines days ago, but it seems at least a half dozen have left the facility."

"Left? You mean they snuck out?"

"They convinced some guards to let them leave the facility with military vehicles."

Holland's face deepened in color, and his eyes bulged with anger. "Do you know why they left?"

"Some left notes or internal communications that showed they were concerned for family members, while others didn't think our facilities were secure enough from civilian attacks."

Holland shook his head, his fists clenched at his sides and then crossed his arms as if to contain the explosion building inside.

Stephanie exchanged glances with Lauren, who mouthed the words, "What is going on?"

With a shrug and a head shake, Stephanie sank in her chair as the room grew quiet and the President seethed.

"I want those servicemen taken into custody," he said, "and I want to know what the hell they were thinking letting those critical civilian leaders run into a hotbed of danger."

"That's just it, sir. Not only did the members of Congress convince the guards to let them go, but many of the guards went with them. We obtained camera footage that shows at least a half dozen similar incidents in key military installments across the country."

"Desertions by our civilian leadership and servicemen and women?" Holland stared at Davies for a moment, more shocked at

CHAPTER THREE

the abandonment than he was at the Russian incursion. Anger replaced incredulity, and he punched his fist into his palm with a crack. "Their country needs them, and they fled like cowards!"

"As I mentioned, sir, all indications point to concern about family —"

"This is bigger than that," Holland growled, leaning over the table with his knuckles digging in. "Is anyone here thinking about leaving?" He looked at each member seated there.

Heads shook vigorously, and the buzzing of radio sounds filled the room, the silence alerting Stephanie to her racing heartbeat. Her kids were home alone, and she was thankful they were prepared and knew how to handle themselves. Still, she couldn't blame anyone for wanting to save their families, but if strong people didn't show leadership during the crisis, no one would have a family to return to.

"I want an open channel to everyone who can hear us." Holland gave a firm nod to Davies and then at Atkins. "I want to talk to everyone from Mount Weather to Edwards Air Force Base. Whomever we can reach through radio relays and satellite connections, I want to be patched through and recorded."

Davies nodded at the President's quiet command. The Colonel went over to the Communications Chief and made the connections. The minutes ticked on, and Holland remained in his contemplative position, leaning on the table as emotions warred on his face.

Davies nodded at the President. "Channel six, sir."

The President clicked a button on the desk to his right to choose the channel and then another to connect, followed by a squelch of feedback and murmuring voices from the other side of the line before someone on the communication team muted those listening.

Stephanie's fingers poised over her keyboard as messages popped on her screens, small squares with video feeds monitoring several camps that were filled with action, yet she couldn't take her eyes off Holland as he held thousands of military personnel and civilian leaders in anticipation.

"Good afternoon, everyone. This is President Holland addressing you from an undisclosed location. I've been briefed on the disaster we all face. The state of the country, our friends and family, and our very lives hang in the balance. It started with the drilling incident in Alaska and has escalated into civilian panic and a Russian incursion into Alaska and parts of Canada. They think we have been weakened and are seeking to take advantage, but I promise it will cost them dearly." Holland laughed and took a deep breath. "I guess you could say things have been piling up. But beside all that, my officers have made it known that some individuals put their own needs over those of the nation. I understand the instinct to go home to your neighborhoods to protect your families and homes. While that's a tempting option and correct in many ways, it's more important that we stay together and find a solution to what's happening. If we don't, *no one's* family will survive this. The *country* won't survive. Millions of our citizens are dead, injured, and missing; our brave determination is the only thing keeping us together. Your country needs you, and I need you. Every family out there struggling to survive needs you. You must remain at your posts, follow orders, and do everything possible to help us set things right."

The President stopped to gather his emotions as his last words trembled. When he'd found his voice again, he went on. "I love this country dearly, and I respect every one of you for being a part of the response to this, from our civilian leadership to members of our Armed Forces, from privates to generals. Thank you for your continued service, and rest assured that we'll be taking steps over the next few days to rebalance what has occurred. Thank you."

Holland clicked the button and looked at Colonel Davies. At a gesture from the Communication Chief, he nodded. "You're off the air now, Mr. President. Thank you for that. That's exactly what everyone needed to hear, sir."

Stephanie's throat was tight, eyes watering as she felt embarrassed and frightened by her thoughts of leaving and going home to Amanda and Larkin. She'd been right to stay because Holland was right; only the staunch actions of brave people could hold things together now. Several members of the communication team stood and clapped and then more joined them, cheering and shouting until the officers and leaders at Stephanie's table stood as one and gave rousing applause.

Stephanie stood, too, nodding as her heart swelled in her chest.

CHAPTER THREE

She remembered Craig putting on military fatigues and getting into a Humvee that took him far from home on a mission that could have ended his life. Yet, they'd just spoken to him on camera in Alaska after what they'd accomplished there, and something about him looked different. Even though she was clapping for President Holland, it was also for Craig. It was confusing to feel that way after the terrible arguments and trying to hash out their divorce without tearing their kids apart. She might resent Craig for many things, yet she'd forever be grateful for what he'd done for the country.

"Thanks, everyone." Holland held up a hand to calm the room, his enraged and disappointed expression having lifted. His closest officers nodded, a couple with teary faces. Holland's gaze shifted to Stephanie. "I think we can get back to work. Senator Tracey, Dr. Lancaster, can you update us on the weather patterns and what's happening out there?"

Lauren looked at Stephanie and glanced across her screens in a moment of panic before standing to address everyone. "The domino effect weather patterns continue, sir. Now, I've got a handle on them using Dr. Sutton's modeling program, and we reconnected supply chains on four major highways, and the list is growing."

"Very good. Continue."

"The issue is that while supply chains shore up, people are still panicking. As Colonel Davies informed us earlier, riots are breaking out in almost every major city except a few southern and Midwestern towns where they've apparently been less affected."

"What about the rescue camps? How are those holding up?"

Stephanie nodded. "You have the report to review, but of the twelve hundred camps we've set up, only about seven hundred have survived."

"What happened?" the President asked.

"Every camp we've lost contact with could have gone offline for various reasons. Either their equipment was knocked out, they were overrun, or something else took them out."

"The weather?"

"Yes, sir. Especially at the onset, the competing pressure systems and non-temperate winds took out many before they could even get fully established. Still, as the camps have become more mobile, I've been able to track these weather patterns and make some sense of them. Since then, we've been working with local resources to keep the camps moving and minimize the damage when possible. I just spoke with Genevieve Clark in one of the Baltimore camps. They have an ideal spot for now, and their perimeter is holding, though clusters of armed civilians are taking shots at getting their supplies. There are almost seventy thousand people at that camp, it's at maximum occupancy. Still, we have a supply convoy on the way, and we'll deliver enough supplies to shore things up for several weeks. Multiply that by hundreds of sites, and that's what we're dealing with."

"What do you need from me?" Holland said, his expression both sober and concerned as he absorbed the data.

"Your continued support, sir..." Stephanie gestured haltingly. "The speech you gave will go a long way. We just need our troops to stay on point and hold things down. We might make it through this if we can protect those camps and allow nonviolent refugees in while fighting off the mobs."

Holland glanced at Davies. "I've got someone working on gathering what remains of our local law enforcement. If we need to send Army or Marine units to these towns to help keep the population from exploding, we'll do so. If we manage things until this weather —"

"Mr. President!"

Everyone's attention turned to General Atkins, who stood near the main display and gestured at the images of the Pentagon grounds, the barricades, and defenses, the military vehicles parked on the lawns and sidewalks with a massive tank covering every entrance. They stared at the center display, at drone footage on the east side of the grounds. The view wavered as winds blew the aircraft around and its stabilizing mechanisms attempted to keep it steady and aloft. The feed was good enough to see the angry faces of the civilian mob as they pressed against a section of fencing that had yet to be reinforced by a concrete barrier. The bulge in the chain-link grew as Marines gathered and assumed firing positions while the distorted sounds of

CHAPTER THREE

bullhorns piped indecipherably loud warnings issued repeatedly at the mob.

Some pressed against the fence and tried to turn and squeeze back through, but the pressure of thousands of bodies won out, and the chain link didn't stand a chance. It bulged and bent and buckled as feet pushed it down, steel poles snapping in the cold. At the same time, a barrage of beer bottles, cans, bricks, and Molotov cocktails sailed through the air at the Marines, breaking over their helmets or crashing harmlessly on the pavement in splatters of fire and glass. Bottles with burning wicks struck the sidewalk in fiery gushes in ten-foot bursts that went out quickly. The fence came down, and people staggered and stumbled over it, many falling and trampled by those storming in from behind them.

The Marines opened fire, carbines at first, tearing into the crowd and blowing them back, bodies hitting the ground and forming a wall of bloody flesh that squirmed and groaned and painted the concrete red. Still, the throng rushed in, tripping and falling over one another. Some swung baseball bats and strips of rebar at the Marines but were mowed down and ripped to pieces. Civilians brandished rifles and pistols, firing at the Marines and killing two before a Humvee rolled into position and shifted its fifty caliber Browning machine gun on the crowd, tracers lighting the area, overblown in the drone's sensitive camera, and dozens of civilians twisted and reeled as if tossed into a blender turned to high.

A collective groan went up in the room, and Stephanie felt her stomach grow sour until she was sure to throw up. Others gasped and went pale but held their resilient postures, chins up and shoulders square. Holland, Atkins, and Davies stared at the screens in sheer horror, a deep grimace on the President's face.

"General Atkins?" Holland asked. "Join me in the war room, now!"

Holland, Atkins, and several officers left the command center in a flurry, taking staffers and assistants with them in a flutter of papers and computer tablets, leaving only the weather team and Colonel Davies in the room.

"I'm going to turn this off." Davies reached for the remote.

CHAPTER THREE

"Please don't," Stephanie said pleadingly. "I don't want to watch, but we must know what's going on out there. I mean, those people could get in here. What if they do?" Stephanie's voice was rising on a note of panic, the effects of the President's speech already fading with her fear that the hungry crowds could break in and tear them apart. It certainly looked like they could; for every ten the Marines took down, thirty more rushed in, spreading inside the perimeter like a stain.

"We're going to be fine," Davies assured her, turning away from the screens and glancing at the civilian workers. "This is the Pentagon. It's the most defended building on the planet. What you're seeing out there? Those Humvees and tanks and Marines? That's a tenth of what we have right here, and that's not counting air support."

"I thought air support was off the table," Lauren said, shifting her dark eyes to the left and up at Davies. "They can't keep anything in the air right now."

"We can if we have to," he said. "We just don't want to lose aircraft unnecessarily. If it gets that bad, you'll see Apaches and Black Hawks swarming this place." Squeezing his fist around the remote, he turned to the screen as it seemed the Marines were pushing the crowd back, driving tanks, and dragging more barricades to bolster the ruptured spot. "I can't believe all those people had to die. Why?"

"They're desperate, Colonel," Lauren said. "Those people have already gone through every department store and shopping center in the area, and they'll be spreading to the surrounding farmlands with two things in mind. Food and shelter."

"But these people..." Davies' posture tensed. "They're not just hungry or worried about the cold. They're mad, and they want our heads."

CHAPTER FOUR

Zach Christensen, North Pole, Alaska

Zach held the Spear in both hands with the barrel pointed at the front windshield. They were moving at a good clip along Highway 2 with Grizzly at the wheel and Liza, Craig, and Nikolay in the backseat. The weather was viciously dreary, with storm clouds pressing down on them and yellow streaks of lightning flashing in the sick sky. Rolling waves of green-gold gases spurted in reflected sunlight, ignited by static friction into bulging orange and black explosions that consumed the upper atmosphere. The fumes that didn't burn drifted off in thick currents that had the potential to sweep down and suffocate them if the conditions were right, and Zach made sure everyone had an air filtration mask at the ready.

The firestorms were no longer surprising, but their violent turbulence was as furious as ever as they marched across the landscape in the distance, their twisting, undulating bodies moving at terrifying speed, changing direction on a whim, their funnel skirts grabbing everything and setting it on fire, trees and homes torn from the ground and casting the smoking debris everywhere.

Zach twisted the carbine in his hands, looking over the control

CHAPTER FOUR

systems as Grizzly drove them south through a steady line of traffic, those still escaping Fairbanks and surrounding towns, cars and buses and pickups packed with people and personal possessions, the highway littered with articles of clothing and garbage, most of it run over and soiled by tire prints, the artifacts of people's lives driven into the slushy muck.

"Is good to be behind the wheel again," Grizzly said as he sat back with both hands steering and a hot cup of steaming coffee in the makeshift holder he'd made from some wire he found at the motor pool.

"You've been behind the wheel for days," Zach commented as he experimentally shifted through his firing selections on the rifle. "You don't want to take a break at some point?"

"Not Grizzly. I always love drive. It sets spirits free and fills my heart with a sense of endless travels."

Zach gestured at the stormy horizon and the undulating clouds around them. "Seems like you're setting your spirit free into a nightmare."

Grizzly laughed, and Craig snickered from the backseat.

"It not like that," the Russian retorted. "I like to drive. I weave between the traffic..." Grizzly yanked the wheel and split a pair of pickup trucks heading south, earning some horn beeps from the drivers as he accelerated the Humvee around them. "And I like driving the American Humvee, especially. People see me coming, they get out of way. Not like when I was trucker."

"Not even with a big rig?"

"Most get in way, cut off Grizzly and make very angry."

Zach turned in his seat and peered at Craig. "So, according to Red Hawk, the Russians are coming hard for us?"

"That's what they said," Craig replied, leaning forward from his position in the middle so Zach could hear him over the Humvee's rumbling diesel. "I've got to tell you, the President wasn't happy about it. It was weird watching the guy I've seen give speeches on TV right on the other end of the videoconference about to explode."

Craig had filled him in on what they'd discussed in the debriefing session with Colonel Red Hawk and the President. Zach would have

CHAPTER FOUR

found it hard to believe that the Red Army was invading the United States if he hadn't seen it with his own eyes. The ramifications of the Russians starting a fight were many, and none of them had a good outcome. The thought of nuclear war had always been in the back of the country's consciousness, though it had certainly been thrust to the forefront, at least in the minds of the military.

"They're not worried about nukes?"

"Of course." Craig shrugged. "We all are... but General Atkins doesn't think they'll use them. He thinks this is a local landgrab, just like they've done repeatedly throughout Europe."

"Only this time, it's on our soil." Zach shook his head. "If I were a younger man, I would've thrown in to fight them."

"Not me," Craig said nonchalantly. "I'm a conscientious objector."

"Yeah, I figured you might be." Zach chuckled.

"It's not just that I refuse to fight..." Craig laughed. "I just wouldn't make much of a soldier. My eyesight is fubar, I couldn't hit the broadside of a barn with a bazooka."

Liza smiled and shook her head. "You looked very tough in that tactical armor."

"I'll leave the fighting up to guys like Zach. They do a better job, anyway. I'd be dead in two seconds. How does the map look? Are we on the right path?"

Zach put his rifle away and pulled out a map given to him in Fairbanks. "Colonel Red Hawk said we needed to make our way to the Delta Junction and get to Whitehorse as soon as possible. Some other towns are on the way, though he didn't have any recommendations on which ones were safe. At Tok, we can take Highway 1 if it's open, but we'll make that choice when we get there. Without being familiar with this part of the country, anyone's guess is as good as mine."

"That's as good as plans go these days," Craig replied, then he shook his head as Grizzly squeezed between a pair of vans with a wheel jerk. "Sometimes I wonder if it would be safer back at the rift."

Zach chuckled. "I hear you. This thing might be nearly over if Orlov hadn't played so nasty."

"I must apologize for my comrade's actions." Liza sounded disap-

CHAPTER FOUR

pointed. "Not all Russians are like him. Most of us only want the same thing Americans want."

"It is true," Grizzly said over his shoulder. "A warm truck and good music."

"That is not what I meant," Liza said after a chuckle. "What I mean is we want a good job, a loving family, and a happy life."

"Amen to that," Zach replied. "What part of Russia are you from, Liza?"

"I grew up in Vladivostok and attended Far Eastern Federal University. I won a position in Moscow at the Moscow Institute of Physics and Technology. I also have family in Khabarovsk, though it has been many years since I've been there. I have traveled almost everywhere in Russia by train. It is a vast and beautiful country but also depressing at times."

"What do you mean?" Craig asked.

"My government cares nothing about the environment, and there is no money for clean energy technologies unless it brings an advantage for those who are already rich."

"Same as in the United States," Craig commented. "Nothing changes unless someone can make a buck. Many government agencies *pretend* to care, but most of that is pandering and empty promises. I've driven myself crazy trying to make a difference." Craig gazed through the windshield in thought. "I find almost every facet of our political system ineffectual unless it comes to arms dealings." He waved his hand. "I think we're past all that now. No sense in talking pointless politics."

"You should try living in Russia where no one supports scientific community." Liza scoffed. "I have attended many conferences in the United States, and your people are far ahead of curve in many ways. At least efforts are being made to shrink humanity's footprint on the planet, but it takes the whole world to accomplish this."

Craig smiled in dark amusement. "Nothing's going to stop what's happening now."

Zach watched the scientists leaning shoulder to shoulder, squeezed in close, Liza gazing out her window while Craig looked ahead.

CHAPTER FOUR

"I have been to Vladivostok many times," Grizzly said cheerily. "All over Russia, I've driven truck and delivered many goods, though I spent much time on western border with Ukraine when I was in military."

With the frozen Tanana River on their right, they plunged through the forested landscape as traffic picked up, and Grizzly wound their Humvee back and forth across the lanes with glances over both shoulders and constantly checking his rearview mirrors. The woods rose on both sides, red cedars, spruces, birches, and smaller shrubs crowding in on the highway in an endless field of green that rode up the slopes. In spots, it was burned with black marks to make the otherwise beautiful landscape ugly, and despite being in the middle of the day, the sunlight was weak, and no golden rays shined across the treetops or brought any sign of a change in the weather. The cabin stayed quiet as another firestorm ripped over a hillside to the east.

In time, they came up on signs for North Pole, Alaska. Grizzly said, "Hey, we should visit Santa Claus."

Zach gazed at the abandoned town, at its smoking buildings and desolate streets, and Grizzly's attempt at humor fell flat. To the south, they passed an airport with several flights lifting off the tarmac, one heavy commercial cargo jet rising and turning south into an encroaching firestorm, either by misdirection or the pilot's mistake. It came out the other side with its engines smoking and wings on fire, teetering back and forth for a minute before plunging toward the Tanana River.

Liza swallowed hard and Craig clicked his tongue in disappointment. A sinking feeling hit Zack like a gut punch. They caught up with some more traffic heading south, cars and trucks joining Richardson Highway as people fled the city, many of them fleeing quickly while others were broken down or stranded in the emergency lanes.

Liza pointed ahead where two pickups had been in a fender bender, though the one who'd rear-ended the other had a crumpled hood and a smoking grill. The owners of the first truck were an older couple who appeared to be in their sixties, the man white-haired and

CHAPTER FOUR

sturdy, his wife sheltered behind him with a fearful yet defiant expression. Two larger, younger men stood in front of the smoking truck, gesticulating to their wrecked vehicle and then at the older couples. Both pickups were packed with supplies, covered in tarps, and tied down with bungee cables and rope.

"It looks like they might fight," Liza said. "We should stop and help that couple. Those men..."

Zach glanced at Grizzly. "Don't stop, man."

"Do not worry, Zach. I not stop."

"But look at those two," Liza pressed. "They're about to push that old man."

"It might come to blows," Zach sighed, "but us stopping to help is only going to put ourselves at risk. There's no police or emergency vehicles left in the North Pole, I guarantee it." On a whim, he grabbed the satellite phone on the dashboard, flipped it over, turned it on, and watched as it tried to connect. When it didn't, he powered it down and placed the phone back. "We couldn't call the police if we wanted."

As he spoke that last sentence, the altercation exploded. One of the men shoved the old man and pushed his wife, the two older people holding onto each other to avoid falling. Zach thought the old man might try to swing back, but he turned and nudged his wife toward their pickup as the men followed and yelled. Their Humvee was just thirty yards away and closing at five miles per hour in the congested traffic when the old man whipped his passenger door open, reached inside, and drew out a rifle.

Liza gasped, and Zach sunk in his seat as the old man took aim and went on the offensive. Shoving the barrel at them, the old man screamed, red-faced and furious. The two men backed off, hands up and waving, but just when Zach thought it was over, one man dashed for the driver's side door of their truck and leaned in to grab something. The old man knew what he was up to, and he fired one shot into the door, the crack resounding in the stuck traffic. The cars in front of them shifted to the left, their fenders knocking against the cars in the other lane with a burst of horns and hollers as people hung out their windows and gestured vehemently.

CHAPTER FOUR

The young man returned fire, and the old man retreated to his vehicle, as he repeatedly pulled the charging handle to load consecutive rounds and spread his shots at the men. The woman crouched near the passenger door and screamed at her husband to get inside. He ducked once and threw his door open, spinning and slipping inside his truck in a move a younger man might've been proud of. A round struck their back window, shattering it, and the woman threw herself inside and flat across the seat as the group's Humvee swept by.

"Everyone duck!" Zach called as the two men continued firing.

Liza cried out, and Nikolay spouted something in Russian, but Craig had put his arms over their shoulders and pushed them down. Glancing in his side mirror, Zach saw the old man and his wife peel out and come flying down the shoulder where they successfully joined traffic and put some distance between them and their assailants.

The Humvee proceeded on Richardson Highway until it turned into Highway 2 again. The bridge over a branch of the Tanana River was intact but severely crowded, causing a delay of thirty minutes before they got across. Horn blasts and invectives shouted from vehicles were common, and Zach continued glancing in his side mirror for trouble. They reached the outskirts of town and passed from a highway crowded with trees to wide-open fields on a slow, gentle curve to the southeast. There were two lanes on both sides, though the northbound lane was abandoned except for the occasional military convoy driving flatbeds packed with tanks, Humvees, troops, and supplies. When traffic got worse, some vehicles crossed over to the other side and went south in the wrong lanes, though soon they were stopped by military personnel and forced back onto the southbound ones.

"They must want the highway open to military traffic." Zach watched as another couple of Humvees passed, packed with Marines and massive guns on the turrets. "But if one of those poisonous air currents hits the crowded highway, a lot of people are going to die."

"And that's why we have these," Craig said, holding up his air filtration mask. "Suffocating seems like a horrible way to die."

CHAPTER FOUR

Everyone in the cabin fell quiet, half waiting for someone to ram them or hijack their vehicle, though most respected the Humvee, the wide-bodied truck and its armored sides able to nudge into any lane. Soon, they passed signs for Eielson Air Force Base, where the military traffic was parked with hundreds of troops assembled in the northern fields waiting to be picked up and carried north to fight the Russians. Planes lifted off and landed, big C-130s making runs of troops and supplies to the area.

"Oh, would you look at that! Is it going to hit?" Nikolay leaned against the right-hand door and pointed toward the airfield where a C-130 rumbled along, the fat nose slowly rising into the sky, the quad turbines creating a buzz of noise and its own whipping storm as it thrust off the tarmac to angle slightly south.

"It's heading for those clouds!" Liza said. "I don't think that's a good move."

Zach shook his head. "No, it's not. They need to..."

His voice trailed off as he watched the big jet angle toward one of the dark clouds that slowly spun high up, forming an anvil shape that stretched to the earth. A thin funnel appeared before the C-130, but the pilot only slightly tilted the wings. In less than five seconds, the funnel raced toward the ground, twisting and spinning crazily in front of the approaching plane. When the twirling point touched the surface, it threw debris into the air, trees and the corner of a supply warehouse disintegrating as the tornado gyrated. The plane angled a little further south within a quarter mile of the vicious tempest. As he broke that way, the tornado changed direction, cutting across the C-130's nose. Liza gasped, Craig groaned, and Zach had no words for the ball of dread in his gut. The pilot suddenly banked hard to the east as the firestorm swept past and they somehow flew safely away.

Zach blew a low whisper. "That was close."

"Is it that surprising?" Craig asked softly.

Zach didn't know if he was talking about death chasing them south or the pilot's good fortune. "Based on what we've seen... absolutely not." Zach shook his head, thinking of his run of luck since the first oil rigs had blown up in front of his eyes, remembering how he and Tremblay had found the trucks parked on the floating ice slab,

CHAPTER FOUR

which had given them enough warmth to survive. And then there was the bear that had killed Tremblay because of one stupid mistake. "I feel better when they come out on the winning side."

"Me, too."

They left Eielson Air Force Base behind and entered the forested Alaskan hillsides again, bending south to ride alongside the Tanana River where its freezing waters were muddy with soot and ash.

Craig leaned between the seats. "How many miles to Whitehorse?"

CHAPTER FIVE

Wendy Christensen, Bridgewater Township, Pennsylvania

Waves of stinging rain washed over them, turning streets into streams that carried garbage and flooded yards. It blew sideways and upside down into Wendy's face, as cold and sharp as razors, forcing her to remain hunched inside her rain poncho, the hood pulled over her eyes, though water still seeped in around her shoulders and into her layered clothing. She'd long ago given up avoiding puddles and splashed right through them, her pants from the knees down completely soaked, and her feet squelched in her socks and boots.

She strode on the left side of the wagons, sometimes up close to Morten, other times lagging on weary legs and aching feet. The insides of her knees screamed with the strain, and her lower back pinched whenever she twisted at the hips. David was on the other side, his tall form slouched in the relentless driving rain, the boy not carrying a rifle, but his hand was always near the Springfield holstered at his hip. Behind her, Samuel and Charlie walked near one another, though Samuel's quietness only drove a continual wedge between them. The man had become furious when Charlie tried to put Clyde inside the wagon with Alma, who was in the middle, monitoring Uri's

CHAPTER FIVE

status. Wendy had told him to back off and give them a break, and he reluctantly returned to his side of the road. With Wendy's help, they put the shivering dog in the wagon bed with Alma and Uri, and Alma wrapped him in a blanket despite his low growls, forcing him to lay next to her as she gave him copious amounts of head scratches. They kept these brief dustups from the Amish leader, yet Morten must've known of the growing conflict, though he didn't acknowledge it. The drivers remained dutifully to their seats, sitting on soggy cushions that captured water around their hips, their shoulders hunched and heads hanging low.

Morten raised his hand and whistled, and Wendy sighed and jogged to the front where another large log blocked their way. The forested towns of Pennsylvania had an unlimited supply of branches and entire trees for Hurricane Jane to throw across the road or on their heads, and the high winds often brought clusters of twigs and wood scraps to clatter against the wagon sides, frightening the children as the flexible walls threatened to come down on their heads.

When everyone got to the debris, Wendy shouted, "It's not too big! I think we can handle it."

Samuel turned away while the kids stayed and helped wrap a rope around the branches. Wendy slung her rifle and stepped to the right-hand shoulder where they started pulling to clear the debris from their path. Straining against the storm and the heavy load, Wendy leaned until she was sitting in a puddle, kicking back, slipping on the rough pavement and spraying gravel, David and Charlie behind and anchoring their strength. The enormous piece of wood scraped across the road until they hauled it to the shoulder and let the rope drop.

"Great job, kids! David, get this rope coiled up. Charlie, you're with me."

David untied the rope while Wendy and Charlie walked into the roadway, kicking pieces of debris and car parts aside to give the wagons a clear path. They exchanged a wave, then all three wagons proceeded before coming to a slow stop on the other side. David threw the rope into the back of the first wagon, and they were on their way again.

CHAPTER FIVE

The winds increased to violent gusts that whipped the rain into a maelstrom, and their ponchos pressed around their legs. Wendy grabbed David and Charlie and pulled them close. "This is turning into another hurricane! Stay close to the wagons!"

The kids nodded and returned to patrol. Wendy remained up front with her head bowed against the stinging rain. She hunkered beneath the wagon's protection as trees whipped back and forth, branches cracking and falling, bouncing off the guardrail or zipping across the road in front of them. The townships they passed were just shadows of structures, and the only way to see them was when lightning rippled across the sky, bathing the world in a strobe effect that left Wendy blinking and dazed. Thunder came next, a rumbling sound that washed over them as soon as the light was gone. There was no use looking for looters in the swirling din, the visibility cut even more as the rain drenched them and forced them against the wagons, Wendy holding on to the side as it creaked, groaned, and rattled with the storm's onslaught. In the next residential neighborhood, the road was too full of debris for them to move unless they unhitched the horses and used them to pull, but the job was too large for them to overcome without injuring someone or taking hours to sort out.

Morten seemed to have the same mindset because he stood and glanced around the wagon at Wendy, pointing off to the right where tree-lined yards gave them a path around. Nodding, Wendy turned and grabbed Charlie, and they ran ahead, jumping a puddle to land in the wet, mushy abatement. They carefully stepped over the washed-out sidewalk, parts of it buckling and cracking as the weather began taking its toll on man-made constructions. David met them at the front of the wagon train, and they strode between two leaning oak trees to check the yard, tossing aside blown-over decorations and dragging parts of a busted-up gazebo off to the side. They used their flashlights to search the wet grass and mud for pieces of metal or glass. Once they'd crossed two yards, Wendy waved to Morten, and he drove them through without problems, moving around the worst of the wreckage until they rejoined the highway heading west.

Along a dark and lonely stretch of road, Wendy caught brief

CHAPTER FIVE

flashes of yellow and pink in the distance, fluttering clothes on the left-hand shoulder weighted down with heavy, bloated bodies. The scent struck her long before they got there, a gut-wrenching aroma she'd never get used to, telling Wendy they'd been there for four or five days since the freeze. Children and their guardians lay sprawled on the pavement or curled up together, several sitting near a small camping stove, the top rattled and clanked against the guardrail where the wind had blown it over.

As they passed, lightning illuminated the corpses' marbled skin and fat, bloated faces where deep decomposition had liquefied them. Wendy stared too long, and her stomach was hit with a bout of nausea, but she caught herself before vomiting across the pavement. Glancing back, she saw Charlie's shadowy face turned toward the corpses, though Wendy couldn't read her expression, much less her thoughts. The horses were trembling, their heads low and tails dripping as they slogged through the wide puddles and streams of water that raced across the road, splashing up their legs and wagon wheels to drench everything from above and below. Morten stood and gave the reins a hard whip, and the animals responded for a moment, lifting their heads and picking up the pace. Wendy had to jog to stay beside them. Soon, however, the horses returned to slogging, and no matter what Morten did, they simply wouldn't go faster.

The rain kicked up harder, pouring over them in sheets, cutting visibility to twenty or thirty yards. When Wendy saw one wagon shift and slide across the pavement beneath the shrieking gales, she knew they had to find shelter. Spotting the gray sides of a brick structure off the road to the right, she rushed up to Morten's wagon, grabbed the seat, and shouted, "We've got to get out of this rain, Morten! I think I see a garage up there!"

Squinting with water running off his hat in rivulets, he peered to where she was pointing. "Go back and tell the others. We'll go there!"

Wendy jogged to Charlie and Lavinia and told them, patting the horses before going back and giving Miriam the same news. A few seconds later, she and the kids were up in front, rubbing Marley's and Fitzpatrick's sides, tugging at their bridles with water splashing off their coats, coaxing them with words of encouragement.

CHAPTER FIVE

"Come on, Marley!" Charlie shouted, clapping her hands and hopping up and down in the blasting sheets of rain.

"We got some good shelter up ahead!" David waved his arms in a windmilling motion.

Wendy whistled, made piping calls, and ran up the road toward the gray structure, turning back to see if the horses followed. The mare and gelding picked up on the encouragement by snorting and throwing themselves forward until the wagons started moving faster. Once they'd got going, Wendy jogged ahead with the kids, their breath gusting from their mouths in puffs of steam as they angled into a gravel parking lot with so many pond-sized puddles that it might as well have been a lake. The gray structure was a mechanic's garage, three big bays with one-half open, the building flanked on both sides by junked cars and rusted engines hanging from hoists or stacked near a variety of shelves and cabinets.

"Just what we're looking for!"

She called to David and Charlie and pointed to the right-side door where it was half open. They ducked into the darkened bay with the smells of grease, oil, and old car interiors greeting them. "David, push this one up, and Charlie and I will check the others."

Wendy moved down the line and grabbed the chains on one door while Charlie went to the third one. Chains rattling, the doors lifted on their rollers, opening to give the wagons plenty of room to get in. A nagging panic gripped the back of Wendy's neck, and she realized she'd been so concerned about getting out of the rain that she didn't even check to see if anyone was inside. Reeling and drawing her flashlight from her coat, she flipped it on and swept the light across the garage's concrete floors and oil-changing bay off to the left. She raised the M&P 15, moving the barrel alongside the flashlight, stepping deeper in and searching from one end to the other. She spied a door straight ahead on the north wall and one on the east side, but she saw no light or movement through the small, grimy windows.

"David!" she called. "With me. Charlie, tell your grandfather to hold on a second."

"Okay, Mom."

Pointing her flashlight at the door straight ahead, they went and

CHAPTER FIVE

peered through the glass. It was a small break room with tables and chairs and two vending machines in the back. The east room was a tiny office with a desk covered in invoices, a single laptop, and a standard lamp with a long gray neck that arched over the piles of papers.

"Let's push some of these workbenches and the tool chest out of the way," she said to David. "This place will be perfect. There're no leaks and the floor is dry."

They began clearing the floor to make way for the wagons, shoving heavy tool chests with hammers and screwdrivers sitting on top, power drills, and a hydraulic hose coiling across the bay floor like a dead snake. Several half-filled oil pans were taken to the office so no one would knock them over, and soon they were standing at the first bay door, waving for the wagons to come in.

Morten's trundled in, and he gave a sharp "Whoa!" as they reached the far side. Wendy ran down the line, directing Lavinia and Samuel into the second bay and Miriam into the third. She had to pull slightly to the right to avoid the oil-changing bay, which could have been disastrous if the horses had stepped over the hole in their rush to get out of the rain. The winds gusted through the building, bringing sprays of moisture. Samuel, Wendy, and David grabbed the door chains, pulling and rattling them shut on their squeaky rails.

The last door struck the floor, eerily muting the storm. Wendy panted for a moment, then peered outside through the bay door windows as rain blasted them, bulging inward and sucking outward as the pressure changed, yet the doors held and kept the storm at bay. The horses snorted gratefully and shook, sending water flying in every direction as they nuzzled each other and trembled in the darkness. Wendy turned to see the kids poking their heads out of the last wagon, and Morten stepped to the garage doors, shaking out his hat and glancing outside, then looking around their shelter with all the curious faces.

"Come on out, children. It's safe." He grinned at Wendy. "The storm won't reach us in here. Miriam, Lavinia, please help the children out of their wet clothes. Samuel, get some lanterns and let's give the place some light."

"Is that safe, Father?" Samuel asked, assisting Mara and Noah to take down the tailgate so the other kids could get out.

"Normally, I would say no. But no one will be out in that raging storm. We should be safe for now."

Spitting water, Wendy leaned her rifle against the concrete partition between the doors and stripped off her poncho, hanging it on a nearby hook before helping Charlie with hers. "Hang yours up with mine, kids," she said. "Oh, Charlie, your shirt is soaked through."

"Yours, too, Mom." Charlie gripped Wendy's shoulder and squeezed the moist cloth.

"I guess so," she chuckled, taking her hair out of its ponytail and letting her wet curls fall to her shoulders. "Have a look around, would you? See if there's a generator we can use to get the lights running."

"If they don't have one," Charlie said, "we've got our power station."

"That's right. It was charged to seventy-five percent when we left, but it might be less now. David, can you get that out and see how much juice we have left?"

"You got it, Mom."

Wendy shook her hair out so it would dry better, then she walked over to Morten, where he spoke with Lavinia by the middle wagon, Alma leaning out the back. The tall woman nodded at Wendy and smiled before sobering her expression to give an update about Uri.

"He's doing okay," she said. "His blood pressure is stable and his pulse is strong. Lavinia, that was some excellent work getting that bullet out. You probably saved his life."

The stern woman gave a curt nod. "I do as the Lord asks and nothing more. He surely guided my hand."

"Just say you're welcome, Lavinia," Morten growled. "We all know how the Lord guides us."

Flushing slightly in embarrassment, she said, "You're welcome."

Samuel had gotten the kids out, and they were standing around, curious and frightened, looking out of place in the old garage with its greasy smells and oil stains. Miriam popped from the back of the third wagon with a lamp, stepping down and joining the four children. She took Esther's hand with an assured smile and held up the

CHAPTER FIVE

light. "Blessed be. The Lord has blessed us. We should take advantage of this, eat properly, and get some rest, sheltered from the storms."

Still dripping, Morten crossed his arms and rubbed his beard, gazing into the garage rafters and toward the back. "We have one task before that."

"What's that, Father?" Samuel asked, shooting a not-entirely-hostile glance at Wendy. She chalked it up to them being out of the icy rain for the moment.

"We need to dry everything off, and quickly, too." He turned and pointed at the oil bay. "Let's string up ropes to hang our clothes, and then everyone can change into something dry. We'll need to dry off the horses and wagons, too. Every spoke and wheel, every screw and nail in the undercarriage. And we need to do it all now."

"Can we not rest a moment?" Samuel asked.

"If only we could, son. What I fear is a change in the weather where everything freezes again."

"Any water that's gotten into cracks or crevices would freeze," Wendy said with a nod. "It could break your wagons into pieces. Maybe there're some shop rags around we can use to dry stuff off." Images of the people they left behind in Stamford raced through Wendy's mind. Sue Myers and her kids, Fred, Chase, and Dale out on the road, Roderigo and Rosa cuddled frozen in their sleeping bag. "Morten is right. We should do it as soon as possible."

"Do you hear that, everyone?" Morten called, gathering in his children and grandchildren. "Alma and Lavinia will take turns looking after Uri. Samuel and I will look over the horses, and everyone else will start drying everything off."

"Okay, kids!" Miriam shouted, setting the lantern on the open tailgate and gathering the kids in her arms. "Let's go on a hunt through dark and mysterious caverns. We're looking for rags and paper towels! Whoever finds the most will get an extra treat tonight!"

"Yay!" the kids yelled together.

Memories of when she'd first met Zach at the barn raising came to mind, the way the Amish acted as a community and tackled their chores. Her Amish in-laws, frightful and curious a moment ago,

CHAPTER FIVE

exploded into a flurry of teamwork, diving in with complete devotion. They spread throughout the building and pulled open cabinets and drawers, searching the break room and finding a big box of paper towels. Wendy and Lavinia teamed up to hang the clotheslines, and the men stripped off the horse's bridles and moved them to one side of the garage, where Morten and Samuel began brushing them down, much to the animals' delight.

David discovered a big oscillating fan and placed it near the bay doors, turning it toward the wagons and connecting it to their power station. A strong, welcome breeze circulated through the building, and Wendy helped him angle it to get the best flow of air. Standing in front of it with her arms spread wide, she grinned and enjoyed her drying skin, and that water wasn't dripping off her nose and chin.

For the next hour, they cared for the horses and dried everything off. Morten lifted little Esther and Lena on top of the wagons to dry the roofs, while the boys climbed beneath and wiped down the undercarriages. Wendy, Miriam, Charlie, and Morten did the wheels and exteriors, discarding their wet shop rags and paper towels into a pile. David removed their propane camping stove from the wagon and set it up in the back while others found several chairs and truck pads to place around it for a cozy spot to rest.

Wendy went to the front to grab her rifle and plant herself on the tailgate of the third wagon, high enough to watch outside at the railing storm for signs of people. Morten was right about the weather's viciousness. She doubted anyone would be out in it.

For the first time in days, laughter echoed in the concrete room. Smells of food cooking drifted off the camping stove. The children had mostly stayed dry in the back of the wagon, though they'd often sat next to the tailgate, holding the door flaps shut and getting wet in the process. Their dresses and breeches hung up from the clotheslines, and David had turned the fan so that it oscillated a brisk breeze across the garments where they swayed and dripped. Wendy was still soggy, her clothes clinging to her skin

CHAPTER FIVE

in itchy dampness, though she couldn't complain. They were safe and drying off, and soon they'd be eating and settling in for the night.

"There you are." Miriam stepped from between the wagons and rested her fists on her hips. Her cheeks were rosy, and her thin blondish-brown hair was tucked into a dry bonnet. "I was looking for you."

"I can't go very far, Miriam," Wendy smiled. "I was keeping watch while everyone got situated."

"And we thank you for that. We're finally drying out, and the kids are happy to be out of the wagons for once. It's the first time they've really been able to talk to David and Charlie."

Wendy glanced over her shoulder and past Miriam before she whispered. "Maybe your kids, but little Mara and Noah look at us with that same squinty stare their parents do."

"They'll be fine," Miriam scoffed lightly. "They're as scared as anyone, but they're good people." She grabbed Wendy's knee. "And it's good to get to spend some time with you. The last time we saw you was at the wedding."

"I remember," Wendy laughed warmly. "At first, we didn't think it would happen with all the controversy about me being an outsider, but your father and Zach convinced them it could work, and it did."

Miriam's smile grew wide. "It certainly did. Now, I'm going to change into some wonderfully fresh clothing. You probably should, too."

Wendy shrugged. "To be honest, we've got a couple of spare sets of clothing, but they're dirty and worn and just as bad as what I'm wearing now."

"I thought you might say that, so I brought you something from my closet." Miriam giggled and revealed a soft, dry Amish dress in a plain gray color. The woman swung it around and held it up next to Wendy. "You have a slight figure, you'll probably be swimming in this, but it will feel better than those soggy things you've got on."

Wincing and sucking air through her teeth, Wendy shook her head. "That's okay, Miriam. I should be fine with —"

"Nonsense, Wendy. There's no good reason for you not to get

CHAPTER FIVE

changed while we're here resting. We won't be off the road long, and you should take advantage of this time to get comfortable."

"I'm not that great with dresses," Wendy explained. "I'm more of a jeans kind of gal."

Miriam lowered her chin and looked at Wendy with mock scorn. "Are you saying you'd be *embarrassed* to wear this dress?"

"Embarrassed isn't the right word, Miriam." Wendy thought about it for a moment. "Okay, I guess I *would* be embarrassed to wear it... I'm not Amish. Isn't there a law or something against me wearing your clothing anyway? Won't Samuel and Lavinia just die?"

Miriam laughed, a light and funny sound. "It's not something that is normally done... but it will be fine, especially since it's an emergency. And if Samuel and Lavinia have something to say about it, they can take it up with Father."

Wendy bit her lip and thought how wonderful it would feel getting out of her wet clothes. "Okay, I'll wear it until mine are dry."

"I'll help you with it."

The women climbed into the wagon bed amid the crates of supplies and herbs that hung from the roof, giving the space a fresh smell that made Wendy dizzy, her stomach growling in anticipation of a warm meal. She stripped off her clothing and slipped the gray dress over her head, the skirt wide and billowing, bunching up around her bare feet, though it felt nice on her shoulders, and the material was soft and dry against her skin, drawing a pleasurable shudder through her chest and back.

"Okay, this feels amazing." Wendy hugged herself and smiled.

Miriam fussed with the length of her skirt, using pins to fold it up and get it off her feet. The dress fit snugly around her shoulders and waist, leaving her bare legs unencumbered yet covered. Miriam held out a thick pair of woolen socks. "These are so soft, Wendy. You're going to love them."

"I'm sure I will." With a resigned sigh, she gave in to Miriam's playful and insistent hospitality.

Stepping back and lifting her skirts, Wendy plopped down on a crate and held her right foot up. Miriam put the sock over her heel and pulled it almost to her knee. Wendy wiggled her toes, enjoying

CHAPTER FIVE

the garment's instant warmth and soft caress. A pleasurable sigh escaped her as she closed her eyes and relished the simplicity of being dry.

"I knew you'd like them. Now, let's get you something to eat. Everyone's over by the stove."

Wendy would draw some smirks but she didn't care. She climbed down from the wagon and followed Miriam's bustling form around the wagons and toward the back corner of the building. The stove rested on a crate, its double burners with medium-sized pots and delicious food boiling inside them. The Amish kids were off by themselves on the left, relaxing on the truck pads and pillows they brought out, chewing on snacks of jerky and dried fruits they'd made in their backyards. Samuel sat on a stool to their right, with Lavinia standing behind him, her hands resting on his shoulders. Morten sat on a tall chair with his boot heels kicked back. The family patriarch had changed into dry clothes and a fresh hat, his wet garments hanging by the others. Charlie and David shared a tool chest to his right, Charlie's foot resting on Clyde where he was curled up on some truck pads at her feet. Miriam stepped aside and ushered Wendy through, and she moved to Charlie's side with a wry frown and her arms crossed, expecting jabs and jeers. The rest of the children were scattered around in fresh clothing, sitting on truck pads or stools as they whispered excitedly.

"Oh, wow, Mom!" Charlie exclaimed in wide-eyed bemusement, her jaw dropping as she stared Wendy up and down.

David gave her a second glance, his thin lips drawn into a crooked smile. "Nice outfit. Are we officially Amish now?"

"Wouldn't hurt a bit," Morten called, giving Wendy a look of hilarity dashed with a hint of pride. "You'd fit right in after a few lessons from the Good Book."

Wendy scoffed. "I'll give you my kids, how's that for a deal?"

"If you were to join, your children would be more than welcome in the community."

Charlie's face turned ashen as she glanced at her brother in terror. "Oh, I'm not sure I could handle Amish life. I need my phone and my e-reader!"

CHAPTER FIVE

David smirked. "I think they're just kidding, Charlie."

"Oh."

Wendy spread her hands. "Go on, everyone. Make fun of me all you want, but I'm happy to be warm and dry."

The Amish children grinned and whispered, and Lavinia allowed a crooked smile that didn't appear like a shark's grin for once. In truth, Samuel seemed the only one displeased, his lips drawn tight, and his gaze boring into her. He peered at his father and observed Morten's amusement. Samuel frowned even more, but kept his mouth wisely shut. A soft hand settled on Wendy's shoulder, and she turned to see Miriam holding another dress.

"I'm not the only one joining the Amish community for a day."

Wendy cocked an eyebrow at Charlie before shifting her gaze to Miriam, who swept in with the dress held high.

"We'd be remiss if we didn't provide Sister Charlie with some equally warm clothes."

David was in the middle of swallowing water, and he choked up laughing at the suggestion. "That sounds great, Aunt Miriam."

Charlie shook her head vigorously. "Oh, I don't think so, guys." In the same breath, she turned to Morten with an apologetic look. "No offense, Grandpa."

The man waved her off with a slow flourish. "No offense taken, dear."

Wendy stepped close to Charlie, grabbed her hand, and placed it against her hip. "It's so comfortable, Charlie, and dry, too. Are you telling me you'd rather sit in those wet clothes for the next few hours before going back out in the rain?"

Charlie stared at her mom, at the dress, then at her mom again. She slammed her mouth shut for a moment of steely defiance. "I appreciate everything, Aunt Miriam, but I'm good. Seriously, guys."

Wendy draped her arm over Charlie's shoulders. "I don't know, honey. Once we're back on the road and into that storm again, you're going to wish you'd gotten warm and cozy in this dress while you had the chance. Don't come crying to me then!" Wendy turned, found a padded stool of her own, pulled it up, and stared hungrily at the boiling stew. "What are we having for dinner?"

CHAPTER FIVE

"A bit of stew and oatmeal." Morten stooped and stirred the pots with a pair of wooden spoons. "It's a hearty meal suited to stave off the road's ache. Just like a fresh change of clothes to warm cold, clammy skin."

Wendy glanced at Charlie and caught her skeptical expression as she stared at the dress in Miriam's hands. The girl's face was twisted with emotions Wendy had once known; the need to still look cool despite good old-fashioned comfort right in front of her. Finally, Charlie rolled her eyes, slapped her palms on her legs, and hopped up.

"Fine, Aunt Miriam," she said. "I'll wear it."

The pair disappeared, and Wendy grinned toothily while Morten emitted a lingering chuckle that sounded like thunder rolling through the room. Charlie came out wearing the pink dress, the fit snug around the hips and shoulders, though not uncomfortably so, and her golden hair fell over her shoulders, looking like she'd stepped out of some old-time movie.

"You look beautiful, Charlie," Wendy said.

Charlie was less than amused, but her mother's warm and thoughtful comment drew a slight smile from her. She pulled her hair to one side so that it fell over her right shoulder. "I guess it fits pretty well."

"It's one of Mara's." Miriam stepped back with a critical eye. "She's a little younger than you, but your sizes aren't too far off."

"You didn't say it was one of mine, Aunt Miriam," Mara replied, standing up with her fists clenched loosely at her sides.

Miriam took an offended and confrontational stance. "I made it for you, that's true, though I thought you'd be thrilled to let Charlie wear it. You're cousins, after all."

Mara deflated, and Lavinia's expression faded from calm resentment to something friendlier. Samuel merely stared at the boiling food and didn't spare a glance for anyone.

"As soon as this is over, we'll give it right back," Wendy promised.

"You may wear those dresses as long as is necessary," Morten said with a sidelong look. "We're family here, and we're going to act like it."

CHAPTER FIVE

"Thank you, Morten." Wendy nodded, then she shifted her gaze to Samuel and Lavinia. "Thanks to you as well."

"Dinner is almost ready." Miriam circled to the stove and grabbed a set of nearby bowls and spoons.

"We'll have a prayer," Morten said, and everyone joined hands as he thanked God for the food and for providing them refuge from the storm. "We thank you for your blessings, oh Lord... Amen."

"Amen," they all replied.

"Before we eat I want to change your dressing, Mom." Charlie raised a first-aid kit.

"Oh, okay," Wendy agreed, turning so Charlie could get at the wound. She'd been wearing the same bandage for a couple of days after getting shot by Turley's people, and she was reminded every time she did something strenuous such as clear debris from the road. "It would be good to make sure it's not infected."

As Miriam dished out bowls of food and utensils clanked, Charlie unbuttoned the back of Wendy's dress and pulled the left part aside just enough to expose her shoulder and scapula. She slowly peeled off the original bandage, wadded it up, and tossed it on a distant workbench. "Does it hurt much?"

"It stings sometimes," she confirmed. "Mostly, I don't feel it. Does it look bad?"

"Actually..." Charlie pressed her fingers around the wound, and Wendy winced a little. "It looks pretty good. I don't see any signs of infection."

"No pus or anything?" Wendy asked with a glance around to make sure she hadn't grossed anyone out, though everyone was deep in their food, spoons digging in and mixing up the mush and stew and wolfing it down.

"Not at all. That antibacterial salve worked well. I'll clean it and reapply everything."

"Thank you." Wendy sighed and allowed herself to slouch forward a little, resting her tired shoulders for a moment to let the girl work despite her growling stomach.

"And how did you get that wound, Wendy?" Morten asked as he

CHAPTER FIVE

took another bite, the steam rising off his spoon and from his warm breath.

"Back in the house when those teachers were shooting at us. It was pretty hectic for a while, and I thought we might lose everything until you guys came along."

"I think we could've taken them," David said, eating greedily from his bowl before drinking from a bottled water he held between his knees. "We had them on the run."

Wendy shook her head. "I wish I could agree, son, but without the help of our family, we might not have made it. Thank you, Morten. Thanks to all of you, especially Samuel, Lavinia, and the kids."

"And my brother is doing fine," Alma said, coming up and dusting her hands off.

"You should be sitting by his side," Lavinia shot back with scornful reproach. She thrust her bowl of food at Samuel and started toward the wagons.

Alma's sharp intake of breath stopped Lavinia. "He's resting peacefully! You'll only bother him if you climb in the wagon and dote over him. He's fine, trust me."

Lavinia's scowl lightened, and she turned and rejoined the circle, taking her bowl of food and sliding into Samuel's lap.

"All done," Charlie said, placing the new bandage down and buttoning up Wendy's dress. "I'm going to put this away and get a can of peas. Anyone want any?"

Esther and Lena made disgusted faces and shook their heads, but Noah raised his hand. "I'll take some."

"Two cans of peas coming up!"

"Have a seat, Alma," Morten said with a gesture toward a stool on the other side of Wendy.

Charlie brought back her peas and dumped them into a smaller pot that straddled the two burners, warming quickly until they were ready, and she and Wendy each had a bowl. The meal filled her belly with a warmth that completed a circle of comfort inside, her brain suddenly tired and foggy as the rain continued falling in sheets, pattering against the roof and bay doors, broken by occasional cracks of lightning and thunder rolling across the sky and rattling the tools hanging on the walls.

"I'll take first watch." Samuel picked up his rifle and strode over to the doors to glance through the shivering windows.

Wendy lifted her eyebrows as Alma and Morten continued eating and Lavinia took the kids exploring the room, leading them with a game into the break room where they could sit at a table.

"Father, do you want the rest of this?" Miriam asked with a gesture at the remaining food. "I want to finish this before I take the dirty pots into the break room. There's still some water pressure, and I would like to take advantage of it."

"Good idea, Miriam. Aye, I'll take some."

"Me, too," David added, holding out his bowl.

Miriam dished out what was left into Morten's and David's bowls before taking the pots into the break room where the kids were carrying on and getting loud, though Wendy doubted it would matter with the storm raging just outside.

Charlie finished her food and glanced at Wendy. "I'll wash our bowls. Are you done?"

"Yes, thanks." Wendy handed the girl hers and relaxed on her stool as much as possible, the hard-padded seat tough on the bottoms of her legs, though it was better than standing and walking. "When you're done," she said to David, "why don't you take yours and your grandfather's bowls and help with the dishes."

"No problem, Mom." David stirred around what remained of his food. "I was thinking about taking watch with Samuel. You know, getting to know him a little. Maybe he won't be so…"

Wendy's eyes shifted to Morten, but he continued looking down, and she couldn't read his expression.

Alma nodded to David. "That sounds like a great idea. We've been so far apart for so long that we don't know each other. I'm sure if we hung around more, maybe Samuel would be friendlier." Alma was so tall that she could sit on the edge of the stool with her feet firmly on the ground and crossed at the ankles. She smiled. "Maybe there's some light to see in all this after all. We'll be a family again."

When neither Morten nor Wendy responded, Alma got up and

CHAPTER FIVE

turned back to the wagons. "I'm going to check on Uri and bring back some apple cider. How does that sound?"

"That sounds lovely," Morten said. "Thank you."

The heat from the cooling stove warmed the surrounding space, and David finished his meal and took the remaining bowls and utensils into the break room to help clean up, leaving Wendy and Morten sitting alone. The tall man crossed his legs and reached inside his coat, bringing out a pipe, a pack of tobacco, and a box of matches. While they waited for Alma to return, Morten packed his pipe, lit it, and instantly filled the space with a robust smokey odor.

Wendy breathed a little of it but turned her head to the side so she didn't get too much. "You know, I never liked the smell of cigarettes, but I'll always love the smell of a pipe."

Morten inhaled from the skinny end, the coals of the pipe lighting bright orange before fading. He chuckled as smoke rolled off his tongue. "There's nothing like a good smoke at the end of a long day, especially a rainy day like this." His gaze shifted to Wendy. "How are you doing?"

"As good as I can be," Wendy said, surprised at the emotion that surfaced from the simple question. "Considering I don't know where my husband is. Well, roughly I do."

"When's the last time you spoke to him?"

As Morten's pipe smoke filled the air with a pleasant aroma, Wendy told him the last time she'd talked to Zach, when he'd called them from somewhere north of Fairbanks after surviving the initial oil rig explosions. "He seemed confident he'd make it home," Wendy added to the end of her story. "The way that hurricane hit us... it's got to be way worse up north, so it'll be tough."

"You know Zach." Morten chuckled. "That's a tough boy. He's always been that way, and he'll stop at nothing to get to where he wants to go."

"But everyone has to be tough." Wendy sniffed as her vision blurred. "Whoever is still alive after all this must be doing something right. Who knows what he's up against? Even crazier weather than this? What about desperate people trying to flee south?"

"It might be easier for him than we think," Morten replied.

"Between what I've heard on the radio, and what you and Alma said, it seems like the government is evacuating people south, so maybe there won't be so much to contend with."

"I hope so," Wendy ended with a soft sigh.

"Are you getting along with Lavinia?"

"That's an entirely different problem. Don't get me wrong, Morten." Wendy scooted onto David's stool and locked arms with her father-in-law. "We're so grateful for you deciding to come help us. You saved our lives, but it's clear Samuel and Lavinia don't want us here."

"Everyone is getting along, and David's idea to go talk to Samuel is a good one. Who knows, maybe they'll end up fast friends."

Wendy chuckled with a lilting note. "I wouldn't count on it. If you saw the way Samuel and Lavinia look at us. They want us gone and resent us for the fix we're in right now. According to them, you'd be in Pearisburg already if it weren't for us."

"Or look at it a different way. What if we only made it this far *because* of you and good David and Charlie?"

"What do you mean?"

"Seventy of us left Fort Plain, a big group that would make a big target for anyone wanting to attack us. Sure, we have plenty of guns and ammunition for protection, but you saw what we went through getting this far. The road to Pearisburg could've been as perilous with my people as it was picking up you and the children. There's still Philadelphia, Baltimore, and Washington to get through, and the roads are filled with frightened, desperate people." He shrugged his thin shoulders and took another draw. After he'd blown the smoke toward the roof, he continued. "Breaking away from our people wasn't an easy decision. We've known them for decades, respected and aged families whose roots go back to the start of the community. None of them were too happy about our plans, but once we meet again, everyone will see that things worked out wonderfully."

"I hope so, Father. I really do." Wendy's expression deepened with curiosity. "What happened in Fort Plain? Why did you leave in the first place?"

"The weather turned sour and cold, so that was one reason.

CHAPTER FIVE

Threats from those in nearby towns was another... ultimately, that was what drove us away. They coveted what we'd worked for, sowing fields and harvesting them to feed our own prosperity. Yes, they wanted it for themselves."

The older man creaked as he slowly slouched forward and crossed his arms over his stomach, the tip of the pipe lingering on his bottom lip. "It started as a few people raiding our barns where we stored our harvests, and as soon as they cracked one barn, they saw us as weak and came in a flood. Groups of a dozen or more, sneaking through the settlement in the dark of night, terrorizing our families and plundering our wares. Once we got past the shock of it, we defended ourselves as best we could, pointing rifles and shouting them off at first, then shooting to kill when they grew more desperate. Our streets and fields ran with blood and rain. The skies cracked with God's wrath. Our families were terrified."

Morten's voice took on a gruff note. "We didn't want to kill them, but they forced our hands. After the first few waves, we thought they would stop. We had meetings to organize and form defenses to protect ourselves. But then fifty hit the Yoder barn at once, killing my good friend, James, and his son, Nathaniel. The thieves didn't stop at looting their barn shelves. No, they took their anger inside where the Yoder family cowered in fear... well, you can imagine what happened to them." Morten looked at her glassy eyes. "I've never known such sorrow..."

Wendy squeezed his arm. "I'm so sorry to hear that, Father. It breaks my heart."

"It broke ours, too. It wasn't long before we decided we couldn't stay where we were, so in the dead of night, we packed our things with half the men guarding the settlement's outskirts, expecting to be attacked at any moment, our fearful wives and children quaking in terror, preparing to leave everything behind."

More smoke left his lips and drifted to the roof, and they sat silently before he pressed on. With a smile, he nudged Wendy's shoulder with his own. "That's when Alma suggested we break off from the group and go in search of you and yours. While initially skeptical, Alma updated me on your discussions over the phone and

CHAPTER FIVE

your fears about Zach coming home to no one. While many doubted Zach's decision to marry outside our community, he stood against that disparagement and did what was in his heart, with God's love and blessing. I knew I would face the same resentfulness and spite should I make the same decision, so I only let Samuel and Uri know and urged them to consider their duties to support me in that mission. Uri agreed wholeheartedly, though Samuel required some convincing."

"He doesn't think it's right."

"He will see the truth in time. He is a good worker, but he's always fallen prey to jealousy and paranoia, and his heart isn't as open as Uri's and Alma's, or yours."

"I take that as a compliment, Father."

"You should... ah, here we go."

Alma appeared with an earth-colored jug. She held it with both hands and poured the contents into a pan to about three-quarters full, capped the jug, placed it aside, and took a spoon out of her apron. Stirring the liquid's cloudy, brownish color brought a sweet heat rising up, and cinnamon and spice filled the air, giving Wendy a heady feeling.

Releasing Morten's arm with a pat, she leaned forward and took a whiff. "That smells amazing, Alma."

"I made it myself and have several more jars in the back. I don't want to brag, but my apple cider is a big deal back at the settlement. I will trade it for many good things once we reach Pearisburg."

"It'll be worth its weight in gold, I'm sure," Wendy said.

The smell permeated the garage, drawing the children by their noses, and soon everyone gathered around to take a small cup of cider. The winner of the "find the rag" competition from earlier got a double helping. Alma poured in more to heat for the older kids and adults. With the dishes done, Lavinia took over as server and filled some cups, smiling when she handed Charlie's and Wendy's to them.

"Thank you," Wendy said, wrapping her chilled fingers around the hot cup and letting the heat soak into her palms. The flavor was sweet and tart, smooth and warm as it went down and blossomed in her belly.

CHAPTER FIVE

"This is so good," Charlie said as she held her mug beneath her nose with both hands.

"Why don't you take some to your brother and Samuel?"

"Good idea, Mom."

Putting her own cup down, Charlie filled up two more from Lavinia and disappeared between the wagons with a swish of her dress, giving Wendy a sudden bout of giggles.

"What is it?" Alma smiled while sitting on Wendy's right with her steaming hot cup.

"It's just Charlie in a dress." Wendy rubbed her eyes. "I never thought I'd see her in one. She was already arguing against it for homecoming next year. She's a jeans and T-shirt kind of girl, if you know what I mean."

"We don't wear jeans, Wendy."

"Of course, you don't!" Wendy laughed.

Alma chuckled with a light and pleasant sound. "But I know what you mean. We like to dress plainly ourselves and aren't ones for pomp."

"Alma has her share of pretty dresses." Lavinia stood on the other side of the stove, holding her mug and being friendly. "And if I had her womanly figure, I'd probably do the same thing."

Alma laughed harder and waved off the compliment.

"I'm surrounded by handsome women," Morten said, "and a veritable treasure trove of young children who bring life to our camp. I'm proud of this family and glad we made the trip."

Lavinia fell silent but nodded, smiling hesitantly as if making friends was the hardest thing she had to do. "I'll check on Uri now, and I promise to be quiet."

"I should, too," Alma added. "Let's go together."

The women disappeared, leaving Wendy alone with Morten in a comfortable silence, kicking her legs out and letting her heels bounce against the stool. "Do you think things will be okay in Pearisburg?"

"It's certainly a bigger place with more resources. Many of us make a pilgrimage there each year to trade news and goods and catch up with family. I have distant cousins there, and the Christensen name carries some weight in the community. I hope that's still true, so our transition will go easy."

"Do you think we'll have a home there? I know you and your family will. You're a part of the Amish community. But what about us?"

"I'd like to think they would welcome you with open arms, but the leadership in Pearisburg is more stringent than in Fort Plain. At the very least, I'd expect to argue the case for allowing you into the community. I'll do everything I can to see you safely settled. My people are conflicted regarding outsiders. Many of us believe God's word tells us to accept everyone no matter what, though others are aggressively against it."

Wendy nodded, a little resentful at the politicking that went on with religion, even those in the same communities in parishes who disagreed and held grudges between them. She suspected that in the long run they'd come together when push came to shove, and she and the kids might have to settle elsewhere.

"Thank you," Wendy said. "Either way, we needed to get out of the Northeast. It was too cold and hostile for anyone."

"I think you'll see it's the same near every major city." Morten smiled, slowly leaning forward with his empty cup as he rose. "If you don't mind, Wendy, I'm going to retire for a little while, but I'll be up to take the next watch. First, I need to run this cup into the kitchen."

Wendy reached for the empty cup and took it out of his hand. "I've got that, Morten. You get some rest."

"Thank you."

Morten disappeared into the shadows as he crossed to the first wagon, stepped up, and vanished inside. Wendy put his cup aside and poured a little more cider into her own. She felt so exhausted, her eyes threatening to shut even as her heart remained restless. The sudden low crack of lightning outside would've normally been scary, but it had become commonplace with these new and ever-changing weather patterns. Charlie appeared and slid onto the tool chest with a sigh, picking up her cup and leaning her shoulder against Wendy. They listened to the storm roll overhead, cracking and rumbling, and

CHAPTER FIVE

to the squeaks of the bay doors as the wind pressure shoved them in and sucked them out again.

After a long silence, Wendy said, "Just a couple of Amish chicks hanging out."

Charlie burst into a fit of giggles and leaned harder against Wendy, bowing her head and clutching her chest, unable to stop. Wendy tried to keep a straight face, but her insides jiggled, lips trembling as she attempted to hold in the laughter. Her breath hitched, and she squeezed her eyes tight to release a torrent of tears down her face. Throwing her arm around Charlie's shoulders, she hugged her hard.

"My only complaint," Charlie said, waving her hand in front of her hot cheeks, "is that I didn't get a gray dress like you, Mom. You know me. Pink is way too bright for my disposition."

"Are you kidding?" Wendy's face scrunched, and she squeezed Charlie with everything she had. "You've always been such a bright ray of sunshine... maybe pink *is* your color."

"Ugh!"

With a loud guffaw, she laughed wholeheartedly, hysterically, drawing everyone's attention with curious looks and half smiles. As the storm continued raging, their laughter settled. They wiped tears from their eyes and held each other in the darkness, taking solace in the love and warmth they had for each other.

CHAPTER SIX

Stephanie Lancaster, Washington, DC

The Pentagon's bustling command center purred steadily along. Stephanie was running on a half pot of coffee and continued studying the shifting weather patterns to guide truck convoys to their destinations. Not only had they delivered supplies to Baltimore, but she'd facilitated several dozen more deliveries from Kansas City to Little Rock, Arkansas, which were experiencing super-cell tornado formations that split into double and triple twisters.

At least a dozen tornadoes from the Southwest had struck parts of central Kentucky, including its capital, Frankfort, and nearby Lexington. Even so, the wind-battered state was one of the more prepared as the camp leaders had merged with military bases at Fort Knox, Fort Campbell, and the Blue Grass Army Depot Base in Richmond. Their National Guardsmen and Army units, many of which were still in training, had shored up things west of Frankfort and taken in hundreds of thousands of refugees. Hundreds of miles away from there, New Jersey was stabilizing with camps around Trenton bolstered by the US Marine Corps Reserves and US Army from the north. Encampments in the area sheltered people behind fences and

CHAPTER SIX

walls, and troops had received almost unlimited supplies of ammunition.

Yet, at the Pentagon, people still crowded the gates, clamoring to get in. Things around the building were under control for the time being, giving Stephanie a little breathing room. The disaster recovery experts assumed that civilian unrest and food shortages would increase their fatality estimates to over eighty million dead and countless injured and displaced. When Stephanie absorbed the news, she could only shake her head and wonder how so much chaos could spread across populated areas.

"Glad to hear Baltimore is in good shape," Stephanie said into her headset as the room grew busier.

For the first time, Genevieve Clark was inside a tent that wasn't about to be blown over. She'd combed her hair back, and her face was rosy-cheeked from the quick scrubbing she'd given herself. "Thanks to you. I'll tell you, Stephanie, this place would've exploded if we hadn't gotten those supplies. The troops are happy, and so are our volunteers, and were bringing in a steady stream of good people while keeping the bad ones out."

"That's excellent." Stephanie glanced at her left-hand screen. "I see another shipment coming from a commercial warehouse in Savannah. They were reluctant to give up their supplies, but they heard what you folks were going through with the weather and those millions of people pouring out of the big cities up north, and they released the supplies from their two million square foot warehouse."

"Because you convinced them," Genevieve said. Her gray eyes were tired, though they held a hint of hope. "You're there in Washington with the President's weight behind every call you make. Right now, especially after that speech he made, it's going a long way to getting us what we need."

"Thanks. I'll let you go now. Get some rest."

Genevieve smiled tiredly and clicked off the video feed. The square on Stephanie's laptop screen turned blue. Sitting back, she sipped warm coffee and then rested her hands over her stomach, pleased with herself at how things were coming along. The busy work forced her to multitask more than she ever had in her entire life, but

CHAPTER SIX

she was getting to know everyone in the supply chain process, from truckers to warehouse managers and sometimes the officers guarding them. Working together, they'd come a long way to stabilizing areas around the country.

"Colonel Davies? I'm going to take a quick break."

The President, Colonel Davies, General Atkins, and other officers sat at one end of the table, speaking quietly as they studied data on the big wall-mounted display with maps showing solid supply route lines and green dots where the military had shored up their defenses. Alaska was an entirely different thing, and they kept that on smaller screens where they managed troop positioning and communications with those on the West Coast as the threat of war loomed. While the thought of what was happening in Alaska was nerve-wracking, it was out of her control, and all she could do was continue shoring up things in the Midwest United States one issue at a time.

Colonel Davies nodded. "Sounds good, Stephanie. Thanks for all your work so far. That weather data you're providing is invaluable."

"You can thank Craig when he gets here."

Davies frowned and nodded, then turned to the President and the assembled officers.

Stephanie smiled and stood, grabbing her coffee cup and heading to the service table where the two urns sat. The first one was empty, so she switched to the second and filled up, tossing a couple of creamers and sugar packets in for taste and an energy boost. She glanced around the room as they progressed from a shocked and terrified nation into something that resembled organization.

With a tentative smile, she left the command center, took two steps along a short hall, and entered the huddle room to call her kids. She'd grabbed a nicer chair from another room that had thick padding on the seat and arms and an adjustable lumbar support. Setting her cup down, she reached up and rubbed her neck, arching her back and stretching her arms above her head. Hours bent over her computer had left her shoulders sore and her hips stiff, the edge of her command center chair pressing against her legs and causing them to ache.

Stephanie kicked her feet up on the desk and rested, letting the

CHAPTER SIX

silence settle on her, the air vents pushing out clean, cool air. She closed her eyes and drifted toward a nap. Her thoughts shifted away from current events to better times at home with the kids and even moments with Craig when things in their marriage were going smoothly. And then images of him in military fatigues before he bravely traveled north to fix the Alaskan Rift. While she was sure he loved them, work had always come first when push came to shove, mostly to the children's detriment. He'd often let things slide with the kids, brushing them off for meetings and projects until their resentment grew, and they barely considered him a father. Craig could never understand that relationships required maintenance, care, and attention, which wasn't an attribute he often worked on. Still, he'd looked so brave as he headed north with the Marines.

Stephanie shifted forward in her chair and woke up from her brief nap, yawning as she picked up the phone and pressed the programmed button to dial home. The underground lines were still up, and if the physical connection to their place near Fairlawn remained up, she'd always be able to call. There was a hum of noise in the earpiece before the light ringtone settled her stomach and nerves. After three rings, Larkin picked up.

"Mom?"

"It's me, Larkin. I'm still at the Pentagon. Is Amanda there with you?"

"I'll put you on speakerphone."

"Hi, Mom!" Amanda said, her light voice like music to Stephanie's ears.

Through a smile, she replied, "It's so good to hear your voices. Sorry, I didn't call sooner, but I got wrapped up in some pretty big things here."

"How's it going?" Amanda asked. "We kind of expected you to be home by now."

"I know, but I'll be stuck here for a while." Before she could hear their groans, she quickly added, "But things are going great here. I can't tell you everything, but I think if we keep going at this pace, we should have things under control soon."

CHAPTER SIX

"We hear there're tons of camps everywhere because people are going nuts," Larkin said.

"That's partially true," Stephanie replied with a single slow nod, "but supply lines are coming back online, and we're seeing some patterns in this crazy weather."

"Well, that's good," Amanda said. "The big question is, when do we get to see you? When are you going to be home?"

"I don't know, honey. The bigger question is, how are you guys holding up?"

"We got the generator running, but we're only turning on lights in the basement. All the windows and doors are locked, and we joined a group of six neighbors... err, six houses around us, including the Watterson's across the street..."

"Okay, the Watterson's are good people. That's smart getting with them right away."

"Anyway, we're all watching each other's backs."

"Have you seen anything in the neighborhood yet?"

"I'm usually on night watch," Amanda said, "so I've seen the most stuff. There were some gunshots yesterday, but they sounded far away. Groups of people were walking down the middle of the street and took off between the houses... you know, between the Miller's and Kingsbury's where everyone cuts through to the next neighborhood?"

"Yeah, I know."

"I keep the lights out except for my tablet. Sometimes I get bored and watch an old movie or something. I've got a bunch of stuff downloaded from before."

"Well, be careful with that," Stephanie warned softly. "If someone catches that light, they might come to investigate.

"I'm trying to be careful."

Stephanie thought about what was happening just outside the Pentagon doors with people charging the fences, breaking through, and being mowed down by Marines. "Keep in mind that things can change quickly, kids. It can be calm one second, the next, violence."

The way her voice drifted quietly across the line must've struck a note with the kids because they were silent for a minute before Larkin spoke up. "Did something happen?"

109

CHAPTER SIX

Stephanie chuckled lightly. "No, but I've seen a few things, and I know how ugly things can get. And you know I'd be home now if what I'm doing wasn't super important. It kills me I can't be there with you guys."

"We're okay, Mom." Amanda was trying to be cheerful, though her voice trembled slightly. "We're armed at all times, and if anyone breaks in, we can go downstairs and lock up in the supply room."

"How long do you think this is going to last?" Larkin asked. "The only reason I'm asking is that we took a quick inventory of what we have, and we figure we can get by for about two months before things get thin here. There's oatmeal and eggs that are still good. Some of the bread you bought last week is already moldy, and we just started making those tuna helper meals. There's about thirty of those boxes and some cereal."

"How are you doing on milk?" Stephanie asked, pretending like there was something she could do about it if they were out.

"We're good there. It was such a good idea to buy the smaller containers. That way, if we open one, we don't have to drink it too fast. I say we have a two-week supply of that. You prepared us well, Mom. We'll be okay."

"Okay, good. I'm hoping I can get home before that, but we should be prepared if I can't." Stephanie pursed her lips and tried to remember if there was anything else. "What about gas for the generator?"

"So far, so good. We've got a month at least, maybe more. We were thinking about siphoning fuel from people's cars, but I think almost everyone is home with the lights out, if you know what I mean. Well, everyone except the Huertas. Mr. Watterson knocked on their door, but no one answered. Mrs. Watterson said we should go on in, but no one wanted to get blown away."

"Smart thinking," Stephanie nodded. "The Huertas are avid hunters. You know they've got guns. If anyone breaks in, they'll take some buckshot to the face."

Larkin laughed. "That's exactly what I told Mr. and Mrs. Watterson."

"It sounds like you're doing okay," she said. "Oh, and I've got

CHAPTER SIX

news about your dad. Remember how I mentioned he was on a mission?"

"Yes, but you couldn't tell us where or what he was doing," Amanda replied.

"Oh, that's still true, but I can tell you the team he was on was successful. They did something amazing, and he made it out okay. He's doing..." Stephanie shook her head and blinked back tears. "Better than ever. Your father is good. And he's coming home now, but it might be awhile."

"It's not like he came to see us anyway," Amanda said with a hint of scorn. "He'll just go off and do whatever he does."

Stephanie was going to say that wasn't true, that Craig loved them and wanted to be with them soon, though that would be a lie. Craig was crazy about the kids, but she'd long ago given up on predicting what he'd do or where he'd put his time. "That might be true, but he made me tell you he loved you and wanted to come home soon. He said that just before he left."

"Was it dangerous?" Amanda seemed genuinely curious. "The mission, I mean. Could he have been killed?"

Stephanie started to reply with a simple "Yes," but her chest heaved, and she stared up at the bright ceiling lights as her eyes filled with moisture, throat suddenly tense, squeezing around her windpipe and making it hard to breathe.

"Mom? Are you still there?"

Stephanie swallowed and nodded. "The mission was high-priority and dangerous. Probably the most dangerous thing anyone could have done, and your father volunteered to do it gladly, for the sake of everyone."

"That doesn't sound like Dad," Larkin said with skepticism.

"He's a complicated man. He could check out sometimes, and it seemed like he didn't care, but trust me when I say his mind was always on bigger things, and he sees things from a bird's eye view."

"You mean a *satellite's* view," Amanda quipped. "That's what Professor Hamblin used to say, and he kind of reminds me of Dad. Anyway, Larkin and I still love him, and we're glad to know he's okay. Maybe we'll get to see him soon."

CHAPTER SIX

"I hope so." Stephanie wiped the tear off her cheek and straightened in her chair. "Well, I guess I should be going. Lots is going on here, and we've got to keep pushing if we're going to get through this. You guys remember your gun training and some things we discussed. Don't put yourself at risk. Don't stick your head up and get anyone's attention. Remember what I said about things escalating quickly? Don't get caught with your guards down."

"We won't," Larkin replied.

"It's all under control here," Amanda added.

"Okay, you kids be safe. I hope to see you soon."

"You, too, Mom. Be safe."

After they hung up, Stephanie drew a breath and gave thanks they were still okay. Even if she wanted to rush home, could she? It's not like she had a car out in the garage. Possibly a week ago, but certainly not with the current state of the Pentagon with the angry mob surrounding them. She grabbed her coffee and headed to the command center, when a Marine grabbed her and pushed her to the side, shoving her against the wall with a heavy forearm on her chest. The coffee cup fell from her hand and hit the carpet, spilling lukewarm liquid on her shoes.

"Stay here a moment, ma'am," the Marine said in a tight, professional tone.

"What?" Stephanie danced angrily with hot liquid in her shoes. "What's going on here? Let me go."

"In a moment, ma'am." The Marine shifted his gaze toward the command center table where other Marines were entering through the main door on the opposite side of the room. They grabbed people and shoved them aside, creating a path to President Holland. A man wearing a collared shirt and black tie with one gun on his hip and another holstered beneath his left arm pressed between the Marines and strode up to the President.

"Sorry for the interruption, Mr. President," the man said stiffly, "but you must come with me right now, sir."

President Holland straightened and faced the Marine, not nearly as surprised as anyone else, his expression flat as if he'd expected something like that to happen. He glanced at General Atkins, who stepped to his side and shifted his gaze around the room to rest on Colonel Davies. "Davies, you're in charge of the Pentagon's defense. Please use every means you can to defend its walls."

The Colonel snapped to attention with his hands stiff against the sides before giving a sharp salute. "I understand, sir. I'll do my best, sir."

With that, the Security Chief gestured for the President to lead them to the door, and Holland moved past the dozen Marines with General Atkins on his heels, nodding to each Marine as they saluted him. The Marines spreading through the command center released those they'd been holding back, the pressure on Stephanie's chest let up as the man turned and walked away. They left as fast as they entered, the door swinging slowly shut and clicking in place. Stunned silence followed, with civilian leadership and communications personnel glancing around in confusion. Stephanie rubbed her chest and stepped away from the wall, looking at Colonel Davies for an explanation.

Davies stared at the opposite door before deflating and turning to those gathered in the room. "I'm not exactly sure why they…" The Colonel shook his head and regarded everyone with a combination of understanding and hurt. It was common knowledge, even to Stephanie, that the President's security detail would be on high alert and would take Holland to a safe location when they deemed his current one was in jeopardy.

"I thought everything was under control," Senator Tracey accused, glancing from the door to Davies with a confused expression. "Did something change out there?"

"On the screen," Stephanie gulped and stared past Davies at the center display.

Aerial drones and cameras arrayed around the Pentagon complex fed them up-to-the-second updates on the tense crowds outside. Everyone in the room had assumed things were fine on the Pentagon grounds, and the massive tanks, Humvees, and Marine units stationed around the complex had it locked down. But as they stood there in stunned silence, the mob created another breach in the perimeter and were flooding inside in waves.

CHAPTER SEVEN

Zach Christensen, Salcha, Alaska

The Humvee was quiet as they cruised south along Highway 2 with mostly beautiful green around them, forest and hills with snow-covered tops, the highway constantly sweeping them in a different direction that followed the Tanana River and its hundreds of branching tributaries. The road was slushy with the amount of traffic passing, sometimes turned to ice and gone slick, though drivers were keeping a respectable distance, and Grizzly's superb driving skill gave them confidence they were in good hands.

Zach was cramped in the passenger seat, having to put his foot up and reposition himself often as the miles rolled beneath their tires. The cabin was quiet and warm, and Grizzly had cracked the window a little to let in some cold air. It was smoky and foul, though not as bad as when he and Tremblay trekked through the north with pollution and fire ripping up the skies and dropping dark clouds on their heads. The wind had tapered off, but not by much, and judging by the muffled explosions lighting up the pitch-black sky, the hydrocarbons were still flowing in the upper atmosphere where lightning cracked

CHAPTER SEVEN

like fireworks casting strange shadows across the roadway and causing everyone to stop and gaze up.

"Come on!" Grizzly slapped his heavy palm on the wheel. "You see explosions in the sky many times, yet you still stop and look."

"Rubbernecking," Zach commented. "How are you doing, friend? You've been driving for a few hours already. Let me know if you want to take a break."

"Right now, I am fine. Most I drive is eighteen hours straight, and I only stop because they make me. Trucking industry is cautious about such things."

"It seems like we're hardly moving with all the traffic," Zach said, nervously tapping his leg. "Still, if you need to rest, let me know."

Grizzly glanced over and grinned. "You are getting antsy. You dislike being passenger."

Zach nodded. "I hate *not* being in control. Even up north, driving the snowmobile seemed better than this. It was cold, but at least I had control of where I was going."

"You *still* have control, but there is only one road to follow for all of us. Highway 2 only. You know this."

"Yeah, I know." Zach glanced over his left shoulder. "Craig, what's the next town coming up?"

Paper rustled as the scientist unfolded the map in his lap. "Let's see." He ran his finger along Highway 2 from Eielson Air Force Base and south for a while. "It looks like Salcha is the next town coming up, and we should get through that quickly. The bigger issue is the bridge past Salcha, ten miles south of town, the only place to cross the Tanana River for miles."

"We can't go any faster through this traffic," Zach said. "Maybe we'll find a helicopter at Whitehorse."

"We can only hope," Grizzly said.

"Want to play some road games?" Craig asked, leaning forward.

Zach laughed. "No... I'd rather take a nap."

Slipping deeper into his seat, Zach half closed his eyes and listened as Liza, Craig, and Nikolay played a hybrid punch buggy game where they searched for specific vehicles on the road. One person picked out the car while the other two craned their necks and peered out the windows to locate it. The winner didn't receive anything special, but the competition was intense as they hunted through the passing traffic and tried to trick each other. At one point, Craig chose "find a pickup truck," of which there were hundreds in both lanes, causing Nikolay and Liza to fight over who'd chosen theirs first.

After a few miles of that, they got bored, and Craig settled back and announced, "Okay, we're going through Salcha now."

Mildly interested, Zach rose in his seat and peered out his window where many homes were burning, and a line of retail stores was nothing but a husk of crumbling walls and smoking embers with a collection of soot-colored clouds hovering a few hundred feet above them. Lightning crackled and sparked, and miniature cyclones swept down in thin tendrils of gyrating fire and smoke, only to touch the ground and dissipate as quickly as they'd formed. Zach shook his head and rested it against the window, allowing the gentle rumbling of the Humvee to put him half asleep. It seemed like a few minutes later when Craig informed them they were reaching the bridge past Salcha.

"According to the map, we're approaching the Salcha River State Recreation Site. It looks like a campsite or something. There might be a few stores there and a hotel."

Grizzly slowed the Humvee at the sight of flaring red taillights ahead.

"I knew it," Zach replied dejectedly, rising in his seat as a warm heat rose in his chest.

"This is a small highway," Nikolay said, gesturing to the right-hand shoulder. "I see many minor roads branching off. And look, someone is getting off on the right-hand side there." He poked at the window. "Could we not do the same?"

"Normally, I'd say yes, Nikolay," Craig said, "but I don't see any other ways to cross the river. I think we just need to sit in this traffic for a while until we can get across the bridge. From there, it should be clear sailing for a while."

CHAPTER SEVEN

"Patience, right?" Zach asked, feeling more cramped and tired than ever, his skin itching beneath his fatigues as he rolled his window down a couple of inches to let in some air. No one said anything as the Humvee slowed further with a line of straight congestion ahead of them. "Grizzly, move onto the right-hand shoulder, and I'll try to see around all this."

Grizzly did as he asked, and they swung over, showing him the same line of vehicles curving to the east around a wide swath of trees that went on forever. He groaned in disappointment. "There's no bridge in sight, just endless traffic."

A horn blared on their left, and traffic came to a sudden lurching stop. A line of walkers were crossing the road, holding hands and weaving between the cars with suitcases and backpacks, barely glancing at the angry drivers as they entered the right-hand shoulder and walked toward a dirt street coming up.

Once the people had passed, the vehicles started up again, though the touch-and-go movements turned the twin lanes into a hotbed of simmering anger. A pickup truck bumped into the one ahead of it, a soft blow but causing the driver in the front vehicle to halfway open his door and shout something back before he slammed it shut again and moved forward. That elicited a chorus of horns from the surrounding cars, especially those behind them who were bumping fenders in a rush to get to the bridge. Grizzly stayed back from the car in front of them, a red pickup with every possession the driver owned thrown in the truck bed with no tarps to hold anything down. They passed clusters of cars pulled onto the left-hand shoulder, things speeding up for a moment before stopping dead a second later. Another group rushed by, ten teenagers and two parents sprinting across the road in their jackets and woolen hats, one kid reaching into the truck ahead of Grizzly, snatching a case of soda pop and carrying it off. The passenger started to get out and give chase, but the driver grabbed them and pulled them back inside.

"It's not worth it," Zach muttered with a head shake.

Most vehicles still gave them a wide berth, curious faces peering over to see the Humvee's passengers, but when they saw Zach in his

CHAPTER SEVEN

military fatigues and holding his gun, they minded their own business. Trucks were pulling to the right-hand shoulder, taking Liza's suggestion to get off and park to wait out the worst of the traffic. Fights were breaking out in a dirt lot, men shoving each other with heated scowls, women squaring off at the edges of the brawl. As they passed, Zach spotted a woman grabbing another by the hair and jerking her head down while others jumped in to break them up. Fists were flying, feet kicking as the two sides clashed and stirred up dirt in a vast cloud that rose beneath the darkening sky.

Grizzly scoffed and shook his head but didn't say anything.

Craig clicked his tongue from the back. "People have enough troubles as it is. I can't believe they'd fight with that nightmare looming over their heads."

The sky was angry again, blustery in shades of black and gray, the endless dreariness stretching from one end of the horizon to the other with just a hint of typical skies to the south in a light-orange stripe around the Earth's edge.

"Only one thing matters right now," Zach said, turning. "Getting across that bridge and moving—"

Grizzly whipped the wheel to the right, and Zach looked up in surprise as a white van bore down on them, pushing into a gap Grizzly had left between the Humvee and the pickup ahead of them. Breaks squealed, and the van jerked back the other way when Grizzly wouldn't give them the space. Then they tried again, rushing forward and angling to the right, forcing Grizzly to either take the hit or get off the road.

"What do they expect?" Grizzly growled. "Do they not know I could bash them into oblivion?"

"I don't think they care," Zach said, craning his neck and looking at the passenger and driver, their angry faces and shouting lips, curses pouring from their mouths because Grizzly wouldn't let them in front of them.

The traffic opened ahead of the white van, and they sped up a moment before the lanes slowed them down again. Even as they tried to cut the Humvee off for a second time, Grizzly pressed the gas

CHAPTER SEVEN

pedal and accelerated to clip their back fender and get up beside them, giving Zach a better view of the people inside.

"Oh, crap!" He slid lower and turned away from the driver's side.

"What is it?" Craig said, squeezing between the seats.

"I know them."

Craig backed up and leaned over Liza to see who it was. "Is that a good thing?"

"Definitely not." Zach glanced at Grizzly as he worked his way past them, sweeping into the right-hand shoulder a few feet to avoid taking another hit. "Their names are Scotty and Sandy, and they're a big pain in the backside."

"Oh, no!" Grizzly said. "Those we met in rescue convoy? They steal things and shoot people."

"They were trying to get me back for taking their radios and weapons..." Zach shook his head. "And, I guess, their snowmobile, too."

"That's a good way to make enemies," Craig replied.

"It wasn't my fault. I asked them to let me have one radio, and I would've gone on my way, but they pulled weapons on me instead." Zach shrugged and gave the van a mean look, remembering how they'd threatened to shoot him. "I wasn't going to let them stand in the way of me calling Wendy and the kids. I guess I doled out a little extra punishment."

"You stole their ride," Craig said with a dark chuckle. "And now —"

"How could they only be here?" Grizzly asked. "They should be much farther south by now."

"They could have been stuck in Fairbanks or North Pole," Zach mused. "I overheard them say they wanted to steal a vehicle, which makes me think they weren't looking to ride a bus."

The van swerved into their lane, smashing the door panels up against the Humvee's side and sending everyone inside lurching left and then back again. When they broke away, the van's once straight fenders were crumpled and bent, pieces of their trim hanging off, and the front turn signal breaking in chunks of yellow plastic. Scotty hit the brakes and fell behind the Humvee, and Grizzly stepped on the

CHAPTER SEVEN

gas harder and launched them way ahead, stopping just short of striking the pickup in front of them. Grizzly was looking into his rearview, and Zach glanced back as the van swept in behind them, riding right up on their tail with Scotty leaning on his horn obnoxiously.

"Stupid people," Grizzly complained. "This vehicle... it has armor. They can hit as much as they want but will do no damage."

"Maybe that's not the kind of damage they want to do."

"What do you mean?"

"Look!"

Everyone in the Humvee turned and stared as the van bore down on them, smashing them again even as they slowed in the choking traffic. Grizzly started to circle to the right and slammed his boot on the brake, causing them to lurch, the Russian driver throwing his hands up and shouting at a delivery-style truck drifting onto the shoulder and taking up all the space, leaving them no room to get around.

Zach spotted figures moving in the back of the van, not just Scotty and Sandy anymore, but shapes pushing toward the front, at least half a dozen armed with weapons. The traffic ahead slowed, Grizzly cursing low as he brought them to a halt along with hundreds of other vehicles with squealing brakes and horn blares.

They stopped, the van doors flew open, and people spilled out. Zach slapped Grizzly's arm with one hand and gripped his Spear with the other, prepared to leap out and fire. "We've got to leave now! Drive!"

"Sorry, Zach. No way around." Grizzly made an exasperated gesture toward the congested road, and the number of people spreading out onto the shoulder as impatience overtook them. "We will simply have to deal with —"

"Now!" Zach patted the seat and pointed as three figures got out of the van and aimed at the Humvee. "It's not just Scotty and Sandy. They've got friends with rifles! Go, Grizzly! Go!"

The Russian glanced into his rearview mirror, eyes going wide and mouth falling open as he saw the weapons pointed at them. With a twist of the wheel and his boot coming down hard on the gas, the

CHAPTER SEVEN

Humvee lurched sharply to the right, clipping the delivery truck's corner as he went around, the weight of the Humvee ripping off the truck's fender and dragging the thing five feet before blasting past it. Bullets traced across the back of the Humvee, pinging off its armor with bright sparks, one hitting the bullet-resistant rear window in a splash of spiderweb cracks. Still, it held steady as they whipped around the delivery truck and got out of sight, only to run into another blockade up ahead with two sedans parked bumper-to-bumper in the center of the right-hand shoulder. A second vehicle was nosing over as if to help, giving the Humvee no way through.

"You've got to go off-road, Grizzly!" Zach said, watching his side mirror as Scotty's people came around the delivery truck and took aim. Zach pointed furiously at where the shoulder dipped into a steep bank. "Can you go that way?"

"I will try." The Russian glanced back. "Everyone, hold on!"

The Humvee swung to the far-right side of the shoulder, crunched the rear bumper of a pickup and then skidded over the embankment. Zach felt weightless and leaned to his left, grabbing the seat and holding onto his weapon as the Humvee's knobby tires tried to grip something.

Liza screamed, and Craig and Nikolay made surprised noises, groaning as they slid sideways down the forty-five-degree slope of frosted gravel, swinging around as Grizzly turned the wheel sharply to the left to get them back up the side. The angle flattened out by a few degrees, and the tires spun wildly, sending a spray of rocks and ice out behind them. Grizzly whipped the wheel back and forth, gassing it and letting up as he fought to keep traction on the gravel-covered slope. The slewing motion sent them crashing into a cluster of bushes and shrubs, the Humvee's heavy rear smashing over them in a crash of green and snow dust, leaving switches and branches sticking out of the undercarriage and vines clinging to the sides. A small sapling took a death blow with a sharp snap but produced enough resistance to knock the Humvee straight to the gasps and cries of everyone in the back seat.

Grizzly made it to the roadside with two tires on the shoulder and two on the embankment. Distant shots rang out, and at least one bullet struck them, causing everybody to flinch and protect their heads despite plenty of armor between them. The bullet-resistant glass had absorbed one shot, and Zach didn't know how many more it could take. Grizzly drove on a straight line along the roadside, steering them to the right to bypass a pedestrian and a vehicle skewed onto the shoulder. A steep drop to a dirt road ran parallel to them and getting down there seemed a tricky proposition.

Zach peered ahead and spotted a side street swinging up to the highway on the right, and he pointed. "Can you take that road, Grizzly?"

"I can, but what if they follow?"

Zach glanced into his side mirror but didn't see the van anywhere. "The shoulder is blocked, and there's no way that van can ride the embankment like we did. Just take it, and we can either wait for this traffic to die down or find another way across."

"I vote for another way across," Craig said, his tone low and ominous.

He leaned over Liza and stared at the boiling sky, where spinning tendrils of smoke and fire dipped toward the Earth, flirting with the surface to destroy whatever they touched. "I know it looks bad out there, and you might be right. We might need to find another way to cross, even if it means finding a shallow spot in the river. One thing's for sure, we can't sit in this traffic any longer, not with Scotty and his goons running around armed and willing to kill."

"Okay, everyone. I will take road coming up, and we will get out of danger for moment."

"Thanks." Zach shook his head. "I bet Scotty wasn't even looking for me but saw this Humvee and thought it would be a nice exchange. They probably pulled up beside us to see what we would do, and they saw me. That probably sent him over the edge."

"What a foolish man for attacking us."

"He had some buddies with him. I counted a half dozen or more, and all of them armed."

"We will stay well ahead of him, my friends. Do not worry. You are in Grizzly's hands."

He turned the Humvee onto the road, swerving between another

CHAPTER SEVEN

pair of vehicles parked there before sweeping back again. It was an empty area with silos in the distance and big circular oil tanks or industrial storage units a mile off and poking their yellow heads above the tree line. Gusting winds brought another firestorm to the west, the twisting heat skimming the treetops, burning them to cinders, and carrying them hundreds of yards to set more dry shrubbery alight. Soon, glowing flames filled the dark sky, turning it orange in a surge of billowing gray smoke that rose to meet the clouds.

"Don't go too far, Grizzly. Head south as best you can."

"Roger that, Zach."

The Humvee's occupants fell silent as Grizzly turned west on a side road, shooting through an abandoned neighborhood of about thirty homes before joining another road south along the tree-spotted lane to the industrial area Zach had seen from a distance. Surrounding the big yellow cylinders were various warehouses and signs for machine shops in a hodgepodge of gravel and dirt parking lots, some of them iced over and covered with snow.

Grizzly eased up on his frantic driving and slowed to a stop in the middle of all of them. Around them were huge piles of cement and tar mixtures. Giant excavators and bulldozers were left abandoned at the foot of the mounds, one vehicle with its door wide open. Zach saw why; the woods nearby had been scorched by firestorms, as well as three warehouses on the east side of the grounds, one of them still smoking from the simmering coals. Otherwise, no one appeared in any of the surrounding buildings or offices.

"Where now, Zach?"

"Let's try that one at the far end." Zach pointed to a large warehouse with a garage-sized door on each end, wide open. The structure was probably a ten thousand square foot facility and twenty feet tall, its roof gable-style and angled upward to a shallow peak with the walls painted a dirty gray color. A sign on the front read *Maclin Machine Parts,* and a smaller sign below it read, *drop-offs at the side door.*

"I'd say we're dropping off, wouldn't you?"

"Yes. That is good."

Grizzly sped up and swerved off to the left, then trundled slowly around the building where skids and odd pieces of metal racks rested

CHAPTER SEVEN

against the brick walls. They reached the side door, and Grizzly started to turn inside.

Zach raised his hand to stop him. "Hold on, man. I want to get out and look around."

"Very good."

Zach popped the door and climbed down. Deep tire tracks created furrows in the gravel, and large delivery trucks were parked neatly near the building. Past those was a wide swath of green trees that flowed north and south, rough ferns and pines nestled together in a crush with few bare spots to see through. Everyone got out, stretching or standing with their hands on their hips and looking back toward the entrance.

Zach squinted and tilted his head.

"What is it?" Craig asked, coming to stand with his knees locked and seeming a little wobbly after the gunfire and rough ride.

"Do you hear that?" Zach looked around.

Craig cocked his head, shifting his ear to catch whatever Zach was talking about. A slow smile spread across his face, and he nodded. "Sounds like water to me. Could be the Tanana River."

"We'll check it out once we figure out if we're safe here." Zach hefted his Spear and circled to Grizzly's side where the big man had rolled down his window. "I'll walk you in. Everyone else stay back."

Grizzly nodded and edged the Humvee forward, bumping over the lip of the concrete warehouse floor where he slid quietly inside, Zach moving next to him as his vision adjusted to the darkness.

"Whoa!" Zach called. "Wait right here."

Rifle in hand, Zach strolled out in front of the Humvee, searching the shadows for signs of anyone lying in wait, his gaze moving up across endless rows of shelves with small to medium boxes stacked perfectly with their labels facing outward. Walking up to one row, he studied the titles as he went, noting they were various-sized gears and engine parts.

With a smile, he turned and waved to Grizzly. "There's nothing anyone would want in here! Pull in."

Nodding, Grizzly drove about fifty feet inside and parked. He got out and stretched like the others had, raising his meat hook

CHAPTER SEVEN

arms above his head, big round belly stuck out as he flexed his hips.

"What is in boxes?" he asked.

"Just a bunch of machine parts. Nothing anyone would want to fight over."

"Good. This will be perfect for now while we get bearings."

"Can you stay with the truck, Grizzly? I'll go see where the water source is. We'll leave Nikolay with you."

"Sure, sure."

Zach walked toward the entrance as the others approached. "Craig, Liza. Let's go to see where that water is. Nikolay, can you hang out here and guard the Humvee with Grizzly?"

"Fine." Nikolay waved amicably and circled to Grizzly, crossing his arms and breaking into conversation with the man in Russian.

The scientists followed Zach to the tree line, and he picked a spot to enter the forest where the underbrush was thin. Their boots crunched on dead leaves and twigs, patches of snow and frost covering everywhere they stepped. The trees rustled gently overhead, sometimes breaking into a violent roar brought on by the turbulent skies.

"Do you think it's the Tanana River?" Liza asked.

"One of its offshoots," Craig corrected her politely as they picked their way through the woods.

Zach remembered the scientist had been out of breath often when he first met him, though a couple of weeks of hard work, climbing, and traveling in the cold north seemed to have toughened him. "I like the idea of an offshoot. That means there could be shallow places to cross. Maybe we'll find a narrow spot."

They soon discovered the truth as they came to the edge of the forest and stepped onto a rocky shore, relatively flat, with tall grasses growing in patches in a field of fist-sized rocks. The transition to the water was smooth, snow-covered dirt and frozen sand, with ice along the edges and the water flowing freely and sluggishly out toward the middle. Standing on the shoreline, Zach eyed the river warily, unable to tell how shallow it was.

"It could be two feet deep or ten feet deep," he observed. "We won't know until we get in."

"Not entirely true." Craig raised a finger. "If we can climb one of those trees high enough, one of us should be able to determine the depth based on the shadows. I'm not a geologist, but I know the river may be at a shallow point at this time of year." He patted Zach's shoulder and pointed at the other side. "There, see that. You can tell by the broken bank and the exposed tree roots the river is likely shallow there."

With hope growing inside, Zach nodded. "I see. How would we know if we can cross?"

"Wherever sand or stones are high, the water might appear lighter, though I'm not sure how it would look under these dark skies." The scientist glanced up as a pair of explosions went off far above in twin bursts of firelight.

"In there," Liza pointed across the thirty yards to the other side, where the trees were rustling wildly as cinders spun within the tree trunks. "It looks like a fire is starting over there. We will want to avoid such places if we make it across."

Zach nodded, tallying up their chances. "At the very least, we could bring the Humvee down and ride along the shoreline. It's flat enough, and the tires on it are good. With Grizzly driving, we could spend an hour looking for a place to cross and take our chances that way or wait for traffic at the bridge, which none of us wants to do."

Zach walked along the shoreline west and stared across at the other side. He'd gotten twenty yards before he saw the tops of structures on the opposite shore, their squarish shapes counter to the flushing trees that swayed beneath the wind gusts. "Look there. I see some buildings. If we can find a place across, we could scout ahead and find a road on the other side."

Craig rubbed his forehead and winced. "It's a long shot. We could get caught out there in the middle of the river, but that's still better than being shot at."

"Exactly." Zach stood next to the scientist.

"Whatever it is we are going to do," Liza said, "we better do it soon because we don't have much time." She raised a finger and

CHAPTER SEVEN

pointed at more spots in the woods where the greenery had caught fire. Cinders swept the treetops like fire dust, as if to light their way ahead in the deadly conflagration.

The trio walked up through the swath of woods, across the lot, and reentered the warehouse space. Grizzly and Nikolay stood side-by-side at the front of the Humvee and watched out the opposite door where an odd mix of ash and cinders fell.

When he heard them coming, Grizzly turned and waved. "Did you find anything?"

"We're pretty sure we found a way across," Zach replied. "We may need to drive along the shoreline and do a little scouting, but it's doable. Craig thinks the water level is lower than normal, which could mean a shallow place where the Humvee wouldn't have too much trouble. And the current seems sluggish."

"If you point me to place, I will take across." Grizzly's chest puffed out, and he gave it a light beat with his fist.

"I know you will, man." Zach patted him on the shoulder and turned to Craig. "Why don't we take a quick break and review the maps? Let's look at the roads on the other side of the Tanana River."

"Good idea," Craig replied, popping the door and reaching inside for the map.

While he spread it out on the Humvee's warm hood, Liza and Nikolay grabbed some water and high-calorie snack bars from their supplies, bringing them around and handing them to everyone. Zach ripped his snack bar open and ate half of it, relishing the flat, sweet peanut butter.

"You better have two of those." Liza chuckled and gave him another.

Zach accepted it with thanks and popped his water bottle top. He took a swig, then glanced around. "We should post some guards while looking at the maps."

"I will go to the other side and keep lookout." Nikolay patted the pistol holstered at his hip. "Maps bore me, and I should make myself useful besides playing games on my phone in the backseat."

"That's fine, Nikolay," Zach agreed. "Just holler if you see anyone."

CHAPTER SEVEN

"I will go to the other side," Liza said, and when Craig protested, she replied, "I have little to say about the map. I trust that you three will pick the best path across." With that, Liza took her snack bar and a small bag of trail mix and strolled over to the entrance where the dim daylight cast weak shadows from outside broken up by an occasional wash of cinders that bathed the forest trees in orange flickers.

"We should make this quick." Zach stared at Grizzly and Craig. "Liza was pointing out some spots where the forest was burning, and we don't want to be caught between forest fires."

"Will only take a minute." Grizzly leaned over the map where Craig was tapping their current position just north of the Tanana offshoot.

"We are right here or thereabouts," he said.

"And you have been to the shoreline?" Grizzly asked.

"That's right."

"What is there? Rocks and dirt? How bad is ice?"

Zach put his Spear on the hood with the soft clatter and leaned over the map, tracing his finger along the river. "Rocks and dirt, yes. There is some crusted ice on the edges, but nothing too thick. There are a lot of sandy parts, too."

"Normally, I would not want to drive on sand. However, it may not be so bad if cold and icy."

"And look up here, guys." Craig tapped his finger on the other side of the river where some marked highways and roads were plain. "Lots of places over there will put us back on the highway less than a quarter of a mile from the river."

"That's what I was hoping for," Zach said. "We can get over there and —"

Gunfire erupted on the west side of the building. Two quick clusters of shots. The trio reached for their weapons and looked toward the bay door Nikolay was guarding, but he was nowhere to be seen. A smaller gun fired, and more return gunfire popped off. The young Russian staggered into sight, arms windmilling as he toppled backward, hitting the ground with his pistol clattering across the floor. Grizzly grabbed for his gun but took a second to get it free, his bulky

CHAPTER SEVEN

stomach in the way. Zach picked up his Spear and turned when a hard steel barrel pressed against his hip and froze him with his hand on his weapon.

"Drop the gun on the hood and backup."

"You, too, fatty!" another man shouted at Grizzly. "Drop that pistol, now!"

Grizzly dropped his gun on the concrete, and Craig raised his hands with a trembling breath. Squeezing his eyes shut, Zach sighed, placed the Spear on the hood, and held up both hands, mirroring Craig.

"Good man. Now, turn around."

Zach turned as Liza sprinted in from where she'd been guarding the east entrance, gun still in its holster, a look of horror on her face.

"Nikolay!" As soon as she reached the Humvee, Sandy stepped into Zach's field of vision, stuck her foot out, and kicked Liza's feet from beneath her, sending her tumbling to the ground with a pained grunt. Sandy squatted and drove her knee into Liza's back, pinning her.

"My friend is shot!" Liza cried. "Take my weapon, but at least let me help him."

"No way," Sandy smirked.

"Nice catch, babe," Scotty said, shifting to Zach. "Now, finish turning around. I want to look at your ugly mug."

Zach turned slowly and faced the barrel of an AR-15-style rifle and Scotty's leer. Another man with a blue beanie and a dark wool coat had a similar weapon on Grizzly, then he shifted it to Craig.

"Hey, little man," Blue Beanie said. "Why don't you drop that little pistol and kick it over here?"

"All three of you," Scotty added.

Grizzly kicked his weapon across the floor. As Zach and Craig were taking their guns out, Sandy got Liza up and shoved her in their direction, giving her a final push so that she stumbled forward and forced Craig to squat to catch her before she hit the ground. Sandy backpedaled and raised a pistol, holding it on Zach a moment before shifting it to Craig and Liza.

Craig's eyes flashed with heat. "Are these the lovely people you're telling us about earlier? The ones who shot the firefighter?"

"One and the same," Zach replied. Holding his pistol out, he placed it on the ground and kicked it over, motioning for Craig to follow suit. Then he fixed Scotty with a stern look as his mind raced to think of a way out of the situation. They were too far away to go for their weapons, and another figure lingered in the shadows behind them.

As if reading Zach's mind, Scotty said, "Don't even think about doing something stupid. We've got you covered."

Instead of making a rash move, Zach tried to buy them time. "We have to quit meeting like this. What do you want?"

"That should be obvious. We want your sweet ride there. The way I figure it, it's the only way we'll get across the river and back up to the highway." Scotty's smile widened. "I'm pretty sure that was your plan, too."

"The thought had crossed our minds," Zach agreed. "Let us go, and you can have everything inside and the food."

"Oh, we're taking that," Scotty held his rifle in one hand and made a flourishing gesture with the other. "But we've still got some other unfinished business to take care of."

"Your beef is with me, man," Zach said. "These other people... they're government scientists." He shifted his eyes to the west side of the building. "One of them you just shot. When the Army boys find out what you did, they'll come down on you hard."

"You're full of it."

Zach took a bold step and lowered his hands a little. "Okay, genius. Then why are we suddenly in a Humvee and wearing military fatigues? You think we just picked this stuff up at an auction?"

Scotty glanced over the armored truck and their equipment, his eyes lingering on the Sig Saur Spear with a hint of doubt flashing across his features.

"This is a government mission," Zach continued, "sanctioned by the President of the United States himself."

Scotty slowly shook his head, eyes darting across the lot of them in self-doubt. "It doesn't matter. We're taking all your stuff, and I'll

CHAPTER SEVEN

teach you a lesson. When we're done with you, there won't be anyone left for the government to question. They'll never know it was us."

"We should let them go." A woman stepped from the shadows, short and stocky with a curved figure and a chestnut brown mane falling in waves over her shoulders and down her back. Dark eyes beneath a strong brow took Zach's group in before shifting to Scotty. "All we need is their Humvee. We don't need anything else. Let's just let them go. We don't need the Army after us, too."

Zach's eyes widened. "Gina?"

CHAPTER EIGHT

Gina Morosov, Wiseman, Alaska, Days Earlier...

Gina stood at the front window of her house and watched Zach pull away on his snowmobile to disappear into the early morning darkness, the troubled man she'd taken in for a night, the good one who'd saved her from ruffians and helped her defend her store. Part of her wanted to go with him like he'd asked, but she couldn't leave without Hank. There was still time for him to come home, and they had so much to lose: the store, their savings, their vehicles, and everything they'd worked to attain for so many years.

"Good luck, my friend," she murmured and went inside to fix some breakfast.

Soon, the smell of bacon and eggs filled the house, fresh coffee made from the water she'd gotten from her storage containers since the faucets weren't working anymore. She spent the rest of the day in quiet loneliness, pacing from one end of the house to the other, standing at the front window of her store as the snow fell heavier and the firestorms increased. Despite it being the middle of the day, it was as dark as dusk, with glowing cinders drifting through the air as

CHAPTER EIGHT

more things caught fire around her. From her porch, she peered down the lane at a house on the far end burning bright, while to the north, the sky was a terrifying mosaic of turbulence. The once quiet, dark clouds had turned more tumultuous, drifting downward to settle on the ground.

Lightning rippled through the dense underbelly as the hydrocarbon fumes Zach had warned her about erupted across the sky, heat blowing down in warm gusts that fluttered her hair. The roads were empty, and the lights were dark, making her feel like she was in a ghost town. Gina rushed inside, shut the door, and threw her back against it, taking a trembling breath as her intention to stay turned into indecision. Over the next hour, she listened as the rafters shook and the floor rumbled, walls rattling against the screaming winds.

Outside, the last few looters were cleaning out the stores, packing everything they could into the backs of their pickups while throwing panicked glances at the sky. After the display the previous evening, no one bothered her or tried to get in, and she almost would've welcomed it as a strange feeling of loneliness crept up her spine and into her head. Hank still hadn't called on the radio or cell phone, and there was no sound of his boots stomping up the porch stairs like he often did when he came home. Sitting at the kitchen table, she wondered if she'd be the last person left in town. She couldn't convince herself to move and only sat there with a cup of coffee in her hand, imagining any other normal day after breakfast, with Hank minding the store and her having a couple of hours of free time before she worked a later shift. Back then, their main concerns were what they were having for dinner. Now, her worries were of Hank and whether she'd be in her house when it fell in on her head.

Sometime around 4 p.m., a deep vibration rolled through the floor and the ceiling, rippling up through her boots to her hips, and when pieces of other houses began crashing into hers, small at first but growing into loud bangs, she knew it was time to go. Leaping from her chair, Gina put on her heavy winter boots and rushed down the hall and stepped into their general store. Already layered with sweaters and thermal protection, she left her regular coat hanging on a hook in the kitchen. Gina glanced around at all the survival pieces

CHAPTER EIGHT

and hunting equipment on the shelves. Memories flashed in her mind, like the time she and Hank had first moved into the place and it was just an empty shell, yet through perseverance and imagination, and a heckuva lot of hard work, they'd transformed the store around them, filling it with coats and parkas and digging tools, knives and axes and hunting rifles and a regular supply of ammunition.

That was just a tiny part of the sales. Many tourists came to the Alaskan wilds to camp, so they had a vast array of sleeping bags, mats, thermal covers, stoves, and a hundred different ways to build a fire. The rear of the store held supplies for RVs and vans like batteries, generators, jerrycans, antifreeze, vehicle jacks, and cargo trays. While it seemed like a lot to remember, Gina had gotten to know all the merchants and warehouses they ordered products from and even the drivers who purchased their regular supplies. People came from neighboring towns, even small ones that weren't on a map yet but were being laid out over the months and years.

Gina had wanted to share more of that with Hank, to grow their dream as big as they could before time and old age demanded final payment. She rushed behind the counter to the other end and pressed into a storeroom between their house and the shop, a simple spot with a desk and computer where she kept inventory, invoice records, and petty cash. She left the cash drawer alone and proceeded to the far wall, where her bug-out bag hung from a hook.

It was a nondescript backpack, like any other a hiker might wear in the Alaskan wilds, and she'd even cut a few shallow holes in the material to give it a well-used look. Being only ten percent of her body weight, it slipped onto her shoulders and nestled her back so she could carry it miles through the wilderness. Beneath that, also on hooks, was her multi-tool axe which she fixed to her belt along with a holster, a Ruger American pistol, and a small magazine pouch with four magazines, each with seventeen rounds. As she adjusted her belt so it rested comfortably on her hips, the ceiling rattled, dust trickled from above, and the walls groaned. Debris clattered against the store's front glass, sharp pebbles and thick branches flung about by the wind.

"I know, I know!"

CHAPTER EIGHT

On the last hook hung a long, warm coat with plenty of inside pockets already packed with things she might use in the wilderness, each piece meticulously thought out in its imagined use. She and Hank had talked through hundreds of situations over dinner and breakfast, making up the wildest conspiracy theories to laugh about, everything from Russian invasions to alien landings, and working out what they'd do. Her gaze lifted to Hank's backpack, coat, and weapons. It was tempting to take some of it, at the very least his gun, but there was only so much she could carry, and if he *did* come home, and the house and store weren't burned down, he'd have his supplies ready to go.

Blinking away tears, Gina turned her back on the room and went up the hall to the living room and into the kitchen where the smells of bacon and egg still lingered. There, she did a full circle, her gaze landing on the table and simple chairs where she and Hank had spent most of their time, like talking about tactical gear and what to stock the store with. They'd spoken about the trends coming to Alaska, the yearly influx of curious travelers on the Dalton Highway after watching all the trucker's shows and survival documentaries based on folks who lived up that way. Hank even wanted to start a line of T-shirts with goofy sayings like *You Moose Vacation in Alaska*, hoping tourists would go nuts over them. Gina argued those kinds of things were fads, and she feared they'd be left with a lot of extra inventory.

She sniffed and started to turn away, but couldn't. Emotion filled her heart and spread upward to her head, her sinuses stuffy as the tears built up and streamed out. Hand on her stomach, she tried to keep from throwing up, but she kept it down because she was tougher than that. With the house about to fall around her, Gina let the tears flow as everything shook and trembled, the floorboards filled with tremors, the walls groaning, pots and pans clanking where they hung above the stove. She wiped the last tear away and went outside to the front door, pulling it shut but not bothering to lock it in case Hank didn't have his key.

Gina moved quickly down the porch stairs, turned left, and crossed the yard to the sidewalk, where she angled toward a row of garage doors at the end of the lane. Glancing around as she went, she caught snippets of hollers and yells, diesel engines revving up, and tires tearing out of gravel lots. A few people seemed jovial and reckless, hooting and yee-hawing like they were in a rodeo movie. When Gina was halfway there, there was a whoosh above her, and she ducked as a blast of cinders washed off the woods to the north, carried by a gust of wind to blanket the house on her left. Gina ran the rest of the way, huffing and puffing until she reached the garage. She circled to the back and unlocked the door of unit two, slipping in to the smells of old oil and dust. She didn't need any of Hank's tools that hung from the walls or were in his chest and cabinets, though she *did* need to decide between the GMC pickup or the snowmobile parked to the right of it. The truck was the obvious choice because she could stay warm inside, but the terrain would be rough on it, and there'd be a chance she could get stuck. There probably hadn't been anyone shoveling or deicing the roads for weeks, and there was no way she could get warnings about avalanches or obstructions. She imagined herself sitting in front of a massive pile of snow with no choice but to abandon the truck and try to outrun the storms on foot.

Her gaze shifted to the snowmobile, anticipating a cold ride with the wind getting beneath her clothing and freezing her skin. Still, she'd be able to get over almost any obstacle, or at least go around, and for conserving calories out in the wild, she couldn't think of anything better than to be on the snowmobile. It had a cargo tray on the back with three jerrycans of gas, and the tank was full. There was likely plenty more gas out there in abandoned vehicles and sheds, even though a lot of cars and houses were already on fire, but if she had to stop, she was comfortable knowing she'd survive. Besides, Zach likely could've scavenged any other vehicle, but he'd picked a snowmobile as his mode of transportation.

"Snowmobile it is," Gina said, grabbing the key from a nearby drawer and walking to the garage door to open it and move some empty cardboard boxes.

The door rolled up on its rails with a clatter and slammed when it

CHAPTER EIGHT

reached the top, leaving Gina staring at three people on the other side, led by Yellow Coveralls, who had a gun in his hand, the same one Blue Coveralls had threatened to shoot her with. The weapon wasn't particularly frightening, but any minor bullet wound could fester and end her, and she wouldn't survive without her things. A woman stood on Yellow Coveralls' right, several inches taller than Gina but slight of frame inside her heavy coat. The other was a native man with dark stains on his coveralls that had to be blood.

"What happened to your friend?" Gina asked casually as her heart went into overdrive and her brain whipped through a dozen ways to get rid of them.

"He died of a gunshot wound," Yellow Coveralls said. "The one you all inflicted on him."

Gina held up both hands and took a step back so her boots were behind a small stack of cardboard boxes lying haphazardly atop one another. "You guys shouldn't have tried to rob my store."

"Doesn't matter now," he said. "What matters is that we're here now, and I'm going to make you pay before we bug out."

Gina glanced up, her eyes reflecting the amber lightning and billowing flames as the sky seemed to slowly drop on the town, and the first hints of fiery cyclones touched the roads and whipped snow and sleet into the air.

"Look, I can appreciate you're not happy with me, but we've got to get out of here." She nodded to her house. "I left the door open, and you can have all the supplies you want. And you can have this truck, too. Keys are right over there in the drawer. Take it and get to safety as soon as you can. I just want to take my backpack and snowmobile and get out of your hair."

Yellow Coveralls snickered at his friends, the gun wavering at Gina's chest. "Oh, now she wants to help us out. What an angel."

"Yeah, a real saint," the woman said with a wry frown. "It's people like you who are part of the problem... people who won't share when others are having a tough time."

"You're right, but the storms are coming hard." Gina nodded pointedly. "This will all burn to the ground shortly."

CHAPTER EIGHT

"I say we tie her up and leave her to get torched with all her stuff," the native man said.

"That's an excellent idea, Sam." Yellow Coveralls nodded toward the woman. "See if you can find some rope, and we'll make sure she gets nice and comfortable before we head out."

Gina drew back her boot and kicked the boxes as high as she could, cardboard flying everywhere with one solid piece hitting Yellow Coveralls right in his gun hand and knocking it aside. Gina was already turning and running behind her pickup truck, swinging around the rear as bullets zipped by and pinged the shelves against the garage wall. Her hand dipped into her pocket, bringing out the Ruger. Footsteps pounded along the side of the truck. Sliding sideways, Gina fell onto her back with her pistol at arm's length, firing between her knees as the woman rushed around with a big piece of jagged metal in her hand. She met the bullets face-first, her head twitching, the back of her skull flying to pieces and decorating the ceiling and far wall with chunks of red and gray matter. Before Gina registered what she'd done, she spun right, moving around the truck to the left-rear fender where she crouched behind the back tire.

"Oh, crap! She shot Mel!" Sam shouted, his boots scraping across the pavement as if he was getting ready to run.

"Hang on, Sam!" Yellow Coveralls growled, and everything went quiet as the two shuffled around and whispered harshly.

Gina couldn't hear them over the raging sky. She was breathing hard, gaze darting up and shifting to the front of the truck, heart thumping as she tried to think of what to do. One of them had a gun, and they were likely going to surround her, but she was crouched behind the wheel so they couldn't shoot her beneath it. The truck shook, rocking on its springs like someone was grabbing the edge and pulling.

"Hey, girl," Yellow Coveralls said. "I'm waving the white flag. Come on out and join the crew. We're down one gal, and we could use someone with your skills. Mel wasn't worth a crap, anyway. She was always complaining, but I can tell you're not that kind of person. You're tough, and that's the kind of person I want to travel south with. I assume that's where you're going?"

139

CHAPTER EIGHT

Gina didn't say a word but squeezed her eyes shut as the man continued rocking the truck, but what was he trying to gain? With a soft curse, she realized it was probably a distraction, and the other man was coming around to shoot or hit her, but when she glanced toward the front of the truck, there was no one there. Gina rolled to her right on a whim, landing on her belly and peering beneath the undercarriage. Across from her, Sam was on his hands and knees and staring back at her, eyes flying wide when he saw the gun pointed at his face.

"Merle, she's —"

The gun blast took him in the side of the neck. Pain flashed through his eyes and he tried to rise for a moment but lost all strength in his body as he flopped forward onto his chest, left hand plastered to his neck where blood was pumping through his fingers. Gina was already up and scooting down the truck's side, reaching the front and sliding along the grill where she rested back on her heels with her gun held against her chest, shaking her head, lips trembling, and jaw pressed tight. She wanted to jump up and run away, but Yellow Coveralls, Merle, was waiting for her on the other side, and he had his weapon. The truck stopped juddering, and Merle's boots scuffed on the cement, but the noise wasn't precise, and she couldn't tell if he was still on the side or had gone around to the back.

"Damn! What are you doing, lady? You got Sam, too!"

Something scooted across the floor, a box or bin, and the truck shifted again, like someone was climbing into the bed.

Merle lowered his voice, sounding resigned and amicable. "Okay, I get it. You win, and now I'm trapped in here with you."

After a deep breath, Gina shouted, "Then get out of here! Get the hell out!"

"How do I know you won't shoot me?"

"Because I didn't threaten you in the first place. Just get out of my garage and let me leave. Once I'm gone, you can do what you want, but you will *not* hurt me. I won't let you."

The man fell silent as the storm grew wilder, from a small cluster of explosions and spinning cyclones to intensifying winds carrying pieces of trees and bushes, shingles, and glass. Another house at the end of the lane collapsed on its front side, the porch beams falling in and a gout of flames shooting up from the rubble.

"It's up to you! But we've got to get out of here now, or we're both dead!"

Still, silence. No scuffling of feet and no sight of him anywhere. Leaning to her right, Gina fell to her hands and peered under the truck, scanning the shadows where Hank kept his tools, but there was no sign of Merle. She thought maybe he'd slipped out the back door, but then the truck bounced again, followed by a crumpling of the roof and hood like he was walking across it as softly as he could. Already on her hands and knees, she rolled to her left, landing on her shoulder, swinging the gun up as Merle jumped to the edge of the hood and fired straight down where she'd been.

With him dead to rights, Gina took her time with the shot, giving him a second to glance her way with a wide-eyed expression of fear before she fired six rounds into him. Merle squealed and squeaked as he tried to dodge the bullets, performing a staggering dance on the hood with the metal crumpling and buckling beneath his boots. When he reached the far side, he raised his pistol to fire back but lost his balance, slipping on his blood as he plunged into the rakes and shovels that hung off the wall on the other side. It all came down with a clatter, hooks and racks with a mess of tools that landed on top of him before it all fell dead quiet.

Gina scrambled to her feet, assumed a firing stance with her arms extended, and stayed low in case he was still alive. She circled the truck's front and swept her weapon up to find him lying dead amidst the clutter, a post-hole digger resting on his chest. The screaming wind broke her stare. She walked to the boxes still blocking her snowmobile, kicked them aside, and moved everything out of the way. After checking the bungee cables securing the jerrycans, Gina holstered her weapon and inspected her ride. She went to one of Hank's cabinets and took out some heavy goggles, a helmet, and an air filtration mask. After putting her headgear on, she slung her leg over the seat and started the machine, listening to the well-maintained engine throttle up to a low roar before settling into a purr. Gina stared at the maelstrom growing in front of her eyes, parts of

CHAPTER EIGHT

houses collapsing, crackling timbers and snapping branches as they were tossed everywhere. A snow-covered car at the end of the lane took a direct hit from a flying tree trunk as wide as Gina's torso, glass shattering, the entire frame rocking and shifting and sliding across the icy pavement ten feet before crashing to a stop against the curb. Fiery debris whipped past her as tears streamed from her eyes. Hank was probably dead and gone, and only her memories of him would remain.

It was time to move on and survive, though she struggled to decide on why.

In her gut punched emotional state, she couldn't have put the reason into a sentence, only that she *should* carry on, put the snowmobile into gear, and find a way out of the turmoil. Carefully and slowly, she drove ahead and leaned back, trying not to grate the steering on the pavement until she moved out from beneath the garage cover, where the wind hit her like a punch and almost tore her from the seat. Finding some frosted ice, she turned right, kicked up the throttle, and shot up a shallow bank to leap the sidewalk. Landing in the side yard, she gave it more gas and bolted up into the snow-covered grass, moving along the edge of the woods where deadfall and burning branches fell all around her. She buzzed by her row of houses, which were collapsing slowly but surely, and then past tourist areas in new hotels they'd just built, putting what remained of Wiseman behind her. She hit a wide-open field and raced south into the fire and ice.

With Wiseman behind her, and the firestorms fading into the distance, Gina followed the Dalton Highway south, running parallel to the snow-covered road with a spattering of abandoned trucks and cars, some of them packed with stolen goods and footprints leading off into the woods. Gina imagined someone reaching out of the shadowy forest to grab her off her snowmobile, so she angled away from the tree line and shot across the open fields where she could move as fast as she dared. It had been a while since going out with

CHAPTER EIGHT

Hank, and when they did, he usually drove, so she was getting back into the habit of driving. Not that she couldn't, but she'd simply enjoyed riding on the back with her arms around his waist and her cheek pressed against him.

Life had changed drastically. Gina was on her own, and she had to remember all the things they'd practiced together in the woods, camping with the bare minimum to build their skills. As the night wore on, she grew tired, her arms shivering as she clung to the handlebars, her knees pressed tightly against the snowmobile's sides, and her lower back and hips ached from trying to keep her balance. The whole time, snow whipped against her goggles, half blinding her with the wind's intensity. She had to find a place to rest soon, get warm, and eat.

Gina studied the tree line and the fields beyond, scanning the rocky slopes for a protected ridge with a little forest cover but not too much, and a good view of the surrounding land. Then again, if someone saw her fire, they'd certainly come to investigate, so she angled off to the west, flying over a woodsy hill covered in wide spruces and shifting around trees that seemed to cling together in fear of the pounding firestorms. Plowing over the crest and riding down the other side, Gina wove into a valley and up to the left, keeping her eye on the compass to avoid getting turned around. Instead of a high rise, she selected a shallow dip in a tight cluster of woods, using the snowmobile's girth to push her way through the tangle of brush until she reached a clearing. She angled so she was facing to the south and stopped. Flashlight out, she flipped it on and got off, wobbling a little as she shined the beam at her surroundings. The silence was jarring after hours of riding, and her legs and arms trembled as she staggered around the site, using her feet to clear deadfall off the ground and position a ring of rocks to start a fire.

Gina walked off into the trees, bending to pick up easy pieces of wood, inspecting them to ensure they were dry before tossing them by the campsite. Taking the multi-use ax off her belt, she shaved some smaller pieces to use as tinder and kindling and broke the others over her knee to get a bit of starter wood. With a paraffin wax-covered accelerant from her pack, she placed it in the kindling and

CHAPTER EIGHT

struck a flint stick with the back of her axe, which had a good amount of carbon in its makeup, sending big fat sparks into the wood and setting it alight. Gina squatted behind the growing flames, putting in twigs as the fire grew from sputtering flickers to flames that reached knee-height. She added a few more sticks on top and then went to her cargo tray and retrieved a battery and a silicone heating pad. With the engine having cooled off enough for her to touch it, she put the pad beneath it and connected the wires to the battery terminals, ensuring the oil would be warm enough to start quickly if she had to get away fast for any reason. She placed a foldout grate over the fire and filled her stainless-steel water container with snow. With that on the grill, she sat on her heels and rested, letting her body return to normalcy after the rattling ride across the tundra.

When the water boiled, she poured it into a second container with a filter inside. Gina placed that into the snow to let it cool down, and after a few minutes, she drank the whole thing, repeating the process twice and pouring what remained in the filter container into the stainless steel one, sealing it up for later use.

With her water needs out of the way, she retrieved a high-calorie granola mix from her bug-out bag and ate slowly, chewing every bite and taking her time swallowing. Tired, antsy, and wanting to rest, she forced herself to enter survival mode, moving slowly around the camp to conserve energy. After she finished her meal, Gina walked out into the woods and cut some long saplings down, stripping them and placing one end on a three-foot stone, with the other side angling to the forest floor. Piling them on, she covered the top and let some of the longer ones fall over the back, adding layer after layer until it was thick. Beneath that, she placed fir boughs and took a thin wool blanket out of her pack to lay on top. Grabbing a thermal blanket, she tossed it inside and squatted by the fire to get warmer. Gazing up, she saw the restless trees swaying in the pitch-black night, not a single star nor any moonlight to give her a shred of hope that the storms would end. In the distance, Gina swore she heard raging flames burning some other part of the forest, and she was at risk where she was, but the trees would offer protection from prying eyes in the short term. If the fires descended on her in the next few hours, she could quickly pack up and buzz out, and she wasn't too far from the edge of the forest where reaching the wide-open fields would give her some reprieve.

Throwing a few more logs onto the fire, she waited until her eyelids drooped and she swayed in her crouch. She rolled into her shelter, sinking into her heavy coat and drawing the thermal blanket over her shoulders. It was warm and cozy, and she wished Hank was there to share the moment with her, their hopes of taking care of each other into old age dashed in the space of a few days. The worst part was that she didn't know what had happened to him out on the road helping people. With tears of anger, sadness, and resentment blurring her vision, Gina fell into a restless sleep where she tossed and turned to stay warm and keep from thinking about whatever terrible fate had befallen her husband.

The following day, she got moving, pulling out of the cluster of trees with wildfires racing through the countryside, spreading across the northern horizon, the dark and angry skies pressing down. Chased by gusts of cinder-filled winds, she sped south for hours, hill after hill rolling beneath her track, weaving between tree trunks and massive stones, learning to spot where the weather was getting worse and where she should turn aside.

She drew closer to the Dalton Highway, reconnecting with Highway 12 and spotting some abandoned vehicles along the road. It was a surprise when she crested a rise and flew over the other side to find a half-dozen people standing around a campsite, tilting their heads as they listened to her revving engine. They quickly jumped into action. Hands reached for her, grabbing and snatching at her arms as she swung to her left. Someone came from that direction, lowering their shoulder and trying to knock her off her seat, but a quick twist of the throttle, and she shot past them and cut through clusters of woods, glancing back to see them chasing her, waving branches and cursing.

Keeping an eye out for similar groups, Gina continued south between the sweeping mountain slopes and their frosted spurs. Like folds in the land, they stretched off to the east and west as her snow-

CHAPTER EIGHT

mobile engine roared and echoed. Wiseman was almost completely abandoned. The only people there giving her dark glances as they packed the last of their things into trucks and got on the road. She found an abandoned truck and used a one-inch hose from her backpack to siphon the fuel out, filling up the jerrycans she'd emptied. Refueled, she checked the area and picked up a few food items before driving onward.

On the fourth day, Gina spotted some signs for Fairbanks, and she remained leery as she passed small towns where a few people lingered. Many of the towns had burned down, caught by firestorms that had raced ahead of her. The clouds continued spreading, covering everything in choking soot. Donning her air filtration mask, she kept on, focusing on reaching Fairbanks and finding help.

She crossed a bridge over the Chatanika River with few signs of civilization, just some people camped by a town's wreckage. When she was within a few miles of Fairbanks she heard the rumbling of massive diesel engines that drowned out her high-revving snowmobile. Stopping at the edge of the ridge overlooking Highway 12, she put it in park and stood. Ten black armored military vehicles with angled noses and machine guns ran north along the highway. Antennae and communication dishes were arrayed across the tops, and they trudged northward with snow flying from beneath their tracks, the lead vehicle clearing the way with a wide snowplow in the front.

"I don't know why you're going north," she said, "but you're crazy."

Back on her snowmobile, she passed the town of Fox and buzzed through partially occupied areas, ignoring the waves and gestures for her to stop, putting her head down and flying right on by with the throttle on high. Past neighborhoods locked in flames or long ago burned out to leave charred husks behind, Gina roared ever southward, reaching the streets of Fairbanks and gazing with jaw-dropping incredulity at how hard they'd been hit. Buildings raged with fresh fire as if they'd just gotten destroyed by another storm, and from a distance, she spotted charred corpses lying in the streets or inside cars sitting skewed on the roadside. Unwilling to go deeper into town, Gina turned east, intending to run along the Chena River that circled the city until she found a bridge to cross and more vehicles to siphon. She knew there was an airport on the west side of town and Fort Wainwright was to the east. Angling that way, she spotted the first C-130 lifting off and heading south away from the firestorm, chased by fiery tendrils reaching down to grab it, though it seemed the pilots were incredibly skilled and kept away from the worst of the storms with a constant string of evasive maneuvers.

Hoping to make friends at the base, Gina leaned over the handlebars and throttled up through paved parks and frosted pavement, glancing south where abandoned residential areas and closed shops stood everywhere, many structures still caught in flames or turned to coal and ash. APCs and Humvees ran out on the tarmac, and a couple thousand troops were forming outside one hangar with others overseeing the removal of jets from the backs of C-130s to be ferried to one side of the runway, where they directed windshields and fire trucks. The Chena River swung south again, and she spotted a bridge past a wide cluster of green trees that would lead almost into the base.

Riding close to the tree line, Gina became so excited to reach the bridge she wasn't paying as much heed to the forest. Three groups of people sprang out and jumped her, kicking up snow as they tried to get in front of her, one person standing right in her way with her palms out for Gina to stop. She throttled harder and plowed into the woman, whose face smashed against her windshield before she rolled off with a cut-off grunt. The impact sent her snowmobile slewing sideways, her rear end coming around as the tracks spit out snow and chunks of ice.

Someone ran in from the road on her left, diving for her, trying to knock her off the snowmobile. Axe in her left hand, she swung wildly, her aim off but inspired, the blade sinking into the man's chest as she flew by, the force ripping the axe from her hand and jerking her backward as the lanyard around her wrist drew taut and yanked the axe from the man's chest. Barely controlling her snowmobile one-handed, she whipped it right, rode up a slight rise, and jumped. The attackers dove out of the way, but her left skid caught someone on the hip,

CHAPTER EIGHT

swatting them aside in a backbreaking collision. She landed awkwardly, the snowmobile balancing on its left track and slewing for twenty yards before pitching her off to the side where she hit the snow and rolled three times.

Dazed and spitting white powder, her left wrist weak after being wrenched so hard, she pushed herself to her hands and knees and gazed at the group of people closing in on her. There were maybe ten of them, none with guns but armed with branches and blunt things they'd picked up from their surroundings. To even the odds, she climbed to her feet, drew her Ruger, and swept it along the lot of them, saying the same thing she did in Wiseman.

"I've got more rounds in this pistol than you've got people. Back the hell off, or someone's going down."

A tall woman with long arms and loose brown hair sticking out from her hat grinned and spread her hands, replying with the same answer Blue Coveralls had given. "You can't kill us —"

Gina didn't wait for her to finish. Starting on the left, she popped off shots, backing up as she fired, hitting the first person and then the next. The third one took a round in the arm, threw his hand over the wound, and screamed. Gina kept shooting down the line as the people on her right charged at her. She incapacitated two more attackers before someone tackled her low, a big heavy shoulder nailing her in the ribs, lifting her off her feet and tossing her five yards where she hit the ground on her left-hand side, her axe rolling beneath her, pistol flying away. Spinning in the opposite direction, she swung backhanded with her right fist and struck him, but the thick glove softened the blow, which barely bothered him. He laughed and crawled on top of her, pinning her, raising a fist and dropping it across her chin with a heavy strike that knocked her head against the ground. While his glove was soft, too, the weight of the punch sent stars zipping through her brain and the iron-tinged taste of blood flooded her mouth.

"Sue, go check out that snowmobile. I'll take care of —"

Gripping the hand axe, Gina swung it with a snarl, not knowing which end would hit him but finding out when the blade chunked into the side of his face, crunching through his jaw and eye socket with a wet and brittle sound. The man reeled with a gasp, his hand going to the axe and feeling the thick blade where it had sunk into his face. His remaining eye twitched in its socket, and his lips trembled as something guttural and unintelligible squeaked out. Gina went to shove him off when a roar swept over them with a wave of heat and cinders. A growing wind sucked up all sound into a drawn-out pause of silence. Swirling, oddly patterned yellow-gold winds blasted in just before lightning cracked and tore the sky apart, creating a maelstrom of orange heat and flames. A woman screamed as her coat caught fire. A voracious gust of glowing embers struck the man astride her, and he flew off of her into the melting snow. Gina threw her arms over her face, rolled, and plopped into a cold slush puddle. With sweeping movements, she splashed herself, the crimson-colored sludge drenching her head and clothes. Waves of flames flowed over her with a hiss of steam and smoke as she continued crawling, staying wet and cold while others burned alive.

The wind stopped, and the smells of cooking flesh filled the air, hitting Gina full in the face. Rising onto her elbows, she lurched forward to throw up in a melt puddle, leaking drool from her bottom lip and tasting bile and blood. After that, she raised higher, gasping and spitting as a soft mist drifted over the field where burned bodies lay in freezing slush, arms bent and twisted in pain, fingers locked in grotesque formations. The air was silent except for the nearby woods, which were smoldering and crackling like a massive campfire. When she looked around for her snowmobile, she spotted it thirty yards away, lying on its side, seat burning, and one ski bent inward and broken.

Rising, she wiped the wetness off her jeans and coat. "There goes my ride."

Someone screamed, and Gina fell into a squat just as the lead woman with the loose brown hair hit her. Being shorter and stockier, with a lower center of gravity, Gina didn't fall but shouldered the woman upright and shoved back, the two grappling, clutching each other by their coats, sliding in the slush before the woman's leg swept out and kicked Gina's left foot from beneath her. As she tumbled, Gina grabbed her jacket and held on tight, dragging her

CHAPTER EIGHT

down, both hitting the cold sludge with a splash. Coming up on top, the woman seized her head and scratched at her eyes. Writhing, Gina knocked her aside with her forearms and punched, connecting twice, bucking and kicking to get her off. The woman spotted something on the ground near Gina, and she snatched it out of the slush, raising it with a sneer of victory. It was Gina's axe, ready to drop and split her skull just like she'd done to the man's face.

Gina blinked into the woman's hate-filled eyes and put her hands up to block the inevitable strike. A gun cracked, and the woman convulsed atop her, blood spurting from a head wound and streaming down her right cheek. With a choking gasp of confusion, the woman sank sideways and slumped off her. The mist rolled by again as Gina shifted her hips to dump the woman to the side, flipping toward where she thought the gunshot had originated. A pair of shadows strode through the slushy field, boots crunching the already freezing water. She could tell by their shapes it was a man and a woman, both carrying the sharp-edged forms of assault-style rifles. Desperately rolling toward the dead woman, Gina searched for and found her axe lying nearby. She snatched it up with her left hand and held it over her head as she flipped onto her back, ready to swing or throw it to distract her attackers and escape. The pair stopped ten yards away, neither aiming their guns at her nor making any other threatening moves.

After a moment, Gina said, "What do you want?"

The man laughed and glanced at the woman. "I'm waiting for you to say thanks for saving your butt. If I hadn't shot that lady, you would've been eating that axe."

Gina relaxed her arm and fell back into the slush. "It was *my* axe... and... thanks. I appreciate the assistance."

"No problem."

Gina sat up, rolled to her left, and slowly got up, dripping in the cold. "Who are you?"

"Name's Scotty, and this is Sandy."

"I'm Gina. Good to meet you, I think."

"You too, Gina," Sandy replied. "Are you looking for a group?"

Gina pointed to the west with her axe. "I was thinking of trying the military guys. Maybe they could —"

Scotty scoffed and spat toward the base. "The Army guys don't have time for civilians. Those bastards watch thousands of people die while they play war games with the Russians."

"Russians?"

The pair glanced at each other, and Scotty stepped forward with Sandy behind him. A breeze swept the mist away, and their forms took on a more defined shape. Scotty was bald with a short, stocky frame and strong shoulders inside a form-fitting black winter coat. Sandy was a native with round cheeks, big brown eyes, and hair dyed a deep auburn that snuck out from beneath her beanie.

"Yeah, lady," Scotty said. "Russians are attacking. Bastards are all over the place. We should stop fighting each other and start fighting them." He shrugged. "At least the military guys are keeping them off our backs. I repeat Sandy's question... are you looking for a group?"

"Depends on what you're doing."

"Going south quickly and safely. Doing whatever it takes to get there."

"You're not assholes, are you?"

The two looked at each other and laughed, and then the man turned his stern eyes on Gina. "Some people might think we're not so nice, but I think we're pretty cool, huh, Sandy?"

Sandy shrugged. "We try. What's it going to be, Gina? We're heading out in five minutes. Got a van on the south side of town..."

"What were you doing over here?"

"Trying to put together a team." Scotty nodded at the charred corpses slowly getting encased in the refreezing slush. "Was going to ask a few of these guys, but I guess they didn't make it. You did. That means you're tough enough to get through this, and that's the kind of person we're looking to roll with. What do you say?"

Scotty stepped closer, letting his rifle hang in his left hand while reaching with his right. Gina glanced from one to the other and then at her wrecked snowmobile. The vehicle was shot, and the only option she had was the military, or... Scotty had saved her from a bludgeoning, and that meant *something*. She'd seen enough evidence

CHAPTER EIGHT

of stinking corpses and refugees around Fairbanks to believe the military might not be the best bet.

Gina nodded and reached out to slap her hand in his. "I'll ride along, at least for a little while."

"Outstanding!" Scotty grinned. "You won't regret it. I promise."

CHAPTER NINE

Zach Christensen, Salcha, Alaska

Zach saw the hesitation in Gina's eyes, yet her gun remained pointed at them, and she was with the two people in the world Zach didn't want to see.

"You know this guy?" Scotty asked with a sneer.

"Yeah, I do. He's good people."

"Bastard stole from me up in Deadhorse." Scotty raised the rifle and pointed it at Zach's face. "Which is part of why we're in this position to begin with. He took our snowmobile, supplies, and both radios."

"Shouldn't have shot at me," Zach replied with tension squeezing his throat. His gaze darted between Gina and the other two. "I told you back at your house, Gina."

Gina gaped. "These were the two you fought with by the military helicopters?"

"That's right. I was trying to teach them a lesson by taking the stuff. Anyway, they made it to the rescue crews."

"Right, you got us kicked out of there, too."

Zach scoffed. "Don't listen to him, Gina. He was so mad about

CHAPTER NINE

me taking their stuff that they threatened us in front of law enforcement and shot a firefighter up there." He shifted to Scotty. "The guy lived, if you care."

"Of course I do," Scotty replied. "You think I enjoy hurting people?"

"Yeah, I think you do." Zach glanced at Gina, wanting desperately to get to his Spear, which was sitting on the truck hood behind him. If he tried to move in any direction, Scotty would mow him down.

"Let me go to Nikolay!" Liza screamed, squirming to get away from Craig even as he held her close. "He is hurt."

"Let her go see to him, man," Zach said. "That guy was just a technician. You didn't have to shoot him."

"Everyone is an enemy these days," Scotty replied.

"Unless they're a friend," Gina added hastily. "Hey, Scotty. Why don't we get that guy some first aid and join up with these guys? They've got weapons, and I know they're tough."

Zach and Scotty scoffed simultaneously, but then he glanced toward the west entrance, where Nikolay barely moved, lying in a pool of blood as he moaned for help. "It would be a good start if you'd let us help our friend. Come on, man."

Scotty stared hard at Zach, then he nodded. "Fine. Go help the guy for all it's worth." With a nod at Liza, he added, "Just you, lady."

Craig released Liza, and she popped the Humvee's rear hatch with Sandy pointing her rifle at her the whole time. After going through layers of supplies, she grabbed a first-aid kit, sprinted around the other side of the Humvee, and raced to Nikolay.

Grizzly started to follow her. "I will go help. I have training in Russian military."

Scotty snapped his rifle on Grizzly. "No way, buddy. Stay right where you are. She can help him, but not you. Sandy, watch her. And tell Rick and the rest of them to stay outside and watch for strangers. We've got things under control here."

"Okay." Sandy jogged after Liza with her weapon pointed at her.

Scotty turned his attention to Grizzly and then to Zach. "Now, back to the real reason we're here." He nodded to the Humvee. "We want that truck of yours, so why don't you all step away and join your wounded buddy and friend over by the door?"

"We're not giving up our things." Zach shot Gina a lingering look but couldn't read her eyes. "We were on a military mission north to stop what's causing all this."

Scotty scoffed and then realized he was serious. "Did you?"

"Partially yes. Maybe even enough to give humanity a chance. We barely survived it, and now I've been ordered by the President to guard these people and get them to Washington, DC. With the American military on high alert and Russians all around us, you'd be smart to let us go and not cause any more damage than you already have. That technician there..." Zach nodded toward Nikolay, where Liza worked furiously to bind the wound on his stomach. "He's part of the Russian science division, and so is she. The man to my left is Dr. Craig Sutton, another US government asset. They want these people back safely, and you're standing in the way."

Scotty's jaw wiggled, and his eyes shifted to Grizzly and back to Zach again. "I call bullshit. They would've flown them if they wanted them back so bad."

"Have you seen the skies? We watched a couple of planes try to get in the air and go down in flames. We're supposed to keep heading south until we run into a base that's clear of this weather and can fly us back. Craig can show you the orders."

Craig blinked in surprise, and then covered up his confusion with a nod. "That's right. I've got orders from Colonel Red Hawk right here in my pocket. I can show them to you."

"Doesn't matter," Scotty replied defiantly, though Zach detected a hint of doubt in his eyes, and his gun barrel wavered slightly. "You might be telling me the truth about those orders, but another thing's true, too. It's hell out there, ten kinds of confusion, and the military boys got their hands full with the Russians. Come on, man! We're on the verge of World War III. By the time they figure out what happened, we'll be long gone and too far away for them to care anymore. Either that or Alaska will be one enormous sheet of ice along with the rest of the United States." Scotty stepped forward, and Blue Beanie followed suit. "Now, back away from the truck."

CHAPTER NINE

Liza wailed, the anguished sound sending a shudder up Zach's spine, and she'd thrown herself over Nikolay who was perfectly still where he lay inside a swath of daylight. A bloodstain was growing around him, Liza smearing it on the floor with her knees as she clutched and pulled on his coat as if her shaking him would raise him from the dead.

"Noooo!" she cried, that single word rose from a deep chest groan and crescendoed upward into a high-pitched note that set Zach's teeth on edge. Drawing her arms along Nikolay's form, Liza turned her rage on Sandy. Snarling, she spat something in Russian and then switched to English. "You people killed him! Why? Why you do this? He was just a young man!"

Scotty had his head down and was peering with fixed concentration at the grieving woman and dead technician. "Sandy, would you shut her up? I'm trying to do business here."

Sandy nodded and stepped closer to Liza, raising her rifle and jamming it pointedly at her as if ready to fire. "Shut up, or you'll be next!"

Although he'd only known Nikolay briefly, Zach's eyes watered with emotion, and an angry heat stirred in his chest. He openly glanced at the Spear, tempted to grab it, turn, fire, and damn the consequences.

Scotty clicked his tongue and stepped closer with his rifle barrel less than a foot from Zach's chest. "Whatever you're thinking, Zach. Don't do it. You can still make it out of here without your truck and supplies. You're a tough guy; you can do it. But we're taking your Humvee and weapons now."

"At least trade us this for your van," Zach offered, swallowing hard and not wanting to do it, but he had his friends to think about. "Make that trade, and we'll walk away... no more trouble. I just don't want anyone else to die."

Scotty seemed to mull the offer, then he shook his head. "Not a bad play, but we can't do that. I'm giving the van to Rick to bring over if they can make it through traffic, but the rest of us are taking the Humvee and going now."

"Okay, I've heard enough." Gina swung her weapon around,

CHAPTER NINE

covering Scotty and Blue Beanie. "Put the gun down, man, or I'll pull the trigger."

Scotty left his gun on Zach but turned his attention to Gina, staring at her, blinking, and finally chuckling. "Are you sure this is a path you want to take?"

Gina tucked the rifle tighter into her shoulder. "Put down the weapons. Both of you."

"You shoot Bruce and me," Scotty said, "and Sandy will shoot that poor woman over there."

"Maybe. But I won't watch this turn into another massacre like before." Gina gave him a grim look, her eyes filled with finality. "This time, it'll be your blood, too."

Scotty relaxed, one hand coming off his rifle and a plaintive gesture even as he kept the gun pointed at Zach. "Seriously, Gina? You're going to betray us after we saved your butt?"

Zach watched Scotty's gun, waiting for it to drop or turn or move in some different direction, and his nerves thrummed with energy, adrenaline surging through his veins. Nikolay was gone, and Liza's continual groaning and sobbing filled his heart with sorrow. One false move for any of them, and it would be a bloodbath, so he focused on looking relaxed even though a storm was growing inside him.

"I appreciate what you guys did for me back at the base," Gina nodded, "but Zach saved me first. Back in Wiseman, he fought off a couple of guys trying to hurt me. Then he saved my store when they were coming to loot it. Since I joined you guys, I've seen you do some questionable things… like with that family who owned the van before we did. You all threatened to kick me out, or worse, when I said something about it. I didn't want to do that…" A sob broke from Gina's throat, and she shifted her hold on her weapon, drawing it in even tighter and lining up the sight so she could sweep across both of them with a couple of shots. "This time, I won't let you do it. Not to Zach. He's my friend. Just put down your weapons and back the hell up."

Scotty froze for a second, and Zach saw the wheels spinning inside his head as he tabulated his chances of shooting Zach and then Gina before he received a couple of rounds himself. Over near the

CHAPTER NINE

entrance, Sandy looked caught between turning the gun on Gina and keeping it on Liza, who glared with hot scorn as if wanting to pounce on the woman. Scotty's rifle pointed at Zach's chest, and he tensed to lunge in a last-ditch chance to keep from being shot.

Scotty scoffed and smiled, raising his left hand, palm out. "We're not dropping our guns," he said, "but we'll back off. Just for you, Gina. Because you were so helpful and sweet, we'll back off. Come on, Bruce."

Blue Beanie, *Bruce*, still had his gun pointed at Craig, though he was glaring at Gina. "Come on, man. We can take them."

"We can *probably* take them," Scotty agreed, keeping his weapon trained on Zach as he paced backward. "But Gina's right. It'd be a bloodbath, and it doesn't need to be that way. We've got the van. We'll figure something out."

Zach watched as the two backed off toward the door where they'd entered, their guns still raised with Gina cross-stepping with them so Scotty and Bruce didn't get an angle on her.

"What about me?" Sandy called. "What do you want me to do with her?"

"Go on out and meet Rick," Scotty said as Bruce turned to grab the door and pull it open. "Tell him to get the van ready. We're moving out."

"I don't want to see you again," Zach called.

Pausing in the entrance, Scotty lowered his weapon and smirked. "You better hope that doesn't happen." He shifted a dark look toward Gina. "We'll deal with this traitor, too." Before anyone could reply, they slipped outside, and the metal door fell shut behind him with a clang.

Zach turned, grabbed his Spear off the Humvee hood, and swung it around toward Sandy, who was running off into the woods. Liza stood next to Nikolay, fists clenched at her side and screaming in Russian at the fleeing woman.

"Liza!" Craig called, sprinting past Zach with Grizzly on his heels.

Zach lowered his weapon and turned to Gina with a half grin. "Thank you for that. Could've gotten ugly."

Shifting her gaze from guarding the door to Zach, she rested her

CHAPTER NINE

rifle on her shoulder and gave him a big, sweet grin. "It's good to see you, Zach. I'm glad you made it out." The husky woman took two strides and threw an arm around his chest, squeezing him tight as her thick chestnut locks fell over her shoulders.

Zach returned the embrace. "I'm glad you took my advice and got out of there."

Gina stepped back. "Waited until my house was about to fall on my head. Probably should've left a little sooner, I guess."

"Hank?"

Gina's smile vanished, and she glanced to where the others stood over Nikolay. "I'm really sorry about him. I didn't realize it was you we were chasing. If I'd known it'd turn out the way it did, I never would've joined them."

"It's a crazy world," Zach admitted. "We have to make decisions on the fly… some of them regretful."

"Yeah, well… Scotty and Sandy did a few things that weren't too cool. And threatening to kill you and your friends… I couldn't let that happen."

Zach clasped her shoulder. "Again, thanks."

With a hesitant smile, she asked, "Got room for one more? I don't take up much room. I'll ride in the hatchback if I have to."

"That won't be necessary." Zach stared at Craig and Grizzly, who had their arms around Liza and helped her up as she looked longingly at poor Nikolay. "As much as I hate to say it," he whispered to Gina, "it looks like a seat just opened up."

"Yeah, I'm sorry about that." Gina frowned. "I should have known Scotty was going to come in firing."

"Nikolay was a good guy."

Zach gestured for Gina to follow him, and they walked to where the men were doing a poor job of consoling Liza, whose eyes were bleary and bloodshot, snot running from her nose as she clung to the men with no strength in her legs.

When she saw Gina, her expression lit up with an angry fire, and her body exploded in a burst of windmilling arms, breaking from the men's grasp. "You!" she shrieked. "You killed my friend. I will kill you!"

CHAPTER NINE

Grizzly lunged and caught Liza's arm, holding her easily as she reached for Gina's neck with her hand twisted into a claw. Gina put her head down but didn't respond, instead backing up a few steps to let Zach move between them.

"Gina didn't shoot Nikolay," Zach said, his gaze shifting to the dead young man where he lay in a spreading pool of blood, his eyes shut, hands resting on his chest in a semblance of peace.

"She was a part of that group!" Liza spat, her tiny body suddenly lunging forward and almost tearing from Grizzly's grip, but the larger man caught her in the nick of time. "Murderers!"

"That's not true," Zach said, shouldering his Spear and holding both hands out in a plaintive gesture. "She's a good person. I met her back in Wiseman, and she let me stay at her place and get some rest. She fed me and gave me some extra fuel for the road. I owe her a lot."

"I don't care," Liza snarled, wiping snot and tears off her lip with the sleeve of her coat.

Craig circled and whispered urgently to her, trying to calm her, holding her wrists as she pushed away from Grizzly with her heated glare fixed firmly on Gina. "Nikolay was my friend since the first day he came to the science division. He looked up to me, and I got him killed."

"That's not true, Liza," Zach said, his baritone voice softening. As a police officer, he'd dealt with many angry and distraught people, and some of his civilian situational training clicked in his mind, bolstered by an emotion that tightened his chest. "It's not your fault, either. It's a hard road out here, and people die. I've had friends die, too…" Zach glanced at Nikolay's prone form. "And Nikolay was one of them. I didn't know him for long, but he was talented and kind. We're going to have to deal with it and move on."

"Move on?" By then, she'd stopped struggling and stood there hunched over, her dark hair hanging lank to her shoulders, tears streaming from swollen eyes. "We cannot simply move on! I am tired of moving on and dealing with such crazy people on the road." Collapsing a little more with Grizzly and Craig there to catch her,

CHAPTER NINE

she glanced down and to the side at Nikolay's still form. "We should have stayed in Fairbanks."

"I understand why you feel that way, but this is the best course." Zach walked to Liza and placed both hands on her shoulders. "Look, I'm sorry this happened to Nikolay. He was a good guy, and he didn't deserve this. None of us do. But you have to stay strong, and we've got to keep moving. I'll do everything I can to keep you safe."

Liza's tone was soft and flat. "You could not keep Nikolay safe."

"You're right," Zach admitted, tears stinging his eyes fiercely. "I should've never sent him over there to keep watch. I thought we were safe here, but we weren't. That's on my head, and I take full responsibility for it. If you want to be mad at someone, be mad at me. Not Gina. Be mad at me."

Liza stared daggers at him, her tears trickling to a few sniffles, her legs strengthening beneath her until she jerked her wrists from the men's grasps and stood on her own. She swayed and seemed about to fall, then she stood straight and packed her emotions behind a wall. Slowly but surely, her face turned stoic, eyes hardening, body tensing.

"I assume we do not have time to bury my friend?" she asked, accepting Craig's sweat rag to wipe her nose.

"I'm afraid not, Liza. I'd say..." Zach looked at the body and then outside. "We should put him by a tree where he can rest until the fires take him."

"Very well." Liza stifled any protest behind a stony expression. She nodded and moved to Nikolay's feet. "I will get his feet if someone can get his shoulders. I see just the spot to place him."

"I'll help you with his feet," Craig said.

They each grabbed a leg while Grizzly lifted him up by the shoulders, the big man's eyes dribbling tears over his chafed cheeks.

Zach stepped outside with his Spear, sweeping across the forest, making sure Scotty and his people had gone. Gina stayed inside while they took Nikolay out to a cluster of white spruces, the lower branches forming a cone of soft needles that stretched to a point at the top. Between those, they placed him, everyone stepping back in a semicircle as Liza kneeled with her hands resting on his, and she bowed her head. She whispered something in Russian, and cried for

CHAPTER NINE

another couple of minutes, and while Zach's heart broke for her, he knew they needed to get away.

The distant crackling of burning trees, the whipping winds, and the first signs of drifting embers fluttered through the air, telling him they were very close to where a storm had struck. Soon, fire would surround them. Still, he waited for Liza to come to peace with what had happened until she stood on wobbly legs.

"I am ready to go now. Thank you for waiting."

Craig put his arm around Liza's shoulders, and they returned to the warehouse. Gina remained off to the side, keeping a respectable distance, until Zach came over and patted her on the back to bring her into the crowd. Retrieving their weapons from the Humvee's hood, they packed inside, Liza insisting on sitting opposite Gina in the backseat.

Grizzly pulled the Humvee outside and pushed through the woods. Everyone bounced and bumped shoulders, the distant fires raging closer as the cinders grew thicker, blasting the branches above them and trickling down to glance off the Humvee's windshield.

The cabin was silent but for Liza's soft sniffles.

CHAPTER TEN

Wendy Christensen, Allentown, Pennsylvania

Chains rattled as the garage doors flew up, letting in a warm breeze. Water dripped on them. Puddles lay spread throughout the gravel lot, though the rain had faded to a drizzle. Wendy and Charlie had changed into their regular clothes but had donned ponchos again, able to leave the hoods pushed back and hair hanging free as they slowly backed the wagons out. Morten, Lavinia, and Miriam spoke soft but expert commands to the horses, and they carefully walked backward with awkward clopping and snorting, not the graceful creatures they were when moving forward. The animals tossed their heads and nickered, but Morten got them moving and backed them out, followed by Lavinia and Miriam, who seemed to have the toughest time of it.

Eventually, they were all out and fell into place, with Morten in front and the others behind. Everyone jumped in a wagon, and they drove west along the highway, the light uncharacteristically bright despite the dark clouds above.

Wendy stretched her legs and walked down the road. On the left stood a line of trees that looked a little thin and beaten, a clutter of

CHAPTER TEN

stripped branches at their feet with pieces of shingles and garbage that blew out over the field. She stared between a break in the trees across endless flat pastures where there might've once been crops but had turned into a group of conjoined lakes. In the distance, something monstrous churned, spinning winds connecting the clouds to the ground in a massive funnel shape, gathering debris and carrying it high into the sky as it cut between a series of hills with a freight train sound. Pieces of houses, vehicles, and every bit of rubble and junk it could suck up went into the maelstrom and spun like dust.

Charlie came up with an awestruck expression. "That's intense. I've never seen anything like that."

The movement mesmerized Wendy, the sheer size of it as a destructive force as it moved across the fields and between the hills before it slipped out of sight. She gulped. "Me neither. Not in all my years on this earth."

"Come on, Wendy and Charlie," Morten called from his wagon as he stared past them with a hint of fear. "Best we vacate."

"You don't have to tell us twice," Wendy said as the two hustled to the back of the wagon. David helped them up with Clyde whining happily and wagging his tail.

"I'm going to sit up front with Grandpa," David said, heading to the front to slip between the loose canvas that made the flaps.

"Be careful, David," Wendy called. "Bring me up if you need a break."

"Okay."

The two women rested against the tailgate with their weapons ready and watching the road behind them. Lavinia rode stiffly in her seat, facing straight ahead yet somehow looking past them without a hint of a smile, pieces of her light red hair breaking out of her bonnet and whipping around her face. Alma was in the back with Uri, checking his status every few minutes to ensure he remained stable throughout their shaky ride. The light rain built up on the horses' coats, and water dripped from their snouts, tails, and tack, making Wendy's skin itch just watching. Still, she received plenty of spray whenever the wind blew sideways and tossed it into her face.

CHAPTER TEN

Charlie used a soft towel to wipe her own cheeks before handing it to her mother. "Do you think Uri will be okay?"

"Alma seems to think he'll be fine. He's stable and even opened his eyes for a bit to take some soup and water. I'm not a doctor, but that seems promising."

"Good, because I like Uri." Charlie turned her head slightly to the side so Lavinia couldn't read her lips. "And the better he gets, the less evil eye we'll get from Samuel and Lavinia."

"That's the truth," Wendy nodded as she scanned the fields off to the south and then to the north, farmland and hills shrouded in mist, sometimes flattening out in great stretches of road.

"Do you think she ever smiles?" Charlie asked with a grin tugging at the corners of her mouth.

"Actually, I saw her smile last night when she brought us our hot cider." Wendy snickered softly. "You know, I think she has a sunny side. She's probably got a lot of jokes she's not allowed to tell, being Amish and all."

Charlie cracked up. "You're killing me, Mom," she said, giving Wendy a playful shove on the shoulder before she returned to her watch.

Things went smoothly for a while until David called back. "Stuff in the road!"

Rifle in hand, Wendy climbed out with Charlie, hopping down beside her. David met them and gestured toward a scattering of evergreen branches with wilted brown needles in front of the wagons. In the mix were parts of bushes and brush, which didn't appear harmful, but it was best to clear their path.

Samuel jogged up with his coat buttoned tight and the usual black hat with the wide brim perched on his head. "Is there a lot?"

"Not much." Wendy scratched her head. "Just a bunch of brush and bushes. Shouldn't take too long."

They made quick work of the branches, not needing any ropes but sometimes double-teaming the bigger ones to drag them to the side. Then they used their boots to sweep away the path through the remaining needles to ensure no nails were sticking up that could get stuck in the horses' hooves. When they were done, Samuel raised his

CHAPTER TEN

arm and waved Morten through, and soon the creaking wagons pulled safely by.

"Why don't you stay down and walk for a while, folks?" Morten called. "I already see more debris ahead that might need to be cleared."

"Charlie, drift back by Lavinia and keep an eye out."

"Yes, ma'am."

Wendy walked close to the wagon as the rain went through many moods, from drizzle to the threat of big fat drops, always with whispers of wind or all-out shrieks that knocked her off balance. Looking up at Morten, she called, "Do you have any clue where we are?"

"Should be getting close to Allentown, but we're not going through. We're going to take a side route south around the city."

Wendy nodded and continued walking, her body energetic after the long night of rest, keeping dry and sleeping six or eight hours straight for the first time in days. Jogging ahead, she made quick work of some more debris, clearing a path and waving Morten through. They turned south for some time, splitting the broad, rainy fields until she caught signs for Highway 29. On a lonely township road filled with deep puddles, they headed west, leaving drenched subdivisions behind and driving around Allentown. Wendy heard the roar of a car engine and looked in every direction, spotting headlights winking through the shadowed streets of a distant neighborhood.

Charlie ran up and tapped her on the arm. "Did you see that, Mom? It looks like there are cars out there, after all."

"It sure looks like that, honey."

Morten had slowed the wagon to a stop, standing in his seat and peering back toward the houses. As he watched, several more vehicles buzzed in the neighborhood, and the distant honking cut through the stormy sounds.

"Cars!" Morten called. Lavinia and Miriam stood and looked around, with David and Samuel walking between the wagons and wearing curious expressions.

Wendy nodded. "I'd say they avoided the worst part of the freeze. But the road is falling apart in places."

CHAPTER TEN

"That's going to be a problem," Morten agreed. "Fortunately, we can go places cars can't."

"But if we bust an axle or wheel," Samuel added as he walked up, "we'll have a tough time replacing it."

"Don't worry yourself too much, son. We've got tools in the back and three spare wheels that should see us through to Pearisburg. Let's get back moving, wouldn't you say? Looks like clear roads ahead, so hop on and we'll keep this train moving." Morten waved his hat at the others, and Lavinia leaned out and waved back.

Wendy and Charlie climbed into the back of the first wagon while David climbed into the seat next to Morten, and Samuel took his spot in Miriam's wagon where he could watch their rear. Thankful for a break, Wendy absently rubbed Clyde's head and hugged him.

She noticed Lavinia watching her with a stoic expression, so she looked at Charlie, where she sat on some blankets, leaning against a crate. Her daughter breathed a sigh of relief. "Boy, I'm glad to be off my feet."

"Me, too. After a little rest, I should be ready to get back out there."

"You're crazy, Mom. I'm ready for a nap."

"You slept through most of the morning," Wendy said pointedly. "You should be ready to run laps around me."

"Maybe I will," Charlie replied snidely and fell backward as Clyde attacked her face with licks. "What are the chances we could find a car or truck out here?"

"That's not out of the realm of possibility. We've already seen several, but I'm a little surprised we haven't seen more yet."

Even as she spoke, a car approached in their lane, speeding up from behind with a high-revving motor. Wendy leaned out through the flaps but couldn't see around Lavinia's wagon. The growling engine came up fast, and a pair of headlights appeared in the road. Shifting into the oncoming lane, a white sedan came toward them, dripping mud and rain, its windshield wipers flipping back and forth and shedding rainwater in gouts.

Gun at the ready, Wendy leaned out and watched them fly by, a man gripping the wheel and a woman in the passenger seat who glanced up

CHAPTER TEN

with a hollow expression as they passed. Ducking and settling into a crouch with her rifle clutched against her chest, she avoided a spray of water shooting up from the tires before turning her attention down the road in case another came up behind that one. The sedan's motor and spraying tires faded into the distance, and silence fell upon them once again except for the ever-dripping rain that struck the wagon roofs and pattered the pavement. The farther southwest they went, the more cars they heard, another flying past recklessly and shouting out the window at them. Morten pulled to the right-hand shoulder as they zipped by, the wind sending his coat billowing around him.

Soon, another trouble crept from the dark, dismal landscape, starting with a grinding of the tires on gravel. Morten called out, "Trouble ahead! Big trouble!"

Wendy shifted her weapon and hopped out. "More debris?"

"No. Bit of a mudslide. Don't get out. I can get us past it."

Wendy climbed back in and crouch-walked to the front of the wagon and pushed through the canvas flaps. She rested her hands on the back of the seat. "Is it bad?"

"It's crazy, Mom," David replied excitedly and pointed. "I've never seen anything like this."

Wendy steadied herself on the rocking, creaking wagon floor, and peered between the two men. The mudslide had swept down from the hill on their right, forcing its way between clusters of maples and cherry trees and stripping them clean of brush and fencing like floss between teeth. It had pushed out onto the road in a flood of brown muck that had spread across the yellow line, carrying pieces of yards, half a wall with the window still in it, and a child's swing set with its plastic and wooden slide crushed to bits. Morten turned them to the left-hand lane where the flow was thinnest, the horses pulling the wagons on the leaning road, stepping into the three-inch layer of muck. The wagon lurched when the front wheels hit the mudslide. The horses lowered their heads and pushed on.

"H'yah! Hey now, Marley and Fitzpatrick! Easy does it! Go easy now!"

The wagon sloughed sideways as the horses hauled. The wagon's

CHAPTER TEN

thin wheels cut through the stagnant mud, and rivulets of water coursed over the flow, creating tiny furrows and creeks that spread off the road and into the lower grasses. A small lake had formed with garbage and debris floating on the surface, and a lone duck looked cold and miserable as it swam in it. Wendy went toward the back, watching as Lavinia's horses plowed through the muck and hauled the wagon behind them, trying to follow in Morten's tracks but having the same slewing problems. Lavinia handled the reins gently but firmly as she half-stood and called to the snorting animals, encouraging them with sharp words that held a hard edge.

The horses did as Morten bid them, and soon they'd gotten through, mud flying off the wooden wheels' rubber edges. Morten and Lavinia kept driving hard to keep the way clear behind them so Miriam could take a run at it. Wendy could barely see around the second wagon as they hit the mudslide, one horse braying, slipping, and almost going down. Though they remained on their feet, they'd killed their momentum and were slogging through the mess, sliding to the right, tromping over thick bushes that had gotten ripped out of the ground by the force of the mudslide, trudging deep enough that they couldn't see what was below their hooves. Miriam cried out, half for help and half pleading to the horses.

Lavinia glanced at Wendy fearfully.

"They're getting stuck!" Wendy called to her. "We might need to pull them —"

Movement caught her eye, and she glanced up the hill past the tree line at another fast-moving mudflow. It seeped down atop the other, moving like living clay as it spread in globs to devour everything in its path. Icy fear gripped Wendy's stomach, and she drew a soft gasp of surprise when part of a house cracked and broke over a ridge, pouring itself over the crest even as it came apart.

"What is it, Wendy?" Morten called through the back of the wagon, shocking her awake.

"Up there, Morten!" she yelled, throwing her leg over the tailgate and shouldering her rifle. "A second mudslide. Miriam is right in its way!"

CHAPTER TEN

"H'yah!" Morten called with a snap of the reins as Wendy leaped off and waved at Lavinia to halt.

Circling to the back, she met Alma, who handed down a coil of rope and climbed out with another. Wendy stooped and began tying it around a steel cleat bolted into the wagon's frame, then turned and ran toward Miriam's wagon, trailing the line behind her. The women pulled the ropes up to the mud spilling across the road, and Wendy retreated when a sudden surge pushed toward her.

Samuel was standing behind Miriam and waving. "Toss me the ropes! One at a time!"

"You go first, Alma," Wendy said, stepping aside.

Alma took the rope coil in one hand, swung it back and forth twice, and hurled it over the horses' heads and into Samuel's arms with loose rings falling free and toppling over Miriam.

Samuel tied his end of the rope around a cleat hitch attached to the front of the wagon's frame, and he waved for Wendy to do the same. Mimicking Alma's movements, she held the coil with both hands, swept it back and forward, and let go with a grunt when her arms were fully extended. The rope sailed slightly to the left, but Samuel leaned out and caught it midair. He crouched and tied it to a cleat on the other side, waving to the ladies, who jogged back to the second wagon.

"Go slowly," Alma said, standing in the road so she could see Lavinia and Miriam.

Lavinia urged her horses forward, and the rope stretched taut and creaked until Alma held up her hand.

"Hold!" she walked back toward Miriam's wagon a few paces, where the Amish woman was controlling her spooked horses. The mudslide was coming faster with rolling clusters of debris and wreckage that swept off the top of the hill. It was only ten yards from the trees but getting closer by the moment.

"It's going to roll over them if we don't go now," Wendy warned.

Alma returned and waved Lavinia ahead. "Go slow and keep them moving."

Lavinia did as she was told, and her horses strained forward, the rope squeaking and stretching nearly to its breaking point. Alma

CHAPTER TEN

jogged toward the stuck wagon, stopped at the edge of the mud, and waved to Miriam.

"Urge them forward," she said, gesturing and backing up. "Come on, Miriam!"

The heavyset woman nodded and stood, giving the reins a snap and shouting at the horses. "H'yah, Shadow and Ivory! Go! H'yah!"

They were geldings, opposite in color, Shadow as dark as night with a glistening wet coat, and Ivory a bright shade of white with his mane stained by the constant rain. The big sturdy beasts strained against their traces, leather and chains pulled tight and clattering as they snorted and grumbled, leaning forward to get the wagon wheels moving again. They were racing against time as the mud pressed between the trees and squirted down the embankment, seeking to smother the wagon as it spilled off and rushed toward Alma's boots.

The tall Amish woman stepped backward and hollered at Wendy. "Tell her to go! Give it everything they can!"

Wendy had drifted away from Lavinia, but she jogged back, her boots splashing puddles until she could see her. Waving forward frantically, she called, "Go! Give it everything!"

With a firm nod, Lavinia barked at the horses and whipped the reins, using her palm to slap the seat next to her. "Hup! Wild Step and Bravo! Let's go! Move it out, dogs! Hie!"

The ropes groaned, and Miriam's wagon picked up speed with all four horses straining in their harnesses, dragging free from the sucking mud. Shadow and Ivory reached the pavement, slipping for a moment before finding a clean spot, leaning forward with quivering shoulders and flanks, hauling Miriam's wagon from the muck as the rushing mud caught her back wheels and swept them sideways a few feet. The wagon straightened with a lurch of the frame and the jangle of equipment hanging on the walls.

"Great job!" Alma cried, clapping as she jogged up to Wendy with a joyful expression. The two grabbed hands and squeezed before Alma let her go and ran up to Lavinia with her fists pumping in victory. "Perfectly done, sister! That was very close."

Lavinia stood with a half-pleased smile. "Unhook us so we can be gone from this mess!"

CHAPTER TEN

Morten was coming back to help. Wendy waved him off. "We did it, Morten. She's through and safe. We're going to untie from the cleats, wind up the rope, and get moving again."

"And I'll check on Uri as soon as we're done," Alma added with water dripping from her bonnet.

Samuel had already untied the rope from Miriam's wagon while Wendy and Alma unhooked the other, and they coiled the ropes around their forearms. Alma's was perfectly done, but Wendy's was sloppy, curls slipping free and tumbling off her arms. With a deep breath, she started over and took her time until she'd wound the rope into organized loops and handed it up to Alma, who'd climbed into the back of Lavinia's wagon.

"Great job, Wendy," Alma said with a knowing nod.

"Great job yourself. See you soon."

Wendy returned to Morten's wagon, grabbed Charlie's and David's open hands, and allowed herself to be pulled into the back, where she unslung her rifle and collapsed on the floor with a grin.

"I saw the mudslide coming down from here," David said with rapt excitement. "It brought the whole hillside with it."

Wendy rolled to her knees and leaned against the tailgate, watching more mud push across the road and down the opposite embankment, carrying refuse and fragments of homes. Bodies tumbled downhill with the flow, someone's arm and parts of his T-shirt flipping up and forward as if they were doing the broad stroke across the road.

"Poor soul," Wendy said with a head shake. "Didn't get out of his home fast enough."

David returned to Morten's side, and things grew quiet once more with just the clopping of horses' hooves and the rolling wagon wheels, thundering skies and cracks of lightning ripping through the gloom and lighting everything with a strobe effect. The rain picked up and faded several times, showing no signs of letting up as the endless gray skies stretched as far as they could see.

"Is it ever going to end?" Charlie asked where she sat curled up on her side of the wagon floor, her arm thrown across a crate, head resting on it as she absently played with Clyde's ears, much to the

CHAPTER TEN

snoozing dog's delight as his tail twitched sluggishly as if he was in a pleasant dream.

"I don't know, honey," Wendy replied while blowing a long, soft sigh. "I hope so."

Life was a smooth ride for another thirty minutes, but for the remnants of flushed-out homes and water flowing across the road in massive, rushing streams. Morten guided them through the worst spots, not stopping long enough to be washed away. Allentown faded behind them, and the quiet road rolled beneath them until David brought a new danger to their attention.

He leaned into the wagon with a sober expression. "People out here, Mom. Lots of them."

Wendy carried her gun to the front, stepped through, and stood in the short space between the wagon seat and the opening to the back, balancing there and peering ahead. Her jaw dropped when she saw what her son meant. They'd reached the city's outskirts, where stores and strip malls were becoming more prominent. Everything to the south turned into farmland and rural space with lakes for fields and slowly degrading farmhouses and barns, herds of animals left out in the open stood miserable in the rain, up to their knees in the water, while ducks and geese flapped and quacked as they swam in circles around them.

From the residential areas and surrounding neighborhoods, clusters of apartment complexes stretched as far as she could see. Masses of refugees shuffled along, four or five thick lines of them hurriedly flocking south and looking for dry ground. The temperatures were certainly easier on them than closer to Stamford, despite the harsh rain and storms. Wendy marveled at the constant trickle of people, mothers and fathers in ponchos holding umbrellas, guiding their kids by their hands across the highway and onto southbound country roads. They cut from the woods on deer trails and marched up the driveways and backyards to disappear into the misting rain. Hundreds and thousands of them moved in a slow procession, carrying suitcases and luggage, children with over-packed backpacks on their slumping shoulders. A group of older folks shambled along with one lady holding a tiny black umbrella with a pink floral print.

CHAPTER TEN

She glanced up as the wagons approached and shuffled faster to get out of the way.

"What are we going to do?" she asked.

"We're going to push through," Morten replied.

"Can't we stop and wait for them to pass?"

"There're thousands of them, it'll take hours, maybe days. We're already on a back road, there's no quicker way through."

"Can we go back and find another road?"

"Nothing but mudslides behind us," Morten replied stoically.

"What if they attack us for trying to bully our way through?"

"If we sit here waiting, we're certain to be attacked."

"Fair enough. What can we do besides fly through them? I don't want to hurt anyone if we can help it, especially not kids."

"We're going to give them a show of force. Ready?"

Hefting her rifle, Wendy stood behind them, leaning her lower leg against the back seat and openly brandishing the weapon. "I'm ready."

"You, too, David."

With a nod, David took out his Springfield and rested his arm across his knees, showing the pistol and fixing himself a grim expression, looking dangerous with his lank, longish hair falling over his eyes. Charlie had been inside the wagon up front to check out what was happening.

"I'll go back and warn Lavinia and Alma. Tell them to be ready."

"Thank you, hun." Wendy flashed her a smile.

Bedraggled and soaked refugees glanced at them as they rolled up, though they expressed only mild curiosity at the horses and wagons and the ominous-looking people with the guns. Wendy noted they all wore short sleeves or hoodies at most, some with sweatshirts and baseball caps, an assortment of jeans and jogging pants that hung off their thinning hips. Wendy shook her head, glad they had their coats at the ready if they needed them, and images of Sue and Fred and their group back in the frozen neighborhood shifted through her mind.

Morten didn't slow as they approached the first line of citizens, three or four people wide, as they trailed back into an empty parking lot. It was a quarter filled with cars with broken windows and a scattering of corpses lying in twisted poses, bloated in various stages of decay. The refugees stepped over or around them, barely sparing them a glance as they crossed the sidewalks and sodden swaths of grass. Most were unarmed, though a few men and teenagers held blunt weapons while dragging suitcases and carts. Morten kicked the horses faster and shouted for people to move, but only a few stopped and stared at Marley and Fitzpatrick, bearing down on them with flaring nostrils shooting steam, heads tossing as they prepared to plow them over.

"Out of the way, ya hear me?" Morten called, waving his hand as if he could part the crowd. "Coming through! Out of the way, I say! Come on, or you're going to get hurt!"

Wendy's entire body balanced on the wagon while holding her rifle, her formidable stance getting hard to maintain. Feet wide, hips flexing, she rode the buckling pavement as their wheels cracked over small pieces of debris in the road. Wendy wondered if the refugees would hold their ground, but once they realized Morten wasn't stopping, they scrambled out of the way, staggering and cursing and clearing a path as the wagon flew past. The next set of refugees didn't move as fast, their ranks made of fathers and young men who saw the wagon coming and formed a barrier between them and their people. None had a gun Wendy could see, but their expressions were grim, water dripping from their hair as they fixed the approaching wagon with steely eyes.

"Sorry, folks, but you'll have to clear a path!" Morten shouted ahead, barely slowing the horses when they came within forty yards. "And if you don't move, you're bound to be shot!" He hiked his thumb at Wendy, and she put her M&P 15 to her shoulder and ran the sights across the lot of them, crouching to keep her balance as they rocked. At first, the men didn't move but shifted into more aggressive stances, a pair on the end looking ready to attack the horses, whispering to their comrades.

"Give them a warning shot," Morten ordered.

"Shoot them?"

CHAPTER TEN

"Fire one at the ground or over their heads. I care not! Best do it quickly before Marley and Fitzpatrick trample them into the mud."

Nodding, Wendy shifted the rifle's barrel at a cluster of trees off to the left, aimed, and fired. The sharp crack sent dozens of refugees flinching away, more than a few scrambling off to the sides. Wendy had pegged a spruce dead center in its trunk to send wood chips flying before swinging the weapon back toward the men, leveling it at them.

"He's not kidding!" she shouted. "We're coming through! Move or die!"

The men hesitated, still looking ready to take them on, but then they divided and shied back. Morten drove through the line and sent the men scattering, except for one who prepared to swing at Marley until Wendy turned her weapon on him.

"Don't even think about it!" she snapped, committed to laying the man out if he carried through with his assault on the horse.

The man spat and sought out his family in the crowd. He joined them on the other side, and they disappeared down the bank and into a field of soggy grass.

Wendy leaned out to see Lavinia and Miriam coming through right behind them, driving hard until they caught up. The crowds ahead thickened, not so much a line but a massive flock of refugees migrating south. The going got rough, the wagons slowing as Morten threatened and shouted, with Wendy and David joining him until people stopped caring. Still, no one attacked the wagons with the Amish brandishing their rifles and pistols.

Samuel hung off the back of Miriam's wagon with his shotgun resting on his hip and gave the refugees dark looks. The wagons moved in fits and starts, getting spread out, people cutting between them, some lines forcing Lavinia to halt as Morten went forward. Charlie kept them abreast of what was happening back there, telling them to speed up or stop as needed so they could stay together.

After twenty minutes of moving slowly, Wendy peered up the road and saw an end to the crowd. "We're reaching the end of the township. We should be okay after this, just —"

CHAPTER TEN

A shot rang out, and a bullet struck the wagon above her right shoulder, and wood chips flicked across her neck and cheek.

David ducked, then he raised his weapon at something off to the right. "Over there, Mom. I saw the muzzle flash."

A cluster of old gray commercial buildings squatted with dumpsters in the parking lot. Two buildings had partially burned down before being soaked by the rains, and dark streams of soot ran from the remains. A man stood behind a dumpster with a large caliber pistol, straightening his arms as he prepared to shoot again. Wendy beat him to it, aiming from the shoulder and firing two rounds that struck the metal dumpster with sharp sparks and loud pings. She didn't score any hits, though a piece of shrapnel must have caught him because he drew back out of sight with an angry shout.

Wendy jumped off the wagon, landing with a grunt and a sting in her ankles, wincing and swinging her weapon toward the dumpster. The man appeared on the other side, leveling his rifle. Wendy fired first, striking the dumpster with three rounds and the man retreated behind cover. She kept her rifle aimed at the same spot but swept it away when a group of twenty refugees came out of nowhere and shuffled blindly by with their heads low, seemingly oblivious to anything but getting across the road. After they cleared those refugees, Wendy jogged to Morten's wagon and climbed in, swaying and panting as she balanced on the gently shaking frame. Morten drove them quickly with an empty road ahead, making it a quarter mile before Wendy felt she could relax. Then they were back to moving branches and debris to put as much space between themselves and the crowds as possible.

A half mile later, Morten called a halt and handed David the reins. "Might be a good idea to stop here and check Miriam's wagon wheels after getting stuck in all that muck. David, keep Marley and Fitzpatrick in line while I have a look."

"Yes, sir."

Charlie hopped out with Clyde and let the dog get some exercise at the end of his leash while they made their way past the second wagon, picking up Alma on the way.

"How's Uri?" Wendy asked.

CHAPTER TEN

"Still stable, and he's eating more. I'm quite thrilled at that."

Morten strode ahead with wide, lurching strides, leaning into a gust of wind that blew up the road from the east. "Indeed, a good sign. When a man has an appetite, he's well on his way to recovery."

"Amen," Alma agreed.

They reached the third wagon, where Miriam stood with her fists on her hips, glancing at the left front wheel. "It's got a lurch to it, Father. Could be something in the hub."

"Not so smooth, eh?" Morten scratched his head as he inspected the wheel.

Samuel was already leaning over it, running his hand along the spokes and down to the hub, and even Wendy could tell the spokes were weakening in the middle where they connected. Two of them seemed soft and spongy, and the steel and rubber tire sagged on that side.

"It's got to be replaced, Father," Samuel said. "Another two miles on that, and she'll spill and dump everything."

"We don't want to prolong any repairs as it could permanently damage the axle." Morten scratched his head and looked around. "We best get to it then. Samuel, grab the buggy jack, and I'll grab a wheel from beneath the frame." He turned to the rest. "Wendy, could you get a watch organized? We need to keep an eye out for what's going on. Don't want to get any surprises."

"I'll do it," Lavinia said as she strode up with a shotgun in her hands and a gray cloak draped over her shoulders. "We'll need to create the perimeter with Wendy and Charlie walking the left side, Miriam taking the back, and myself and Alma on the shoulder. David's fine where he is upfront in Father's wagon to keep Marley and Fitzpatrick in line. If no one watches those two animals, and they'll be wandering off in no time. Look sharp people."

Samuel grinned and nodded, circling to the wagon's rear where they kept the tools and repair equipment. Morten looked apologetically at Wendy before getting a blanket from Miriam, which he laid on the ground beneath the wagon so he could crawl under and detach a spare wheel they had bolted to the frame.

"Whatever suits you," Wendy mumbled, jerking her head, grab-

CHAPTER TEN

bing Charlie with her gaze and looking toward the front of the wagon line. "Let's go, Charlie. We've got the side."

"Lavinia *loves* telling people what to do," the girl grumbled as she stuck her hands in her pockets and left off with a scowl at Lavinia's back. "She's so bossy."

Wendy stared at her, appalled. "Charlie Rene Christensen, take that back right now."

"Do I have to?"

"You absolutely do."

"She's just so bossy for no reason." Charlie rolled her eyes and stared at the wet pavement as their shoes splashed through the half-inch of water covering everything. "Her face makes me want to puke…"

"Stop it," Wendy hissed. "I'm serious. Take it back. No matter how she feels about us, she's family, and I won't have you talking about our family that way."

With a heavy sigh, Charlie shrugged. "Okay, I take it back."

The way she said it with droll objection brought a smile to Wendy's face, but she turned away so the girl didn't catch it. Wendy nodded at the deep forest on the left with its sheer wall of gnarled and tangled wood, vines from the upper boughs hanging over the open road like they might stretch down and grab them. "Now, keep an eye out. There are plenty of shadows where someone could be hiding."

Charlie glanced behind her between wagons one and two, where more forest crowded the shoulder with no sign of a house or building. "It's the same over there, but at least it's not a hill. We don't have to worry about mudslides."

"But look at the road," Wendy said, walking into the left-hand lane and stamping down on a spot where the pavement had buckled upward and ran through with cracks. "The rain is doing a number on everything man-made —"

As she said the words, a tree branch somewhere back along the road cracked and broke downward, still partially tangled in the clutching vines, spinning and toppling as it fell to the pavement with a crunch.

CHAPTER TEN

"It's doing a number on nature, too," Charlie said.

Wendy glanced up to see they were mostly out of danger with no heavy branches above their heads. "Just make sure you're not standing under something like that."

"Mom! Mom, get over here!"

David stood from his seat, clutching the reins in one hand and pointing his pistol in the other. Wendy couldn't see what it was, so she jogged to her left to move around the horses, bringing her M&P 15 up and ready to fire, only to lower it slightly when she saw a family of five, two young girls, a preteen boy, a skinny dark-haired woman who swam in her coat, and a tall man with wet, tousled hair and brown eyes. He stared pleadingly at her from a face etched in pain. He leaned on a cane, something wrong with his left foot, a thick bandage around his calf that bulged beneath his jeans. The mother and children remained back while the man hobbled forward a couple of steps, drawing David's ire.

"Stay right there, man," David said in a pointed tone. He waved his pistol at the man.

The man backed off with quick, practiced steps on the crutch, his free hand raised, palm out. "Sorry. I won't come closer."

"Where'd you come from?" Wendy asked and shot her gaze past them to the woods. "We're out of the residential areas. Nothing but farmland out here."

"We've got a farm about three miles from here," he acknowledged.

"Well, shouldn't you be in it?"

He shook his head and flashed his wife a sad glance. "We wish. As soon as the weather changed and worsened, Allentown folks started going nuts. We tried to go to a store on the first day and stock up on a couple of things, but it was a nightmare. People were beating each other..."

The little girl had her mother's dark eyes. "We saw somebody get shot!" She spoke in a mystified tone, beyond the fear and filled with a bizarre curiosity about what was happening. "Some man fell down dead."

CHAPTER TEN

The mother shushed her, grabbed both girls, and held them against her legs.

"We got run out, end of story," the man said. "It ain't something I'm proud of. I should've defended us better, but there was a gang of them. About a dozen."

"A dozen," the woman echoed with a vigorous nod.

"They broke into the front door, and we exchanged some gunfire." He took on a miserable look, glancing at his wife and kids in disappointment. "I wanted to fight for our home, but I had to get my family out of there. You got to understand that."

"What do you want?" Wendy asked.

The man appeared mystified for a second, his gaze skittering toward the wagons and shifting back to them. "We just came out of the woods after spending the last three nights there. Had nothing but what we'd taken from our barn before those bastards took it all. We've got nothing left. Our blankets and clothes are soaked, so heavy we can hardly carry them, and we were hoping to catch a ride on your wagon."

Wendy glanced at Samuel and Morten as they continued working on the broken wheel, getting the other one off and already putting the new one on. "I don't think that's a good idea."

"Come on, lady. Look at us." The man gestured at his family, but when Wendy only replied with a stone-hard stare, he pressed, "Look, my name's —"

"I don't want to know your name," Wendy cut him off. "You can't come with us. These wagons aren't even mine."

"Y-Yeah," Charlie stammered. "We're passengers ourselves."

"But those wagons are huge," the man replied with an exaggerated gesture. "There's plenty of room in there. It's just us five."

"We've got kids in the back of the third wagon," Wendy said. "Four of them. We've kept them out of sight, but they're back there."

"What about the middle wagon? It looks—"

"Man with a gunshot wound is taking up most of that with the rest of our supplies."

"I'm sorry to hear that," the man said with an exasperated frown, "but you can't just leave us out here on the road."

CHAPTER TEN

"We've left a lot more than you," Wendy stated flatly.

"You don't understand..." The man stepped forward with his free hand curled into a fist, but his wife stepped away from their kids and grabbed him by his arm to pull him behind her.

"Please," she said, appealing to Wendy. "We're good people. We've lost everything. We just need a ride to someplace..." She shook her head. "Safe."

Wendy kept her gun trained on the woman, but her heart twisted inside, knowing if it were Charlie and David, she'd do everything possible to keep them safe. Wendy's jaw worked back and forth as emotions warred within her, then she shook her head decidedly. "It's not up to me. It's up to Morten. He owns the wagons. He is our leader."

"Take us to Morten then," the man said, stepping forward before quickly deflating. "Please. Please take us to Morten."

"Come on." Wendy gestured with her weapon for them to follow, shooting Charlie a knowing look, and the girl stayed back with her hand resting on the bulge beneath her coat.

"He won't let them in, Mom," David said, watching them.

"Keep your eyes open, son," Wendy said, leading the group past Lavinia's icy stare, with Alma breaking off and curiously following on the other side of the wagons.

Miriam and the children watched from the deck of their wagon, Wendy conscious of how this must look to the kids. They reached the wagon where Morten and Samuel were finishing the repairs, and the Amish leader was wiping grease off his hands with an old rag as they approached.

"Um, Morten."

He turned, the smile dying on his face when he saw what Wendy had brought with her. "What is this?"

"They came upon David," Wendy said. "They're desperate and want to ride in the wagons with us."

A shadow darkened Morten's face as he gazed at the bedraggled family, picking over each of them. "While it pains me to say this," he said apologetically. "I'm afraid we don't have room for any more people. You're going to have to move along."

CHAPTER TEN

"Come on, please," the father said, hobbling past Wendy to stand a couple of feet from Morten, who stood nearly a foot taller than him. "Can't you see we're desperate? What little food we had is gone. We're on our last leg, and some asshole shot me in the foot back at our farmhouse before they..." He choked out a sob, swallowed hard, and glanced away before fixing Morten with a challenging stare. "Before they took everything."

Morten hesitated, his expression softening as he looked over the children and their mother's pleading face. The man leaned on his crutch, haggard and weary.

Samuel shook his head. "Father, we don't have the means to carry these people. The Lord beseeches us to help our fellow man, but his word preaches devotion to family first."

Morten rested his hand on Samuel's shoulder, nodding at the truth in his words. "And it's these decisions the Lord has asked us to make with faith as our guide."

Samuel stepped up to the father with his shotgun gripped against his chest. "I'm sorry, but you can't ride with us."

A shadow fell across the man's face, and his gaze shifted between Morten and Samuel. "You're condemning us to die out here. We don't have weapons, and people will try to take what we have... We'll be easy targets."

"You don't have anything," Samuel pointed out. "You won't be a target if you've got nothing for them to take."

"What about my precious children? My wife? You don't think they'd be a target?" The man shook his head. "You're being purposefully naïve if you don't know what's happening out here. Backpacks and personal possessions aren't the only things people steal."

"You are right." Morten shrugged. "We cannot allow your family to travel inside our wagons," he said, "but you can walk close to us, and we will provide you protection."

The man looked confused. "Your wagons will outpace us."

"We're often forced to have our people walk beside the wagons to help clear debris in the road and ensure the way through is safe. It's slow going, but it ensures our wagons don't breakdown in this harsh environment. The roads are getting worse by the day. There-

CHAPTER TEN

fore, you may travel in our shadow if you can keep up at a slow walk."

"We won't last long with no food," the mother said.

"We can spare some food, but we're traveling to Pearisburg, Virginia. That may not be your destination. I'm afraid we cannot escort you anywhere else."

The woman stared at her husband hopefully. "That's better than nothing? If they give us food, we could keep up for a while until we find a car or something."

As the man mulled it over, Samuel took hold of Morten's arm. "A word with you, Father?"

The two men walked away and Alma joined them, gesturing as they talked out of earshot. To Wendy, it seemed Morten and Alma were on one side, and Samuel was on the other, motioning at the refugee family and shaking his head. As they discussed the situation, the wind picked up, with more rain falling in a single long sigh before tapering off, and Wendy pulled her poncho hood up to keep water from dripping down her neck.

Wendy stepped back with Charlie. "For once, I'm on Samuel's side here."

"You seriously wouldn't help them?"

"It's not that I wouldn't help them. It's just... we've been through so much and beat every threat and challenge thrown our way. I can't help but wonder how much farther our luck will hold."

"You told us before, Mom. It's not so much luck as it is being prepared, and if it weren't for you having it all together, we'd be in huge trouble right now. We never would've survived back home."

"That's why my instincts tell me we can't entertain taking these people with us. Anything that slows us down is a risk." Tears leaked from Wendy's eyes, and she looked west along the road where it curved south. "His kids are cute, but they've got a father, and he'll figure it out for them. The mother's no slouch, either."

"They probably need a helping hand. If that's the case, I agree with Grandfather. They can walk with us until something comes along."

Wendy pursed her lips in reply, proud of her daughter's big heart

CHAPTER TEN

but unsure if she was thinking the situation through. Morten, Alma, and Samuel broke up their conference, and she could tell their decision by Samuel's sour face.

"We've talked it over." Morten stopped a couple of feet from the family and gave a firm nod. "You may have some food and walk with us under our protection, but only until you find something better."

The man and his wife had been whispering the entire time, and they accepted Morten's judgment with graciousness and trembling smiles. "Thank you for your hospitality," the man said. "This should give me a good chance to practice with this crutch." Balancing on one foot, he held out the crutch and gave it a shake, drawing a broad smile from Morten and a nod from Alma.

Alma pointed to the third wagon, where Miriam and the children looked on curiously. "All right, then. Let's get you folks situated while my father and Samuel finish the repairs."

"We'll be back underway in another fifteen minutes," Morten announced, breaking the meeting up and leaving Charlie, Wendy, and Clyde to watch the family walk excitedly to the rear of the wagon where Miriam was already handing out some food portions. Lavinia stood by Shadow and Ivory, petting the horses as she looked on, shaking her head and gesturing for young Mara and Noah to hop down and bring their shotguns with them.

"Those two are only thirteen or fourteen, but I guess everyone's getting involved in watch shifts now."

"It's about time," Charlie said. "They complained about me not watching, but I jumped right in when Uri went down."

"You're doing great, honey. Let's get back to it."

The rest of the watch was uneventful, and the family got a big share of food: sweet bread and butter, coffee and tea, cold soup, and a pouch of beef jerky to munch on as they walked. Otherwise, they had nothing but the clothes they were wearing and their will to live as the wagon caravan pulled up the road and continued toward Pearisburg.

Mile after mile they rolled, slowly but steadily, only taking breaks when there was something they had to clear or if Wendy needed to run ahead and check how the pavement was buckling. They were often forced into yards or wet fields to bypass rough spots. Soon,

185

CHAPTER TEN

they passed signs for towns like Kutztown, Virginville, and Shoemakersville.

The family kept up well enough at first, the father having the worst trouble as he hobbled along on his crutch, sweating and huffing in the cool, gray mists. The gloomy day turned into a dismal early evening, and they passed small townships of less than a handful of buildings, occasional farmhouses, and barns. The family followed dutifully, though Wendy saw several places they could've stopped to settle, and she jogged over to Morten to tell him as much.

He nodded but kept his eyes on the road. "I am driving as slowly as possible to let them keep up."

"I know, but they're falling behind more and more every second." Wendy sighed. "We're going to lose them if we don't stop and let them rest or ride. It's only the man putting them behind, walking on crutches and all."

"They could've stopped to look through any of these ruined barns and farmhouses. It would be better for them than walking in the rain like they are."

"Whatever happened to them at their farmhouse must've been bad. They're willing to drive themselves to exhaustion just to remain under our protection." Wendy glanced at David to see her son peering at his feet.

Morten screwed up his face in thought, staring into the distance, grimacing with some internal pain until nodding at Wendy. "The next decent place we see, we'll stop and check it out for them, make sure it's safe. Somehow, we'll talk them into staying."

"Won't that be dangerous, too?" David asked. "There are crazy people everywhere."

"You're not wrong, David." Morten put his arm around David and hugged him. "We started putting ourselves at risk the second we allowed them to come along, but it's what I felt was right in my heart and what the Lord would've wanted us to do. But those compromises often have expiration dates, and we must make a hard choice."

"Otherwise, they'll be holding us back," David replied.

Wendy frowned. "Samuel and Lavinia will be happy."

CHAPTER TEN

"That's another fear," Morten said. "There is a possibility we could lose them."

"What do you mean?"

"If Samuel believes my actions are putting his immediate family at risk..." The thought faded from his lips, but the truth of it rang in Wendy's heart.

"He and Lavinia would pull out, wouldn't they?" she asked. "They'd just drive out ahead of us and disappear. If you count Mara and Noah, we'd be down four guns. And supplies, too."

Morten nodded sadly as David stared at him.

"And while I may think Samuel is wrong," Morten continued, "I cannot allow strangers to divide us. My fatherly influence on my children is strong, but there are still things they won't do no matter how much I beg and plead."

"Zach getting married to me was one of those things they will never respect," Wendy replied bitterly.

Morten chuckled. "Zach marrying you was the *best* thing ever, whether they see it or not."

"Hey, hold up, folks!" the father called from the rear of the wagon train, waving and begging them to stop.

Morten allowed it, much to Samuel's and Lavinia's scornful scowls, though Wendy made a play at scouting ahead while the family sat on the road and rested for twenty minutes.

Miriam provided water and extra snacks for the children. The Amish kids were already forming a slight bond with the strangers, who'd become more than a curiosity where they sat in the middle of the road. Soon, Morten called for them to get moving again, and the family stood and shuffled along without complaint.

Lavinia drove the second wagon with impatient whips of the reins, keeping a watchful eye on her two children, who were learning how to patrol with Alma, teaching them what to do and look for. Charlie fell into a quiet mood, walking Clyde until the dog whined, and then she put him in the back of the first wagon where he curled up on his blanket.

They passed more people crossing the road, families like the ones who were following them, all with hollow eyes and shellshocked

CHAPTER TEN

expressions, and while her heart went out to them, it was numb, too. Morten announced his intention to skirt Reading, and he and David navigated upfront, tracing back roads and highways on a map with their fingers, changing directions to go south for a while and then west toward Centerport. There were many spots where they could've picked up the pace, though Wendy realized Morten was delaying as a larger decision loomed in their minds.

Somewhere near Centerport, she stepped away from the wagon and gazed to see the family had fallen way behind. To her surprise, they had been joined by two other families, pushing their supplies in shopping carts or dragging them in rolling suitcases, trailing the Christensens as if on a pilgrimage. A large man helped the wounded father, and the mothers and kids were walking in a tight group, glancing at the vast fields surrounding them and motioning to the wagons.

A faint edge of doubt crawled in Wendy's gut, and a paranoid part of her mind told her they might try to take over the wagons, but she calmed herself and reasoned that the strangers didn't have weapons. If the Christensens wanted to escape, they could climb aboard and outrun the bedraggled stragglers. Still, she drifted back to come even with Charlie, who hadn't noticed the new groups. Together, they monitored them until nightfall when Morten called for those on patrol to get inside the wagons for their safety. Before she got in, Wendy dropped back, looking for the families in the darkness to see how they were getting along. Even though she fell twenty yards behind, there were no voices, shuffling shoes, or squeaky grocery cartwheels trailing behind them.

They'd simply disappeared, vanished like ghosts in the cooling night. Wendy jogged back to the first wagon with aching feet, climbed inside, and did her best to put the family out of her mind.

CHAPTER ELEVEN

Stephanie Lancaster, Washington, DC

The command center had taken on a stale smell. Everyone working inside hadn't bathed properly for days, barely using the extensive locker room facilities spread throughout the Pentagon subfloors. Showers and bathrooms, areas to change and rest, were available, though the ready teams were far too busy for that, hovering over their laptops and dedicated to the cause with skeptical glances at the military officers in charge of protecting them, whispers as the communication specialists and civilian leadership quietly wondered if they would be abandoned.

Outside the Pentagon walls, thousands of civilians continued testing the perimeter, some holding signs and chanting, while others scuffled and fought with the Marines and soldiers guarding the barricades. Stephanie, Lauren, and the remaining team members witnessed it on the big screens and tiny speakers, which piped at a tinny volume that had started grating on her ears hours ago.

Stephanie ended her call with another convoy leader, guiding them from Birmingham, Alabama warehouses to a FEMA camp outside Montgomery as icy winds crept farther south by the hour,

CHAPTER ELEVEN

followed by heavy rains and tornado activity. None of it was as bad as the civilian chaos spreading through the country like wildfire, panic and a complete breakdown of authority, reports from truckers and military personnel about small towns taking up arms and protecting their outskirts from the millions fleeing the larger cities for the safety of rural areas.

Stephanie's eyes were sore from watching computer models run through their paces as she tracked storms and even more hurricane activity presenting itself up the East Coast, flash thunderstorms and cyclones pummeling the shoreline and destroying billions of dollars' worth of homes and businesses. She couldn't predict where the flooded areas, mountains, and hills would wash out next, carrying entire neighborhoods with them, the voices of hundreds of volunteers and workers doing everything they could to salvage what remained of the country's critical infrastructure. Stephanie leaned forward on her elbows and rubbed her itching eyes, dragging her hands down her face and ending with a sigh. Several communication specialists slept at their desks, and Davies sat at the head of the table with other officers as they continued to address the situation outside, though Stephanie saw it could only end one way.

"You should take a break," Lauren said, the senator sitting across from her, still working with the civilian leaders in the room and those able to call in remotely. "You've done an amazing job, Stephanie."

Stephanie blinked as if seeing Lauren for the first time, though they'd been sitting across from each other for days. While doing different jobs, Stephanie had taken a lesson in stoic resoluteness from the put-together senator who still wore her spotless white blouse and pencil skirt, black hose and heels, hair slightly tousled in a pixie cut.

"I haven't seen you take a break for hours, but you look great," she replied. "Whatever you're doing, it's working."

Lauren smiled. "I just stay hydrated and try to catch a little sleep when I can. Otherwise, I try not to stress too much. Gives you worry lines."

Stephanie raised an eyebrow and clasped her hands in front of her. "Are you kidding? Look at what's happening out there. We're

CHAPTER ELEVEN

making a lot of progress, but what do we do if they break in? I'm hoping someone has some secret exit ready to go."

Lauren chuckled with a twisted smile Stephanie thought seemed fake. "We're surrounded by Marines and Army personnel. There's no way anyone's getting in. But I guess it's a little scary. Have you spoken with your kids? You're using an old landline that still runs to your house, right?"

"That's right. It was there when we moved in, and I just kept it around and made sure we had phones still connected. I checked with the facility department and made sure I had access from the DC facilities." She laughed. "I spent so much time working here and at the other government agencies, usually down in the dreary list of basements where I couldn't get a cell phone signal."

Lauren held up her cell phone. "I know what you mean. I've never been able to get a signal anywhere but on the first floor."

"And that's spotty." Stephanie shrugged. "Whenever I'd take a break, I'd go to a meeting room and call to tell them I wouldn't be home for another day or two. That was mostly when they were in high school, but since they've been at college..." She shook her head. "I honestly didn't think we'd use it that much. Now it's my lifeline home."

"Makes me wish I'd done the same thing. My kids are in high school and on spring break, but I couldn't tell you if we have a landline in our house. My husband would know more about that."

"They're all together at the house?"

Lauren shrugged and gazed toward the TV screens with doubt as Davies stood and walked to one, pointing at another break in the line where military forces were converging to seal it, and faint sounds of gunfire rippled through the speakers. One of his lieutenants came up, studied the scene, and turned to the assembled group for an internal discussion.

Lauren shifted back to Stephanie. "They were the last time I checked, but I haven't spoken to anyone. I'm worried about them, but I know we've got a duty to the country here. I just wonder how long we can stick around."

Stephanie tilted her head to the side. "What choice do we have?"

CHAPTER ELEVEN

The senator broke out of her wistful look and found her smile. "We always have a choice, Lauren. The President isn't the only one who can just up and leave when they want."

Stephanie was about to ask what she meant by that when Davies turned away from the screen and pulled his radio off his belt, speaking loudly into it when he'd been more reserved throughout the growing hours.

"What do you mean you can't hold the east grounds?"

The response came back over the radio, though Stephanie couldn't hear what they said, only that the room fell silent and those at the table paused to listen. One was a woman senator from Nebraska who'd been in Washington when things broke down, and she'd been lucky enough to have her luggage with her when they brought her to the Pentagon. She'd changed into jeans and a sweatshirt while others had rolled up their sleeves or found spare clothing provided by the staff. The snack cart along the wall looked more like a family of raccoons had raided it, with creamer and sugar packets scattered on the table, and at least one of the two coffee urns empty. The regular snack bars and pieces of fruit were all gone, when before they'd been replaced as soon as they diminished even the faintest bit.

The Nebraska Senator leaned over her laptop. "Colonel Davies? Excuse me, Colonel Davies?"

Davies put his radio down and stood. "What is it, Senator Olson?"

Olson gestured at the screen. "We're all seeing what's happening here, sir. Should things get out of control, are there plans to evacuate us and any remaining staff?"

"There are protocols in place, and we'll make you aware of those when we feel it's necessary." While the Colonel kept his tone professional and crisp, he wavered behind his hard stare.

"If there is a threat to us, sir," Olson pressed. "Don't you think we should get to safety like the President? Is there a fallback point?"

"For government officials, yes," Davies said softly, voice barely under control as he glanced around the room. "We've got multiple exit points away from any danger, and we'll get you to those when the time comes."

CHAPTER ELEVEN

His radio piped up again, and he put it to his ear to listen and bark back a reply. "I'll be right up." The Colonel ended the call, stiffened, and took a rousing breath as he gestured to another officer sitting to his right. That man clicked the button on a remote, and the TV screens showing the external view of the Pentagon grounds blinked off, leaving only the weather reports and random data on a side wall.

The civilian officials grumbled in panicked tones, and Stephanie sat straighter in her seat, her stomach nauseated with alarm. Davies gestured to the remaining military personnel in the room to follow him to the door that led to the exterior hallways. Just before exiting, he turned to address those at the table, many of whom had stood and watched him with distraught expressions and questions on their lips.

"We're going upstairs to deal with some issues," he said, "but all is well. Just keep working. We'll contact the communications team if we need you to do anything."

The military personnel left the room, the door slipping shut with a loud click. There was a moment of silence before the civilian leadership broke into a fit of angry conversation.

"I don't see how we can continue to work this way."

"Half of us are dead on our feet."

"Do they expect us to keep working when those people break in? I'm sorry, but this is getting too crazy for me."

"What are you going to do about it? Think you can just drive out of here now? Wouldn't they have told us where the fallback point was if there was one? Something's not right."

The anger in the room bordered on hostility. Stephanie sat back in her chair and blinked at her screens, all the interest in helping supply convoys and military personnel navigate the wild storms blazing across the country fading as her concern about Larkin and Amanda rushed in tenfold. She was overcome with a drowning feeling, her breath coming in quiet gasps as desperate thoughts entered her mind.

"We're trapped here, aren't we?" She watched Lauren shut her laptop and lean back with a trembling sigh, her smile fleeting as she looked around.

193

CHAPTER ELEVEN

"There's no reason to think Colonel Davies doesn't know what he's doing. He hasn't led us down the wrong path yet."

Stephanie gestured behind her to the door with an incredulous look. "We're getting dangerously close to the wrong path *now*."

"We're going to be fine," Lauren concluded, tapping her fingers on her desk before standing. "I am going to take that break."

Stephanie sighed and shook her weariness and worry away to refocus on her screens. "Good for you. Get a few winks for me because I won't sleep until this is all over."

"Will do."

Lauren stepped to the end of the table out of Stephanie's view. Still, when the door to the sleeping quarters in the huddle rooms didn't open, she looked curiously around to see the senator wasn't heading that way but had reached the door to the external halls where Colonel Davies had gone. Eyes narrowed, Stephanie followed and caught the door as it closed, pushing through and spotting Lauren as she turned right into the next intersection. With an unsettling dread in her stomach, Stephanie dashed ahead, curious and concerned, rounding a corner to see the senator striding briskly to the end of a long hall where a set of elevator doors stood open.

"Lauren. Hey, where are you going?"

Lauren turned and saw her, but she only walked faster. "What are you doing, Stephanie?"

"I should ask you the same thing. You said you were going to take a break. The sleeping quarters are back off the conference room."

Lauren attempted a professional smile, but it came off as snide. "I know, but that's not where I'm really going. I'm going someplace else." She slipped inside the elevator and punched the button to go down.

"Where?" Stephanie reached the doors and slammed her hand between them as they slid shut. She slipped in beside the senator. "Where could you *possibly* be going?"

"It's none of your concern, Stephanie. You should go back to the—"

The doors shut with a slow hiss, and the elevator dropped smoothly downward.

CHAPTER ELEVEN

"Too late now," Lauren said.

"I figured maybe you needed someone to talk to after everything happening outside with the civilians and all." Stephanie winced sheepishly and attempted to connect to the senator as a friend. "I just want you to know that everyone's afraid, even me. You can lean on me if you need to."

Lauren seemed confused, then she smiled. "Oh, bless you, Stephanie. You think I'm coming down here because I'm too scared to stay up there and deal with all that? You're partially correct. I'm *terrified* of those people outside, and I'm afraid this is a losing cause."

"Seriously, Lauren?"

The doors opened to a familiar intersection with halls branching right, left, and ahead. Stephanie stared at the numbers and arrows pointing off in different directions, but before she could blink, Lauren was out the doors and moving along a passage labeled *Motor Pool B*. With a gasp, she leaped from the elevator on Lauren's heels. The senator had taken a small radio with an antenna from her handbag and whispered into it.

Stephanie struggled to keep up with Lauren's longer legs.

"Wait a minute. This is where we took Craig to get a Humvee out of here." Realization dawned in Stephanie's eyes. "There are no offices down here."

"There's that scientific brain working hard," Lauren gently chided, pointing to her temple and striding faster. In no time, she was yards ahead of her again.

Stephanie surged to keep up. "Where are you going?"

Lauren pushed through two sets of double glass doors to enter the starkly lit motor pool with its rows of vehicles and more empty spots than Stephanie had seen before. A pair of Army guards stepped from both sides to bar the senator's way, each holding a loaded carbine and fixing her with neutral looks.

"Senator Tracey," a soldier asked. "Are you ready to go."

"I'm ready," Lauren nodded. "We'll pick up your families on the way. Are the roads clear?"

"We won't know till we get out there. But we can go."

CHAPTER ELEVEN

Stephanie grabbed Lauren's arm, turning her thin frame around. "Where are you going? How can you leave?"

Lauren scowled at Stephanie's hand on her arm and then tore herself free. "I'm going home to my kids. You got a problem with that?"

"But we're all stuck here," Stephanie said. "There's a bigger cause."

"Look, there's no bigger cause than my family, and I don't have a connection to them like you. I've no idea if they're alive or dead, and I can't know unless I go home and check."

Shaking her head, confused and hurt, Stephanie said, "But are you even allowed to leave? Who's driving you?"

Lauren backed up with the soldiers. "I'm a senator. I pulled a couple of favors with the higher-ups and promised these boys I'd get their families to a safe spot until things stabilized. In return, they're going to drive me to my house and pick up my husband and kids on the way."

"Trading political favors," Stephanie spat. "You think Colonel Davies would allow this?"

Lauren shrugged. "It's not his call. It's mine, and I'm going home to take care of my kids. You should, too."

"But there's so much work left to do. So many people need our help. Don't you think that's more important?"

"It was until President Holland took off, and that only confirmed something I'd been thinking about it for a long time. This is a decision I've made."

Stephanie followed her, but one soldier stepped around Lauren and pushed her back with his weapon, sending her heart leaping with fright and shock. "You can't put your hands on me."

"I can today, ma'am." The soldier ensured she stayed where she was before backing up with the other two.

Diesel engines roared, and three Humvees appeared from the lower floor, swinging across two rows of armored vehicles before coming to an abrupt stop in front of them. The soldier went to the first truck's rear door and pulled it open for Lauren as she slipped sideways and put one leg in.

CHAPTER ELEVEN

"I'm telling you, Stephanie. Things are falling apart here, and Davies can't hold it together much longer." Her voice rose with apparent certainty. "When this place falls, those people will get in here looking for supplies or whatever else they can get their hands on. They're going to be pretty mad at the government's response, helpless and hungry as they tear apart the storerooms in the subfloors. And when they're done with those, they're going to take all that anger, roll it up into a fist, and use it to beat everyone to a pulp. Don't be here when that happens." The senator gave her a lingering look before ending the conversation with a brief Nod. "Good luck, Stephanie."

The soldier shut the door and got in the passenger side, and the armored vehicles tore off through the lot with a squeal of tires, leaving Stephanie standing there in disbelief and shock, blinking as the taillights swept up the ramp and disappeared. Realizing she was alone in the motor pool, she turned and pushed past the double doors, striding along the maze of passages in her pumps, taking the elevator up where she found her way to the conference room. A few people glanced up as she stepped in, though they quickly went back to whispering over their laptop screens, dutiful worker ants doing their jobs. Still breathing heavily, Stephanie walked to her seat, noticing the lack of staff and that half the communication officers were missing.

Senator Olson had gotten busy again, and Stephanie tried to get back to work, checking the insistent blinking messages on her screen. Still, she couldn't help glancing at the blank TVs on the wall and wondering what was happening on the Pentagon grounds. They were too deep to hear any signs of battle, and they wouldn't know if anyone had gotten inside until they'd infiltrated every hall and, as Lauren put it, beat them to a pulp. A shudder of fear ran through her, and when she thought of Larkin and Amanda and what they might be dealing with, waves of panic grew in her head, and her hands shook when she rested them on her table.

Colonel Davies returned with his officers an hour later, to everyone's relief. He was red-faced and sweating, his demeanor wary as he

CHAPTER ELEVEN

announced, "It was another break in the perimeter, but we handled it. Everything's okay now."

Senator Olson smiled, saying, "Thank you, Colonel. Can we get the screens back on? Having them off makes it claustrophobic down here."

"Yes, of course." Davies nodded to an officer who brought back the TV on the right but left the other one off with no explanation. Olson didn't argue and returned to her seat.

"Colonel, I need to talk to you," Stephanie said as she stood and gestured toward the huddle room. "In private, please."

"Sorry, but it's going to have to wait," he replied, glancing up from his laptop where he and two other officers were conversing. "We've got some troop coordination to facilitate."

"Please, sir. It's important."

"Not now, Dr. Lancaster. I can speak with you when we're done here."

A rising heat blossomed in her chest, and the frustration and hurt of Lauren abandoning them overflowed. "Senator Tracey is gone, sir."

Davies glanced up. "She's probably taking a break. She'll be back."

"No, sir." Stephanie stood stiffly like a soldier giving a report. "I watched her go with three Humvees and drive away."

That got his attention. Davies came around to face her with his hands on his hips and a wild look in his eyes. "What do you mean she left...? A convoy of Humvees? With soldiers? three "

"That's right."

Davies' face grew redder, his breathing rapid as anger filled him. "Well, where the hell did she say they were going?"

"Home, sir. She said they were taking her home."

CHAPTER TWELVE

Alexei Petrov, Moscow, Russia

Stretching across the horizon, the skies over Moscow were as blue as Alexei had ever seen, so clear it hurt his eyes. The time was just before noon, and he was off work and enjoying the unseasonably warm weather. He'd texted his wife that he was taking Pavel to the park and had immediately left, eager to get out there and spend quality time with his son.

On their way to Neskuchny Garden, they'd stopped at an ice cream parlor to pick up his son's favorite flavor, chocolate chip, and a strawberry-vanilla cone for himself. They both licked around the edges of the cones to keep the sweet cream from dripping down the sides, though Alexei was cautious not to get too distracted and crash in midday traffic. They were halfway done by the time they reached the park, and he whipped the wheel one-handed to get them into the lot and pulled in between two other vehicles. Russian citizens packed the place after taking off early and making excuses to get outside to see the incredible weather.

He got out and circled to Pavel's door, opening it so the boy slid from the seat and happily splashed in a puddle. On any other day,

CHAPTER TWELVE

Alexei might have been angry with the boy and chastised him or made him sit in the car for a few extra minutes, but he let the behavior pass and locked up. Taking his son's hand, they walked the edge of the parking lot until they came to a paved path through the beautiful park. The sun was brilliant overhead, warm on the back of his neck and arms, the temperature rising to seventy-eight degrees as mist rose off the grass puddles and snowmelt on the concrete. It was bright and growing brighter, pouncing through the treetops to send golden light pouring across the grass like honey. The park was filled with people, all smiling and laughing, and he nodded to them as they strolled by and breathed the scent of the suddenly vibrant greenery all around them.

"Where're all the flowers, Papa?" Pavel asked.

Alexei finished crunching part of his cone and swallowed the creamy chill, which was melting a lot. "Well, it's just warming up now, and the flowers won't be growing for some time."

"It feels like summer," Pavel replied, scratching his head and squinting into a burst of radiant light peeking in through the treetops.

While the weather had been up and down lately, Moscow had been covered in snow until yesterday when a sudden warm-up had gripped the city, starting a melt the weather people said was a temporary thing as a new cold front was moving in over the city. Yet, when they'd woken up, the winds were even warmer than the day before, and the balmy evening had melted most of the snow, the runoff soaking the ground everywhere until around 10 a.m. when the sun had strengthened and burned everything off, filling the park with a heavy mist that clung to the ground. They took a path deeper into the garden, heading toward the Moskva River with news reports from earlier showing mist rising off its murky surface, the whole place feeling unseasonably humid and warm.

Pavel was enjoying himself. Having finished his ice cream, he let go of Alexei's hand and ran along the pathway, splashing in puddles and laughing as he hurried past the magnificent flowerbeds sectioned off around the fountains and squares dispersed throughout. The

CHAPTER TWELVE

gardens seemed drab without their usual blossoms and carefully pruned trees, yet it was still a magnificent start to spring.

At a wide-open grassy field in the middle of a stand of thick woods, birch and maple clustered together, their branches stripped clean from winter with just a few leafy buds to hold off the sunlight. It wasn't too soggy out there, so Alexei took Pavel by the hand and led him near a magnificent stone fountain resting on a red-brick patio surrounded by a circular bench where people were sitting and laughing, some enjoying their lunches while others played with their kids. Encouraged by the crowd and the excitement of spring in his blood, Alexei cast aside any fears of getting wet and allowed Pavel to pull him out through the grass. They tromped though puddles, and he noted some grass was still brown from winter while patches of it seemed like new growth but dried out and yellow. He questioned the strange discoloration when Pavel tugged sharply and pointed to the trees.

"What about the squirrels, Papa?"

"I'm sure they'll be out soon. It takes some time for the spring to get rolling."

The wind gusted through, and dark leaves fluttered past, looking burned-in with golden color, more like fall and not the vibrant green foliage that signified the beginning of spring. Pavel laughed and burst ahead, splashing from one puddle to the next until he made it to the red-brick patio with the crowds of playing children and adults eating their midday sandwiches. The boy landed hard with two feet and a squelch of water. Other kids saw him, grinned, and pointed, rushing over to look down at his shoes and the tracks he made as he dashed between them and took off around the fountain.

Alexei hurried to the red-brick patio to catch Pavel, but the crowd was too thick and the sun too bright and warm to give chase, so he fell back on his heels with a sigh, crossed his arms, and let the boy play. Smiling and squeezing his eyes shut, he raised his face to the sunlight and let it warm his skin, the heat soaking into his bones and sending shudders across his shoulders as if shaking off the last vestiges of the winter cold.

"Amazing weather."

CHAPTER TWELVE

Alexei glanced over to see a pretty young mother next to him, dressed in a pair of snug blue jeans and a pink blouse, arms folded and hip hitched as she watched the kids play. Judging by the lack of makeup and hastily assembled bun of hair on her head, the trip to the park was likely a last-minute thing.

Alexei laughed. "I haven't seen anything like this in my entire life. One minute it's cold and snowing with ice everywhere, the next it's…"

"A beautiful spring day?"

"Exactly. I had the day off, and Pavel wanted to come to play. I figured it would be healthy for him to see some other children after being locked inside all winter."

"Same with my Greta. She's always begging to be outside the house, but it's such a mess in winter. She tracks in so much snow and slush."

"Now it will just be mud," Alexei responded and gestured to the puddles around them.

"What do you make of the old dead leaves coming down?" The woman nodded at the crisped and browned leaves still fluttering from the treetops where some green had sprouted.

"I figured it must be those that had been caught in the upper branches before winter, and when this warm weather came, the frost melted and released them."

"I thought the same thing… but this grass." She walked to the patio's edge and used the toe of her shoe to sweep across a swath of crispy brown grass. "See what I mean?" she said. "It looks burned."

"Yes, I noticed that, too." Alexei looked up. "I'm not sure what to make of it, but —"

His phone buzzed in his pocket, and he pulled it out, checked the caller, and gave the pretty girl an apologetic smile. "Sorry. This is my wife."

She grinned pleasantly. "Oh, no problem at all."

"Hello, honey."

"Hello, babe," Katerina replied. "Are you at the park already?"

"Yes. It's beautiful out here. I can't wait for you to get here."

"Is Pavel enjoying himself?"

CHAPTER TWELVE

"More than you know," Alexei said as he tracked Pavel playing with the other children. "He made some friends in less than a minute. They're chasing each other around the fountain."

"Oh, that's wonderful," she said, and Alexei could hear the smile in her voice. "I knew it would do him so well to be with other children. Winter was very tough."

"It feels amazing out here. Get here soon?"

"That's what I was going to tell you. I can't get off work as early as I wanted, but I'll come in an hour, if that's okay. Will you still be there?"

"Normally, I wouldn't think we would be here very long, but it really is so beautiful I think we will stay."

"Okay then. See you soon, my love."

"Bye."

Alexei put the phone back in his pocket and turned to the young woman when Pavel came flying up and slammed into his leg, throwing his arms around Alexei's waist and wearing a disgruntled frown.

"Excuse me," Alexei said before kneeling and holding Pavel out. "Are you okay? Aren't you having fun anymore?"

The boy rubbed his eyes but quickly stopped, glancing over his shoulder at the other kids. "Yes, but it's hot."

"I know that. We were just talking about how wonderful the weather is. It's almost summer."

"No, Papa. It's burning me."

Alexei blinked at his son in confusion, noticing his own skin tingling with intense heat. He took Pavel's chin and turned his face toward him. Alexei's eyes widened in surprise. "Son, your cheeks are red, and your ears, too. Your forehead looks like you've been under a heat lamp. What is happening?"

Other children and adults were experiencing similar effects, one man wiping a rag across his forehead as he squinted at the sky. Two kids cried and held out their arms, the exceptionally pale children with raw, red skin and complaining that it was hard to breathe. Coupled with his own burning skin, Alexie pulled his phone out and opened the national weather app.

203

CHAPTER TWELVE

"It can't be that hot," he said, then he shook his head in disbelief and stared at the young woman. "It's ninety-seven degrees."

"Something's wrong." She ran off to fetch her daughter.

"This is crazy." Alexei glanced around in confusion and read the growing terror on the parents' faces. "We've only been out here fifteen or twenty minutes. Ow!" He cupped his hands over his ear, surprised at how warm it was, reminding him of how it might feel if he stood outside in the sun with no sunblock on the hottest summer day. Waiting for the woman to see if she and her child were okay, Alexei took Pavel's hand to guide him away. "Come on, son. We need to find some shade."

The only problem with that was that the leaves were still dead and missing from most of the trees except the firs and evergreens, which had a browned appearance wherever the sun struck them, and more of the grass patches were smoking; it wasn't just the snow melt steaming off but actual *burning* grass. Picking up the pace, he pulled Pavel behind him, the boy staggering and crying when he couldn't keep up. Another man rushed by with his son in his arms and steam coming off his clothing. Alexei's panic elevated, and his pulse raced. He scooped up Pavel and hurried past the wilting trees and growing screams. He wrapped the boy in his arms, covering his face with his hand as his own neck and arms burned. The sun was like a lancing fire, needles of light piercing his skin to the bone, and he didn't dare look upward for fear of what it might do to his eyes.

"It hurts, Papa. Ow, it burns!"

"I know, little man. We're almost to the car. We'll be safe there."

Alexei raced past the dead gardens, wilting and turning brown beneath the sun's brutal gaze. He spotted the parking lot, rows of cars with citizens rushing to them, cutting between them, snatching at door handles to whip them open and throw their children and themselves inside where the sun couldn't touch them.

Alexei reached the pavement and ran between two sedans, stopping on a dime and lurching back when a red sports car raced past. He didn't even take time to curse them as he searched for his car, holding up one hand to halt traffic and dash ahead until he stood at the passenger door. Face stinging, ears burning, he carefully put Pavel

CHAPTER TWELVE

into the back seat and climbed in the front, glancing in the rearview to see his cheeks with a few small blisters and a couple more on his forehead, the skin bright red and irritated as if he'd fallen asleep beneath a sun lamp. When he looked at Pavel, he saw the boy had burn spots above his eyebrows, and his face was twisted in confusion and pain, only growing worse when he touched the blisters and popped them so the fluid ran into his eyes.

"Hush, now, Pavel. It will be okay. We're going home now..." Alexei started the car and changed his train of thought. "To the hospital. We will go to the hospital, and they will fix it."

Even as he eased into the frantic traffic, he doubted his ideas about getting medical attention. All the lanes leading across the bridge to central Moscow were overflowing with vehicles, so he pulled out and turned south, heading home to an urgent care center near there. The sting set in, sending needles of pain dancing over his skin as traffic piled up and cut off his chances of getting anywhere. He worked the steering wheel, whipping them into the next lane and around a string of cars and a truck, forcing his way in front of it to pass through an intersection as the light turned green. Someone else was racing to beat the light when Alexei cut him off, the car beeping, the driver cursing as Alexei flew through it and continued.

"You've got to be more careful," he mumbled, glancing in his rearview, ears ringing with Pavel's whining and crying. "The last thing you want to do is crash while trying to get to a hospital."

His words were sharp as his pain grew, and any time he shifted his facial expression, his skin screamed, drawing tighter by the second, shiny in the scorching midday sun. Steam was baking off the streets in curls of smoke that drifted upward, leaving mist-like pollution over the city.

Several feet of snow had fallen on them last week and melted in two days. It seemed impossible, yet it was true. Ideas about how it could've happened circled in his brain. Alexei had read articles explaining how the Earth's poles could shift and potentially leave inexplicable thin spots in the atmosphere where excess radiation could leak through. He'd seen news reports about how global warming would do the same after decades or centuries. But if that

CHAPTER TWELVE

were happening, someone should've predicted it or warned them. A recent story on Russian news mentioned an explosion in Alaska where joint US-Russian oil companies were drilling, though he didn't see how it had anything to do with what they were experiencing.

"It's not just the heat," he murmured. "It must be UV radiation. What were we told about that and how to protect ourselves from it?"

Alexei was tapping his palm on the steering wheel, listening to Pavel's staccato hiccups when the skin on the back of his hand stung him. He held it up in front of his face to see it had turned red and was blistering. With a pained cry, he lowered his hands out of the direct sunlight and gripped the wheel at the bottom, still whipping it back and forth, his foot working the brake and gas and punching his horn whenever someone got in the way. At first, he tore around cars and cut through with good progress, but it was slowing as more people entered the highway and congested the lanes.

"Come on, come on!" He hissed, eyes watering with intensifying pain, and he yearned for a salve, ice, or a cold bath. Pavel had popped several blisters on his head. "Stop touching your face, son," Alexei said. "Don't touch yourself. Do you hear me?"

The boy nodded but continued whimpering and snuffling, growing to a high-pitched mewling that stabbed daggers into Alexei's ears.

"Please, Pavel. I'm trying to drive. Can you please hold it down?"

Pavel settled a little, but the child was in so much pain he couldn't help himself and started up again before too long. Alexei didn't stop him but focused on the road as shouts and panicked cries echoed in the streets. A man was running down the sidewalk of a tall apartment building, his coat covering his head as he hunched over. Others rushed in the opposite direction, eyes on the pavement and not looking where they were going as they slammed together, bounced off each other, and recoiled from the sunlight. Someone screamed, and something crashed up ahead to bring traffic screeching to a halt.

Alexei yanked the wheel to the right and maneuvered to the roadside shoulder, where he got around three cars before hitting a tight spot and slamming his brakes, lurching to a stop with nowhere else to go. More people raced by with umbrellas, books, newspapers, and

CHAPTER TWELVE

anything to protect them held over their heads, screaming and yelling in pain, cursing and shoving each other as they scrambled for shade. Many more were pounding on the doors of buildings, demanding to be let in, filling restaurant lobbies, and rushing away from the light. A window shattered nearby as someone threw a brick through a storefront and dove inside, disregarding the sharp shards of glass littering the floor.

Alexei searched for some way to drive through the crowded streets, but cars in the northbound lanes were slipping across the yellow line, making things worse as fenders crunched and people leaped out and started fighting. The sun scorched them, and they scattered back to their vehicles or into alleyways. With no end to the traffic in sight, the sun only grew stronger and burned off any moisture it could reach.

"We have to get out of here," Alexei concluded, realizing they'd have to make a run for it just like the others out there.

Keeping to the shadows, he took out his phone and dialed his wife with blistered fingers, getting her voicemail. "Hello, Katerina. I hope you haven't left the office yet. Please, stay inside. Something is happening with the sun, and it's burning everything. I've got Pavel with me, but we're stuck in traffic. We're getting out and running for it. Maybe try to get home or find someplace safe to hide until night. Pavel is fine..."

At that moment, the boy's agonized wail filled the car.

"Yes, clearly he is in pain, dear, but it's just blisters and redness on his skin. I have him inside the car now, and we are in the shade. Okay, we're getting out and will cover up and run until we can reach a hospital or get home. I think we will need to run a cool bath and see if we have any of that sunburn balm in the closet. Do you remember the stuff we used on our last vacation at the beach?" Realizing he was rambling and only putting off the inevitable, Alexei finished the call. "Okay, I've got to get Pavel somewhere safe. We'll see you soon. Be safe and stay out of the sun!"

A swath of sunlight had been shining across his dashboard. Toward the middle, a crack formed in the vinyl and split with a pop that frightened him. A car in the opposite lane had been sitting in

CHAPTER TWELVE

the sunlight for some time, and Alexei noticed the driver was passed out at the wheel, her blonde hair glowing in the direct sun, blisters boiling off her skin as her head began smoking. Whatever was attacking them would eventually get them as the sun completed a slow arc across the sky, driving people into the shadows until none remained.

"We have to go now, Pavel."

"T... To the hospital?"

"No, we're going *home*."

Turning between the seats, Alexei grabbed a pair of coats he'd left there in case it got cold that morning. With his larger coat over his head, he popped the door and slammed it against a car that had pulled too close.

"What are you doing!" he cursed the driver as he tried to squeeze into the ten-inch space, sucking in his gut to get through, finally making it and whipping Pavel's door open to slam it purposefully into the other car with a sharp *crunch*. When the driver didn't argue back, Alexei stooped and saw a man lying passed out beneath his windshield, moisture from his cooking skin drifting up to stain the glass with greasy smoke.

"Come on, Pavel! Get out, son!"

As he looked into the pained eyes of his son, Alexei grabbed his arm and hauled him from the backseat. He put the boy's coat over his head and stooped to keep the dangerous rays from touching him, even if it meant exposing his own skin for a second or two.

Covered, he guided the boy through the jammed-up cars, sometimes having to step over two touching bumpers to get to the other side until they'd reached the sidewalk where people huddled in the shadows of the buildings, staring in fear as light slowly crept across the pavement to touch the tips of their shoes. With one finger hooked into Pavel's belt loop, he guided them through the crowd and tried to enter a store, but the doorway was blocked, people shoving him out of the way.

Alexei lifted Pavel to keep the boy from tripping over someone lying in the bright light with a reek coming off them that made Alexei want to puke. Any attempt to enter buildings or retail stores turned out the same way, hallways packed with people cowering from the sun, pounding on apartment doors and breaking in.

"Home!" he growled. "We have to get home!" Alexei glanced up to read the next street sign, looking south where they lived on the city's outskirts. It was just two miles to their tiny apartment building, and they could make it there if they kept their heads down and ran. Ignoring his son's plaintiff yowling, even though it broke his heart to do so, Alexei focused on getting home. He pushed his son ahead of him through the growing chaos.

All across Moscow, people ran screaming as the heat rose from the mid-nineties to a hundred and five in the space of ten minutes, continuing to climb as the city's citizens ran from the burning radiation. What had been enthusiasm and curiosity turned to sheer chaos as they panicked, fell, and were trampled by their fellow citizens. Cars smashed into each other as drivers passed out at the wheel. On the Bolshoy Kamenny Bridge, a truck swerved and raced up the slanted front end of a sports car, flying sideways into the rail, teetering on the edge, and plunging into the steaming Moscow River. Car interiors caught fire, and door mechanisms malfunctioned, trapping people inside, pounding on the glass until they cooked and filled the cabins with greasy fumes. Many successfully broke the glass, but they collapsed half-way out of the windows, dying feebly in the harsh sun. Some made it farther, tumbling from their cars into the streets, leaping up and instinctively seeking either darkness or water, even though those weren't always guaranteed protection.

Moscow cooked beneath the stinging rays, the snow melting for miles around the city's outskirts in an oval patch of atmospheric weakness that had exposed them to the sun's deadly radiation, leaving emergency services crippled and the streets littered with crawling, screeching forms. Within an hour, thousands of bodies floated in the Moscow River or fountains and aqueducts around the city, and by nightfall, the stench of cooked meat hung thick in the quieting streets.

CHAPTER TWELVE

Mateo Alvarez, Iquique, Chile

The sun above Iquique on the Chilean coast looked down from blue skies, touching its citizens with tropical warmth and painting the coastal high-rises and relaxed beaches with beautiful light. The city sat perched on the western coast, surrounded by tall hillsides made of shale and fine-grained limestone with highways that cut brown lines across the slopes. Way up high and overlooking the town were parks and viewing spots, trails, lush greenery, and an outskirt village called Alto Hospicio. Off the sandy shore, the frothing waves glowed as they swept toward beaches teeming with tanned people, and delighted vacationers walked the pathways between the hotels, restaurants, and cafes, ready to spend their money at the start of the weekend. Laughter filled the air, and smiles were everywhere as the lazy day stretched from late morning to afternoon. The skies were blue with a smattering of dark clouds in the north to add enough shade to keep people cool on shadowy corners where partiers smoked or drank in large groups, listening to music and laughing the day away. Deeper in the city on Orella Street, strumming guitars jammed to the beat of shakers and light horns.

Matteo Alvarez held Maria's hand as they strolled along the gorgeous boulevard with its gardens of bright flowers and green fern bushes. Matteo was dressed in new jeans and a purple collared shirt, buttoned up neatly with a modest gold chain around his neck. Maria was beautiful in sandals and khaki shorts, her white tank top with the thin shoulder straps accentuating her neckline gorgeously.

"Where are we going, Matteo?" she asked coyly, giving him the impression that she might know what was up.

Keeping his voice even, he played it off. "Can't a boy take his girl out for lunch?"

"Yes, of course," she laughed, her dark hair falling across her face in a gust of wind. "But you've been so busy with your job lately, I thought you might not have any time for me any longer and were looking for another girl."

"You are the only one for me." He smiled evenly and gave her a playful pinch in the side, and she fell against him with soft giggles.

CHAPTER TWELVE

"Well, at least tell me where you're taking me."

"Right here," he said, gesturing to a doorway where the old-fashioned swinging doors stood open, and the smells of spicy chili and cooking meat wafted out to tease their senses. Matteo was looking forward to his first shot of tequila, something to get him through the next hour and not break down in laughter or tears.

"Oh, the Caleta Buena!" Maria declared, clutching her hands to her chest and laughing. "This must be an auspicious occasion indeed."

Matteo had been working so much to save enough to take her to Caleta Buena after purchasing the expensive ring he hoped to put on her finger in a short while. The past few months had been hard to get through, riding waves of optimism and fear, wanting to make her the happiest woman in the world. Things were already going well with his new job, and he'd been working hard to save for a home and a future they could look forward to.

Brimming with confidence, he put his hand on her back and guided her inside, where the hostess brightened and beamed a smile at them. "Hello, Mr. Alvarez! We have your table ready. Right this way. You'll be up on the second-floor patio, with a magnificent view of the city and the beaches."

Matteo guided Maria in front of him, but she turned back and dropped her jaw with a look of bemusement and disbelief. He only smiled and let her get ahead of him, glancing at her beautifully tanned legs as she went up the stairs behind the hostess, who led them to their table. Matteo held Maria's chair and pushed it in, then he took the seat opposite her and looked around. It was a quiet afternoon, with just a few patrons occupying nearby tables. The wraparound balcony gave them a view of the sea where its salty flavor drifted by on a cool breeze, and they could watch the Punta Negra countryside off to the north with its brown hills and highways cutting through them.

Maria studied the drink menu, and Matteo watched her, his heart racing with a sense of pride he'd taken them that far, being the man his parents had wanted him to be. Maria glanced up, and he didn't

CHAPTER TWELVE

look away but held her gaze, allowing a loving smile to form, matched by her but even brighter.

"What's gotten into you, Matteo? You're acting so strange today."

"Is that a good or bad thing?" he asked, looking at the menu but already knowing what he was having.

"A good thing, I guess." Maria bit her lip and studied the menu.

The waitress came and took their drink orders. Matteo reached across the table and squeezed Maria's hand. Her expression sobered as the gravity of the moment settled on her. They didn't speak and instead looked out over the brown hillsides to the northeast and back to the Pacific Ocean to the west, reveling in the surrounding beauty with their fingers intertwined. A couple were seated two tables over, where an older woman leaned in and spoke to her husband loud enough for Matteo to hear.

"Do you think the trouble will reach us here?"

"I don't think so," the man responded with a laugh. "Alaska is far away, way up where things are cold and dark. Not like here."

"But they say it's spreading... that it's some kind of pollution causing a lot of cold and rain. Did you hear about Moscow today?"

The man's face darkened. "How could I not? It was all over the news, I listened to it while working in the yard."

"They were hit with a radioactive heat wave. It was just terrible. They're estimating a lot of people are dead or missing, but they didn't give any exact numbers. Can you believe that? And they think it has something to do with what happened up north. Something about hydrocarbons flooding the atmosphere and the weather and... oh, I don't know, Joseph. It's so frightening!"

Matteo's smile faded, the global events were worrying, especially with the other news reports coming from parts of Canada and the United States. There was even some flooding in Peru and Ecuador to bring matters home, though the governments weren't issuing national warnings yet. News anchorpeople stated government sources were more concerned with breakdowns in the supply chains and how the tragedy up north might affect products and goods traded between the United States, Mexico, and South America. While there'd been several brownouts over the past week because of disruptions in the

CHAPTER TWELVE

oil and gas coming from America, not much had changed for them in Chile, and Matteo had barely kept up with the news because he was so worried about setting up this date with Maria.

He absently dropped his hand into his pocket to make sure he still had the ring, and he sighed with relief when he felt the modest but pricey stone between his fingers. It had cost him a half year's wages, and he didn't have it paid off yet.

The waitress returned with their mixed drinks, apologizing for the lack of ice because of the recent power outages. The ice machines had only been working a few hours earlier that day. Matteo was in too good of a mood to care, and he graciously accepted her apology and let her get on with the day's specials, commenting on several of the garnishes and other items that had been pulled from the menu because of the power shortages. She assured them the main courses hadn't changed much at all.

Matteo made a joke and nodded for Maria to order first, then he selected a light meal so he didn't upset his nervous stomach. The waitress smiled haltingly and took their menus, then she glanced at the sky. Matteo followed her gaze to the north to see dark clouds sweeping in, the composition like billowing smoke rather than drifting pockets of water mist. Still, he smiled at Maria, and they continued looking around at the beautiful day despite the darkness creeping in.

By the time the waitress returned with their *palta riena*, a drizzle had started, and she quickly brought an umbrella and placed it into the hole in the center of the table. With the help of a waiter, they erected it and turned the crank to get the umbrella open. Matteo thanked them, and he and Maria shared the appetizer quietly with loving looks and smiles that sent butterflies flittering through his stomach. Still, the sky continued to close over them, the dark clouds twisting into nightmarish shapes as they spread across the city, and the rain escalated from a drizzle to fat drops that struck their umbrella hard. It was an almost calming downpour until the wind kicked up and blew Maria's hair around her head, with fat raindrops falling as the umbrella strained and bent, scooting their table a couple of inches before Matteo put his foot down to block one leg.

CHAPTER TWELVE

As he did that, his drink fell over and spilled everywhere, tequila and fruit juices rolling off the side and partially into his lap as he leaped up and kicked his chair aside in surprise. A scowl formed on his face, but Maria dashed the dark mood again, laughing and covering her mouth with her hands.

"Oh, I shouldn't laugh," she said apologetically, grabbing a napkin and circling to pat off his shirt and pants. Before she could touch the ring in his pocket, he brushed her hands away harshly but followed up with a smile.

"Come on," he said, giving up on the table but still in good spirits as she stared up into the fat rain droplets. "Let's get inside."

The waitress caught them as they were moving away from their spilled drinks and bucking umbrella, ducking as it was ripped from the table and tossed onto the floor. With heaps of apologies, she guided them to the covered alcove, where they stood beneath the concrete awning and watched the rain come down in violent sheets.

Maria leaned against him, reaching for his hand, her hair wet but still beautiful, her dark eyes looking at him with pure devotion. "What's wrong, Matteo? You look so sad."

He tried to smile, but it faltered into a frown. "I'm not sad. I just thought... I wanted today to be special."

"Any time I'm with you is special," Maria said, squeezing his hand.

A blast of wind pushed Matteo against the wall, but he caught her up and pulled her with him as she gasped.

The waitress rushed over and spoke to everyone who'd taken refuge in the alcove. "We're sorry for the inconvenience," she said, "but we'll re-seat everyone and remake all your drinks and food as soon as this rain passes. Please —"

A rumbling started in the distance, at first vibrating the hairs in his ears and then the stone tiles beneath his feet. The restaurant shuddered and quivered under tremendous force. Knees trembling, pulse racing, Matteo held Maria close and saw the older couple doing the same thing, the woman gasping and looking around in fear as glasses rattled and plates fell off tables.

"Is it an earthquake?" Maria asked.

It was a fair question. Earthquakes were frequent occurrences in

CHAPTER TWELVE

their part of South America, though it didn't feel like any quake he'd ever felt. "I don't know, Maria. It seems... different somehow."

To the north, a wall of gray had consumed the hills surrounding them, the rain blasting the countryside and only falling harder so they could barely see. He looked up a long slope where the highway stretched across the slopes and saw a section give way and roll downward in a sudden gush of mud and shrubbery. Matteo blinked, thinking it was a trick of the light. He stepped to the edge of the awning and squinted, spotting more pieces of the highway falling off beneath the sliding hill, taking cars and trucks with it, metal, concrete, and road signs churning in a sudden flush of dark mud gaining momentum.

"That's a mudslide!" The older woman clutched her chest as everyone turned their gazes in that direction, watching the hill roll swiftly downward, rushing faster toward the north part of town.

A collective gasp of shock rose as a wide swath of the hillside suddenly cracked across the top section and broke away, sliding off in a massive sheet of earthen force and filling in the roads and ditches on the outskirts of town, the tops of buildings shaking and disappearing, telephone poles shivering and flipping down as the dark powers swept through. The mudslide spread into the center of Punta Negra, and collective screams rose above the roaring rain. Matteo and the rest of the onlookers rushed to the stone rail and peered at the streets. By then, the restaurant was shaking terribly, glasses rattling from their shelves to crash on the floor as frantic employees tried to keep them from falling or hurried to clean up the shattered glass. People hurried through the streets, at first a few handfuls and then growing to dozens, sprinting and stumbling, couples clutching and keeping each other on their feet as torrents of water rushed along the gutters and carried away refuse and garbage.

"Is the restaurant going to collapse?" Maria gripped Matteo's arm with nervous tension. "Should we leave?"

"I don't think so, Maria," he replied breathlessly, slipping his arm around her and pulling her close. "We are up very high, and look..." He pointed down to the street where the water swelled from the gutters to encapsulate the sidewalks, carrying bicycles and rubbish,

CHAPTER TWELVE

sweeping people's feet from beneath them and washing them away as they cried in frantic terror with their arms and legs flailing in the swirl.

The flood grew from a foot of water to four feet, pushing small vehicles down the lanes, rushing into restaurants and corner stores to swamp them and wash their contents out through the windows. Lobby chairs and cushions, potted plants, knickknacks, and picture frames gushed out and flushed past them in a foamy spray. Screams grew louder as those watching from the upper floors saw what was happening and gasped in terror and disbelief, leaning from the windows and trying to catch people sweeping by. One woman reached to grasp someone and fell headfirst into the waves to disappear and not come up again. Maria slammed her palms over her ears as cries for help grew to a gut-wrenching crescendo, and Matteo's eyes watered as he held her tight, rain dripping from his nose and chin.

"Should we jump down and help?" the older woman from before said, but her husband shook his head and stared at the rushing waters.

"It would be a death wish, dear," the man said. "There's nothing we can do up here, and we can't go down."

More buildings on the west side of town shifted. They started sinking at the corners as if resting on quicksand, but soon they moved toward the ocean, slewing sideways as they crashed into other buildings and brought them down. Two dozen structures collapsed, and still more mud broke off the hillside, rushing swiftly through Punta Negra and tearing the town apart in a thick, sticky sludge. A wash of people flew by, screaming as they clung to each other or floating furniture as the water level continued to rise. They rolled in the powerful tide, some going under and never coming up again. Building material, timbers, and parts of houses rushed in from the outskirts through the streets and back alleys, bedraggled refugees clinging to housing frames and floating barrels, staring ahead as they rushed by and crashed, the nailed-together pieces breaking up and sinking fast.

Matteo reached for them as they passed, though he couldn't grab

CHAPTER TWELVE

anyone. He seemed to see the tragedy from a distance, looking at events through someone else's eyes. While part of him was horrified, he was glad they were up high on a steady building and Maria was safe. Then, the restaurant started to crumble, the corner on the left shaking and trembling, finally knocking loose when a compact car crashed into it. Brick, wood, and plaster came down on the car's roof, shattering glass as everything floated sluggishly away. Matteo grabbed Maria and drew her from the concrete rail toward the alcove where the building seemed more stable. A small group of people standing by the disintegrating corner leaped to safety and knocked others aside, the throng pressing against Matteo and Maria as they hugged the wall.

He stepped in front of her, protecting her, scowling at the shoving crowd. "Everyone needs to calm down!" he shouted. "Panicking won't do us any good. We need to think about getting even higher." He grabbed the waitress, who was staring at the crackling lightning ripping through the sky. "Are there some stairs we can use to get to the roof?" When she didn't reply, Matteo shook her and broke her out of her terrified trance. "Can we get to the roof?"

She blinked, glanced at the sky, and nodded. "It's this way —"

They turned to go deeper into the restaurant when something coughed in the building's internal structure. A puff of dust swept upward and was captured by the falling rain as the remaining upper patio shook and collapsed. It dropped right in front of them, washing into the street, slow at first but gathering momentum as the flooding pressure continued its relentless push to the ocean. The older couple slipped off the edge, spun with horrified expressions, grabbing each other and gasping in surprise. What remained of the edge flashed out of sight, striking the growing pile of stones below, and tumbled into the hungry stream.

More people fell with the collapsing balcony, the survivors pushing inside, knocking each other and furniture aside as they retreated to the most central portion of the building. One moment, the waitress was in Matteo's hand, and the next, she was swaying and clawing at a chair before she fell and was trampled by clambering feet. The rushing water grew deafening in his ears, louder than

CHAPTER TWELVE

Maria's screaming, and more parts of the building chipped off and swept away. They backed toward the bar, some climbing up and kicking aside mixed drinks, scrambling up as the tile beneath them broke apart with water spraying over their feet. A woman had taken off her shoes and was tip-toeing backward, but then she slipped and fell, landing hard on her right hip, reaching and grasping for her friends as the water rose, captured her legs, and dragged her under the submerged floor.

Matteo grabbed Maria and helped her onto the bar, looking around for a set of stairs or any way to get higher above the flood. Pieces of other buildings battered the restaurant. Someone grabbed Maria's foot, and Matteo kicked them in the face, feeling no guilt as they slipped off the jagged edge and went under. The bar quaked, stools and chairs sucked down, glasses and tequila bottles kicked by patrons into the muddy swill. He turned Maria and pointed to the ice cooler behind the bar, and the pair leaped over and landed on it, falling against the shelves of hard liquor where they clung for their lives.

Seeing nowhere else to go, Matteo grabbed Maria in a hug, kissed her face, and pushed her wet hair back with his hands as she clung to him. "I love you, Maria, and I wanted this day to be special. I'm so sorry..."

She shook her head, terror in her eyes, then slammed her face against his chest, seizing him, nails digging into his skin, giving in to the realization of what was about to happen. More people screamed and fell in, and soon they were the only two standing on a small section of the restaurant, bolstered by a couple of primary steel beams running through the subfloor.

"I love you too, Matteo," she responded, spitting rain and kissing him long on the lips, and then she threw her arms around him and squeezed tight as the world raged beneath their feet.

The northern section of Iquique turned to sludge. The rushing mud swept away entire buildings filled with thousands of people and churned in the mixture before being driven through the tourist areas. Oceanside strip malls dumped over the public docks and into the sea. On the south side of town where Alto Hospicio sat high up, the hillside disintegrated, with Highway 16 sliding off in pieces, driven by the violently crashing rains. Lightning cracked and thunder rolled as entire neighborhoods swept down the muddy slope, the wreckage piling into the valley atop train tracks and loading yards. As the hours passed, the rain continued falling, and the shifting hill gained momentum. It pushed the debris through narrow valleys and beach dunes to swamp the south portion of Iquique and smother it in a suffocating layer of sludge, leaving thousands dead in its wake.

The city of Iquique was not the only victim of the flash rains and flooding. Hundreds of small towns along the South American West Coast flushed into the sea without a trace, from Lima, Peru to Santiago, Chile, where the landscape was firmer and greener and riddled with clinging rain forests to stem the tide.

The storm ravaged the remaining coast beyond repair as the South American governments monitored the turbulent weather patterns in the north and began executing emergency plans to save anyone left alive.

CHAPTER THIRTEEN

Zach Christensen, Salcha, Alaska

The Humvee rumbled along the shoreline with Zach walking off to its right, finding trees and stable deadfall to climb. He peered across at the other side, taking Craig's guidance to discover a shallow way through. The Tanana River offshoots were sluggish, yet still deep and dangerous to anyone trying to cross, and he didn't want to get too far into the wilderness. They needed to find streets on the other side to return them to the highway.

Zach forced himself to breathe easier, taking deep breaths that puffed out warm in the cold, and the ever-churning black skies spread above them like an inkblot. If they wasted any more time, they could be stuck out there and left without transportation, a potential death knell with the forests growing smokier by the hour. With Grizzly behind the wheel, the Humvee rumbled over dead branches and stones, water lapping at the tires. Gina, Craig, and Liza followed Zach, crowding around him where he stopped to stare at the near shore with its semi-sandy beach. The opposite side looked a little rougher, the bank steeper and muddier with larger pieces of wood and stones and no way to drive the shoreline.

CHAPTER THIRTEEN

"What are you thinking?" Craig asked.

"It would be easy to cross here." Zach pointed. "We could slip across and use the winch to climb up the other side. It's crowded along the shore, but once you're up that bank..."

"There is a grassy field up there and potentially a way to the roads." Craig crossed his arms and rubbed his chin. "Seems like as good a spot as any."

Gina came trotting up from behind, leaping from one rock to the other, holding her rifle against her side so it didn't rattle. When she got there, she hiked her thumb back toward the bridge. "I haven't seen any sign of Scotty and his gang, and the bridge is still packed. There're a couple of cars burning up there. They'd be roasted if a firestorm hit it right now."

"Good work, Gina," Zach said with a curt nod. "I still think we need to hurry. Scotty will see what they're dealing with on that highway, and I think they'll come looking for us. You say there's six of them now?"

"That's right, but at least three aren't totally on board with Scotty's methods, being that he's kind of an asshole which I found out later. I doubt they'd want to go up against any armed force for no good reason."

"Good. Hopefully, that's the last we see of him."

Gina turned to the water and looked across. "How deep do you think it is out there?"

"Only one way to find out." Zach strolled off the stone he'd been standing on and waved at Grizzly to stop. The big Russian rolled down his window, and Zach leaned in. "I'm thinking about crossing right about here. Why don't you nose into the water here at the edge, and I'll tie the winch around myself and push across to see if it's shallow?"

"Sounds good, Zach," he replied but glanced up at the fading daylight as it glowed orange, with sweeping forest fires dotting the landscape. "Hopefully, we can get across now and avoid trap."

The others had come up, and Zach stepped back and spoke to the rest of them. "If the smoke gets bad, Colonel Red Hawk provided us with air filtration masks and plenty of filters. We should be okay

CHAPTER THIRTEEN

there, but it's the heat we'll eventually have a problem with, especially if we end up in one of the dryer spots where there's no snow or ice. I'll wrap the winch around myself and cross here to check the depth."

"It's going to be cold, Zach," Craig said pointedly.

"Yeah, I know. I'll strip down and go barefoot, too."

Gina winced, and Liza shook her head.

Zach glanced out to the sluggish waters where a dead branch floated by. "No time like the present."

Grizzly got the Humvee turned around, and Zach sat on the stone, removed his boots and socks, and then his fatigue pants and one layer of long underwear came off. He gave his dry garments to Gina and stood there with the brisk wind biting his legs and backside.

Grizzly had pulled up so the Humvee's tires sat in a few inches of water. "Okay, Zach. Ready."

Zach stepped in and circled to the front where he unwound the winch, wrapped it around his waist, and hooked it, then he turned and backed into the river as Craig, Liza, and Gina watched from the shore. Grizzly let out the cable so Zach could keep moving. "Just keep feeding it to me steady," he called, and when the icy water reached his knees, he spun and lunged forward, pulling the line tight as he trudged across the slowly slipping river.

A quarter of the way out, the current pushed at his legs so that he had to curl his toes around the rocks to stay upright. About halfway across, it rose to his thighs, the bald iciness of it gripping his legs in a cold vice as he kept his breathing steady in the event he was swept into the flow and went under. Just like with Trembley up north, it was essential to keep a calm head when dealing with chilled water.

The water splashed against him and soaked his long underwear up to his chest, and pieces of logs and deadfall bumped him as they drifted by. Still, the flow grew shallower as he moved past the midpoint where it reached the tops of his thighs. Then he was striding up through the silt and sharp rocks to the sandy shore, turning and waving. Gina and Craig gave him a thumbs up, and when Zach got Grizzly's attention, he marked the point on his leg where he

CHAPTER THIRTEEN

felt the water had risen to, and the Russian stuck his thumb out the window and told everyone to get in.

Removing the winch line, Zach held it up and dropped it, and it wound its way toward the Humvee through the rushing waters. Zach backed up the bank where it broke upward at a sharp angle and picked his way to a spot about twenty yards to the east which was relatively shallow. At that point, he climbed barefoot up over rocks and sticks, shivering with the cold that clung to him, his feet numb from the river crossing. Grabbing dead branches and deadfall that littered the grass, he tossed them aside and returned to the bank to hold two thumbs up.

The Humvee burst into the river with a splash, Grizzly keeping the gas pressed as exhaust poured from the side pipe and water flowed up over the grill to roll off the hood. The vehicle wove back and forth, cutting quickly through the water with little problem, and about halfway across, Grizzly turned on the windshield wipers to sweep it off to the sides. The passengers wore worried expressions as they clung to handholds and watched the sluggish river surge against the vehicle, spraying up over the windows and top. The big diesel roared, and the wheels churned through the muck, still weaving slightly as Grizzly worked it up onto the shore, took a sharp right, and rode up the beach with water dripping off the frame and pipes. They made it to the shallow spot in the bank and broke hard left, riding up it with the suspension rattling and shocks springing, bouncing everyone inside around as the undercarriage scraped the ground.

Zach had stepped out of the way but shook his head when Grizzly went a little too far to the right, where he'd tossed some of the deadfall, crunching over the thick underbrush and rocking the vehicle hard. As the Humvee tore up the slope and followed the path up to the woods, Zach jogged behind it, stomach sinking as something rattled and pounded in the suspension toward the front. He waved and shouted for Grizzly to stop, and the Humvee lurched to a halt before a stand of spruce, tamarack, and poplar intertwined in a thick cluster. Gina, Craig, and Liza got out, the scientists visibly shaken and pale.

CHAPTER THIRTEEN

Gina grinned and held out Zach's clothes. "That was a ride and a half. Why don't you get changed over there in those trees? I'll toss you some towels."

"Thanks." Zach turned to Grizzly as he was getting out. "Did you hear that sound from the suspension?"

"Yes," he replied, falling to one knee and looking beneath the left front wheel. "We hit something while crossing. I try to shake free, but it caught in axle. Something bent. Will need to bend it back." He stood and scratched his head, sizing up the truck's position on the slope in relation to the trees. "I get this far so we would be out of the way if river rose. I can use scissor jack plus winch to hold steady. I look under and make repair."

"You do that, and I'll get warmed up." He took a blanket from Gina. "We can rest and have a meal if everyone wants, but we're getting out of here as soon as Grizzly's done."

Gina nodded and returned to the group as Grizzly backed the Humvee up to a flatter spot with its nose at the trees. Body shivering, lips trembling, Zach picked his way through the forest to find a private place to change, riddled with concern that the Humvee's mechanical problem might throw a major wrench in their plans.

Grizzly had the Humvee jacked up at a slight angle with rocks beneath the rear tires and the winch line wrapped around a tangle of thick trees. Grizzly was under the vehicle, feet sticking out, one leg bent at the knee and his belly almost touching the frame despite it being raised. Hammer blows rang off the undercarriage, echoing through the forest as the smoke grew thicker around them.

Zach kneeled by the tire with his hand resting on the front fender. "How does it look?"

"Not as bad as first thought," Grizzly replied. "Truck is fine. Log is jammed in the wheel well and screw up steering. I will have it out in moment."

"Do you need my saw?" Gina came up with her axe in one hand and backpack in the other.

CHAPTER THIRTEEN

Grizzly scooted out from beneath the Humvee, his heels kicking at the grass and gravel. He twisted and looked up at Gina. "What kind of saw?"

She pulled a folding saw from a pouch and opened it to reveal the serrated edge. "There's this one, my favorite field saw, but I have a couple of smaller ones, too."

"That one is perfect," he nodded, reaching forward. "I only bring hammers, ratchets, and screwdrivers. Who knew I would need to cut wood?"

"Do you need some help with that?" Zach asked. "I can get down there and do some of the work."

"I do not need your strength for this job. I will cut little piece at time. Give me twenty, thirty minutes."

Zach patted the fender and stood, walking to the small fire they'd built where Liza and Craig kneeled and poked at the food in their heated MREs. Gina followed him, and the two strolled down the hill a few paces, Zach crossing his arms and staring at the Tanana River offshoot drifting by. The night was coming early without actual sunlight to keep it at bay, and the sky was lit with the familiar orange fire blossoms they'd gotten used to seeing.

He glanced at Gina. "So, that's how you found Scotty and Sandy? Just outside the base?"

"That's right. And can you believe they convinced me to go with them and that the military guys wouldn't help me?"

"They were probably right. There were some National Guard members helping refugees get out of the city on buses, but otherwise they were too busy fighting the Russians."

Gina glanced at Liza and scoffed. "It's hard to believe we've got Russians in our country now. I guess we always thought it could happen, and here it is. Do you think it's going to be World War III?"

"Craig and Liza were privy to some conversations with the President and his generals and colonels. They seem to think it's a land grab for resources."

"They think they can get away with it?"

"With our country in such a vulnerable position... it's possible."

CHAPTER THIRTEEN

"Still, Russians on US soil. You'd think the retaliation would be swift and hard."

"Exactly. But I don't know what's happening around the world. We know the United States East Coast is in terrible shape." Zach swallowed, thinking of Wendy and the kids and hoping they were safe and sound with his family in Pearisburg. "If the rest of the country is as bad, there're probably a lot of riots happening. That would be enough to keep a lot of our military resources busy."

"But wouldn't nukes be on the table?"

Zach shrugged. "Who knows what's happening in Russia right now? If they're not having any of the troubles we're having with the weather and the firestorms, they might actually be in a position to win a war with us, or at least hold Alaska hostage. I'd assume nuking the oil and gas fields would only worsen our current situation."

"The politicians in my country are experts at taking bits and pieces slowly without incurring the wrath of any one country or the world. Or sometimes they do and just not care."

Zach glanced to his left to see Liza and Craig walking up, the Russian scientist mirroring Zach's stance with her arms crossed and watching the river flow.

"But this is the United States, honey," Gina scoffed. "This isn't Crimea or Ukraine. There'll be repercussions for this. We've got a gun behind every blade of grass if the Russians want to play."

"I would welcome someone to stop our military leaders, especially Commander Orlov." Liza looked at Gina with a hint of a challenge. "As long as we don't begin launching tactical nuclear missiles. They'd be foolish to deploy those without fear of destroying themselves. But with the United States in disarray, they could opt to deploy thermobaric weapons against your country in strategic places... like Fairbanks."

"And if the President hasn't declared war already," Zach said, "I'd wager he'll be doing it pretty soon."

"Well, we've got bombs, too," Gina added. "And a bit of bad weather won't keep us from deploying them."

"I'm sure everyone is considering that," Liza replied flatly.

"Actually, I'm not sure they are," Craig said with a head shake.

CHAPTER THIRTEEN

"I've been dealing with government officials most of my life, and they're all idiots. No matter what side you're on, it's all agenda driven and pushing for outcomes none of us could imagine." He crossed his arms like the rest of them. "No, I'm pretty sure both parties are making the dumbest possible decisions right now. Even at a time like this, someone will be looking out for their own hides and trying to make a buck."

"Until they bomb us back to the Stone Age," Zach said.

The banging behind them had stopped, and Grizzly was grunting beneath the Humvee as he sawed at the wood with soft bumps and knocks, his arms and elbows hitting the frame.

"And even then, someone will still take advantage of others." Craig stared up at the sky wistfully. "These firestorms are scary, but I half expect to see a gigantic mushroom cloud rising over Fairbanks at any moment."

"Would we even see it?" Gina asked.

"Not with the sky the way it is, but with the nuclear fallout mixing with what's already up there..." Craig's gaze drifted across the Tanana offshoot and above the trees. "That would be some real dirty air."

There came one final bang from behind them, and wood tumbled from the undercarriage to land on the gravel.

"It is fixed!" Grizzly said. "We can probably — ooof! Help!"

Zach spun as the Humvee wavered on its jack, sliding to the left and threatening to crush the Russian beneath it. Without thinking, he knocked Liza and Craig aside and sprinted toward the drifting vehicle, two strides carrying him to it, throwing his shoulder against the fender with a crunch to stop it mid-swing before it crushed his friend. Spinning, Zach slammed his back against it and dug in with his heels, his entire body straining and kicking backward to hold it in place.

"Get his legs!" Zach growled through clenched teeth, and every muscle in his body strained and trembled as the stab wounds in his neck blossomed into lancing pain shooting through his body. "Pull him out before it crushes him."

Gina and Craig rushed over, each grabbing a foot and hauling him

CHAPTER THIRTEEN

backward across the ground as the massive Humvee shoved Zach aside and crashed on its wheels.

Grizzly sat up, sweaty-faced and breathing hard, staring at the truck and then at his friends. "Thank you, my friends!" He rested his hand on his fat belly, chuckling with a relieved smile. "That was close. Grizzly would have been much skinnier if you had not taken swift action."

Gasping and rolling the tension out of his shoulders, Zach stood. "Definitely would've gotten some broken ribs, at least. Can someone look at my neck? I think some stitches might've popped."

Gina gestured. "Over here. Kneel." Zach knelt in front of her, and she pulled down his fatigue jacket to inspect the wounds. "Yep, you popped some on this long cut. You said a Russian fighter did this?"

"That's right. When we were leaving the rift area, the Russians tried to leave us for dead."

"They didn't consider what happens when you make Zach mad." Craig walked to the back of the Humvee, opening the hatch and grabbing the first-aid kit.

"I'm going to need the one with sutures." Gina leaned in and cocked an eyebrow. "I'm not a professional at this. I'm just going to get that out of the way."

Zach laughed. "Don't worry about it. Just pull out the old ones and do the best you can."

As they packed up their tools and supplies, Zach sat on a log with Gina standing behind him, patching him up.

"Was the guy stitching you drunk?" she asked. "These sutures aren't exactly symmetrical."

"We were floating in waves when the medic was doing it. I wouldn't expect them to be perfect."

"It's actually a good thing... here comes a stick. It leaves me a little room to work with... another stick."

Zach winced every time she said "stick," but the torture was soon over, and she cleaned the area and put a new bandage on top. With everything packed and ready to go, they climbed inside the Humvee and pulled up the curving slope to reach a high ridge and navigate through the forest spotted with trees and heavy underbrush. The

CHAPTER THIRTEEN

Humvee made easy work of it as they used their compass to keep pointed south. The map came out, and Zach spread it on his lap, finger resting at a point south of the bridge.

"We should be right around here," he said. "If we continue heading south, we should come across one of these three roads going east and west. Any of them will get us back to the highway."

The trail was more treacherous, Grizzly bumping over tangles of brush and through bushes with Zach and Gina getting out to move the bigger obstructions. They worked their way up the hill and sat at the top of a rise overlooking the surrounding valleys. Farther south, more fires burned, though the higher elevation didn't reveal any buildings or roads they could get to. The Humvee slid off the rise and dipped into shallow valleys with stretches of open fields enveloped by endless forests. Liza pointed to something off to the left, a squarish shape set into a hillside, and as they drove closer, bouncing and jostling inside the Humvee's cabin, Zach saw it was a barn and, beyond that, a farmstead with a driveway leading to a dirt road. With whoops of joy, they headed due east and perceived the distant glow of headlamps trickling south. It wasn't long before Grizzly found the ramp to get on the highway, and they joined the sporadic flow of traffic, pushing the Humvee to fifty.

"Finally!" Zach said, putting his heels up on the narrow dashboard with his toes touching the glass and his Sig Sauer Spear resting in his lap. As darkness descended on them, the crew got quiet, lulled into a daze by the sounds of the road sliding beneath them. Farther away from the antagonizing skies and forest fires, Zach sleepily closed his eyes to the clattering diesel engines. "Let me know if you see a white van pulling up," he mumbled to Grizzly before resting his head against the window.

"I will let you know." Grizzly sat back happily with one hand thrown over the wheel. "But do not worry. They are far behind us now."

"Don't count on it." Zach fell into a deep sleep with visions of home flitting through his mind, going way back to when he lived with his Amish family near Fort Plain. His early years were spent outdoors in fields and gardens, doing hard labor, working his summers away

CHAPTER THIRTEEN

but having fun, too. Samuel and Uri always fought with each other but never with Zach because they knew what they'd get, and he remembered Alma's short temper. It all seemed so far away, but he was comfortable in the Humvee's passenger seat as long as they were moving and putting the uncertainty and fighting behind them. He needed to get home to the people he loved. Somewhere in the back of his mind, he promised the first thing he'd do was apologize for being away from them so much and so often.

As the hours passed and the night wore on, Zach sporadically woke and blinked at signs as they went by; the Delta Junction, Tok, and Beaver Creek, all with the countryside flushed of color with just an occasional vehicle flying past them. With a top speed of about seventy miles per hour, the Humvee wasn't the fastest mode of transportation, but it was powerful and gave him a sense of machine reliability. The whole while, Liza and Craig chatted in the back, discussing what was happening with the weather, remarking about the sky and what they'd found north at the Alaskan Rift, and Craig was even learning a few Russian words. Gina didn't speak but rested her head against the window like Zach, snoring lightly and waking up to fuss around in the back for something to drink or eat.

At some point, Zach looked at Grizzly. "Do you want to trade? I can drive for a little while."

The big Russian woke from his focused daze and glanced over. "I am fine, my friend. Not as wide awake as before, so we make coffee?"

Liza leaned forward. "I would like to use the restroom as well."

"Me, too," Gina added.

Zach gestured to a dirt road coming up with a pair of broken-down vehicles sitting nearby. "And we need to fill the jerrycans, too. That's probably a diesel truck."

They pulled off the highway onto a dirt road next to a stand of thick forest. Soon, they were all walking stiffly in the cold, stretching, yawning, and dipping into the woods to do their business. Gina returned with a handful of sticks and twigs, building a small fire surrounded by stones in just a few minutes, while Zach and Grizzly went to siphon the abandoned truck. Not only did they top off the Humvee, but they got two of their four cans filled. They found the

CHAPTER THIRTEEN

water kettle and a package of Army coffee from their supplies in the back of the Humvee. Soon, the smells of the bitter roast drifted through the air, and they were standing around the small campfire, sipping from cups or travel mugs they'd gotten from the Fairbanks motor pool, everyone quiet, Zach still shaking off the grogginess of sleep.

"When I get home, I've got about a month of sleep to catch up on," he said.

"I'll probably never sleep again," Gina replied as she squatted and stared into the fire.

"I will not sleep until the hydrocarbon flood has stopped and we step back from the precipice of war." Liza stiffened where she sat on a log, gripping her coffee cup tighter.

Craig raised his hand. "I second that motion."

Back on the road, they looked forward to the next small town where they might fill up some of their jerrycans, realizing just what a gas hog the Humvee was. On the way, they passed broken-down vehicles on the roadside with blank faces peering through the windows. A few people got out and tried to flag them down as they approached, but Zach and Grizzly shared a look, and they drove past the stranded refugees without stopping. After the fifth one, Liza's face appeared over Grizzly's shoulder.

"Are we not going to stop for anyone?"

"We're not stopping for anyone, no," Zach replied. "I know what you're going to say... that it's cruel and mean to leave people stranded like that."

"Yes. That's exactly what I was going to say. Could we at least offer them some fuel or food?"

"There is a long way to go, and we've got more important things to do. We need to get you guys to the air force base and somehow take you to Washington. That's our mission."

"Everyone says they have this mission. They have more important things to do than helping others. Maybe these missions that do not help others should be put aside. Maybe they are not the most important things." The Russian scientist stared at him with tears running down her cheeks.

CHAPTER THIRTEEN

"I get what you're saying," Zach replied with a slight flush of embarrassment. "I really do. But we can't stop and help everyone, and we don't know what we'll run into on the road. We've already seen that from the bridge traffic and dealing with Scotty and Sandy. If you think these people care about us, you're mistaken. Many of them would hurt us to take our car and supplies."

When Liza's expression didn't change, Zach fixed her with a firm stare. "Look, I don't want anyone to get hurt, and my heart goes out to everybody stuck on the side of the road, but we're not stopping for anything. I'm getting home to my family, and in the meantime, I'll do my damnedest to make sure you folks are protected. That's as far as I'll go at this point. If we part paths, you can go around helping all these people, but I'm moving on until I get to Pearisburg."

Liza nodded to the road. "What about them?"

They were coming up on a medium-sized sedan half jacked up with a woman standing near the front tire, hands on her hips and staring at it with her hair whipping around her face. In the backseat, two kids were peering through the rear window, fog on the edges of the glass as their wide eyes stared at the approaching Humvee.

Grizzly leaned forward and squinted. "She is having tire problem. Lugs probably too tight, and she can't get them off."

"We can't spare ten minutes to help the family?" Liza was staring daggers at him.

Craig leaned forward to give his input. "We need to make good time from here on out, Zach, but this one looks like an easy win. Mother with two kids who needs some lugs turned. If you guys stop, I'll do it myself."

Zach glanced between the two men, noting Grizzly was already slowing down. The big Russian shrugged. "Ten minutes work and done."

With an icy stare that softened, Zach nodded. "Okay, fine. You guys help the woman with the wheel, and I'll walk the road to ensure no one is lying in wait. But I'm warning you, we are *not* stopping for every person out here."

Liza smiled in agreement. "Certainly not everyone."

When the Humvee stopped, she popped the door and got out,

CHAPTER THIRTEEN

waving to the woman to show they were friendly. With his Spear in hand, Zach walked to the shoulder, nodding to the woman before sweeping the forest bank with his weapon.

Grizzly and Craig attended to the tire while Gina guarded the north side of the road, standing stoutly by the Humvee's hatch and watching for any approaching vehicles. As promised, Grizzly declared the repair finished in ten minutes, and he lowered the jack while Liza spared the small family a few MREs from their supplies and sent them on their way. Everyone climbed into the Humvee, and Grizzly pulled out and got behind the sedan, keeping up for a while before it got way ahead of them and disappeared.

A hand fell on his shoulder, and Zach looked to see Liza peeking over the seat at him with a beaming smile. "Thank you, Zach. Just that bit of light in all this darkness makes my heart happy."

Zach smiled faintly, nodded, and turned his attention to the long road ahead.

Craig leaned in. "Zach, why don't you hand me the radio back here, and I'll see if I can tune in to any military chatter."

"There wouldn't be any of that so far from Fairbanks."

Craig shrugged. "Still, maybe we'll catch some other people on the emergency channels. If anything, it would be nice to see what we're working with here. Yeah, it's got to have some range with these whip antennae on it."

"It looks pretty complex," Zach admitted, staring at several squarish components set into the dashboard in front of the gears, the knobs and dials like a mix between a CB radio and something more advanced. Nothing like the old radios they used in the NYPD police cruisers.

"From here, it looks like it can receive and transmit..." Craig leaned closer. "It looks like there're two radios. They probably use one to monitor certain channels. Turn it on."

Zach pressed the power button, and the radio popped to life with static, red and white lights glowing as the signal gauge needles bounced wildly until he grabbed the tuning knob and started dialing through various frequencies. More squeals and rips of interference

CHAPTER THIRTEEN

filled the cabin, squelching off as he moved from one signal to the next.

"Wait, go back," Craig said. "I heard voices."

Zach reversed the dial, hitting the spot and working the knob until voices piped into the cabin in military stiffness.

"... round out and check the perimeter."

"Uh. Roger that, Canada Base. SF-10 heading to the perimeter to check for signs of enemy forces. Standby."

There was a spattering of noise and more squelching before a reply returned. "Roger that, Scout Force Ten. This is Canada Base standing by."

"Sounds like some maneuvering," Zach said, preparing to move on to a different channel.

Craig raised his hand. "Wait. Leave it here for a second. Sounds like it might be important."

Zach shrugged and left it where it was, sitting back in his seat as they waited for whoever SF-10 was to report to Canada Base. Thirty seconds later, a reply piped through the tiny speakers, with the soldier on the other end breathless despite his professional tone.

"Canada base, this is SF-10. I repeat, this is Scout Force Ten. We've encountered a small enemy force. Engaging now." Before the soldier could release the talk button, a light spattering of machine gun rounds exploded through the line, followed by cursing.

"Roger that, SF-10. Fire team support incoming."

Craig leaned farther between the seats and fixed Zach with a questioning look. "Would the Russians be this far into the Yukon?"

CHAPTER FOURTEEN

Wendy Christensen, Pearisburg, Virginia

"Grandpa says it's coming up on the right," David said as he leaned between the flaps to tell Wendy and Charlie.

"It's about time," Charlie replied drearily, grabbing Clyde's head and rubbing his ears. "I thought we'd never get here."

Wendy rose from where she'd been resting on a bed of crates with two blankets beneath her, her dreams scattered with thoughts of Zach and their home in Stamford. Blinking in confusion, she put her hand to her head and looked around. Charlie was right there with her blonde hair turned greasy and dark, dirt streaks on her face, and her cheeks with a gaunt appearance after days of walking in the dreary rain down a long highway filled with dangerous people and violent storms. There'd only been two or three times over the past week when the rain had stopped, though it had started right up again almost immediately, sometimes with a drizzle while other times it arrived in an explosion of slashing droplets with ripping lightning and growling thunder that shook the pavement.

"Pearisburg? Really?" she asked.

Charlie had put on her shoes and was tying them. "That's what

CHAPTER FOURTEEN

David said Grandpa said. We should get out and walk ahead. I'm so excited to sleep in a real bed." The way she said the last part in an ecstatic voice, Wendy laughed and swung her legs off the crates, wiggling her toes in her musty socks.

"You and me both. I'd kill for a shower, too." Wendy shifted to the back of the wagon and peered outside to where Alma and Samuel patrolled with Mara and Noah.

Alma rushed forward with the kids and waved Wendy down with an excited look.

"We're here! Pearisburg!"

Charlie climbed over the tailgate and jumped off the back, waving at Lavinia, who nodded with the same stern gaze she'd held for the past week or more. Wendy went slower, putting her shoes on and tying them tight, her feet already hurting with the thought of walking for miles again. Her fingernails were grubby, dirt caked beneath them from moving logs, branches, and blown-over trees out of the way, working stoically with Samuel and getting along under Morten's watchful gaze. Wendy stepped to the tailgate and jumped down, exchanging frowns with Lavinia before walking toward the center of the road with her rifle slung on her shoulder. She nodded at Miriam, who waved happily and pointed ahead. The woman's enthusiasm was inspiring and a little contagious, and Wendy turned and jogged to catch up with Charlie and Alma and the kids, who walked beside Marley and Fitzpatrick.

The ditch along the side of the road was filled with water flowing slowly east toward some drainage, but beyond that was a long black fence stretching as far as she could see. Endless fields, woods, and Amish farmhouses dotted the landscape from the flat areas into the hills. A big, bright white barn sat at the top, surrounded by a spattering of other buildings peeking through the treetops. Homes of all sizes lined roads that branched in multiple directions before sweeping down to join a gravel tract that ran parallel to the highway. Up ahead, Wendy spotted a turn in where the black fence changed to a neat rock wall with no mortar to hold it in place. Bracketing a black gate to the Amish community was a well-made brick wall with old wooden signs decorated with rustic writing: *Pearisburg Arts and*

CHAPTER FOURTEEN

Crafts, Fresh Canned Food, and *Trader's Market* with an arrow pointing right.

Wendy glanced at Morten and smiled. "We made it, Dad."

"That we did, my dear." Morten looked as haggard as the rest, with sunken features and water dripping from his wide-brimmed hat and beard, but his hardened eyes remained strong and committed as always. "It looks like the village survived. No traces of interlopers that I can see."

Wendy nodded, though she knew danger often hid in the shadows, so she studied the passing houses with a critical eye, only giving Morten's words credence when she saw faces peering out at them through the curtains, though no one ran out onto the porches with open arms to welcome them.

"I wonder if our cousins still live here?" Alma hurried to the head of the line with her skirt swishing around her legs. "I'm not even sure I remember all their names... there was Rita and Clem and Naomi. All of my mother's kin and distant relatives." Alma walked faster as they faced the brick walls bracketing the driveway and the black steel gate barring their way.

They moved past a series of buildings and signs pointing to the Trader's Market up a road to the west. At the corners were a pair of quaint shops with colorful awnings boasting fine Amish products inside, but the doors had closed signs on them, and the blinds were shut tight.

"Maybe they shut down and left," Charlie said with a skeptical look.

"I don't think so, child," Morten replied from the driver's seat. "They've probably closed all the stores because they realize no one will buy anymore. They'd only come from the cities to *steal*."

Morten pulled the wagon into the entrance and stopped at the gate with Lavinia and Miriam driving up and parking beside him. The Amish leader leaped from his bench and landed heavily, looking around with a troubled glare.

"Is everything okay?" Wendy asked.

"I think so, but I don't see any signs of our brothers and sisters from Fort Plain, and no one is here to welcome us."

CHAPTER FOURTEEN

"Would they be throwing a welcome party?" She gestured toward the rows of houses. "The people we saw back there looked at us strangely, but I know some mistrust runs through these communities. With all due respect, Dad."

"Yes, dear. That would be the expected response to a group of travelers coming out of nowhere and showing up on our doorsteps. Still, I'd think our people from Fort Plain would have someone out here watching for us." He shook his head and wiped his frown away. "Let's go in and see if anyone is awake."

"Uri wants to come, too," Lavinia called from her wagon, motioning for Mara and Noah to assist her at the rear.

Alma shook her head and gasped in frustration, though she still circled back to help. Everyone joined them, the whole family smiling with no dark glances from Samuel or the girls. Inside the second wagon, Lavinia held Uri by the arm and walked him to the tailgate. David and Charlie lowered it so Lavinia and Samuel could sit Uri on the edge, where he looked around with a wide smile.

"How are you feeling, son?" Morten gently rested his hand on Uri's shoulder.

"Thanks to all of you, I'm feeling much better." He glanced lovingly at Lavinia. "And I thank God for guiding Lavinia's hand to pluck the bullet from my belly. All of you, thank you."

With tears in her eyes, Charlie took a step back, and Wendy put her arm around the girl, drawing her away so that Uri could hop down and hobble using a crutch Samuel had fashioned out of a long piece of wood. The end was cut into a U-shape that fit perfectly beneath his arm and was wrapped with layers of padding and tape to give it some cushion. Gathering around Uri, they marched toward the gate, which was still shut to them but didn't appear padlocked or chained. Morten led the way with lanky strides, his coat hanging off his broad shoulders as he approached and waved his hand.

"Hello there, brothers and sisters of Pearisburg. I am Morten Christensen, husband of Elvesta Raber from the Fort Plains community! We come seeking refuge from the storm and the warm company of our brothers and sisters of God."

Wendy, Charlie, and David walked off to the left and pressed their

CHAPTER FOURTEEN

faces against the black gates. Charlie gripped two of the bars and peered across the road at two large, abandoned barns and a scattering of smaller buildings behind it. The gravel tract went north and south, weaving deeper into the Amish community and surrounding hills, its secrets hidden by dripping forests with trees that were just budding green. Firs and spruces gave the hillsides some color but stood quiet beneath the flat gray sky.

"I think I see someone back there!" Charlie called, putting her hand through the bars and pointing at the shadowy buildings.

Two men stepped from behind a barn dressed in traditional Amish garb, wearing hats and long coats glistening in the rain, one carrying a shotgun but the other with no visible weapon.

"Hello there!" Morten waved. "Can you hear me over there? My name is Morten Christensen. We've traveled all this way from Fort Plain. We mean you no harm but seek shelter and an audience with Lee Smithson. He'll know me by relation to my wife, Elvesta."

The pair exchanged a glance and descended the short slope to the road, stopping and looking over everyone behind the gate, from Wendy down the line to Samuel, Alma, Lavinia, Miriam, and all the kids surrounding Uri. They had another quick talk and came ahead until they stood ten feet from the gate. One was tall, wearing thick rubber galoshes and a dark beard covering his jaw. The other had on leather boots with his pants tucked inside them.

The taller one who carried the shotgun strode closer. "I'm Ray Glick, and this is my friend, Liam Swarey. You say you want to see Smithson?"

"First, I'd beg some information from you," Morten said. "Have there been any other folks in from Fort Plain? There would've been dozens of them with a big line of wagons stretching up the road..." Morten gestured back the other way and laughed, but his grin faded when the two young men looked confused.

"There have been no others of our kind at our gates," Ray said. "And none from Fort Plain. We would've known if that many people had shown up."

Morten gripped his chest, face twisted in anguish, turning to appeal to Alma, who clasped his hand and lowered her head in grief.

CHAPTER FOURTEEN

"They didn't make it. How could they not have? They'd gotten a great head start. Alma, I fear the worst has happened. They might be —"

"Don't say it, Father." Alma's words were rushed, and her eyes brimmed with tears. "They could've been delayed for several reasons, especially with the large group. We talked about what it might mean if we showed up and they weren't here."

Morten nodded that he understood, yet he still fell against the gate with a sob, slouching forward with one arm wrapped around his belly as if poisoned. "I hear your words, daughter, yet sorrow still lives in my heart, for I have no faith that they're okay. God's voice has abandoned me on the matter."

Wendy glanced at Charlie and walked around David to rest her hand on Morten's back. "It's going to be okay." Turning her attention to the two Amish men standing inside the gates, Wendy asked, "So, can we see this Smithson person?"

Ray nodded and gestured to Liam. "Go grab the elders and tell them who's here."

Liam jogged to a barn and came out a moment later on horseback, turning north and taking off fast up the road. Ray stood with his hips forward and one arm crossed on his chest, the other draped over the shotgun which rested on his shoulder.

Wendy pressed. "Can you let us in while we wait?"

Ray shook his head, and Wendy snorted disgustedly and walked away. Charlie followed her to the wagons with Clyde obediently by her side, and when they got out of earshot, Wendy fixed Ray with a dark scowl.

"You should probably knock that off, Mom."

"What do you mean? I wasn't expecting them to welcome us with open arms, but if they won't even let Morten in..."

"They won't let us in. And don't look now, but Lavinia is staring holes in you."

"She's always staring holes in me, more or less, with intermittent moments of kindness."

"Right, but this seems worse than usual."

Wendy glared at the woman, holding her hand out and saying, "*What?*"

CHAPTER FOURTEEN

Lavinia glanced at Samuel and then left the gate, storming up to her with a heated glare. "You should stay back here with your family."

"According to Morten and everyone but you, we *are* all family."

Lavinia retreated with a wicked grin. "You know what I mean, Wendy Christensen. They'll take one look at you and your kids, and none of us will get inside, especially if you're not the kind of person who shows gratitude. Keep talking like you did to those two young men, and we'll find ourselves locked out and truly homeless. I'm asking you to hold your tongue until our father has spoken with Smithson. Father is likely still held highly amongst the Pearisburg elders, and if you speak out and start demanding things, they'll see him as weak." She stepped back and looked Wendy up and down. "And they'd be right for the favoritism he gives you."

Wendy started to say something mean but glanced at Charlie and then at Ray, who was observing them. Instead of spouting off, she gave Lavinia a cool nod. "Yeah, I get it. I don't want to do or say anything that will keep us locked out. You're right. I'll keep my mouth shut and stay back here."

Lavinia nodded, blinked, and backed off. "Thank you."

As she walked away, Wendy stepped toward David and hissed his name. Her son came to stand with them while they waited for Smithson and the elders.

"Lavinia is asking us to lie low and not say much," she told him. "Both of you stick by me, and we'll just hang out here by the wagons until Morten talks to them."

"What if they get here and Grandpa can't convince them to let us in?" Charlie asked. "What if they kick us out? Where are we going to go from there?"

"I don't know, Charlie," Wendy replied, slapping her leg in frustration and circling to stand on the other side of Marley and Fitzpatrick, turning to pet Fitzpatrick along his smooth flanks. "If it doesn't work out, we'll find someplace close to settle down. It won't be perfect, but we can start over somewhere and wait for your father to get here."

Charlie's face was screwed up with fright. "But what if he doesn't come home? What if he never sees the message we left and —"

CHAPTER FOURTEEN

Wendy grabbed her by the arm. "I told you about that kind of talk. I'm not trying to shut you down, but I won't hear *that* kind of talk. Dad will make it, and *we'll* make it. Do you hear me?"

"Yeah, Mom. Okay. Not trying to be negative, I'm just —"

"I know, baby." Wendy let her anger drain away and hugged Charlie. "I'm sorry for being so harsh with you."

The sounds of running horses reached them, and Wendy peeked around Fitzpatrick to look up the lane where a group of a dozen swept in from the south and came to a halt next to Ray, all of them dismounting and pulling rifles from saddle holsters, led by a short, portly man with an exceptionally scruffy black-gray beard and a bulging belly. He squinted at the lot of them before settling on Morten, a broad smile breaking out on his face.

"God is good," he said with wide arms. "It is Morten Christensen and his brood. Go on, Ray. Open the gates for our guests."

Ray's stoic expression fell away, and he jogged to the gates, flipping the latch up and throwing them wide with a welcoming gesture. Morten went first, followed by Samuel and the boys, with the women lingering and helping Uri hobble in. Wendy nodded to David and Charlie, and the three strolled behind their Amish kin with Clyde staying back by the horses, mistrustful of the new people. Wendy resolved to stay quiet and listen. Morten and Smithson locked arms in a firm embrace, looking each other up and down with gleeful expressions.

"It's been a long journey from our enclave to your door," Morten said graciously, "but it is well worth it to see the smiling faces of our brothers. These are my sons, Samuel and Uri, their wives, Lavinia and Miriam, and my beautiful daughter, Alma."

"Well met," Smithson said, pushing his thick, black-rimmed glasses higher on his nose as he studied the group curiously. "I'm truly sorry to hear that Elvesta passed two years ago, and our prayers are with you."

"Yes, it was a tragedy, and we wanted to visit sooner, but..."

"Don't mention it, my friend." Smithson appeared confused. "Pardon my questions, but why are you here? You left your enclave

CHAPTER FOURTEEN

where you had your homes and protection. In these dire times, such a journey would seem unwarranted."

"It would seem that way, but the weather up in the north is even worse than here, my brother. To make a long story short, we were forced to leave, and the rest of the enclave went ahead of us while we took a detour to pick up some other family members." Morten glanced up into the hills with his own confused expression. "I would've thought they'd made it here before us. Imagine my surprise when I arrived to find out I was wrong."

"I cannot speak for them, but we are glad you're here." Smithson looked around the taller man yet again. "What is this about an extended family you had to find? Are they from another enclave —" Smithson's words fell flat as he spotted Wendy and the kids, their clothing identifying them as outsiders. Pulling Morten close, Smithson whispered something harsh, and Morten huffed and gestured angrily in response.

"Here we go," David commented.

Charlie rolled her eyes. "This is where they kick us to the curb."

"Hush," Wendy hissed, stepping a little closer to hear the men.

The other leaders drew in, all of them no younger than thirty and wearing an assortment of farm clothes, overalls, coveralls, blue jeans, or threadbare Amish pants with suspenders or homemade belts to hold them on their hips. They wore scruffy beards that were unkempt and untrimmed. Many held shotguns or thirty-aught-six rifles, though none of them were the AR-15 style that Wendy carried.

Way off behind the men, a group of women had gathered, staying in the shadows with their variously colored cape dresses and umbrellas as they whispered and pointed at the newcomers.

"It's so weird how they keep their women back there like that," Charlie said with a sniff. "They're always back there, not doing much of anything."

"I'd say they do a *lot*. Look at Lavinia and Alma. They had a lot of responsibility for getting here, and we might not have made it if not for them."

"I know, but —"

"People are just different here. They have a certain way of doing

CHAPTER FOURTEEN

things, and it's neither good nor bad. It just is. As long as people are happy and not being abused, I've never had a problem with their ways."

"I guess."

Smithson and Morten broke up the meeting, and both men stepped through the waiting women to stand in front of Wendy. The enclave leader hooked his thumbs in his pocket and stuck his chest out haughtily as he looked down his nose.

Morten stepped in and spoke. "Wendy, we decided you must find your own place to stay for now."

"I thought you said we'd be fine here, Dad." Wendy wasn't surprised at the decision, but it still hurt. "Did you tell them I'm married to Zach?"

Morten nodded. "I told them exactly that, but it doesn't matter to them. Under normal circumstances, it would be difficult for them to accept you and the kids for any length of time, but in these dire times, it's more important than ever to know who you bring into your communities."

"But you can vouch for us, Morten."

Morten spread his hands as Alma stood close with a suspicious look. "I'm sorry, Wendy, but I will help you find a place to stay and ensure you have supplies. It will just be outside the protection of the community. There's bound to be an abandoned house along the old highway here."

Wendy glanced at Lavinia and Samuel, who both wore smart grins.

Anger raged through her blood, and she stepped aside and addressed Smithson. "I know how you feel about outsiders, and I don't have a problem with that. But Morten said in these dire times it's important to know who your friends are. We helped Morten and his family, your people, get here. We guarded their supplies and fought for them. We protected these kids and made sure they got here in one piece, and that means we're friends of the community. You could use our help."

Morten started to say something, but Smithson held up his hand to stop him. The portly man stepped up to Wendy, leading with his

CHAPTER FOURTEEN

gut and sticking it out before bucking up to speak. "That may be well and true, ma'am, but it doesn't hold any weight when it comes to being a trusted member of this community. Faith in God is what we require here."

"You don't know what my beliefs are," Wendy replied, keeping her voice low and common. "And it shouldn't matter when a mother and her children are looking for a place to lie down. All we want is a roof over our heads and a chance to wait here for my husband."

"A husband who was away from his family," Smithson said, turning and pacing. "Morten says Zachary practically abandoned his family to work up north."

"I did not say it that way, Smithson," Morten interjected with a finger pointed at the man's chest.

"All the same... anyone who runs three thousand miles away from their family certainly doesn't love them."

That drew snickers and laughter from the other men, and Alma rushed in to interject, but Morten held her back with a curt headshake.

"Zach needed that job," Wendy said. "He was going through some trouble as a police officer. Something shook him, and he was just trying to find himself."

"Find himself," Smithson said sarcastically with a glance at the other men. "The world is full of people trying to find themselves and see where that has got them. Everything is falling apart, and they don't know who to turn to for guidance. They're separated from their families and crushed by this wicked world, yet here we stand against the world as one. That's exactly why we don't let outside influences into the community. You people may not be evil, but the influence is within you." He pointed at Wendy. "The second we let you in is the second we plant a poisoned seed. Furthermore—"

Shooting erupted in the distance to the west, and the Amish men turned and exchanged sudden, worried glances. A bell rang up on the hill at the top of a steeple... three clangs and then a clatter, throwing the Amish into a confused rush as they leaped onto the horses and started to turn away.

CHAPTER FOURTEEN

Morten gestured to Smithson and the others. "What is it, Smithson?"

The Amish leader turned his gelding in a circle before facing Morten. "An attack on the west side of town. We've got to go now. Keep your people here until we can return. I don't want any of them entering our enclave."

"We've got extra guns. We can help."

Smithson glanced across them, his eyes settling on Wendy and David before flicking back to Morten. "You and your sons would be welcome, but the women and the outsiders must stay. What's it going to be?"

Morten clenched his fist at his side, then turned and gestured to Samuel. "Samuel, bring my shotgun. We're going to fight."

Samuel reached into the driver's seat and grabbed his father's shotgun, carrying it with him as well as his own.

Smithson deftly guided his horse backward and turned. "Jump on with John and Amos. Come on, men. Let's ride to defend our homes!"

Morten glanced at Wendy apologetically and climbed up behind another Amish man on a big, black stallion. The horsemen took off, riding a little north and then cut west again on a dirt lane that led deeper into the Amish enclave, splashing through puddles as the rain fell.

"What a bunch of idiots," Charlie said, coming up.

David rested his hand on her shoulder. "But you did real good, Mom. You told that dude exactly what he needed to hear. We helped get our family here, but if they want us to leave, then to heck with them."

The Pearisburg women across the street rushed over to the gleeful shouts of Lavinia and Miriam and the children. They all embraced and held hands, introducing themselves in a gaggle of voices, many whispering and pointing at Wendy and her kids. Still, others gazed worriedly west to where the men had ridden.

Alma approached Wendy and the kids, resting her hands on her hips and sighing. "I'm so sorry about all this, guys. Father did his best to make sure you could fit in with us."

CHAPTER FOURTEEN

"Thanks for the support," Wendy said with a shrug. "It stinks, but we don't want to be where we're not wanted. We'll find a place to stay close by because we're not leaving the county. Not with Zach on his way here. And when he gets here, he won't be happy with this Smithson guy."

"Dad's probably going to rearrange his face," David said, tossing his wet hair out of his eyes.

"That probably won't be necessary, but he'll definitely give the guy a piece of his mind." Wendy sighed and rested her hands on her hips. "I'm almost thinking we should take our stuff and leave now."

"Please, don't," Alma pleaded. "There still may be a chance. At the very least, let me and Father help you find a place. He's a great judge of houses and how to ensure you find one that's good. I promise we will." Before Wendy could reply, Alma wrapped her long arms around her and hugged her close, drawing Charlie and David in. "And I won't take no for an answer."

"Okay, Alma." Wendy laughed, her heart twisting with a mixture of emotions. "At the very least, we'll stay until this trouble is over, and if you and Father want to help us find a place to live, we'll set out right away. But don't you want to get settled —"

Wendy cocked her head to the side at a strange noise coming down the road from the north. She broke away from the embrace and walked out around to check the highway.

"What is it, Mom?" David asked.

"Can you hear that car?"

David's brow wrinkled as he tried to listen, not seeming to hear it at first, but then he brightened. "Yeah. I can hear it now. Not just one car, but a couple."

With a chill running up her spine, Wendy jogged the other way past the kids and around the wagons, looking south down the road and not seeing anything. Yet the engines revved louder, coming fast and closer by the second with squealing tires as if they were rounding a bend. She glared the other way, squinting and then raced toward a cluster of trees north of the wagons.

"They're coming!" she shouted. "Charlie and David follow me. Over here! The rest of you take cover!"

249

CHAPTER FOURTEEN

The other Amish women scattered, screaming and crying out and running for the protection of the buildings. Alma, Lavinia, and Miriam shoved their kids after the Amish women and took Uri by the arms and led him to the brick wall where he could take cover. In his weakened condition, he was in no shape to fight. Alma grabbed her shotgun out of the driver's seat of the first wagon, hunkering down and moving to the rear to peer around at the road. Wendy, the kids, and Clyde splashed through the grass puddles to a cluster of oaks and maples just inside the black fence line with a clear view of the road and the vehicles racing toward them. Liam and Ray took positions behind the brick wall with their shotguns resting there, ready to fire.

Wendy checked her M&P 15 and eased between the two enormous trees, with the oak on her left shoulder as cover. "Back me up, kids," she whispered.

"You got it, Mom," David said, drawing his Springfield and creeping around the big maple to peek around the other side with Charlie right behind him and Clyde whining on his leash.

Leaning out, peering through the mist, Wendy caught sight of headlamps moving toward them, a Dodge Charger and a heavy pickup truck, their frames jumping and jostling over the uneven pavement, speeding up along the straightaway and seemingly about to lose control before the drivers put on the brakes and slowed.

"They're doing it. They're going to stop and try to attack the enclave from the rear."

"We're going to let them have it," Charlie said.

Wendy felt the weapon's power as it aligned perfectly with her arms, her left hand gripping the hand guard and her elbow bent in a firm position. Finger inside the trigger guard, she let the cars pass and tracked them smoothly in her sights. They started to turn in but then stopped and swung to the side with a shuddering of brakes by the wagons parked in their way. The windows rolled down, and weapon barrels flashed. Wendy squeezed the trigger, the powerful gun bucking her shoulder as she punched round after round into the back of the pickup, dotting the windshield in three places and putting holes in the tailgate. She switched to the Charger, where the

CHAPTER FOURTEEN

man was firing a handgun at the wagons, the horses spooked in their harnesses, tugging this way and that and trying to take off, though something held them in check.

A shotgun blast from Alma at the back of the first wagon shattered the Charger's right-side windows, and a man howled and cursed. Ray and Liam fired buckshot, strafing the pickup truck in the side and front to bust the glass and elicit another shriek from the passenger.

Wendy hit them from behind, squeezing the trigger repeatedly and placing her shots evenly along the back window, three quick strikes, hoping to get the driver and at least one passenger, sighing with disappointment when both vehicles hit their gas pedals and tore off in a squeal of tires and exhaust. She kept firing until they were fifty or a hundred yards away, still getting hits and punching holes into the Charger's trunk before finally lowering her rifle as rain sizzled on the barrel.

"Great shooting, Mom," Charlie said, smiling. "I didn't have to cover you at all."

"I hope it's that way every time," Wendy stated flatly, riding an excited high. "I don't want you kids to have to shoot people." Shouldering her gun, she jogged toward the wagons, calling, "Is everyone okay? Alma? Lavinia? Miriam?"

"I'm okay!" Miriam replied, circling Shadow and Ivory. "I held the horses so they wouldn't break."

"Me, too," Lavinia said, moving around Wild Step and Bravo while glaring after the cars as they raced away, their engines fading in the distance. "I bet those evil men will not try that again."

"I hope they don't," Wendy nodded as Alma came out to greet her, the two women clutching arms and grinning.

"Excellent shooting," Alma said. "I did not sense any panic in you at all. Your shots were very steady."

"Thanks. I've had lots of practice."

Ray and Liam rose from their hiding spots and stepped into the gated lane, walking up between the wagons but not saying anything to the women.

Uri hobbled around the corner behind them, giving Wendy and

CHAPTER FOURTEEN

his sister a respectful nod. "Ladies, that was as wonderful a defense of an enclave as I've ever seen." He laughed. "Not that I've seen many, but your shooting was on point."

"No problem," Wendy said, glancing at Ray and Liam. "Maybe I can get some work here as a guard."

The ladies laughed, and David snickered. Even Lavinia wore a crooked smile as she sneered at the retreating vehicles. Within a minute, the sounds of racing horses reached them, and from the western lane came Smithson, Morten, and the rest of the Amish men. They drew up, guns raised, and glanced around.

"Ray! Liam! What happened here?" Smithson bellowed.

The two guards moved between the wagons and entered the broader intersection where everybody gathered. "They attacked us from the road, but Morten's wagons blocked them from getting in. Still, they stopped and tried to shoot, but we drove them off with the ladies' help."

"The attack on the barn was surprisingly weak," Morten said, "and we chased them off, which is why we returned as soon as we heard gunshots from this direction."

Wendy nodded. "It was a feint on that side, and they were hoping they could break through the gates and cause some trouble, I'd warrant."

Smithson blinked at Wendy from behind his thick spectacles and turned his wide-eyed gaze on Morten. "If you hadn't parked your wagons there, they would've broken right through."

"And if my daughter and Wendy hadn't protected the entrance, they would've broken in to cause a great deal of trouble. We owe them our thanks."

"Is this true?" Smithson asked.

"They protected us well," Ray agreed, and he nodded at Wendy. "The lady with the rifle filled them full of holes. She picked them apart easily."

Wendy kept her mouth shut as she stared at Smithson. He turned his horse one way and then the other, sizing Wendy and Alma up as Morten's words hit home. Face tightening and lips pressed tight, he reluctantly doled out some praise. "Then we owe you an immense

CHAPTER FOURTEEN

thanks for helping defend our enclave. From now on, we must be wary of raiders coming up with creative ways to trick us."

"And it sounds like we could use their guns after all," Morten added with a cocked eyebrow.

Smithson shook his head and seemed about to say no, but the surrounding men mumbled and nodded, looking at Wendy and Alma appreciatively. It swayed him in a different direction. With a calculated breath, he said, "They may stay while we take this discussion to my home. There, they'll remain in our protection until we can decide what to do with them. Post double guards at the gates."

With that, the Amish leader turned and galloped away, followed by the rest of the riders. The Amish women brought Miriam's and Lavinia's kids back with words of praise and affection.

Morten had dismounted and approached Wendy with a mischievous grin. "Whatever you did, it will go a long way to being accepted into the community. Excellent work. I'm proud of all of you. Now come on! Get in the wagons! We're going to Smithson's!"

CHAPTER FIFTEEN

Wendy Christensen, Pearisburg, Virginia

Wendy stood in the two-track gravel driveway in front of Smithson's house, listening to Morten plead his case for allowing her and the kids to stay. The massive three-story farmhouse sat atop a rolling field, a beautiful but straightforward construction with sweeping decks and white siding stained by the new rains. A rail fence surrounded the property, and a bright red barn with a grain silo sat out back. Inside, the men had parked the horses, leaving their care to the younger men in the group as the elders argued with raised voices and heated gestures.

Wendy walked down the driveway a little, so she didn't have to see or hear them, and sheltered beneath a concrete patio with an awning. She took a seat on an extended bench. Off to the left, floodwaters gathered in a small valley to form a growing lake which, to her, appeared likely to spill over and rush downhill toward the other Amish homes.

On the high spots, people stood in rain ponchos with shotguns and rifles, their wide-brimmed hats dripping water as they scanned

CHAPTER FIFTEEN

the woods for looters and thieves. Indoors, the women made meals and served drinks, and the debate continued.

Charlie and David arrived at the patio with mugs in their hands. They sat on either side of her, and David offered her a hot coffee.

"Thanks, honey," she said and smothered the warm mug with her hands. She had a sip and brightened at the robust flavor. "Ah, this is wonderful."

"I'm not a coffee drinker," Charlie said with a nod. She sat with her knees pressed tight as she let the steam from her mug roll over her face. "But the Amish make the best coffee."

"Handcrafted or something, right?" David said with a grin.

They remained silent after that, listening to the rain falling on the grass and in the lake. Creeks and small streams flowed from the mountain and split around Smithson's farmstead. In some places, they'd erected barriers to direct the water downhill and keep his home from being swept off the hillside.

"Is it going to rain forever?" Charlie asked.

"I was just thinking the same thing," Wendy replied. "It's like Noah and the flood or something."

"How long are they going to argue in there?" David sniffed and leaned forward. "It's not a huge decision. They either want us to stay, or they don't."

"Who knows what kind of politics are going on in there."

"I agree with David," Charlie said, glancing toward the house where they could see through the windows at the men's shadows gesticulating by candlelight. "It's so silly."

"I agree, but it's not our call."

Charlie scoffed. "Let's just leave."

"It's not that simple, honey," Wendy said. "You've already seen how dangerous it is on the road, so protection and a safe place to put our heads down would be amazing right now. Not to mention your father is coming, and we want to be around when he gets here."

"Do they have running water?" Charlie asked. "I mean, if they have hot, running water, it would be worth all this arguing. I feel like I'm wearing layers of dirt."

"I hear you." Wendy frowned and peered toward the house. "This

CHAPTER FIFTEEN

is going long because we won some of them over. They know we're not going to poison them like Smithson implied."

"Right. We'd keep to ourselves," David agreed.

"Hey, guys!"

Alma called to them as she was coming down from the house along the gravel path. She'd changed dresses and cleaned up, her long blonde hair tucked into her bonnet, and her bright blue eyes shining. In her arms, she carried two platters covered with soft towels.

"David, help her with those, please."

David placed his coffee cup on the seat next to him and took a platter from Alma.

"Thank you." She smiled and stooped in front of Wendy and Charlie, then uncovered a plate of homemade bread, peanut butter, tiny pickles, beets, and strawberries.

Wendy blinked with surprise. "Wow, Alma. Is that cherry marshmallow dip in the middle?"

"It certainly is." She looked at the other platter. "I believe David has the plate with the crackers."

David knelt next to them and held out the platter, pulling off the cloth to reveal slices of bread and crackers. "Thanks, Aunt Alma." He grabbed a cracker, dove into the dip, and popped it in his mouth.

"That good, huh?" Wendy put a strawberry in her mouth and chewed slowly, savoring the burst of sweet flavor as it rolled down her throat. "This is amazing, Alma. We haven't had fresh fruit in so long."

"Has it been a few weeks yet?"

"I lost track of time back when we were at the house," Wendy admitted. "This dip is incredible. How are you still getting all this stuff?"

"We've got greenhouses in the lower parts of the enclave, and we're still harvesting things that started growing weeks ago, though I must admit the crops are starving for sunlight. Still, we've got an almost unlimited supply of canned goods in our cellars, homemade cheeses, milk, and enough food for a small army I'd warrant. Some of the women were telling me about alternate ways of growing crops or changing what they grow."

CHAPTER FIFTEEN

"In case the rain doesn't stop." Charlie asked and jammed another smothered cracker into her mouth.

"That's right. Most everyone thinks it will stop soon, but it's impossible to predict." Alma glanced behind her at the lake. "I want to believe that, but something has changed. A lot of folks think it's the end of days, and the events of the Bible are playing out right here and now."

"Honestly, I can't argue with that," Wendy replied. "I can see how sticking together and having a big community to rely on would be comforting."

"I admit I feel better being out of the wagons and in a nice, clean home," Alma said with a smile. "Smithson has done well for himself over the years, and his wife, Amelia, is lovely."

"We might disagree on who's lovely and who's not," Wendy responded and quickly regretted her words. "Sorry, I'm just a little annoyed at all this. On the one hand, this is a beautiful place with so much potential. You're so nice to us, and Miriam and Morten, too. But there are people like Lavinia, Samuel, and others who are violently opposed to us being here. Then again, you come out with this delicious food."

Charlie laughed. "You hit the nail on the head, Mom."

"I understand how you feel, but people are stubborn," Alma said. "No one will admit when they're wrong or go the extra mile to take outsiders in, but Father is making a great case. I don't want you to go. Whatever they decide, we'll make it work."

Wendy dusted crumbs off her hand and squeezed Alma's arm. "Thank you. You've truly been a sister to me, and we're so grateful for you and Dad."

"Yeah, Aunt Alma," Charlie said. "I'm so glad we got to see you and travel with you. I learned a lot from you, Grandpa, and Lavinia, even if she doesn't like us."

"She likes you, it's just —"

The commotion in the house shifted, and Wendy turned to see Morten stride from the side door and stand out in the rain, looking for them. When he saw them on the patio, he gestured for them to come up.

CHAPTER FIFTEEN

"What do you think it'll be?" Wendy asked as she, Alma, and the kids covered the food and carried it back up the path to the driveway.

"I couldn't say," Alma replied flatly. "I hope they make the right decision and let you stay close by so I can see you guys every day."

Once they reached the door, Morten held his hand up. "You can enter the debate room, but David and Charlie need to go into the kitchen with the women."

David scoffed. "No thanks, Grandpa. I'll stay out here if that's okay."

"I think that would be fine," he replied. "Please stay close and don't go walking up in the fields. There are men up there with guns."

"Stay very close," Wendy said.

"I'll sit at the patio." David handed the platter to Charlie and left with his coffee in hand.

After hanging up her wet poncho and rifle on a hook in the entranceway, Wendy followed Morten down a long hallway, her boots heavy on the hardwood floor, the place thick with the scent of delicious food and a bit of dust. The walls were devoid of pictures except for religious knickknacks of Bible sayings and rustic pieces of farm equipment. They stepped into an open area where the kitchen and great room adjoined. Alma and Charlie broke to the right where the dining room bustled with women in cape dresses boasting cheery smiles, although some gave Charlie and Wendy skeptical glances. She followed Morten into a quaint space with a wood-burning stove, shelves full of books, several Amish-made couches, and old furniture that gave it a traditional appearance. Wendy took two steps in before Morten turned and held up his hand.

"Right there is fine, Wendy."

"Okay." She clasped her hands in front of her, gazing across the allotment of men staring at her with mixed expressions, some with hostility and others nodding at her with an air of acceptance. Part of her wanted to walk out, but she kept her feet planted for the kids, hoping to have a safe, comfortable place to wait for Zach to come home. She saw Samuel on the far left next to a table with his hands in his pockets and an unreadable frown. Smithson was seated in a

CHAPTER FIFTEEN

leather-bound chair in front of the fire. The chair had been turned to face the center of the room. She caught whiffs of hot apple cider and coffee and figured they must've gone through pots of the beverages for the past two hours. The Amish leader leaned back and regarded Wendy with a neutral expression. His gaze never left her until he stood and approached. Stopping a few feet in front of her, Smithson hooked his thumbs into his suspenders.

He glanced at the gathered men, then he shifted his gaze back to her. "First, our gratitude for helping protect the enclave. It was brave of you and something we would only ask of our women in the direst of circumstances."

Wendy nodded.

"For that proven dedication to our people, we've decided you would not be a poison to our community and that you have good hearts despite not following our ways."

Wendy raised on the balls of her feet and eased back. "Thank you. I'm glad we could—"

"But I cannot allow you to live among our general population. Instead, you will be sent to the outskirts of the community where we have an older home you will certainly find comfortable."

Wendy didn't know what that meant, but a glance at Morten's dark expression told her it was bad news, and Samuel's slow smile confirmed her uneasy feelings. "Thank you, Smithson, I think." Wendy picked her words carefully. "Does that mean we can't enter the community?"

"That's correct," Smithson said. "Of course, you may receive visitors from your family, Morten, Alma, and the others, but you'll not take part in regular gatherings, and you'll have the responsibility of ringing a bell should anyone suspicious enter our property."

"So, you relegated us to guard duty?" Wendy said bluntly.

"If you carry out your duty properly, it's possible we could find better arrangements for you down the road."

"Down the road? One reason we're here is for protection..." Wendy crossed her arms. "What if I stay on the outskirts, but you allow David and Charlie to stay with Morten and Alma? Surely, you would be amenable to protecting children?"

CHAPTER FIFTEEN

Smithson shook his head. "They're hardly children. Your son David is practically a man and should be looking forward to meaningful work. Perhaps he could attend church services to learn more about our ways."

"That hardly seems fair to Charlie."

Smithson stiffened. "Morten assured us that for the sake of your children, you'd be willing to make compromises to remain under our protection."

Wendy stepped forward and peered into Smithson's pretentious face. "We'll guard your outskirts and help around the enclave where we can, but we're not interested in the other parts."

"Now, Wendy," Morten said. "We'll worry about all that after we get you settled in. If something doesn't suit you or the members of the enclave, we can make different arrangements later. For now, we should get the children to a place where they can rest and shed the worries of the road."

Wendy mulled over Morten's words and stepped back, then gave a curt nod. "Thank you. We appreciate you allowing us to stay on the outskirts for now. All we want is a place to lay our heads and nothing more."

Morten continued with a subtle wink at Wendy. "This is a suitable compromise for now. We'll have someone at the edge of town who can help protect the property. At the same time, we'll offer help when we can. We'll be distant neighbors, as I understand the location is off the beaten track."

"It's on the south side of the enclave in a series of homes built for future expansion," Smithson said. "But we never filled the homes."

"What is this about a bell?" Wendy asked.

"You may have noticed when the looters attacked our barn," Smithson said, "we use bells to raise the alarm. Despite the distance between our homes, the bells are extremely loud, and the sound carries for miles. If you see people not of the enclave, ring the bell, and we'll come."

Wendy took a deep breath. "Fine. I just want to get the kids there and settled. They haven't slept well in days."

Smithson tugged on his suspenders, rose on the balls of his feet,

CHAPTER FIFTEEN

and settled again. "I agree to this arrangement. We'll revisit the matter in seven days."

Someone shouted and pushed through the side door with heavy footfalls on the hardwood. Wendy glanced to see David tromping toward her, dripping all over the floor as his chest heaved in anger.

"What is it, son?"

"I was sitting out there and saw some men go up to Grandpa's wagon where we had our supplies."

"Had?"

"They started taking the bins with our guns and food."

Wendy reeled on Morten and Smithson. "What's the meaning of this? We don't get to keep our things?"

"It's standard for us to share much of what we own," Smithson said, seeming genuinely surprised. "Especially now with what's happening to the world, we pool our resources and dole them out as needed. Any guns and ammunition are stored to protect the community."

"We purchased that stuff ourselves," Wendy protested. "We've got canned goods, MREs, and other things I saved over the years."

"Not the type of fresh food we would normally eat, but it may come in handy down the road." Smithson held his hands out. "This is one compromise you'll have to make if you want to stay here."

"How can we defend the outskirts with no weapons?"

Smithson closed his eyes and took a deep breath as if explaining the situation to a child. "You may keep the weapons you have on you for that purpose and a sack of food, but everything else, including Morten's supplies, will go into the community barns and warehouses to be kept as inventory."

Morten stepped closer, towering above everyone. "It is the way of things, Wendy. This is no ruse to trick you or take anything from you. If we're going to work as a community, you must learn to make concessions."

Lips pressed tight, Wendy glanced around the room at the men's flat expressions, Samuel's crooked frown mocking her. Her anger rose but faded just as fast, for the kids' sake. "Okay. It's your community. We'll live under your rules only until Zach comes home."

CHAPTER FIFTEEN

Smithson swept his gaze around the room at all the men and gestured at Wendy. "It's good to know we can make this compromise. Now, you'll have to let us discuss other matters. Morten and Alma will take you to your new home. We sincerely hope you like it."

"Thank you." Wendy bowed her head and turned to grip David by the arm, ushering him toward the door.

"Are you kidding, Mom?" he whispered as they moved down the hallway, water dripping off his poncho. "We've got so much ammo and food."

"I know, son, but Morten is right. We can't live under their roof and not expect to have responsibilities and make compromises."

"Dumb compromises."

Wendy grabbed her poncho off the hook and slipped it on, followed by her M&P 15. "They may seem dumb to you, but the Amish have their rules, and these elders are the people who make them. So, we're obligated until your father gets here, then we can find a different place to go." She shook her head as they stepped into the rain to wait for Morten. "To be honest, maybe we're the ones being paranoid. They are offering to give us a house... a safe place to stay."

"Yeah, after we drove off a bunch of jerks."

She saw the line of Amish men around the wagons. A couple were taking the supplies from Samuel's and Uri's wagons and carrying them to carts that were wheeled into a big red barn. Some of those were their supplies, but Wendy resisted any resentment and resigned herself to the compromise she'd made.

"We showed them what we can do and that we have value," she said. "We can be part of this community if we do the work. It might not be perfect, but it's the best we can do for now." Wendy crossed her arms as emotion welled up in her chest, and she gasped shallowly. "I don't feel great about it, son, and you giving me grief doesn't make it any better."

David deflated and wrapped his arm around her shoulders. "Sorry, Mom. I just feel like they should've left us keep our things. You're the one who put all that food and ammunition together, and now it's going into some big pile."

The door flew open, and Charlie rushed out, slipping her arms

CHAPTER FIFTEEN

into her poncho as she came. "What happened? I was in the kitchen with Alma when I heard David's voice. I just caught the last part of the conversation."

"We've got a place to live," Wendy replied.

"But our food and weapons are going into some community chest," David said.

Charlie looked confused. "What? That makes no sense."

Wendy glanced between the two of her kids. "It makes sense to them, and they want us on a leash for a while, at least until things settle and they get used to us. Maybe when your grandfather's people get here, things will change."

Charlie shook her head. "I doubt it, Mom. They're all the same. They'll always judge us no matter how much we do for them."

Wendy rubbed Charlie's back. "You might be right, but I don't want to worry about it right now. I'm happy we still have each other, and we're going to get out of this rain."

"Amen to that at least," Charlie said.

Morten's hulking figure appeared in the doorway, and he stepped outside with an apologetic look at Wendy and the kids. "I appreciate you working with us, Wendy. Smithson is not one to go against doctrine, so we did very well." He gestured toward the wagons. "Let's climb aboard, and I'll take you to your new home."

Charlie went to the barn and retrieved Clyde from where she'd tied him up near the horses. As they climbed into the wagon, Alma came outside, shuffling through the rain, the end of her long cape draping to the ground. Wendy and Charlie helped her into the wagon's rear, where they sat on benches along the wagon walls. David took his position next to his grandfather in the driver's seat. Morten flicked the reins and got the horses moving, and they did a circle at the top of Smithson's driveway to head back the way they'd come.

Alma gazed across the space at Wendy.

"Are you okay?"

Wendy cracked a smile. "I'm not entirely happy with the arrangement, but I understand why it went down that way. If we want to be part of the community, we must give a little."

Alma nodded. "Well said, Wendy. And don't worry. You won't be

CHAPTER FIFTEEN

far, and I'll visit every day and help you get the place fixed up to make a happy home for your husband's imminent arrival." She spoke the last part with a flourish and a smile that made Wendy laugh, and even Charlie grinned.

Marley and Fitzpatrick snorted, and the wagon wheels ground over the gravel lane, sweeping them down into the dripping woods where they joined the main road running through the Amish community. The wind whipped up, stirring the upper boughs and sending heavy drops across the wagon roof in heavy drizzles. They drove past dozens of Amish farmhouses, which were many at first until they reached a small cluster of abandoned homes a half mile from the enclave farmsteads.

Morten guided the wagon up a slightly sloping lane with a creek trickling down the middle. They passed quaint Amish houses placed fifty yards apart with open spaces between them and small barns and sheds out back, almost cookie-cutter if not for the occasional unique floor plans with some single-story ranches while others had multiple levels. Curious about where they'd be living, Wendy knelt by the tailgate and checked out the places as they passed. Weeds and bushes choked the yard, and a few had roofs and porches in disrepair.

Alma kneeled beside her. "What do you think?"

"I don't know, Alma. These look like they're in pretty terrible shape."

"Everything's a fixer-upper, Father always says."

"Oh, I agree, but I can't help feel we're being put in no-man's-land."

Alma laughed. "It might seem that way, but I heard the men talking. With the news that more people from Fort Plain might come, they plan on putting them out here, so while it might seem lonely at first, you'll have plenty of neighbors before long."

Wendy sat back on her heels, waiting to see which one they'd be moving into. Morten slowed and pulled into a driveway on the left, angling them toward four homes clustered in a rough circle, all single-story spaces with small plots of land out back.

Alma's excited expression dwindled, and she gave Wendy a troubled glance. "You're right, these are terrible."

CHAPTER FIFTEEN

Charlie stepped to Alma's other side as they stopped at the end of the lane. "Yeah, these look bad. The windows are dirty, and the porch on that one across the street is falling in."

They climbed out, and Morten grabbed a burlap sack from the seat and slung it over his shoulder. Alma crossed to him with a stern stare. She pulled him aside and whispered. He replied with a sharp word and a head shake. His faltering smile returned, and he turned to Wendy, David, and Charlie, gesturing at a dilapidated structure with overgrown bushes and tall, drooping grass around the sides.

"Charlie, tie Clyde to one of the porch rails," Wendy told her daughter. "I don't want him getting into anything."

"Okay, Mom."

Wendy moved ahead and led them up a weed-choked stone path to the front porch, stopping there to see the plants grown up through the floorboards and Virginia creepers crawling up the sides of the house and porch beams that held up the drooping awning. Her heart sank.

"How long have these been here?"

Morten stood next to her, took off his hat, and scratched his head, then glanced at Wendy. "I admit this does not look promising, but Smithson said they are better on the inside than the outside. Other projects around the community delayed their upkeep, but he assured me as soon as the weather breaks, teams of workers will come fix things."

"Alma said that when the Fort Plain people get here, they may occupy some of these homes."

"That was mentioned, but now I have doubts." Morten turned to Wendy with unease. "I'm sorry, but I swear by my family's name, we'll make it right." He took the burlap sack off his shoulder and smiled. "And you'll have these supplies that should last you a few days until our return."

Wendy hugged him. "Thanks, Dad." She glanced at the dilapidated home and sighed. "Well, let's see how bad this is."

The floorboards creaked beneath her boots, and water dripped through holes in the covered roof, but the door was not locked, and she pushed the old-fashioned knob and walked inside an empty

CHAPTER FIFTEEN

house. On the right was a simple living room with a fireplace and built-in wall shelves. A kitchen with a wood-burning stove sat off to the left, and a narrow hallway stretched ahead into the darkness. Open ductwork ran along the walls and ceiling, and the dripping sounds were accompanied by a moldy smell.

Morten walked to the fireplace where a couple of old oil lamps sat. He picked one up and lit it. It glowed big and bright, and he dimmed it by adjusting the wick. The light revealed discolored paint, a slightly slanted ceiling, and a few thin cracks in the walls, nothing that couldn't be repaired. A layer of dust coated everything, and the hardwood floor was a delicate cherry color and stained beautifully.

Wendy glanced at Alma. "Fixer-upper may be an understatement."

Alma chuckled and then sighed. "You're right, Wendy. This is just an absolute mess. I'm so sorry you guys have to stay here."

"To be honest, ladies," Morten said. "This home looks like it was never finished, which might explain its current state. Smithson mentioned these were built several years ago until the enclave split, and half of them went to settle another part of Virginia, which sometimes happens to communities when they grow too large." He looked around with an educated eye. "But all these cracks and small things are fixable, and I know Samuel and Uri will join me in helping with the repairs."

"I will, too!" Alma gave her a quick hug, took the lantern from Morten, and strode to the hall in a swish of skirts. "Let's see what's down here. Bedrooms, no doubt."

"I'll find some additional light," Morten said, walking through the living room while Wendy and the kids followed Alma down the hall.

It was more of the same, with three bedrooms in the back, the largest on the southwest corner with a jagged crack in one wall and water leaking in. The other two were on the north side of the house, perfectly dry with no leaks they could see and dusty mattresses on the bed. David went to the first one while Wendy and Charlie walked through the second. Charlie did a full circle of the room, coming back to square up to Wendy, arms crossed and staring at the floor with a trembling chin.

Wendy reached out and grabbed her. "Aw, what's wrong?"

CHAPTER FIFTEEN

Tears streaked down her face. "Are you kidding, Mom? This place is an absolute *disaster*. How are we going to stay here? Honestly, I'd rather sleep in the wagons."

Squeezing her arms, Wendy leaned in and kept her voice low. "I know what you're saying, honey. Right now, we need to appreciate what we have. We'll clean the place up, and look..." Wendy walked over to the simple bed with its wooden frame and squarish posts, turning and sitting on the mattress, bouncing on the springs with a puff of dust.

Charlie watched the cloud rise and shook her head, more tears bursting from her eyes. "Geez, Mom. This is terrible."

"No, sis," David said sarcastically as he stepped into the room. "This is all handcrafted. Don't you know?"

Charlie's face twisted, and she cried harder.

Wendy shot David a dark look. "You're not helping, son."

"Sorry, mom," he replied sheepishly. "Just trying to bring a little humor into this."

Charlie shook her head. "There's nothing funny about it."

Alma entered the room with an armful of blankets. "I found these in the closet. They don't smell perfectly fresh, but they're not as dusty as everything else." She placed them on a nearby dresser, then she studied the room with her hands on her hips, biting her lip and peering at Wendy worryingly. "A little work and it will be cute."

Wendy's smile was flat. "Nice try, Alma. Seriously, no need to talk it off. We'll get to work and at least make it habitable for one or two nights. We may walk around and see if there's anything better in these other homes."

"Wise thinking," Morten said, stepping into the room and placing a lit lantern on the dresser. "I looked around back. There's some covered wood that's still dry."

"David, will you bring some wood in and get a fire going? We'll look for the furnace later. I'm sure it's downstairs, but I don't think I can stand to see what it's like down there right now."

"Roger that, Mom," David said with a loose salute before he moved past Morten and strode down the hall to the back door.

Seeing Charlie's distress, Morten wrapped a long arm around her

CHAPTER FIFTEEN

and pulled her tight. "I hate to take our leave so soon, but we have our own houses to get in order. After this, I question what we might be walking into." Patting Charlie's back, he said, "It's not for us to complain in the light of the Lord's blessing. May he keep us this night, and may we sleep well after such a long and arduous journey."

"I'll walk you to the door," Wendy said. "Charlie, see if you can find any more blankets in the closets or bathrooms. The best thing we can do is start getting this place together, okay?"

Charlie sniffed and nodded, uncrossing her arms. She moved to the dresser, where she searched through the drawers. Wendy accompanied Alma and Morten to the front porch where they stepped onto the wet planks. After handing Wendy the remaining lantern, Morten removed his hat and scratched his head, staring out into the dreary gray mist.

"We'll turn this around, Wendy," he said, "Don't worry."

"I don't want to be ungrateful. The trip was tough on us all. I was hoping things would be easier once we got here." She laughed darkly and gave him a playful slap on the arm. "Better hope your place isn't worse than this, or you'll be moving in with us."

Morten chuckled deep, an honest sound that lifted Wendy's heart. "Yes, my daughter. While you have seen your fate, we have one step left to explore."

They watched the rain fall for another minute, then her kids came out and they said their goodbyes with tearful hugs and assurances they'd turn this into a home if it killed them. Morten and Alma walked into the growing darkness to the wagon. Poor Marley and Fitzpatrick had been in the rain for hours, so they stroked them a few times before climbing into the driver's seat and pulling off, leaving Wendy and the kids on the porch with Charlie's low, worried whine sounding like a sad song.

"Okay, kiddos," Wendy said, holding up the lantern and turning to the door. "Let's get inside and make something of this place. What do you say?"

The replies were less than enthusiastic, but David got a fire going, and a slow warmth filled the house. The mattresses came next. They dragged them onto the back porch where water leaked through the

CHAPTER FIFTEEN

awning. Bushes grew tall along the rail, and vines crawled over everything. David found a piece of wood and whacked the mattresses while Charlie and Wendy held them up, faces turned away as big clouds of dust puffed out into the rain. They kept at it until there was nothing more to beat out of them. Wendy noticed a big brass bell hanging in the porch corner with a heavy ringer, its thick sides covered in grime.

"I guess this is what we ring if someone attacks us," she told the kids.

By the time they'd finished with the second mattress, Wendy was sweating in the chill. They dragged them inside, placed them on their frames, and covered them with the blankets Alma had found. The dresser drawers from both rooms yielded pillowcases and old picture frames, but nothing else of substance. The kitchen had a bottle of oil for the lamps, a box of matches, and some old, chipped dishes. Charlie tried the faucet, and a burst of sludge shot out and splashed the sink, causing her to jump back and hold her nose.

Inside the sack Morten had brought were four cans of vegetables from their original supplies, a steel tripod grate-grill for the fire, a small pan, three bottled waters each, a pouch of smoked beef jerky, and assorted snacks. They mixed the corn and green beans into the pan and heated it while they munched on the smoked meat, resting on chairs they'd found in the various rooms, old broken-down things on the last legs of their life but perfect for the Christensen's new beginning.

While the vegetables warmed, David went outside, grabbed a few more logs, brought them in and stacked them.

"One thing we've got a lot of is decent wood," he said, sitting back down. "There's a bunch out there."

Wendy nodded. "Well, that's a good thing, I suppose. Food might be a little sketchy, but we'll go out first thing in the morning and check the other houses around us to see if there's anything there."

They took turns eating vegetables out of the pan with utensils they found in the sack. Wendy felt better with a full stomach. When they were done, she set the pan off to the side and stood on the front porch, walking from one end to the other in thought.

CHAPTER FIFTEEN

David joined her. "What are you looking for, Mom?"

Wendy leaned against the rail and gazed into the rain. "I thought we could find a barrel and some extra gutters or building material and make us a rain catcher. We could find some coffee filters or something to filter it and then boil it to make sure it's clean. That would take care of our water problem."

"Yeah, we can take our time on that. It's going to rain forever."

"Don't be so sure. The weather can change quickly, just like it did back in Stamford." She winced and shook her head. "Darn it, we left our heavy coats back with the other supplies. I'm sure they're sitting in Smithson's barn right now."

"Yeah, we gave up a lot."

Wendy frowned. "I trust Morten and Alma to keep us in the loop. They'll be back with more supplies tomorrow, and we can start looking at the reality of staying here long-term. We want to look around at the different houses and take anything that might help us. I know they said people from Fort Plain might move in at some point, and Smithson's people will help *them* before us, so we need to gather what we can."

"Thankfully, we've got Aunt Alma and Grandpa, or we'd be in big trouble."

A half scream pierced the gloom. Wendy and David rushed inside to the fireplace, and Wendy grabbed her M&P 15 and tromped down the hall. "Charlie! Charlie! Where are you?"

Flying past the bathroom and David's bedroom, Wendy ducked into Charlie's room to find the girl standing next to the back window and looking out beyond the porch with Clyde's leash in one hand and muzzling him with the other.

"What is it, Charlie?" Wendy hissed, walking to the window but retreating a pace when Charlie blocked her.

"Stay there, Mom." The girl peeked through the glass and jumped back with a gasp. "I saw some people out there."

"Did they attack you?" David asked, drawing his Springfield.

"No. I was dusting some blankets and saw some guys standing in the field and ran back inside. I forgot to ring the bell." She glanced at Wendy. "Sorry, Mom."

CHAPTER FIFTEEN

"It's okay, honey." Heart pounding, Wendy edged around Charlie and peeked out the window. Sure enough, two shadows stood about fifty yards out in the gray mist, their shapes showing they held rifles or shotguns, though they weren't moving furtively like looters would.

"Who are they?" Charlie asked. "Are they going to attack us?"

Wendy bit her lip and hefted her rifle. "I've got an idea who it might be. You guys stay here."

"Wait, Mom," David said, following her. "I'll go, too."

"No, you won't." She reached the end of the hall and pushed outside. With a quick turn, she pressed her palm against his chest. "Stay here and protect your sister. If my guess is right, we have nothing to worry about."

David shook his head and spoke through tight lips. "Fine."

Wendy marched down the three back porch steps into a puddle-filled backyard. She angled toward the barns and sheds that dotted the property. As she splashed toward them, one of the men saw her coming and poked his buddy, both Amish with long coats, wide-brimmed hats, and clean-shaven jaws, which told her they were unmarried men.

Stopping fifteen yards away, she held her rifle casually with the barrel pointed up. "Are you patrolling for Smithson?"

The young man shared a questioning look before nodding. "You are the outsiders?"

"That's right. You might want to come to the front door and introduce yourselves instead of standing out here like creeps." She hefted her weapon. "You can get yourself killed, scaring people like that."

The one who'd spoken to her gave his buddy a worried look. "Sorry, ma'am. We'll remember that."

With that, they tipped their hats, turned, and walked into the mist, leaving Wendy standing there with water leaking into her shoes.

Wendy's dreams were plagued by a constant pattering of rain on their ramshackle roof, distant lightning crackling, followed by the rumble of

CHAPTER FIFTEEN

thunder that shook the walls and floor. The bed beneath her was five inches of creaky springs and dust, yet it was the most comfortable thing she'd slept on in weeks. Despite the worry nagging at her mind, she had passed out quickly, knowing she wasn't supposed to sleep that long, but every time she started to rise, she would turn on a different side and sink into the soft cushions, pulling the cover over her shoulders.

David shook her awake at some point, and she blinked into the dismal gray daylight as it seeped into the windows. "Mom. Get up, Mom. It's kind of an emergency."

Jolting awake, head swimming in grogginess, Wendy threw off the blanket and swung her legs off the bed. David knelt and shoved her boots on her feet.

"Thank you. What is it? I wasn't supposed to sleep so long."

"I had first watch, and Charlie got up in the middle of the night and couldn't sleep, so she watched the back."

"You should've woken me up and gotten some sleep."

"Not with those creepy Amish dudes hanging out in the backyard." David was tying her boots up tight, and Wendy leaned forward and brushed his hands away, tying them herself.

"Those guys are with Smithson. I told you about them. I talked to them."

"We know, Mom, but they keep walking through the backyard, and Charlie saw one of them standing at the edge of the porch last night." David stood, took out his Springfield, and double-checked that it was loaded.

"Did they say anything?"

"Nope."

"Okay, so what's the other problem?"

"You just have to see for yourself."

David left the room, and Wendy sat on the edge of the bed with her stomach growling and sleep still pulling at her despite the potential danger. With a shake of her head, she ran her hand through her golden curls and searched for her rifle, finding it leaning against the end of the bed. She staggered up and grabbed it, blinking wide as she exited the bedroom and shuffled down the hall where David stood at the front window and looked outside.

CHAPTER FIFTEEN

Charlie was right behind them, and she glanced back as Wendy came up.

"You won't believe this, Mom," she said. "These people just get creepier and creepier."

"That's what I'm hearing." Wendy stood next to David and pulled the old, dusty curtains aside.

"Did he tell you those guys were on the porch last night?"

"Yes. Were they looking in your window?"

"I don't know." Charlie placed her fists on her hips. "I had my lantern off, but I woke up in the middle of the night to Clyde growling by the window. Then there was lightning, and I saw one of them standing there. I don't know if he was looking in, but I couldn't get to sleep after that, so I went up front with David and let him know. Then I sat in the hall by your door with Clyde and my gun. I'm telling you, Mom. Something weird is going on."

Wendy peered outside at some commotion two houses down, one of the better homes she had her eye on to scavenge for supplies, only there was an Amish wagon sitting out front with a couple of people carrying things up the sidewalk to the house. "Is someone moving in over there?"

"That's what I was thinking," David replied. "No one came up to tell us, and I wasn't about to go talk to them."

"No, you did the right thing coming to get me."

Charlie shuddered. "What are we going to do?"

"I don't know. Maybe Smithson put them out here to keep us company."

"Come on. You don't believe that." Charlie's soft blue eyes glanced from Wendy to the window. "You know how these people think they're better than us. We're outsiders, and they're monitoring us."

Wendy started to protest, but Charlie could be right. "If they were moving in as friendly neighbors, they would've come to the door and introduced themselves."

"Exactly. They saw David on the porch, and they were giving him weird looks the whole time."

"Is that true?"

CHAPTER FIFTEEN

David nodded. "I wanted them to know we were here and didn't want them creeping around, but they said nothing and kept moving their stuff in. I even waved to see what they would do, and nothing."

"Well, they may not have answered you, but they're going to answer me." She checked her weapon, hung it from her shoulder, and glanced at the kids. "You guys have my back?"

"Always, Mom." Charlie hugged her. "Do you want to take Clyde with you?"

Wendy looked around to see Clyde sitting by the door, head cocked to the side, floppy ears perked up, tail sweeping back and forth. The dog had filled out well, his ribs no longer showing, muscle bulking his chest and shoulders. There were no more bony spots on his hips, and he'd been running and prancing every time Charlie led him out of the wagon.

"You know what? That's a great idea. I'll take him with me."

Charlie gave her the leash, and Wendy held it in her left hand and cradled her M&P 15 in her right, the magazine fully loaded with thirty rounds, though the rest of her ammunition was with the things Smithson took.

Charlie popped the door, and Wendy stepped out onto the wet porch, moving down the stairs as she watched what was happening across the street. The father was a short man with broad shoulders, a pasty-face, and clean-shaven, head down as he lifted a chair out of the back and walked toward the house. A diminutive redheaded woman wearing a bonnet, who looked about sixteen years old, stepped into his place. She appeared tired, with strands of hair falling around her cheeks. A heavy cape covered her shoulders and was wet where it skimmed the surrounding puddles. She reached into the back of the wagon and retrieved small pieces of furniture and set them on the ground. Wendy's footsteps must've spooked her, because she backed up with a start, hand pressed against her chest. She glanced from Clyde to the rifle to Wendy's eyes.

Wendy nodded and smiled flatly. "Hello, neighbor."

"Oh, hello," the woman gasped. "Sorry for having such a ghastly reaction, but you scared me."

"If I did, I'm sorry," Wendy said honestly. "We just noticed you moving in over here."

CHAPTER FIFTEEN

"That's right. My husband and I..." She turned haltingly and pointed back toward their house. "We accepted Elder Smithson's gift and are moving in today."

"Today of all days? It's raining hard, and you must have already noticed your house needs a lot of work."

"Oh, yes," she laughed nervously. "Elder Smithson let us know all the details, but we'd been planning this for some time and thought we should come on out."

"Because we're here?"

The woman looked taken aback. "Well, no. We were just supposed to move in."

"You said you're married?"

The young woman brightened. "Oh, yes. A year now."

Wendy nodded doubtfully and shifted her eyes as the man walked up the path with a wary expression, taking his supposed wife by the arm and pulling her aside so he could move in front of her. Clyde growled low in his chest, his tail swishing in agitation as he backed up a step. The dog glared at the man but didn't bare his teeth.

The man stared at Wendy darkly with pale eyes that sent a shiver down her spine. His gaze shifted to Clyde. "You need to get that dog under control."

"He's not bothering anyone."

The man stared, then reached inside the wagon to pull out a small table, eyes never leaving Wendy and Clyde as he turned and guided the woman down the pathway. "Not supposed to talk to them, Adele."

"I know, Jed. Sorry."

Wendy called at their backs. "Why aren't you supposed to talk to us? I know you've got these weird rules about outsiders, but it's a little strange..." Her words trailed off as they disappeared inside, the screen door squealing on rusty hinges. She thought about challenging them, demanding to know why they were there and what they wanted, but the way the man had looked at her told her most of what she needed to know, and Clyde's reaction only supported her instincts. Stepping close to the wagon, Wendy peered inside at the assortment of furniture the couple supposedly owned, most of it

CHAPTER FIFTEEN

marked up and dented, two chairs with broken legs, certainly not the type of pieces a young, fruitful married couple would own. It seemed like they'd taken them from a repair shop and thrown them in the wagon.

Wendy waited a full minute for them to come out, and when they didn't, she turned on her heel. "Let's go, Clyde."

When she got inside, the kids crowded around and followed them to the fireplace, where Wendy found a stool and sat, resting her rifle on her knees and rubbing her eyes with both hands. The fire had dwindled, nothing remaining but ashes glowing orange.

"David, can you get the fire started back up?"

Wordlessly, David went to the wood, grabbed a piece, and stepped past Wendy to put it into the fireplace. Charlie sat next to her with her hands held out as if seeking an explanation.

"Well, Mom?" she asked. "What's up with them?"

Wendy picked up a bottled water, twisted off the top, and took a long drink. "They're definitely not married, though they claim to be."

"How do you know?"

"Generally, men in the Amish community stop shaving their beards when they get married. That guy has a baby face, as clean-shaven as they come. And she's all of sixteen, though that might not mean much here."

Wendy patted Clyde on his chest, glancing at his empty plate of food where a few morsels remained with some streaks of gravy. "And Clyde doesn't like them, either. The furniture in their wagon is all beat up, not something a young Amish man would have. Heck, Zach could take two months and build us an entire furniture set when he was younger."

Charlie crossed her arms. "They sent those people to spy on us."

Wendy nodded. "Smithson doesn't trust us, so he sent his patrols out wider and put a couple of guards on us to ensure we stayed out of trouble. I shouldn't be surprised."

"What are we going to do?"

"I don't know, Charlie." Wendy reached for the pouch of smoked meat, took out a piece, and bit off an end, giving the rest to Clyde.

CHAPTER FIFTEEN

"What do you mean you don't know? They stuck us in this hole, and now we are under guard."

"Prisoners," David said as he stirred the fire.

Charlie gestured at her brother. "Who knows what they're going to do next? In case you didn't notice, they're a little strange, and the only reason they've put up with us this far is because of Morten and Alma."

"I know, and you're right. But think about the options we have."

"Let's just leave," Charlie said, her voice growing more plaintive with every word.

"And abandon Morten and your aunt? I know things are bad, but they've been bad since all this started. We have to consider our options."

"Like what?"

"While this isn't perfect, at least there are guards in the field, and at least two more of Smithson's people are here in case anybody attacks the enclave from this direction. What if this isn't as creepy as you think, and Smithson is just doing what he normally would've done, anyway?"

David and Charlie got quiet before David spoke up. "They barely gave us anything to eat. We could probably do better out there on the road scavenging."

Charlie nodded. "Right? I think so, too."

Wendy shook her head. "I don't know about that." When she looked at the kids, her eyes were watering, the pressure building until tears streamed out. "I get what you're saying, and I'm not negating your opinions. But think about all the people we passed on the way here, washed out of their homes, listless victims preying on each other and looking for a safe place just to sleep. I don't want to end up like them, wandering the streets, trying to find a place to live."

She gestured at the fireplace and the hallway to the bedrooms. "This place isn't great, but it's a roof over our heads, and there's a fire. That's something we have to appreciate."

They fell quiet and Charlie gazed at her mother as David finished with the fire and began to pace the hardwood floor. Eventually, he

CHAPTER FIFTEEN

shook his head and announced, "I'm going downstairs to see if there's anything we can use."

"I'm on watch," Wendy raised her hand. "Charlie, you need to–"

"I can't sleep, Mom," she said with a vigorous head shake. "Seriously, did you think I could sleep with those creeps out there?"

"Take Clyde into David's bedroom. There's a side window, but it's got curtains. Use a blanket to cover it if it's still not dark enough." When Charlie only sat and stared at her, she shot her a motherly glare. "I'm serious, Charlie. You need to get some sleep."

"Mom —"

"No, Charlie." Wendy swung her legs around, facing her daughter, and taking one of her hands. "Listen. You need to get some rest. Give me some time to think, okay? We're right here, and no one will hurt you." Wendy raised the M&P 15 and gave it a little shake. "I've got more firepower in my hand than those guys have out there, so don't worry. And Clyde..." Wendy nodded at the dog as he followed the conversation, his tail wagging with curiosity and excitement the second Wendy mentioned his name. "You were right about Clyde all along. He's a good dog, and I'm glad we got him. He'll protect you."

Charlie sat back and absently rubbed Clyde's head, scratching between his ears with long, dirty fingernails and causing the dog to go into a fit with his rear leg. The girl laughed and reached down to hug him, and when she shifted back to Wendy, her eyes were moist with fearful emotion.

"Okay, Mom," she said. "I'll do my best, but I can't guarantee anything."

"I love you, honey." Wendy stood and kissed Charlie's forehead.

"Love you, too, Mom."

Wendy walked to the front window, watching the neighbors as they continued moving things into their house. The pair didn't seem to speak much, nor were there any other Amish people there to help, which was odd considering the Amish community's work ethic.

"Not being very Amish," she murmured.

With Charlie going to bed, Wendy turned and strolled to the back of the house, glancing into David's room to see Charlie roll beneath her covers with Clyde at her side, the dog watching her until

CHAPTER FIFTEEN

she got comfortable before he lay down and rested a paw on her leg. Grinning, Wendy walked to Charlie's room and stood by the window, staring into the perpetual dusk with the cloudy skies and constant rainfall, the fat drops striking the roof. Leaning against the wall, Wendy put her hand on the glass and stared into the midday mist, the flooded yard, the barns and structures with water stains six to ten inches up the sides.

Pieces of wood and shingles lay in the wet grass, probably blown off when the winds were rougher. After thirty minutes of standing there, Wendy was about to turn away when a pair of shadows walked across the lawn, splashing through the water out in the open, barely glancing toward the house as they stopped by one barn, lit cigarettes, and smoked. David's words rang in her mind, suggesting they were prisoners in their own loaned home. Wendy tried to imagine living with the guards every day, always under the watchful eyes of the Amish and Smithson. Her skin turned hot as she grew more aggravated. She had a son and a young daughter in the house, surrounded by people who didn't like them and likely would control them rather than allow Wendy enough agency to protect their interests. They were squeezed in and trapped, and they'd only been there less than twenty-four hours.

Exiting the back bedroom, Wendy walked down the hall and found the basement door. She opened it to a set of steep stairs and a narrow passage angling downward. The musty smell was even worse, though David's lantern light added some warmth to an otherwise creepy view.

"David? Are you down there?"

"Yeah, Mom. I'm here."

"Good. I'm coming down."

"Be careful. The stairs are wet."

Wendy descended slowly, some steps worn and angled downward, making them extra slick. With both hands on the wall, she reached the floor to stand in three inches of water.

"Anything good down here?"

"A lot of old junk, mostly," he replied from across the room where he was going through some shelves. "A lot of old tools and stuff."

CHAPTER FIFTEEN

"Any food?" She picked her way over, stepping carefully to the least flooded parts, noting that the water was worse on the north side of the house under the front porch, one-inch cracks running up the walls and water bugs scattering in the lantern light.

"Two burlap sacks full of oats and rice, but it looks like mice ate through it."

"Gross."

Wendy stepped up behind him and leaned in to peer at the items. It was an old wooden shelf, sturdy, mostly bare except for the mouse-ridden grain sacks and a few coffee cans with screws and bolts inside. David picked up his lantern, shifted to the side where it rested on the second to top shelf, and gave Wendy a little room.

She stepped closer and looked deep into the shelves, squinting, sniffing at the mustiness in the air, and spotting something that caught her attention way in the back. Reaching in, she drew a box to the edge of the shelf, coughing and waving her hand in front of her face to clear the dust. She stood on her toes to peer in, finding several decorative ceramic candleholders and knickknacks. Pushing them aside, she uncovered a dozen candles of various sizes and colors, greens and purples and pastel whites.

"Hey, maybe Charlie will feel better if I liven the place up a bit."

"I doubt it," David replied, still looking around, "but you can try."

Wendy picked up the box and carried it to the foot of the stairs, turning back to David. "Don't be long down here. I can't imagine there's much else we can use, but if you find any candles or flashlights, bring them up."

"You got it, Mom."

Wendy marched upstairs with her decorations, turning to her left to listen to Charlie's weeping from the other room. With a sad heart, she walked into the living room and looked around at the dusty floors and leaking walls, still surprised that how hastily and poorly the Amish had maintained the house.

"Okay, Wendy, interior decorator." She took a deep breath and blew a raspberry between her lips. "Let's see if you can make this place livable."

CHAPTER FIFTEEN

The room glowed with warm candlelight, lending a soft texture to the harsh walls, penetrating the shadows and casting off the cold wetness in the air. She'd tidied up a bit, finding some old rags in a cabinet beneath the sink, dusting the counters and tables. Without water to clean, the place would have to stay mostly dirty for a while. It was midday, but it was as gloomy as early evening, with the dense cloud cover still filling the sky with shades of gray and black hues, jagged shapes in the lower atmosphere descending into a mist like a child had scribbled crayons across the horizon. Wendy stood in front of the fire with her arms crossed and her rifle leaning against the hearth, alternating walking to the window and watching the neighbors as they finished moving in and pulling their wagon into a small barn behind the place. Soft illumination seeped from their windows, though it did nothing to warm the chill in Wendy's heart.

David stood watch in the last room of the house, monitoring the Amish guards as they walked by. There were the two from earlier, but those numbers had grown to six in total, though Wendy couldn't tell them apart in the gloom. The original agreement had been for Wendy and the kids to ring the bell if intruders attacked them, yet the more she mulled it, the more she realized David and Charlie were probably right. They were being watched, monitored, tracked, whatever she wanted to call it, though it all amounted to them being prisoners. Morten's word should have been enough to earn some modicum of trust within the community, but it wasn't. Releasing a thin breath of air between her lips, Wendy walked back to the stool and sat in front of the roaring flames, reaching for a piece of wood and tossing it in. A moment later, shuffling feet got her attention, and she turned to see Charlie entering the room with a dusty blanket around her shoulders, hair back with strands coming loose from her ponytail and hanging in her face. Clyde walked next to her, licking his chops as she sat in an old lawn chair facing the fire.

"Oh, hey, Charlie. Did you get any sleep?"

"No, not at all. I'll never sleep again. Not with those guys out

CHAPTER FIFTEEN

there."

Wendy started to say it wasn't that bad, but she wasn't in Charlie's head and couldn't imagine what she must've been thinking when the men were looking in on her. "Well, you can try later, huh?" When Charlie didn't answer, Wendy glanced around the place with a half-smile. "I tidied up a bit and lit some candles. What do you think?"

Charlie sighed. "Clyde's hungry... do we have anything for him?"

Wendy nodded and leaned to her left to grab the sack Morten had given them, pulling it close and looking inside. "We have two cans of dog food. I'll open a can for him now and save the other one for later. In fact, we could all stand to eat something. There are canned vegetables and cured meat, plus —"

"I'm not hungry, but I wanted to make sure Clyde got some food."

"Sure, honey. Let me see if I can find a can opener."

Wendy carried the dog food into the kitchen, going through the drawers and cabinets and looking for utensils, eliciting a sigh of frustration when there were none. "Do you believe this place?"

"See, Mom. How are we going to get the cans open?" Charlie asked, rubbing Clyde between his ears. "This place is terrible, and I'd be surprised if they even bring tus food tomorrow. We're reliant on them for everything right now, just like —"

"Enough, Charlie," Wendy replied with an angry edge.

"We don't have a choice. That doesn't sound like the mom I know talking."

Wendy marched over to her chair and kneeled in front of her, resting one hand on her knee and the dog food on the arm of her chair, staring up at Charlie's surly, sour face. "Look, missy. You're not the only one who doesn't want to be here. I'm tired of seeing you kids in danger. All I wanted was a night or two to be under a roof and..." Wendy shook her head, eyes turning moist as frustration swelled inside her. "Keep you safe."

"You do keep us safe, Mom." Charlie leaned forward, spreading the blanket and putting her hands over Wendy's. Her soft blue eyes stirred with turbulence, an uneasy expression she wasn't used to seeing on her daughter's face. "You did great keeping us alive through

CHAPTER FIFTEEN

the hurricane and the cold spell, and now it's nothing but storms and rain and floods. Tornadoes, too. And I know we're supposed to stay here and wait for Dad, but something in my gut tells me we need to keep moving. It's not ideal, but —"

"We may need to change our way of thinking," Wendy said, nodding, flipping her free hand to hold Charlie's. "It already crossed my mind, and I can't stop thinking about what might be out there. Some abandoned house or barn to hole up in for a while. A place that's ours, and we can come and go freely. It's got to be better than being in the line of fire should someone attack the Amish."

"Exactly," Charlie replied with a brightening expression. "At least we'd be in control of things. I'd be worried about Grandpa and Aunt Alma, but we can't help if they choose their people over us."

Wendy pursed her lips and nodded, squeezing Charlie's hand. "I'll tell you what. Let's see if David can tell if there's been a pattern in the patrols. Maybe we can pack up what we have..." Wendy glanced around and settled on the sacK Morten had given them. "Which amounts to nothing, and trek on down the road a bit. We can walk a few miles and search for a new place, and if we don't find anything by tomorrow evening, we can always come back and sneak in."

"Won't they know?"

Wendy shrugged. "We'll leave some candles burning, so they'll think we're still inside. That should keep them satisfied for one night, and we'll have to hope we get lucky walking around. On the way in, we saw a lot of farmsteads and houses."

Charlie rose in her seat and rubbed Clyde's head vigorously. "We saw a bunch up in the hills and nestled in the fields. There were even some barns that would be better than this. Do you mean it, Mom? Are we leaving soon?"

Wendy glanced out the front window. "Might want to get out of here while the getting is good. But we should wait until evening anyway, so let's hold tight until then, okay?"

"Sure, Mom. Okay!" Charlie started to get up but sat back. "I was going to pack up our things, but I guess we don't have much."

"David found some garbage bags downstairs, so maybe we can make some rainproof hoods since Smithson took the rest of our

CHAPTER FIFTEEN

things." Wendy looked around. "They're over on the kitchen counter. In the meantime, I'll bust some of these cans open, and we'll have a meal before we leave."

"Some calories for the journey," Charlie nodded as she stood and started into the kitchen before pausing. "How are you going to do that?"

"Something your father taught me when we were camping one day. I just need a rock."

Charlie's eyebrows wrinkled. "Um, okay, Mom. There are some rocks in the garden off the front porch."

Wendy smiled, doing her best to hide the stirring emotions in her gut, the uncertainty of what might happen the second they walked out that door. Yet, she couldn't guarantee their safety where they were.

With Charlie busy, Wendy took the dog food and a couple of cans of vegetables and placed them aside. Then she went outside in search of a rock.

Sweeping rain rattled off the roof, falling in waves again, heavy drops pounding the old shingles and dripping through new cracks in the walls, trickles of moisture pooled around the baseboards. Lightning exploded outside, growing from an occasional spark of light in the sky to a repeated series of sharp bursts ushering in rolling thunder and winds that gusted across the roofs in shrieking voices, whistling as if in warning of what they were about to do.

Charlie had fallen asleep on the floor in front of the fire amid a pile of blankets and old pillows they'd found, Clyde curled up beside her with one paw resting on her leg, his baleful eyes watching David and Wendy as they switched positions at the front and back of the house, meeting in the middle and exchanging information.

"I've got the pattern down now, Mom," he said on their last pass. "Looks like three groups of men spaced thirty minutes apart, give or take a few minutes. That should give us plenty of time to get past them."

CHAPTER FIFTEEN

"Seems that way," Wendy shrugged and scratched her head. "Unfortunately, we don't know how far they are going or if they're hiding in one of those sheds. If they see us leaving, they might come after us."

"Then again, they might not." David scoffed. "They didn't want us here, so why would they care if we get up and leave?"

"You've got a point, son. Still, let's try to avoid any confrontations if we can."

David glanced at Charlie. "Should we wake her up?"

Wendy didn't have a watch to tell how close it was to midnight. It felt late, and any semblance of daylight had long ago faded. "I'll wake her up now. Please light a few candles and place them around the house."

David nodded and went off to do it, and Wendy kneeled by Charlie, closing her eyes against the warmth radiating from the fire, reluctant to leave what little peace and safety they'd achieved after the long trek from Stamford. She patted Clyde's side and gave her daughter a gentle shake.

"Honey, it's time to go. Come on, baby. Get your boots on. Your brother and I are ready."

Charlie rolled over with a groggy expression. "So, you decided we're going to do it?"

"I was going to make it work, but I don't think we can. This place is moldy and bug infested, and I don't know who to be more afraid of, Smithson's people or the ones who attacked them when we arrived. No, we're getting out of here right now. Come on, get your boots on. Let's go." She gave the girl a slap on the leg and stood as the room grew brighter with candlelight.

"It's probably not a positive thought..." David finished with the candles, put the lighter in his pocket, and checked his holstered weapon. "But I wouldn't be upset if one of these candles fell over and burned the place down. Not that it would happen with all this rain."

"Let's keep the energy level positive, huh?" Wendy hugged David and guided him toward the back door, then turned to see Charlie finish lacing her boots and standing.

CHAPTER FIFTEEN

"Come on, Clyde. Time to put your poncho on."

While they'd been sitting there bored, Charlie had fashioned him a doggy-style poncho with holes to put his head and front legs through. The long end laid back over his flanks and legs to leave his tail sticking out and wagging to the sound of rustling plastic. Wendy covered her mouth and stifled an uncontrollable giggle. "I didn't think Clyde would let you put it on him."

"Look at that tail, Mom. He's just as excited to get out of this dump as we are. Let's go."

They walked to the rear of the house, keeping to the sides of the hallway and stopping at the back door, where they looked out the window into the voracious storm. The flooded yard stretched off to a thick tree line on the left, and the road continued west into nowhere. The wind ripped branches from the trees and tossed them through the air, where they struck the house and skimmed across the ponds that had formed everywhere.

"Looks like we picked a bad time to leave," Charlie said. "The storm's not letting up anytime soon."

"It might be a perfect time, too," Wendy replied. "Those guards won't want to deal with this weather, and if they're out in a shed or standing nearby, I doubt they'll raise their heads long enough to look for us. David, when was the last time they were by?"

"About thirty minutes ago, and they'll be back any time now."

They waited for the patrol to pass, then peeked through the glass, Wendy's gaze shifting from off to the right where the barns and sheds were. The structures sat in a lake that had gotten so deep the grass only stuck above the surface a few inches. Wendy dreaded having to run through that to get to the road. Shadows played tricks on her eyes, and it was nearly impossible to tell if anything was moving in the ever-shifting patterns of mist and rain. Charlie stood between them, ducked low with her hands on the glass, stiffening suddenly as if she'd spotted something.

"Is that them, guys?" she asked, pressing her finger against the glass at a pair of dark forms moving off to their right.

Wendy put her hand on Charlie's shoulder and pushed her away from the window so the girl wouldn't be seen. Sure enough, two

CHAPTER FIFTEEN

shapes were trudging through the darkness, boots splashing in the shin-high water, their coats whipping around their legs as they ducked into the wind. Gesturing for David to get back, the trio slunk into the shadows to keep the living room light from giving them away. They didn't need to hide because the Amish guards walked straight on by without a single glance at the house, plodding down a gentle slope to the tree line, climbing a rail fence there, and moving across to the other side to disappear into the night.

"Let's go," Charlie said, grabbing the doorknob and pushing past David to get outside.

When she threw open the door, howling winds burst into the hallway, throwing rain into their faces as it knocked them back. Before she could tell Charlie to stop, the girl rushed through with Clyde's leash in her hand. She made it two steps with Wendy and David on her heels when a monstrous shape appeared at the bottom of the porch steps, the billowing coat and wide-brimmed hat pulled tight over the man's hawkish features, his white beard flipping back and forth on his chin. Clyde erupted in a fit of savage growls and barks, his paws splayed in front of them, head low as he snapped. Wendy grabbed Charlie by the jacket and hauled her backward so her shoulders smacked into the door frame. An instant later, Wendy raised her rifle and pointed at his chest with her finger moving inside the trigger guard ready to squeeze off a shot. Rain whipped into her face, her homemade plastic hood flapping against her cheeks. Just as she was applying pressure to the trigger, the man lifted his hand, palm out.

"Hold on, Wendy! Don't shoot. It's me, Morten!"

Wendy blinked at the big man and lowered her weapon, sputtering as she exploded on him. "What are you doing out here? I almost shot you!"

"I apologize, Wendy, but I had to make sure none of Smithson's men saw me!" Morten shouted above the rain, then motioned to the house. "Let's go inside a moment, and I'll explain."

Nodding, Wendy backed off and gestured for the kids to go inside, where she came behind them with Morten following with

CHAPTER FIFTEEN

heavy steps. David pulled the door shut, and they stood in the hallway, dripping and shivering from the brief burst of chilly rain.

"What were you doing, Wendy?" Morten said, forced to duck in the crowded passage. "The storm is terrible tonight."

Wendy fixed him with a stern look, uncertain she should tell him what they were up to, especially since he might be working with Smithson to keep the family close. Then she remembered his support of her marriage to Zach and the trouble he'd gone through to fight to get his community to accept her begrudgingly.

"We're getting out of here, Morten. We appreciate what you've done for us, but we don't trust them. Smithson put guards on us and moved some people in across the road. They're shifty, and they barely spoke a word to me when I tried to talk to them. It's just... weird."

"We can find someplace better down the road, Grandpa," David added, standing a few inches shorter than his grandfather, though he lacked his bulk. "We can't stay here. Two of them came to the back porch window and scared Charlie."

Morten looked between the three of them, nodding his understanding. "It is as I feared. When I returned from getting you settled out here, I was told to return to Smithson's, where I was grilled before a small group of elders. They asked me to do things I didn't want to."

Wendy's jaw clenched, and she stepped forward with narrowed eyes. "Like what?"

Morten scoffed and wiped the rainwater off his chin. "They spoke about Charlie and David, specifically. Smithson was interested in knowing if I might influence the children to learn more of our ways."

"What's that supposed to mean, Grandpa?" Charlie asked.

"Well, they wanted to know if David could attend some of our religious meetings and be swayed to join the community."

"And what about me?" Charlie pressed.

"He, um... he asked what your interest might be in joining the women to learn our ways and marry into the community."

"Marrying an Amish guy?" Charlie was more confused than ever, though it quickly dawned on her what he was saying, and her face

CHAPTER FIFTEEN

twisted up with disgust. "No thank you, Grandpa. No offense, but that's the last thing on my mind right now."

"Yeah, Grandpa. I'm not joining the Amish and growing one of those weird beards. No offense... yours looks pretty cool."

"No offense taken." Morten laughed. "I told them the very same thing. I explained that you hadn't grown up in the community and would struggle to get used to our way of life. Still, they pressed on and threatened what might happen if an arrangement couldn't be made."

"What about me?" Wendy asked, one hand on her hip, rifle pointed at the floor. "Do they have any big plans for *me*?"

Morten smiled in the flickering candlelight. "No, Wendy. I'm afraid they fear you're a lost cause, but they might've tolerated you here if they could sway the kids to join them."

"We were about to leave anyway," Charlie said with a hint of anger. "And how dare they talk about marrying me off to one of their guys! I'm only fourteen."

Wendy silenced Charlie with a glance and turned back to Morten. "If you're here to talk us into something, I'm warning you—"

"Quite the opposite, I assure you," he said with a humble bow. "The opposite is true. I was hoping you hadn't gotten too comfortable here because I came to suggest that you move down the road a bit. Farmsteads line the highway, and even more are up in the hills. While many of them will be occupied, there may be several warmer places to live than this doghouse they put you into." Morten looked anguished, hands on his hips and shoulders trembling. "I'm sorry, Wendy. I thought they would welcome all of us with open arms, but I was wrong. You must hate me."

Wendy's disgruntled expression faded, and her anxious rage was replaced by love for the man, who'd only ever fought for them. With a relieved sigh, she stepped forward and locked arms with him. "Don't apologize, Dad. I should've known you wouldn't betray us, even though you could have many times."

"I would never abandon you," Morten replied gruffly with tears gleaming in the candlelight. "While others may not see it as I do, I've come to understand you are a blessing to us through the light of the Lord, and I'd die before I let anyone hurt you."

David and Charlie stepped in and wrapped their arms around them, clinging to Morten's slim form and bony arms, and Wendy smiled and basked in the warmth for a moment, the smell of the old man's musty coat drenched with rainwater. Releasing him, she stepped back and gestured to the door. "We should go now. The patrol will return in what...?"

"We've got about fifteen minutes, Mom," David replied.

"I timed them as well," Morten said. "I had to maintain secrecy and didn't want them to report to Smithson that I'd been here to help you."

"Help us? Aren't you just here to warn us?"

"No indeed, daughter." Morten's grin grew wide and pleased. "I ran across some supplies they'd taken from us and brought you three backpacks full of your food and supplies, as well as most of your ammunition and two more pistols you left with us."

Wendy looked around in confusion. "Where?"

"I drove my wagon on the back roads and parked a bit down the highway, and everything's in back. Just follow me."

The four descended into the night storm with high winds striking at them from every direction, water splashing off their ponchos and into their faces as they trudged through the veritable lake surrounding the property. Heads down and plodding forward, David, Charlie, and Wendy held hands with Clyde coming last at the end of his leash. They walked fast to keep up with Morten's wide steps, using his height as a shield as they moved toward the road. Through the stormy gale, Wendy glanced around for the Amish guards and saw that the candles they'd lit gave off a warm light from the house windows like someone was home. Passing through the tree line, getting tangled on stickers and brittle brush, they climbed the fence and landed in a stream of water running alongside the road. Charlie handed Clyde over to David, and the boy shuffled up a bank to the buckling pavement half washed out from the storms.

They splashed through shallow puddles into the thick gloom, with lightning cracking above them to cast their way ahead in stark

CHAPTER FIFTEEN

but brief light flashes. Soon, Wendy saw the squarish shape of one of Morten's wagons, the canvas flaps blowing in the breeze, the horses standing there dripping with their heads down and looking miserable. They stopped at the rear of the wagon with Morten releasing the tailgate and climbing up.

"Poor Marley and Fitzpatrick," Charlie said, moving past them with Clyde trotting behind her. She patted the horses' sides and necks, circling to grab their harnesses and pull their muzzles close. They chuffed, snorted, and nuzzled Charlie's shoulders and head, pushing the girl around until she was laughing. "Poor babies can never get out of this rain."

"Don't worry, Charlie," Morten called from inside the wagon. "As soon as I have you situated, I'll put them away where they're dry and warm. Don't worry too much."

"Come get your backpack, Charlie!" Wendy said as she peered around the rear of the wagon.

"Okay, Mom."

Charlie kissed the horses and brought Clyde to the back, where Wendy gave her a backpack bulging with food and supplies. David was shrugging his on when Morten handed hers to her, and she placed her rifle on the tailgate and put it on, loving the weight of it settling on her shoulders and the simple freedom of having their own provisions.

"There you go," Morten said, then raised his finger as if suddenly remembering something. "Oh, and there's these." He handed down a rag with two pistols inside, and Wendy took them and put them in David's backpack, along with several ammunition boxes.

"This is awesome, Morten," she said, buckling the pack flap and peering up at him. "We thought we'd be stuck in that house with nothing to eat or drink, dependent on Smithson for supplies. After what you just told us, I can believe he'd use it as leverage to keep us under his thumb."

Morten was standing in the back, arms crossed and nodding. "Unfortunately, some elements of our flock would force our beliefs on others, but I've always believed a man or woman can only find their way through self-reflection and the learnings of time. If you and

CHAPTER FIFTEEN

Zach ever wanted to join our faith, you would have done it long ago. That doesn't mean I don't love you all."

Wendy reached up and took his hand, smiling into the rain as it dripped from the back of the wagon into her face. "I know, Dad. Thank you for everything. We'll be down the road, I think." Wendy looked west with uncertainty.

"You'll find a small can of paint in David's backpack. Just mark W, D, and C on a sidewalk or side of the house, and we'll know you're nearby."

"Okay. We'll do that for certain." Wendy grabbed the kids and pulled them close to the tailgate. Morten knelt and leaned forward, embracing them as one with his long arms. They held each other for a long moment, and then Morten grunted and struggled to rise, gripping his back with a laugh.

"I'm a little stiff with all this rain. I must be getting old."

"You've got a lot of years ahead of you," Wendy smiled. "You be safe, Dad."

"You, too, Wendy. You kids take care of your mother."

"We will, Grandpa," David said, gripping his arm and squeezing.

"Tell Aunt Alma that we love her," Charlie added with a smile, water dripping from her hair and chin.

"Will do."

Wendy backed away from the wagon and pulled the kids around, and with no idea where they were going to go, Wendy led them past the horses and walked westward into the night.

CHAPTER SIXTEEN

Stephanie Lancaster, Washington, DC

The conference room was cool and dry, and Stephanie had donned a sweater provided by a staffer as she continued to pour over weather data to help guide and strengthen the country's supply lines. They had it down to a science, working with multiple internal team leaders in refugee camps across the United States, many hanging by a thread as they faced outside threats and kept civilians calm. They'd gotten ahead by rerouting supplies, guarding the highways, and stopping marauders. The mental toll on the refugees was showing as the days wore on. Fights broke out inside camps where people were packed by the dozens into large tents with rickety cots. The refugees were soft, not used to roughing it in the wilderness or battling for their survival every day. Priests and psychologists were in high demand as they made rounds through the camps to restore faith and hope to those who'd lost it. And while Stephanie was aware of how hard life had become for them, she pushed aside her emotions and focused on what was in her control.

"Correct, Genevieve. I've got two big storms descending on you guys, completely independent of each other, with southwesterly

CHAPTER SIXTEEN

winds reaching fifty-five to sixty miles per hour. Not hurricane speeds, but enough to tear up some of your tents and equipment and carry them off to the coast."

"All the same," Genevieve replied over the crackling connection, her face on the video screen wavering and freezing every few seconds. "It'll make a lot of people around here nervous, but we'll keep them busy battening everything down."

"Smart thinking."

"Any idea on when all this will start dying down?"

Stephanie closed her eyes, fingers hovering over the keyboard, shaking from lack of sleep and too much caffeine, and she squeezed them into fists to steady her nerves. Opening her eyes, she scanned the three screens in front of her, depicting various weather stations across the nation to provide a complete picture of the ongoing crisis. She'd even had time to look into Canada and Mexico, which were worse in many ways. The Gulfstream had become increasingly disturbed and agitated by the domino effect from the Alaskan Rift. Much of the warm water they would typically expect to see heading north in the spring and summer simply wasn't there, and colder temperatures were creeping across the Northern Hemisphere by the hour. Anything north of Baltimore was freezing up again, and that wouldn't bode well for anyone still alive up there.

Her contact with the President's scientific team, Jerrick Nilsen, had suggested to Holland that they start an evacuation of the affected cities to the south when he'd found out the news. The thought of millions of people making a journey on highways washed out and shattered by the rainstorms across the Midwest and East Coast gave Stephanie a miserable, hopeless feeling that threatened to overwhelm her. And the places that needed those warm currents, like the British Isles and some of Northern Europe and Iceland, weren't getting them. Stephanie rubbed her hand down her face as if she could wash the information away.

"Are you okay, Stephanie?"

Stephanie shook herself out of it. "Sorry Genevieve. I'm good. I was pouring over this data to get an answer for you, but there's just nothing I can say that's going to make you feel any better. There are some small signs that weather patterns are fighting to return to normal, driven by the Earth's rotation, but the hydrocarbon disruptions are making it too difficult to recover. What's the temperature like there? Does it feel like it's getting any colder?"

Through the flickering screen, she caught Genevieve's doubtful expression. "Why? Should it be?"

"I'm just asking because we're seeing some disruption of the Gulfstream, which might make it a little chilly for you."

"Great. Just what we wanted to hear."

Stephanie winced. "I'm sorry. Just so you're aware, if things get cold, you should be prepared to move the entire campus out."

"Are you kidding me? Can't they provide heating units to fight the cold?"

"That's not for me to answer, but someone in supply could. I just heard from Jerrick Nilsen that he's suggesting moving as many people south as possible."

"There are over two hundred thousand people in this camp," Genevieve said flatly, "and it's growing all the time. We finally developed a good screening process, and now we might have to move."

"It's out of our control. You don't want to be caught in a deep freeze like New York was. I hear it was brutal, and the death toll..." Stephanie couldn't even mention it.

Someone slammed a cup down, and Stephanie jolted in her seat, shifting to where Davies was standing by the coffee urns, scolding one of the Pentagon staffers who wore the gray uniform of an attendant. The Colonel's left hand was working the urn handle obnoxiously as coffee dripped onto the table, and he turned his cup upside down to show it was empty.

"The world's flipped on its head, and I can't even get a cup of coffee?" Davies glared at her.

"I'm sorry, sir," the staffer said, her frightened expression looking up from the other side where she was picking up one urn with shaking hands. She hugged it to her chest and turned to carry it around to a door that led to the kitchen and food prep area that served the entire Pentagon sub levels.

CHAPTER SIXTEEN

"We need both filled pronto, understand me?" Davies flipped his mug onto the table, where it clattered around and rolled to a stop.

"Yes, sir. I'll have that for you right away."

At first, the staffer couldn't get the door open with her arms occupied, but one of the communication team got up and came to her assistance, grabbing the door and holding it so she could go through. As the door closed behind her, Davies scoffed and returned to his place at the conference.

Lips pursed in sympathy for the girl, Stephanie shifted back to Genevieve. "Genevieve, that should do it for my update for you. I've got to go."

Stephanie ended the call, stood, and moved off to her left, shooting Davies a furious glare as he crossed on the opposite side of the table. He caught her look and softened, but Stephanie only shook her head and continued picking up the remaining empty urn, lifting it from its stand, and shuffling to the door. Grabbing the knob, she walked back to get it open, caught it with her foot, and flipped it wide enough to pass through, taking three steps down the long dark hallway that led deeper into the facility, glancing past supply rooms, restrooms, janitorial closets, and finally the kitchen. With a sharp left, she nudged the door open and entered a large kitchen area with shelves full of big ketchup containers, tomatoes, corn, and many other goods.

On the far side were industrial-sized, stainless-steel stoves with big ovens beneath them. A handful of people went about their business, one cook in the very back with a few of the serving staff. Stephanie moved to the left, looking around the urn to find the woman off to the right at prep tables with massive brewers where the coffee urns fit. The staffer had just placed her urn beneath the brewer and was digging out scoops of coffee into a filter when she turned to see Stephanie.

With a flush of embarrassment, she said, "Oh, Miss Lancaster. You didn't have to do that."

"The hell I didn't. Colonel Davies was acting like a child , and I don't care that he outranks me." With a definitive nod, Stephanie slammed the urn down with authority and pushed it into a locked

CHAPTER SIXTEEN

position beneath a second brewer. "Now, how does this thing work?"

"It's pretty easy," the staffer replied, grabbing another filter and scooping coffee into it. "You just put five scoops in here, flip out the basket, and put it in. Then just hit the red button, and the machine does the rest." She crossed her arms, leaned her hip against the table, and grinned.

"Well done. Too bad we could be court-martialed if we put something in the Colonel's drink."

The staffer covered her mouth to stifle a giggle. "Oh, my. I haven't laughed in days. Thanks for that. I'm Laney. Laney Dixon." The young woman looked to be in her late twenties, with light brown skin and a thick bush of curly hair pulled back in clips to keep the wild locks under control.

"Nice to meet you, Laney." Stephanie crossed her arms to mirror her new friend. "We've been down here for days and never met."

"Weeks, actually." Laney corrected her.

"You knew my name, but I didn't get yours. Sorry about that."

"It's not your fault. We started with so many people it would've been impossible for you to get all our names."

"Speaking of which..." Stephanie turned and looked around. "You seem a little understaffed here."

"Yeah, a lot of people took off home."

"Are they allowed to do that?"

"When our manager found out what was happening outside with people trying to get in, he offered to let everyone go home. I guess he got wind of a few people slipping out and figured it would happen, anyway."

"How are they slipping out?"

"I guess you know about all the catacombs beneath the building and around the area. They lead to exits all around town, and I guess people are using them to bolt."

"You mean, the ones that lead to the motor pools and garages?"

"Those, and some that connect to other buildings around town. You wouldn't believe how many ways there are to get out of here."

"You didn't want to go?"

CHAPTER SIXTEEN

"Sure, I did, but they couldn't provide escorts for us. We'd be on our own. And after seeing how crazy people were acting outside, there was no way I was going to drive out in my Honda. My family lives out in the suburbs west of the capital. A place called Luray. Not too far, but..."

"I know right where it is," Stephanie stated flatly. "You didn't want to go it alone."

"I figure it'll take a lot for those people to break in, and how much safer could we possibly be? I mean, we're surrounded by military."

Stephanie nodded but thought about the thousands of citizens pressing up to the barricades on the external cameras, and she wondered if Davies knew the staff manager was allowing his employees to leave. "Do you need any help? Is there something you need to get done right away that you're behind on?"

"Everything," Laney gestured in exasperation. "There are three other staff rooms we're working on, almost seventy people here on the sublevel we're serving, and they all need coffee."

"Coffee delivery it is."

They filled the first two urns, carried them to a rolling cart, and drove it down to the main conference room. Davies gave Stephanie a guilty look from the head of the table as she and Laney muscled the heavy urns into position and refreshed the sugar and creamers. Returning to the kitchen, they brewed up two more big urns and carried them to a second space where military officers were buzzing around a table filled with communication gear, their faces bathed in the glow of laptop screens. After that, Laney took Stephanie back into the supply room, a warehouse-sized space with rows of goods that reached the ceiling.

"Wow."

"I know." Laney glanced around with a smile before grabbing big cans of vegetables from a shelf and placing them on her cart as Stephanie wheeled it behind her down the row. "You could feed an army for a couple of years with all the stuff. That's another reason some of us don't want to leave. There is food here, and it feels safe, right?"

CHAPTER SIXTEEN

Stephanie raised her eyebrows. "Mostly, I'd agree. The crowd outside..."

Laney stopped working and fixed her with a stare. "What? What's up with the crowd?"

"They've been growing crazier by the hour, and with the President being whisked away..."

"That was pretty creepy." Laney placed a final can of vegetables on the cart, grabbed the front handle, and wheeled it to the cold storage area with Stephanie helping to push it. "Kind of made me feel like we got abandoned."

"It was just protocol," Stephanie shook her head. "I'm sure the President didn't want to leave us, but he didn't have a choice."

"That's what our manager said earlier. But with the crowds getting crazier, how long do you think we can hold out here?"

Stephanie shrugged. "It's the Pentagon, so I thought forever, but maybe not."

Over the next thirty minutes, Stephanie took a break from her responsibilities and helped Laney get caught up, delivering urns of coffee and bringing supplies to the two remaining chefs. The rooms had thinned out and the hallways were empty, and it wasn't long before they stopped to take a break and steal a couple of pieces of chocolate cheesecake from the freezers, giggling and laughing between the quiet rows as they ate.

"I haven't done this since my first job in a kitchen when I was eighteen," Stephanie said. "Ah, the days of my youth."

"I'm on my third piece today." Laney shrugged. "I might as well indulge in the good stuff before things get worse."

"Not a bad idea, actually. What's next?"

Laney finished her last bite and put her plate on a shelf. "That's it. I'm all caught up for now. Thanks so much for helping me get this stuff taken care of, especially when you've got way more important things to do."

"I needed a break anyway. And if you need anything, ask. I'd be happy to help."

"I don't think I'll need it, considering how empty it's getting." Laney glanced around. "But I'll ask if I do."

CHAPTER SIXTEEN

Stephanie was about to turn away when Laney suddenly embraced her. Stephanie hugged her back, closing her eyes amidst the warmth and embrace of another human being, as fleeting as it was, surprised when tears streamed down her face.

Breaking off, she nodded. "Thanks. I really needed a hug."

Laney laughed and wiped at her eyes. "Me, too. Catch you later."

"Bye."

Stephanie returned to the conference room, noticing how empty the place was with at least two other officers missing and a handful of communication specialists gone, though Jack Brown remained dutifully at his post and gave her a wave as she came in. Stephanie waved back and sat, meeting Davies' eyes, where he looked at her from the head of the table.

"Everything okay?" he asked.

"Everything's fine," Stephanie replied. "Just a little short-staffed around here suddenly."

With a dark look, Davies nodded and returned to his job of monitoring the situation outside and communicating with the officers seated at the table. Stephanie did the same, falling into her usual routine of checking weather reports from the West Coast to the east, replying to queries via instant messenger or email, and joining two quick conference calls to help some truckers through the Missouri back roads where furious storms were causing delays in supply runs in that area. After her second cup of coffee, the words on her screen began to blur, and she finally cleared her last task before resting forward with her head in her hands. Her body shook inside and out, and the depth of the uncertainty surrounding them weighed on her chest like a stone.

Whatever hard shell she'd encased herself in was cracking, and her thoughts returned to home, wondering what the kids were doing and if they were safe. Every time she called, they seemed fine, reporting the goings-on in the neighborhood and relaying the news that the neighbors were working together for protection. Knowing that high-ranking government officials seemed to bug out at the worst possible time along with support staff members plagued her with revolving guilt. One minute, she told herself she should be home

CHAPTER SIXTEEN

with the kids, the next she was scolding herself for even thinking about leaving her post.

When the barricades came down, it broke any doubt in Stephanie's mind about what she needed to do. It started with one of Davies' captains, who stood from his seat and hurried toward the center screen. At first, it didn't get Stephanie's attention until Davies and the rest of the assembled officers stood and crowded around the displays. She could barely see over their heads at what was happening, some flurry of activity on the eastern portion of the Pentagon grounds. The fence butting the barricades wavered and shook, thousands of fingers interlocked into the chain-link, pushing and pulling, the distortion and fury on their faces visible on the fuzzy picture. It had gotten the attention of the rest of the staff as well, and several were walking over to check out the other displays showing different parts of the grounds where similar things were happening.

Davies was on his radio, calling out as he monitored the situation, shifting across the group to the left-hand screen, giving orders, and stepping back when a section of the north fence finally came down. The faint noise coming through the speakers was terrifying to Stephanie's ears even though the volume was low. She stood and looked around at those seated to her left, two senators talking to their disaster relief teams in Virginia and Kentucky. A pair of congresspeople from Pennsylvania who'd been in town at the time of the crisis looked on in fear. Others she barely knew held their hands frozen above their keyboards. All eyes were turned toward the screens, mouths gaping as the fence came down bit by bit, and someone latched big hooks onto the barricades, which were torn apart by vehicles off camera, the crowd pouring in once more, thousands of angry citizens, starving and desperate and willing to sacrifice themselves to see it all come down.

Davies was hollering into his radio, grabbing two officers and sending them out through the door leading to the upper levels. "Activate the tactical teams on the roof and spin up the helicopters!"

"Yes, sir!" one said as they left the room in a rush.

Seeing that everyone was watching, Davies put his radio against his chest. "Folks, get back to work. We'll have this taken care of

CHAPTER SIXTEEN

shortly." Then he barked into his radio, head down and keeping his voice low with the other officers gathered around.

No one paid attention to the last order but kept their eyes fixed on the screen, watching as the chaos grew and spread throughout the Pentagon grounds. More barricades were pulled aside, followed by a swell of refugees pouring in through the gaps, overrunning the military positions even as tracers let the sky with bright flares of light. At the top of the screens, helicopters zipped by in the windy storm, shooting down into the crowd, pops and more flashes bursting as citizens fired back with rifles and pistols.

Stephanie glanced at the two senators on her left. "What should we do?"

The senator from Kentucky shook his head. "We probably should think about getting the hell out of here."

"But Colonel Davies said everything's fine," the Virginia senator replied, her gaze stuck to the screen. "They can't actually get inside the building, can they?"

Stephanie shrugged with trembling shoulders. "I didn't think so either, but... look!"

As they watched, the crowd parted, and a pair of headlights plowed ahead with people scrambling to get out of the way. A massive vehicle rolled into view, big block letters printed on the armored sides, its grill and fender wide across the front.

"What is that?" The Virginia senator asked, squinting. "Is that a van?"

The Kentucky senator was shaking his head. "No, that's not a van at all. That's a bank truck. It has to weigh quite a bit — whoa!"

The heavy truck motored fast toward the open barricade, with the nearest Humvees aiming elsewhere and firing sprays of tracers into the crowd to cut them to pieces. They overran a third Humvee in the top left corner of the camera, the vehicle shaking on its chassis as a soldier was ripped from the turret. Then the doors were flung wide, and those soldiers were dragged out, too. Projectiles flew, Molotov cocktails and grenades exploding everywhere on the screens. The truck continued to race toward the building, smashing over the torn-down fencing and splitting the open barricades,

CHAPTER SIXTEEN

plowing over citizens and soldiers alike. Just as it cleared the left-hand side of the screen, an explosion drowned the camera view in bright light for a second before a rumble of sound rippled down through the building. Those at the table gasped and stepped back, looking up as if the ceiling were about to fall on their heads. Dust trickled on them as the vibrations faded.

"What the hell's going on up there?" Davies screamed, staring wide-eyed at the screen, nostrils flaring with anger. "I told you to reinforce the eastern flank."

Someone replied on the radio in minced static only the Colonel could hear.

"Fall back to the inner halls," Davies growled, grabbing the rest of his officers, shoving, and pulling them toward the door. "We'll make kill zones from those defensive positions and pile up the bodies if that's what they want."

Davies and his officers rushed out without a word to those left in the room, leaving them standing and staring at each other as the displays continued showing them what was happening outside their doors. A moment later, the screens flashed and blanked out, bathing the room in silence.

"Well, this is a bunch of crap," the Kentucky senator said, slapping his hand on the table and sitting heavily.

"What are we going to do?" The Virginia senator held fear in her eyes, and it was spreading through the room. Stephanie glanced over to see the congresspeople from Pennsylvania circle the table and head for the door. Two communication officers got up and followed them, leaving the rest to look around in fear.

Stephanie waved her hands. "Listen, everybody. I know this is a crazy situation, and everyone probably feels abandoned right now, but if you're thinking about going out there —"

"Why shouldn't we?" a specialist yelled from the back of the room. "Everyone's abandoning us. Do we really want to be stuck here with those crazies?"

More people echoed the sentiment.

"Because we don't know what's out there," Stephanie pleaded. "Unless you're going out there with a couple of pretty good-sized

CHAPTER SIXTEEN

guns, you're not going very far." Kicking her chair back, she circled and gestured at the displays. "Didn't we see soldiers dragged right out of their Humvee? And they had a lot of weapons. If they aren't faring well out there, we're not going to. And how many of you could get out of here without an escort? I couldn't, and I've been working here for years. There's the one motor pool..." Stephanie shrugged. "But that's all I know."

Everyone glanced around in silence, with a few nodding in agreement. Still, others continued looking at the door and whispered to those next to them. One man got up from his station and rushed toward the door, glancing back with guilt-ridden eyes.

"Sorry," he said, slipping out with no one trying to stop him.

"What if we hide?" Jack Brown stood up from his console and looked around. "A lot of us have been working here for a few years, and we know how to take the stairs to the lower passages. There're at least two more floors below us and plenty of hiding places."

"That's as good an idea as any," Stephanie nodded, picking up her main laptop, circling the table, and heading toward the door to the huddle rooms. "But I'd wait until Colonel Davies gets back to see what he advises. I'm sure they've got a plan."

The senator from Kentucky started to follow her, pointing in accusation. "And where are you going?"

"I've got a private phone call to make," Stephanie said. "Do you have a problem with that?"

The senator held his hands up. "No, ma'am."

She exited the room and took the first right into her usual space, shutting the door behind her before sliding into her seat. With the laptop open in front of her, she dialed home, waiting patiently for the landline on that side, fingers tapping the table as the fine sheen of sweat gathered and trickled down her face. Her chest tightened as the phone continued to ring with no one picking up. Finally, a click sounded over her laptop speakers, and a sleepy voice piped in.

"Hello? Mom?"

"Larkin, honey." She spoke the words with a heavy sigh. "I'm so glad you picked up. I was starting to worry."

CHAPTER SIXTEEN

"I was sleeping. Amanda is keeping watch, so I was trying to get a few winks."

"Good. You're still sticking to your patrols."

"Oh, yeah. Definitely. Not just around the house, but Mr. Morris has also got us on neighborhood patrols."

"Zeke Morris? Is he running the show there?"

"Yeah, we're seeing more people come to the neighborhood, and the Wilsons got robbed and assaulted last night. It was pretty bad, but nobody died. They got away with all of their supplies and tried to burn down their house. The Etlers shot two more people the other day trying to get in their back door. So, Mr. Morris got some people together and went door to door, rounding us all up, taking stock, and starting the neighborhood watch thing."

Stephanie was nodding, blinking back tears the whole time. "It's something I suspected would happen. People are leaving the cities and making their way to the suburbs and farms, trying to escape populated areas."

"Yeah, it's happening a little too much." Larkin laughed, his voice rough and tired. "But Amanda and I are hanging in there, Mom. You don't have to worry about us. Are you going to come home soon?"

Stephanie started to reply, but her voice was frozen, those same warring emotions swelling in her heart in resurfacing. "Yes, Larkin," she finally spoke. "I want to come home, but it might be too late." Face twisting, fist clenched on the table, she shook her head and cried quietly with only a single sob slipping out.

"What's wrong, Mom? Are you crying?"

"A little. Things are getting worse here, and we might not be able to hold out."

"You've got to get home now, then." Larkin's voice rose with panic. "I thought when you were done, you could just hitch a ride back home."

"It's not that easy, son. The road is dangerous, and I..." Stephanie fell forward with emotion pouring from her chest, tears streaming from her eyes, and her breath hitching as she struggled through the turmoil.

"Mom? Hey, Mom? You don't have to cry. We'll be okay. I mean,

CHAPTER SIXTEEN

it's scary out here, not going to lie, but we'll be fine until you can get here."

Stephanie sobbed again, a throat choking sound she couldn't keep in no matter how hard she tried. Through her blurry vision, she imagined her children sitting in a dark house alone while she worked to save a nation devouring itself from the inside out.

Drowning in tears, Stephanie's hard, dutiful wall fell to pieces, and she spoke the confession she'd hoped never to make.

"I screwed up, Larkin," she admitted. "I should have done something sooner. I should've asked to leave or found a way to bring you here, but I didn't. And I'm not sure I can make it home now."

"What are you talking about, Mom? You had to help with the biggest disaster in the world. Amanda and I knew you wanted to come home, but you had to deal with that. I'll bet you saved thousands of lives... you and Dad."

Stephanie's crying dried up.

"I used to get mad at him for never coming to our games and stuff. He missed just about everything. But when I got to school, I started reading about him—all the protests and people who hate him for his activism. I still don't always agree with him, either. But what I learned about Dad that no one ever told me was that he's a brave guy. He's willing to do whatever it takes for his beliefs, and we have to respect him for that. I wasn't surprised when you told me he'd gone on a dangerous mission to help save people. And we weren't surprised when you couldn't come home, too."

Stephanie's heart swelled so large in her chest that it stemmed the flow of tears as she stiffened in her chair. "Really? You're not mad at me?"

"No way, Mom. At least you prepared us for something like this, and Mr. Morris treats us like adults, not like the other kids who mostly stay inside. There aren't any other college kids out there patrolling. None of them are trained on weapons. They're like babies compared to us."

The hint of a smile tugged at the corner of Stephanie's mouth, and she shook her head, overcome with a simmering joy. Relief and

CHAPTER SIXTEEN

pride rolled into one immense feeling, and she released a thin breath and settled back into her seat.

"Well, thank you, Larkin. I'm proud of you guys, too. It sounds like you've got things under control there."

"We really do, Mom. So, take care of what you have to do there and get home to us as soon as possible, okay?"

"Okay, son. I will. I'll be there soon."

"I love you, Mom. See you soon."

Larkin hung up, leaving a stark silence in the room, though the gnawing feeling in her gut was gone, replaced with a mixture of emotions she couldn't fathom. Yet one thought stuck with her, something Larkin had just said about finding out about his father after reaching college. All that time, Stephanie figured the kids hated him, and she'd done everything to protect them from what she considered bad parenting, even being mean to Craig when she probably shouldn't have been. They saw right through to who he really was, something she'd refused for so long, drowned in her own pride and career aspirations. The realization shined a light on her own failings.

With a wistful smile filled with regret and love, Stephanie began to pack up her laptop when a squeak from the door caused her to turn.

"Colonel Davies?"

The red-faced Colonel stood in the doorway, holding it open about a foot with his head and shoulders leaning in. His hair was unkempt, and worry filled his eyes. "Sorry, Stephanie. I didn't mean to interrupt."

"Oh, no problem, sir." Stephanie lowered her voice and looked away. "What did you hear?"

"Enough. At first, I thought you'd left. Half the team is gone, hiding somewhere on the grounds or maybe escaped, I don't know."

Stephanie bristled and squared her shoulders. "I've been here the whole time, sir. I didn't even think about abandoning my post, even though..." Tears threatened to stream from her eyes, though she got it under control. "Even though my kids are alone at home."

Davies scoffed softly. "All that dedication to duty, and you're not even military."

CHAPTER SIXTEEN

"No."

"Well, maybe you should've been."

Stephanie laughed softly and turned to face him. "I'll take that as a compliment, sir."

The Colonel allowed himself a grin. "Anyway, I came here to tell you the President is safe and still running things, but I'm ordering the evacuation of nonmilitary personnel. You've been dedicated and loyal, but there's no reason you need to be here. There's nothing you can do."

"They're breaking in?"

"It's just a matter of time." His professional tone returned. "The plan is to hold them off until the civilians are away and safe, then we'll seal off any top-secret chambers and evacuate the troops. We're giving up the Pentagon, for now."

"I'm sorry to hear that," she replied sadly. "And thank you for ordering the evacuation, but are you sure we can escape? It's a madhouse out there, and without weapons and soldiers to take us, it —"

"Don't worry about that. I've got a couple of APCs taking some of the staff south, and you'll be traveling with a small contingent of Marines back to your house before they go off on another mission."

"Marines just for me?"

"They'll be taking you out of here in a Humvee," the Colonel nodded. "If they can't protect you on the way home, no one can."

Stephanie shook her head, stumbling over her words. "I don't know what to say, Colonel Davies. That's incredible. You're giving me a chance to get home to my kids."

"As I said, the royal treatment isn't just for you. The Marines I'm sending with you have other work to do once they're done dropping you off. Your house was on the way. Follow me, and I'll introduce you to the men."

"Thanks again, sir," Stephanie replied, packing up her laptop and tucking it under her arm, trailing Davies as they returned to the conference room where it was completely cleared out except for the military staff. The senators from Virginia and Kentucky were nowhere to be seen.

CHAPTER SIXTEEN

"Where'd they take the senators?"

"The civilian leadership is getting on a bus and heading south to a new bunker away from all this. They'll be safe there."

"Good." Stephanie clasped her hands together. "That's good to know. So, I'm the only one left?"

"Yes, and I'm glad I found you. I almost didn't check the huddle rooms for any stragglers. Are you ready?"

Placing her laptop with her others, she turned and raised her voice. "Wait, sir. What about my computers and work? Who will work on feeding the supply chain folks and camp leaders weather information?"

"That will be given to an appropriate resource on the President's team. Jerrick Nilsen, to be specific. In fact, all the data you collected over the past days and weeks using Craig's modeling software will be transferred via hard drive to the President's new location."

"Okay, that's good." Wringing her fingers together, she glanced longingly at the equipment, thinking back on the hours she'd spent sitting in front of the keys, drawing out the data, parsing, and sending it to those who needed it most. With a hopeful grin, she started to follow him again before holding up her finger. "Oh, another thing, sir. There's another staffer here who lives on the way to my house. She said her family lives in Luray. Could we give her a lift?"

Davies turned and locked his hands behind his back. "Oh, which staffer is it?"

"Her name is Laney Dixon. She's the poor girl you yelled at about the coffee earlier."

Davies dropped his stern demeanor and looked at the floor sheepishly. "I remember her. I shouldn't have yelled at her, I know."

"Then if you're going to send me home, you could send her, too. It's right on the way, and she's a sweet girl. You'd be doing her a big favor."

Hands clasped in front of him, Davies rose on the balls of his feet and sank back, seeming to contemplate the strategy before nodding. "The Humvee holds five, and I'm sending three soldiers along with you so, it would work."

Clapping once, Stephanie gestured for the Colonel to go ahead,

CHAPTER SIXTEEN

and she followed through the door leading to the Pentagon's inner chambers. Three soldiers immediately jumped to attention when they stepped out, saluting the Colonel and turning to Stephanie with brief and respectful nods. She briefly scanned their names and ranks, identifying Sergeant Gress, Specialist Jamison, and Private Adelson, all fully dressed in military fatigues with goggles resting on their helmets and the respiratory masks disconnected and hanging loose to the sides.

"Hello, guys," Stephanie said with a brief nod to each.

"These are your escorts back home," Davies nodded to her.

"Stay with her for a minute, men. I need to find the kitchen staff and grab another straggler for you to get home."

With that, Davies turned back through the conference room door while Stephanie stood in awkward silence with the soldiers, all big, burly men dressed in dirt-stained fatigues. Gress had a broad chest and chiseled chin, while Adelson was lanky, looming over the group by a good six inches. Their uniforms only made them seem bigger, ammunition pouches strapped to their chests and waists, carbines hanging from their shoulders, none looking too eager to engage in conversation. When Davies took longer than expected, Adelson leaned in with a nod, his jaw working as he chewed a wad of gum.

"Don't worry, Mrs. Lancaster, we'll get you home no matter what it looks like out there."

"Thanks," Stephanie smiled haltingly.

"It might look like hell out there," the Private pointed upward at the chaos happening on the grounds, "and people might be getting slaughtered left and right —"

"Easy, Adelson," Gress growled. "No need to panic the lady."

"I've been watching on the cameras, I know what I'm getting into," Stephanie laughed. "It's hell out there."

Adelson nodded briefly to the Sergeant but continued addressing Stephanie. "I just wanted you to know we always carry out our orders to the letter, ever since we started running side missions. In fact, we did the one for that family up in Stamford. That was yours?"

Stephanie's jaw dropped, then she smiled. "That was you guys?

CHAPTER SIXTEEN

Thank you so much. You don't know how much that meant to us. By the way, the message you guys took down was written in Dutch, and the father knows where his family went."

"Good to hear, ma'am. Yeah, that's good to know, isn't it, guys?"

Jamison nodded and leaned against the wall while Gress stood with his arms folded and staring at the ground.

"Call me Stephanie. No ma'ams or Mrs. Lancasters with me."

"That's going to be hard," Adelson said. "I was brought up a yes sir, yes ma'am kind of guy. My parents always taught me proper respect."

"Why don't you leave the lady alone for a minute, Adelson" Gress growled, his stocky form shifting toward the door as Davies came through with Laney Dixon behind him, hastily putting on a coat with a bag full of her things in her free arm. She'd changed out of her staff outfit and wore jeans, fashionable boots, and a gray sweater that hung off her thin form.

Seeing Stephanie, she released a sigh of relief. "Oh, I'm *so* glad you're here. They were about to take me down and put me on a bus with all the others, and I wasn't too thrilled about my chances."

"Consider this my official apology for yelling at you over the coffee, Miss Dixon," Davies said.

Looking the Marines up and down, Laney seemed both intimidated and impressed. "Apology accepted. Thanks for the invite, Stephanie."

"No problem. It'll be nice to have another gal along with me."

In a rushed tone, Davies gestured at the Sergeant. "Sergeant Gress, you have your orders. Simply add in a waypoint for Miss Dixon, who should be on the way to Mrs. Lancaster's. Any questions?"

"No, sir. We've got everything we need."

"Good. Now, I need to take care of a few things." Davies' expression turned grim. "I'll be issuing orders to hunt down every single man and woman who abandoned their post. Then I'll join the rest of the Marine and Army teams upstairs. Good luck, men. Safe travels, ladies."

"Thank you, Colonel," Stephanie replied.

CHAPTER SIXTEEN

The soldiers saluted the Colonel as he returned to the conference room and angled toward the remaining communication staff. Sergeant Gress gestured for them to follow him as he descended into the passages leading to the motor pools. Stephanie and Laney came next with Adelson and Jamison behind them, their steps quick but swaggering as they pressed the women down the hall, Gress taking each corner with strategic precision.

"All right, folks," he said. "We're about to get this journey underway. It'll be rough and rocky, so buckle up."

They marched down a maze of passages past magnetically locked doors with key-coded entrances. Groups of staffers carrying briefcases handcuffed to their wrists rushed by with similar Marine or Army units guarding them, some dressed in the black suits of Secret Service agents holding pistols or automatic rifles, barely casting a glance their way as they passed. Soon, Stephanie was half jogging to keep up with Sergeant Gress, his stocky form hiding the length of his strides, his wide shoulders demanding space in the hall. Occasional muffled booms reverberated through the walls, the lights dimming for a moment before returning to full power. They stepped onto a service elevator Stephanie hadn't been on before, and she and Laney stood in the middle, shoulder to shoulder. Gress punched a button and the car dropped. Noticing Laney's trembling chin, Stephanie took her hand and squeezed gently, and Laney gave her a nervous smile and a thankful nod.

Private Adelson cleared his throat and leaned down. "Not to sound any alarms about what we're about to get into, but do either of you ladies know how to fire a rifle?"

CHAPTER SEVENTEEN

Zach Christensen, Whitehorse, Yukon

The lone Humvee rolled down the long and winding highway, still chased by fiery skies and pockets of fumes, the mountains peeling away to either side in great swaths of forested hillsides and rich green mountains covered with snow. Where the firestorms burned the hottest, avalanches and mudslides slid into small towns, burying everything beneath them and sometimes covering the highway in avalanches, forcing Grizzly to go around. They passed lakes with half-melted surfaces, fishing huts and villages on the opposite shores glowing orange as they burned. At night, they could see distant fires tearing through the forests, scorching them to the ground and creating scabbed patches on knobby hills. Lightning and thunder crashed over their heads so often they hardly noticed it, and Zach sat cramped in the Humvee's passenger seat, his carbine as a bedmate, taking turns driving with the big Russian whenever the man could no longer keep his eyes open.

Pockets of hydrocarbon fumes occasionally washed over them, setting off Craig's contaminant detector and throwing them into a sudden frenzy to put their air filtration masks on before they ended

CHAPTER SEVENTEEN

up like the suffocated herd of moose Zach had run across many days earlier. He never forgot to remind them of that story and that they needed to move fast when the alarms rang. All it would take was one person to leave their filtration mask in the Humvee when they took a bathroom break to kill them. According to Craig, ten or fifteen seconds of breathing that air could do them in.

"How many miles have we gone so far, Grizzly?" Zach asked in a tired tone.

Grizzly was massive in the driver's seat, his bulging belly pressed against the wheel despite having put the seat back. His arms rested partially on his middle as he gripped the wheel and drove on an extended stretch of straight highway with their headlamps glowing in the gloomy afternoon light. The windshield wipers were going as rain and snow swept down on them in alternating waves of turbulent winds. Pudgy hands bounced on the steering wheel. "Let us see. We got past the Harding-Birch-Lakes and Delta Junction. The soldiers from Fort Greely were very nice."

"They were a little miffed that we had one of their Humvees," Craig said from the back, "but once we showed them Red Hawk's orders, they were a little more understanding. At least they let us refuel."

"The place was a ghost town," Zach said. "Nothing but military convoys heading north."

"Hogging the road," Liza replied glumly.

That was regarding the number of times they'd had to pull over to let United States military vehicles pass, massive APCs and tanks on the back of semitrailer flatbeds as they rushed north to guard against a Russian attack.

"Based on the radio chatter we picked up," Zach said, "Orlov must be doing a number up there. I hope Red Hawk and his Marines are okay."

Liza smirked. "They will never be okay as long as Orlov is alive. The man is ruthless and will stop at nothing to drive the Americans off their oilfields. It's the perfect time for him to take that opportunity."

Zach glanced back. "After meeting him, I'd agree with you."

CHAPTER SEVENTEEN

Grizzly pointed at the radio that had been on at a medium volume almost every second they'd been on the road. "Last time we pull over to take potty break... I hear Russian soldiers speaking. When I tried to better tune, it go away." Taking his hands off the wheel for a second, he spread them in exasperation before slapping his palms down again.

"Aside from a couple of faint Russian signals," Craig said, "we're getting mostly Canadian Armed Forces, but I couldn't tell you what they're up to... all that military talk goes right over my head."

"I'm not a military strategist, but it sounded to me like they're doing some maneuvering or chasing ghosts."

"Chasing ghosts?" Liza asked.

"They're probably nervous and seeing shadows of Russians if you get my meaning."

"Yes, I see what you mean." The Russian scientist glanced up through the side window. "When will we outrun these storms?"

"I don't think anyone knows," Gina replied from the back seat. "If those skies don't clear, we'll never get an airlift out of here."

Zach glanced upward through his window at the bubbling skies, fumes of yellow gold twirling through the dense black fog. Thick tongues of lightning blasted through them to continue the explosions of billowing smoke that dissipated into a black fog, pushing the storm clouds ever southward. The highway was still littered with abandoned vehicles and car frames blasted and scraped off the road by the winds or the Russian ghosts. While Zach couldn't prove the latter, he stared suspiciously at several damaged vehicles that appeared punched through with small rounds from even bigger guns.

Not wanting to alarm the others, Zach scoffed and shook his head. "Nothing will fly up there except those brave bastards back at the air force base playing cat and mouse with those cyclones. Those are some brave pilots."

"We went by Dry Creek and Tok," Grizzly said.

"Thankfully, that bridge was clear," Craig said. "I wasn't looking forward to another river crossing."

"Whatever I must do, I will do," Grizzly explained with a glance

CHAPTER SEVENTEEN

in his rearview. "I will drive over bridges or through streams. Grizzly will get you there."

"I know you will, buddy," Craig replied.

Grizzly chuckled. "To answer question directly, we have gone four hundred miles or more over the past thirty-six hours, and from what I remember of map, Quill Creek is ahead, and big lake. At next junction, we go east to Whitehorse."

Zach glanced back. "And what do we know about it?"

Craig pulled out a notepad where he'd taken some things down from Colonel Red Hawk before leaving Fairbanks. "Well, it's the capital city of Yukon, and it's usually got about thirty thousand people in it. I don't know about now."

"What about the military presence there?"

"Red Hawk didn't think there was a US presence there yet, but there should be some CAF forces there. That's just a guess, though. The coordination between our two countries wasn't flawless when we left Fairbanks."

"So, we'll play it by ear."

Grizzly laughed and pointed at the road ahead, where a green sign slanted on the right-hand side of the road, reading *Quill Creek*. "See, I speak truth."

"What's that leave us with before we reach Whitehorse?"

Craig unfolded part of his map, tracing with his finger.

"Only a hundred and fifty miles," Grizzly replied.

"A hundred and fifty miles," Craig agreed with a shrug.

"Anyone else need a bathroom break?" Zach asked. "I've got to go."

Gina and Liza both expressed their interest in stopping, so Grizzly drove another ten miles, following signs for Jocuot Hall and Burwash Landing. He pulled the Humvee left into a narrow lane leading through a forested area with houses nestled into the landscape and a campground. They cruised past rental cabins, a restaurant with a moose head on the front, and a small refueling station on the next corner. The trees parted, and Grizzly drove left down a winding lane divided by random patches of dirt and telephone poles and another couple of houses on the right. A gated welcome center

CHAPTER SEVENTEEN

stood next to tall beach grass that disappeared over the hill. Stretched ahead of them was a massive lake, its surface dense and gray with ice, frosted around the edges and in great white patches out toward the center.

"Would you look at that," Craig said. "Must be a mile or two across."

As soon as the Humvee stopped, doors popped open, and everyone got out, standing on the windy landing and looking down from the heights. The shoreline was rough and rocky, with tiny fingers of land curving into the deep gray waters where waves washed over the ice. Snow spotted the shoreline, promising hard-packed earth and slippery slopes.

"It's beautiful," Gina said, hands stuffed into her coat pockets and her chestnut hair blowing around her head. Pressing a hand to her temple, she dragged a lock of hair behind her ear and turned to Zach with wet eyes.

"Hey, what's wrong?" Zach walked over, glancing over his left shoulder as everyone spread out to find private places to do their business. Before turning back to Gina, he raised his hand and snapped his fingers. "Folks, don't wander too far out of sight. The place looks abandoned, but there could be people around just hiding."

Grizzly walked toward a small home next to one that had been burned up, scorch marks on the pavement and patches of ice and frost in the usual configuration the firestorms made when they touched down. The more he looked, Zach saw a swath of torn up vegetation and trees straight down the lake's southern shoreline.

"Careful over there!" Zach called, and Grizzly grunted something and waved back. Craig and Liza wandered over to the visitor's building, poking around along the fence and looking for a way in. When Zach turned back to Gina, he saw she'd walked closer to the edge of the overlook next to a path leading down to the shore. He was about to ask her not to go down, but she stopped there anyway, and he went to stand by her side.

"Sorry about that," he scoffed and adjusted the rifle on his shoulder. "Just trying to make sure we stay together."

319

CHAPTER SEVENTEEN

"You're doing a great job," she said with a glance and a smile.

"It's not something I asked for. I'd be home right now if it were up to me."

"And I'd have my Hank here with me."

"I know you would, and I'm sorry this happened to you." Zach started to put his arm around her but hesitated. "I know Wendy and the kids could be in trouble, too, but at least I talked to them, and my heart is settled. I couldn't imagine what it would be like in your shoes right now."

Without warning, Gina threw herself against Zach, wrapping her arms around his broad chest and squeezing him. She pressed her face into his jacket, heavy sobs hitching in her chest as she clung to him. Zach pursed his lips against the gut-wrenching sounds and put his arm around her shoulder, squeezing her hard against him but not matching her strength.

"When we reach Whitehorse, they'll have a database with lists of names we can search through or something. If we'd picked you up in Fairbanks, we could've checked then... I wasn't thinking."

"It's not your fault, and you don't know our last name anyway." Gina wiped her nose with the back of her hand, sniffling, squeezing Zach one more time before breaking off and gazing at him with teary eyes.

"That's true, and likewise."

"We've been in the car together all this time and never thought to ask."

"I'm Zach Christensen."

"Gina Morosov. Nice to meet you."

They shook hands, hugged again, and laughed.

"Sorry about the crying stuff," she said. "I try to be tough, but I break down every time I think of Hank. And I know other people have it even worse than me. A lot of people died out there in the cold or the firestorms... and who knows what the death toll is in the States now. I should be thankful to be with you guys."

"True, but that doesn't mean you can't grieve for your husband." Zach slapped his palm against his head. "No, I refuse to say it. You don't know if he's dead at all, and the fact that Scotty and Sandy

CHAPTER SEVENTEEN

survived means the rescue teams could have, too. That means your husband might've come in with them."

"I waited a full day after you left." Hands back in her pocket, she shook her head. "Those storms up there are brutal, and I'm not sure anyone could've survived it. But I appreciate your support and your kind words. Makes me feel like I'm not so alone out here."

"You're not alone, Gina. Some pretty good friends surround you. The way Grizzly drives, we'll make it back to the States sooner than later, I promise. After we get to Whitehorse, we'll check with whoever's in charge and get you connected to the national databases, if that's even a thing yet." Zach took her by the shoulders. "We won't give up, okay?"

Gina nodded briskly with the same wide smile that came so easily to her. "Okay, Zach."

"Let's take care of business and get to the Humvee. We've still got a long way to go."

Gina turned in a full circle and spotted a place that looked private, pointing and heading that way. Zach turned back to the vast expanse of the lake and peered across the waters, unable to see the other side. His gaze drifted along the shoreline and the rough-and-tumble waves that broke through the shifting, half-melted ice, the temperatures just high enough to create bumping ice flows out there in a gently-stirring current. With a heavy sigh, he turned and strode off to relieve himself.

The Humvee swept along Highway 1, bypassing the first car in many miles, cruising past a small convoy of vehicles on the right-hand side of the road where drivers were assisting a broken-down vehicle. Another pair of cars passed them, coming the other way, and Zach looked back to see them slowing to pull off a side road leading into the wilderness. Trails stretched into massive knobs of rolling hills, lonely crags in the distance capped with roiling skies and lit by sputters of lightning. The highway rose high above the forested plains with tall green trees spread all around them, the land sheered away

CHAPTER SEVENTEEN

on either side to provide space for rest stops, gas stations, and food marts. There were cars in the lots, and people ran everywhere while casting glances at the turbulent sky.

Roads branched off Highway 1 to neighborhoods where sprinkles of electric light gleamed from windows and headlamps as the first signs of normalcy they'd seen in weeks greeted them. Off to the left, a handful of helicopters swooped in from the south, keeping low to the ground and landing on another part of the tarmac. A small military plane shot through the sky, hugging the mountains and heading to the northwest. The city rested on a wide piece of flat land made of multiple paved strips, with dozens of warehouses, trucking stations, and large department stores scattered around. Downtown spanned several blocks ringed with a spattering of subdivisions divided by stretches of woodland and connected by back roads. The Whitehorse Dam choked off the Yukon River, which swept along the east side of town and provided power to the homes and buildings. Despite tendrils of smoke trailing into the sky, patterns of electric lights glowed from windows all around and up ahead.

"This town is alive." Craig leaned between the seats.

"Doesn't seem they've abandoned it yet." Zach replied.

They turned hard south and were met with four pairs of headlights blocking the road ahead, pointed in their direction, spotlights in the turrets of armored vehicles swinging their way and pinning them in stark yellow light.

As he raised his arm to block the brightness. "Not very nice, my friends. Grizzly cannot see."

"Looks like it could be military, probably CAF." Zach mirrored Grizzly's posture, craning his neck and squinting into the blinding lights as several dark shapes walked toward them away from the vehicles, all carrying rifles pointed at the Humvee. A loud voice piped over a loudspeaker, though he couldn't make out what they were saying. Patting Grizzly's arm, he said, "Stop here, Grizzly. They've got guns on us, trying to figure out who we are."

"Okay."

The Humvee stopped with a growl of tires, and Zach popped the door open, so the loudspeaker voice punched through. "... out with

CHAPTER SEVENTEEN

your hands up. Do not make any sudden moves, or you will be fired upon. I repeat to the driver of the Humvee. Turn off your engine and step out with your hands up. Do not make any sudden moves, or you will be fired upon."

Zach was already halfway out the door, arms held high, frozen as the shadows of soldiers stepped closer and surrounded him. "Get back inside, passenger," one barked. "You heard the orders."

"My name is Zach Christensen, and I'm under orders from US military commander Colonel Red Hawk of the Fairbanks defense unit. I'm authorized to speak with your commanding officer."

The commanding soldier conferred with another before he moved in, a tall man in military fatigues with the symbol of the Canadian flag leaf on the left sleeve. "You're not Russians."

"I've got Russians with me," Zach replied, though he quickly followed up. "But they're on our side. I have a Russian scientist and driver, cleared by Colonel Red Hawk of the US Marines. I'm to escort them back to the US, where they'll be flown across the country to DC."

"I'm Sergeant Cloutier, and I'd like you to step away from the vehicle."

Nodding, Zach moved from behind the door to the right-hand shoulder as other CAF troops circled to attend to Grizzly and the rest of them.

Cloutier met him there, the Sergeant a skinny, pale-faced young man who couldn't have been much older than twenty, decked out in a flak vest and a carbine, his expression lock-jawed and serious. "You say your name's Zach Christensen? Who are the others?"

"My driver is, um, Grizzly Smirnoff. The Russian scientist is Liza Kovaleva, and the two Americans with me are Dr. Craig Sutton and Gina Morosov. I'm sure if your captain checked his orders, he'd see we're on —"

"No need to explain to me." Cloutier cut him off, reaching in to take Zach's pistol from its holster and then gesturing to a spot on the side of the road. "Have a seat on the ground there."

Zach glanced over his shoulder to see everyone else in the vehicle being forced to the side of the road with their hands up. The CAF

CHAPTER SEVENTEEN

troops descended upon the Humvee, stripping their supplies out and tossing them on the ground. One soldier found his carbine and showed it to one of his buddies.

"We don't have time for this, Sergeant Cloutier. As I said, we're under direct orders—"

"And I said sit down, sir. I'll radio to the captain."

With a heavy sigh, Zach nodded and sat on the side of the road, crossing his legs so he didn't tip backward. Cloutier called another soldier over, whispered to him, and gestured toward the four Humvees lined up across the highway. The soldier ran off while Cloutier tucked Zack's pistol into his belt and stepped closer.

"Where'd you get that Humvee, sir?"

"Colonel Red Hawk gave us all our equipment back in Fairbanks where they're fighting on the front lines..." A CAF soldier got in and started the Humvee. "Are you serious? You're going to confiscate our truck?"

"We're at war here, sir, and we can't have civilians driving around in military equipment. We need every piece we can get."

Zach stiffened. "This is a big Canadian military base. You've got American-made Humvees right there." Zach couldn't tell the make and model, but the Humvees' silhouette in the penetrating spotlights seemed obvious.

"I don't have to justify anything to you, sir."

"Well, you better start justifying some things if you value the United States military's help. I'm assuming you're working in tandem?"

Cloutier shifted positions. "Sir, this HQ is seventy-five percent cadets, and we weren't ready for a Russian invasion because of cutbacks. We've got a few armored vehicles and some tanks, but we'll need every piece of equipment we can get."

"Russian invasion? We heard some chitchat on the radio but weren't sure."

"Yes. They're crawling all over the place."

"How could they be crawling all over the place so deep in Canadian Territory?"

The Sergeant glanced back and then nodded toward the west.

CHAPTER SEVENTEEN

"We're only two hundred miles from the Gulf of Alaska, and intelligence reports say Russians are landing on shore."

"What do you think they're up to?"

Coultier shrugged. "Working their way inland for all we know. Maybe an all-out assault on the United States and Canada. If you were in Fairbanks, you'd know this."

"I've had run-ins with the Russians already." Zach rolled his shoulders and winced. "I've got the stab wounds to prove it. I didn't expect they'd made it this far south."

Coultier stepped to the side, craning his neck to peer at the bandages wrapped around the base of Zach's skull before lowering his rifle to a more relaxed stance. "Sorry about your injuries, sir. But, yeah. Several landing parties were spotted in the Gulf area, which isn't far from here. Right now, we're waiting for support from the Americans by carrier strike groups. We expect to see some big fireworks then, but we're trying to hold our ground for now."

"Colonel Red Hawk isn't retreating, I can tell you that much."

"Good to know, sir."

The CAF soldiers hadn't driven their Humvee away, though several had collected all their gear and weapons and were carrying them to a small ATV.

"So, you're still going to take all our stuff?"

"For now, yes. We've got civilians sheltered at the base and in town, and you can get behind the lines and wait there for further instructions from our commanders. It depends on what the captain wants to do with you."

Zach shook his head and bit back a retort. The Sergeant was doing his job, even if it went against a US officer's orders. "No one was evacuated from town?"

"Evacuation orders were given, but people are pretty stubborn about defending their property around here. There are more guns here per capita than in most Canadian provinces. Colonel Leopold probably figures that keeping them here will only help our defense when the Russians show up."

"Colonel Red Hawk won't be happy about this."

"He isn't here now. I'm sure Colonel Leopold will provide you

CHAPTER SEVENTEEN

with another way to get south, but it may take a few hours to process. It's up to him, sir."

Shots rang out, bullets hit the Humvee with pings and sparks of light, zipped by like a gale of hummingbirds, whispering sounds of death. The Sergeant was hit several times, rounds punching his flak armor and then striking him in the arms and legs as he tried to get his rifle up but dropped it and fell. Wide-eyed and spattered with blood, Zach rolled onto his belly, crawling on his forearms to the Humvee as two more CAF soldiers were struck in the barrage, the one carrying his Spear knocked inside the Humvee as the weapon clattered to the pavement, the other spinning and trying to get away but caught with several shots in the back that sent him sprawling, face-first, to the concrete. Zach kept crawling as bullets continued pouring in. He leaned left and grabbed his carbine as rounds hit the side of the Humvee and ricocheted across the ground, striking the fenders and undercarriage. Wincing, ducking, grunting with hellfire at his heels, Zach crawled to the front of the Humvee, rolled once, and came up with his left shoulder against the grill. Grizzly and the others were caught crouched by the roadside, torn between running to the Canadian Humvees and their own truck. A single CAF soldier near them fired back in bursts from his carbine, stepping over two dead men as he went, working his way toward the Humvee where Zach was crouched.

Zach waved his people away. "Get out of here! Find some cover! Now!"

Grizzly spread his arms and gestured for everyone to move. Gina turned with a dead Canadian's rifle in her hands and fired into the woods to the west, cross-stepping as she retreated and covered Craig and Liza as they held their arms over their heads and rushed to the Canadian vehicles. Zach didn't wait to see if they made it and raised above the Humvee's hood, spying flashes off to his left and right, at least a dozen at first glance, ducking again when several rounds hit the Humvee's bullet-resistant glass. Zach checked his weapon, rose, and rested the Spear on the hood, firing between his open door and the frame, the rifle bucking against his shoulder as he gave it a short

CHAPTER SEVENTEEN

burst and then a longer one, leaning into it as the sheer power of the gun forced him back.

He was vaguely aware of the Canadian soldier falling to one knee next to him with a grunt, beads of sweat and blood running down his face at a wound that must have sheared through his helmet strap and knocked it off. The soldier shot him a feverish glance before rising to fire off to the right in wild bursts. Concentrated fire ripped into the Humvee as something whistled over their heads and landed behind them with a heavy thud and an explosion that blew Zach against the grill with a grunt. The pressure almost burst his eardrums as a wave of heat writhed across the pavement and up his back. The detonation dissipated, and he sank as more incoming fire hit the Humvee's armor like hail. The Canadian Humvee on the far-left side had taken the hit and was engulfed in flames, one soldier screaming and leaping from the turret, the spotlight dead as troops fled the fire.

The two inner Humvees came to life, machine guns swinging around and lighting up the sky with tracer fire as they took apart the woods on either side, cutting up spruces, firs, and Russian soldiers screamed. Flesh burned and gun smoke drifted by, causing Zach to turn his face away before a backwash of charred evergreen reek filled the air. Another whistling projectile zipped by, and Zach grabbed the soldier next to him and drew him down, trying to get beneath the Humvee as an explosion rocked the sky. Shrapnel flew in every direction, pieces smacking off the Humvee's hood and windshield. Something stung him in the right shoulder and calf, but he clung to the soldier and kept the man's head low, waiting for the wave of heat to pass and the clatter of falling debris to quit raining on them.

"Are you okay?" Zach shouted, lifting the soldier so they both leaned against the grill. "We need to work as a team…"

The man's expression was blank, eyes staring at nothing as several bloody wounds leaked down his face and neck, the left side of his skull punctured by a piece of smoking shrapnel. Zach let him slide off the grill to flop back onto the road. One of the center Humvees had been taken out with that last shot, and the chances reinforcements could arrive before his position was overrun were extremely low. Russian voices

CHAPTER SEVENTEEN

shouted back and forth across the road, and he sensed they smelled blood and would come hard for the Canadians and his friends, who'd become collateral damage in the fight. Growling deep in his chest, Zach rose and emptied his magazine with a spray of fire toward the tree line where Russian shadows crept. One soldier ducked while another took a hit, blown backward into the shrubs. Sinking behind the grill, he ejected his spent magazine and popped in a new one, charging the weapon and slipping to the right side of the Humvee to raise and fire along that tree line, sending a half-dozen Russians scattering into the woods.

A wave of dizziness hit him, and Zach crouched and blinked in a daze, losing his bearings for a moment. Leaning against the grill, he listened as shots flew at him unhindered, the Canadian Humvees silent with only a few shadows moving back there. Senses sharpening, head clearing, he gripped his weapon tighter and thought about retreating, but the thirty yards between him and the Canadian Humvees was an obvious kill zone. While he didn't know if reinforcements were on the way or if he was simply the only man standing, Zach would keep firing until he had nothing left. The ammunition pouch at his waist held two more magazines plus what he had in the gun. He rose and shot at the encroaching Russians, who were creeping up again, hitting one with a high-powered round as the others charged in.

From the corner of his eye, Zach spotted more enemies sprinting toward their position on the left, and another projectile whizzed by overhead, sealing the fate of one of the remaining Canadian Humvees. Zach focused on those on the right he could take down, firing a brief burst into a group of soldiers who'd taken cover behind some deadfall and stones. Two screamed and fell backward while others ducked back again. The third projectile detonated, sending shrapnel arcing overhead and skittering across the pavement, pieces glancing off Zach's coat and striking the Humvee. Sweeping the Spear to the left, he fired three more short bursts at several enemies before he was out of rounds again. Quick-swapping his magazine, he charged his weapon and focused on the same group of soldiers, knowing at any second that the ones on the left would sweep in and put a bullet in his head.

CHAPTER SEVENTEEN

The Russian soldiers behind the deadfall took a chance and charged. Zach swept his weapon from left to right and back again, firing short bursts every second, mowing them like grass and spraying blood across the rocks and fallen logs. He shot one man in the face, his head seeming to evaporate as he dropped. Another got zippered up the middle even as the man's single return round ricocheted off the hood a foot in front of Zach's face. Still, others were coming, and he was alone. Lifting the heavy weapon and limping one step to the left, he searched the woods, not surprised to see three Russians flanking him and sprinting up the bank. Before he could squeeze the trigger, a shotgun boomed next to him, sending the nearest Russian to his knees and shrieking in pain as he gripped his right side, smoking with buckshot. Zach adjusted his aim and shot the man in the chest as a second shotgun blast exploded closer, followed by a third. Whoever it was continued peppering the enemies on the bank with smoking lead. Another Russian fell and slipped down the incline as Zach blew the next comrade away in a teeth-rattling burst from his Spear. The air was thick with smoke as they thwarted the Russian charge and sent the remaining troops running for the tree line.

Zach turned to see Gina breaking in his direction, ducking as return fire chased her to his side, where she slammed against the grill and pulled him down with her. "Are you okay?"

"Yeah, I'm good. I took a bit of shrapnel to the leg, but I can walk." He nodded at her shotgun as she loaded in more shells. "Where'd you get that?"

"From one of the Canadian boys. Standard issue semiautomatic shotgun of the CAF."

"Nice shooting. I was just about to get out of here."

"Stay put. They've got guys coming up now. In fact —"

Someone climbed into one of the Canadian Humvee's turret and started firing again, tearing into the Russian surge approaching on the left as more CAF soldiers sprinted between the burning wreckage to counterattack. Another Humvee that ripped around the shoulder and came to a squealing halt on the northbound lanes, adding heavy support to the ground troops.

CHAPTER SEVENTEEN

"Okay, now we go," Gina called, pushing off the grill and starting back toward the Canadian line.

Zach stood to follow but nearly fell when his right leg gave out, barely catching himself as he staggered against the Humvee's grill. Gina was there, getting her stocky frame beneath his arm. She was so short, Zach could lean his forearm on her shoulder, better enabling her to bear his weight as they hobbled back to cover, the heat from the burning Humvees searing them as they passed. The ripping sounds of the continuous machine gun fire was ear shattering. More soldiers arrived by the second, many carrying canisters of ammunition and heavier guns.

As gunfire spat both ways, Zach and Gina were joined by Grizzly, Liza, and Craig, marching south as CAF armored vehicles swept in, troops adjusting their helmets and charging weapons as they ran, eyes fixed on the woods to the north and the burning wreckage the Russians had left behind. The ATV carrying their equipment sped by with two injured men, and Grizzly raised his arm to stop them but they kept moving. A hundred yards ahead, two APCs with red crosses on the sides came to a tire-shuddering halt, their doors dropping open with medics rushing out to accept the wounded. Grizzly got under Zach's other arm, supporting him as he limped along with pain radiating up his leg and side. When they reached the armored ambulances with their tall roofs, a paramedic broke off and came to them, gesturing for them to take a spot off the roadside.

Seeing they weren't soldiers, the medic motioned to a pair of guards and began triaging Zach's wound by cutting up his pant leg. A CAF soldier stepped away from a buddy he'd brought in and gaped at Zach's group's weaponry. He confiscated Zach's Spear, Gina's shotgun, and all their sidearms and carried them off. The medic was looking at his leg, spreading the pants material apart to expose the bloody gash on the side of his calf, only two inches long but oozing blood. She removed a bottle of saline rinse from a kit and squirted it over the wound, clearing the dirt and grime.

"I was talking to Sergeant Coultier when he got hit," Zach explained. "We're from Fairbanks, and we need to speak to your commanding officer... Colonel Leopold, I think. Please get —"

CHAPTER SEVENTEEN

"The laceration on your leg isn't deep," the medic said, "but there appears to be small pieces of shrapnel inside. I'll get someone to clean it and give you some stitches, but you'll have to wait. We have more serious injuries to deal with."

Gunfire erupted in the air behind them, and men screamed. Captains yelled orders and dispersed troops into the woods, and Humvees launched off the road and into pastures to give chase to the retreating Russians. Smoke gripped the air and wafted by in waves, and the young medic winced at the bursts of guns and explosions.

"What about his arm?" Liza said, coming over on her knees and pulling Zach so his right side showed small burn holes in his fatigue jacket. "He was hit many times here."

Nodding, the medic took a quick look, cutting the material off his shoulder and up his side, pulling apart his layers of clothing and letting in the cold air. When she sprayed saline on the wounds, pinpricks of pain lanced him.

"These aren't too bad either," she replied. "Scratches compared to these other guys, but we need to ensure it doesn't get infected. We'll get someone to help you soon."

Zach sighed and nodded, waving the medic off as his group had a seat. Grizzly stood and tried to go to the ATV with their equipment but was pushed back by the CAF guards who'd been placed on them. More dispersed from an APC and spread across the road, watching the woods on either side with radio communication and static buzzing as the fighting moved off to the north. With nothing to do for the moment, Zach inspected his wounds as best he could, the bleeding worse than the actual damage. Wet warmth soaked into his socks and boots and ran down his side to saturate his shorts around his waistline.

"They could have at least given us some gauze," Liza said, standing and walking toward an APC where the paramedics were working on reviving the severely wounded soldier. A guard stepped in her way, but Liza pointed back at Zach and then motioned to a foldout table with rolls of gauze, gesturing to him fervently. He nodded and held his hand up for her to wait before he crossed and got a roll of gauze and a bottle of saline for her.

CHAPTER SEVENTEEN

"Nice soldier," Liza said as she knelt by Zack's side, ripping off a piece of gauze to dab around Zach's leg wound, washing it out with the saline, and dabbing at it again.

"Thanks, Liza," Zach replied.

"Did they expect you to bleed out right here?"

"The medic was right. They have bigger problems than me."

Liza scoffed and kept working. Cutting off pieces, she stuffed a small amount into the cut and wrapped the roll around it twice, slicing that and tucking the loose end in to hold it. Then she did the same with his arm, washing it out and commenting on the tiny pieces of shrapnel that fell out. Then she ran out of solution and had to sit with the rest of them.

Screams of pain drew their attention as more soldiers were brought in from the fighting, blood everywhere as medical teams tried and failed to save two soldiers. A doctor slammed his bloody fist on a table and waved for the guards to take a dead man away and bring the next one up. Assistants stepped to the side and made room as another man was placed on the rolling cot with a massive belly wound, the doctor leaning in as flashlights illuminated the gory injuries. The roar of diesel engines filled the air as more trucks rushed up from the city proper, going around the medical units and down off the side of the roads to patrol the woods with foot troops filtering out into the trees.

Shifting as the fighting raged back and forth, Craig stood and looked north, then south toward the city where more armored trucks were coming up. "You think they'll get us away from the fighting?"

"They're trying to stabilize people before they take them back," Zach replied. "See?"

A medical APC backed up to the growing group of wounded with its door lowered, and a pair of guards helped roll two injured soldiers inside, both with bandages wrapped around their middles and heads. The smell of burned flesh rolled over them, and Liza turned away with tears in her eyes. Gina sat with her elbows on her knees, head down as she stared at the ground between her legs.

"Are you okay?" Zach asked, leaning over and grabbing her arm.

She looked up with a pale, dazed expression, her mouth working

CHAPTER SEVENTEEN

but no words coming out. She nodded and licked her lips. "I think so. It didn't hit me at first, but we just went through an actual military battle."

Zach chuckled darkly. "Pretty much. How do you feel?"

Holding up her shaking hands, she stared at them a moment before shifting her gaze back to him. "I panicked and grabbed a shotgun one of the CAF soldiers had dropped, the model was one we'd ordered into the shop for a local hunter. I found a pouch full of shells, took them and the gun and got between the Humvees..." Shaking her head in disbelief, she continued. "I didn't know what else to do. Bullets were flying everywhere, and through the smoke, I saw you alone back at our Humvee. I had to do something."

"You saved my life, Gina." Zach squeezed her arm. "Seriously, thank you."

"You are hero," Grizzly said from the opposite side where the big man was sitting, one leg cocked and the other straight.

"I'm no hero," Gina replied, wiping tears off her cheeks as she laughed. "I'm just glad we made it out relatively unscathed."

Zach looked around as more wounded were loaded into trucks and carried south through the city. "It could've been way worse."

A few minutes later, a soldier ran up to their guard, motioned to them and at a nearby Humvee, and the guard gestured for them to get up and go over. With Grizzly and Gina getting under his arms, they got Zach on his feet and moved to the armored vehicle.

Liza challenged the guard. "What about his leg? Is anyone going to help with that? The medic says he has shrapnel in it."

The soldier shook his head. "I'm sure Colonel Leopold will have someone look at it when you get to HQ. Just get in. The Russians are pushing back this way, and we're getting everyone away from the fighting."

"Help me in," Zach told them, and Grizzly and Gina walked him over to the Humvee, where they climbed in back. Craig and Liza were taken to another Humvee and got inside, their pale faces peering out.

The armored trucks turned and swept south toward the city, keeping to the right side of the road so other vehicles could move by.

CHAPTER SEVENTEEN

From the back seat, Zach looked around, the adrenaline of the fight waning as the situation settled on him. The CAF had their equipment and weapons, and their Humvee was shot to pieces. Zach didn't know if Red Hawk's previous orders would stand under the guard of a foreign military force, and sharp anxiety gnawed at his stomach.

"I hope we can get out of here soon," Zach said to Gina. "They got all our stuff, and I'm not sure if the Humvee even runs anymore."

"At least it didn't get blown up," Gina replied with a sigh as she watched a handful of American-made Humvees with big guns mounted on them drive by in the opposite direction.

"And I hope this Colonel Leopold has enough sense to let us go."

They drove on Klondike Highway past residential neighborhoods and entered the city proper until they reached a bright new sign that read *CAF Central Command*. The Humvees took a right off the highway to drive down a long lane filled with enormous warehouses, open gravel yards, and rig trailers in rows off to both sides. The place bustled with military personnel, tents, and temporary structures built everywhere, the Canadian flag whipping in the wind in the center of the encampment. More armored trucks shot past them to turn north up the highway on their massive frames.

Zach's driver angled off to the left up a side road that led to the most significant combination of tents and prefab buildings in the area. The Humvees pulled into two spots, popped their passengers' doors, and ordered them out gruffly. There were no medics around, so Zach leaned on the vehicle until Gina and Grizzly came to his aid. They followed the guards to a side tent detached from the rest. It had a dirt floor filled with rows of benches all the way to the back with a large propane heater in the middle and a podium up front.

"Wait in here until Colonel Leopold can see you." One guard gestured for them to go inside. "And don't try to leave. We'll be just outside."

"Wouldn't think of it," Zach said. "When can we see him?"

"As soon as the last Russian out there is dead," he frowned. "Might be a bit."

"Thanks."

As Gina and Grizzly took Zach to the first bench, two other

CHAPTER SEVENTEEN

guards brought Craig and Liza in. Craig sized up the place and addressed the soldiers as they started to leave. "Hey, if we're going to be here a while, can you bring some water?"

"And where are we supposed to use the bathroom?" Liza asked, hands on her hips.

One turned back and gave them an annoyed head shake. "We'll bring some water in for you, and if you need to use the restroom, let us know. We'll take you off to the side, and you can go in the woods."

Liza sighed and shook her head at the men. "I guess it will have to do. Thank you."

The soldiers left them alone in the tent with the sounds of the rumbling camp around them, boots running, diesel trucks revving and pulling out to join the fight along with distant booms.

"I hope they're winning," Gina said as she stood and paced, earning an agreeable grunt from Grizzly.

"It seems like they should be," Zach replied, "but based on what the Sergeant told me when we pulled off, this was a CAF training facility with mostly cadets."

"Still, I can't imagine the Russians have enough forces to take over a town of this size so deep in the Yukon," Craig said.

"Like the Sergeant told me. The coast isn't all that far from here, and Russian landing parties were spotted."

"Oh, no!" Liza held her head in her hands as she paced opposite Gina. "I cannot believe this is happening. My government is pushing things too far, and it will end in our destruction."

Craig put his hand on her shoulder to stop her. "I don't doubt some people would love to see that happen, but what can we do now? Let's see if we can do something about Zach's leg."

Liza threw up her hands in exasperation. "How can we do that when we have no medical supplies? They give us nothing."

"My dad used to tell us to rub dirt on it," Gina smirked.

Zach laughed and winced at the stinging pain radiating up the side of his leg to his hip. "At this point, I'd take it."

Twenty minutes passed and then an hour, which extended another hour more, and the group spread out on the first two rows, Zach lying on the ground with his leg elevated while Craig and Liza sat side-by-

CHAPTER SEVENTEEN

side, whispering in scientific jargon Zach didn't understand. Grizzly moved closer to the propane heater and stretched out in front of it, using his jacket as a pillow, his light snores drifting through the air. The guards brought two-gallon jugs of water and some paper cups. Liza washed out Zack's wound twice and re-wrapped it with what remained of the gauze. By that time, his leg and side had begun to stiffen, and a low-grade soreness set in from the sheer tension of the fight. Crawling away from the gunfire and firing the powerful carbine at the Russians had sent shocks through his shoulders and arms.

Beneath the pain of his superficial injuries was the worry they wouldn't get back on the road soon enough, and when he was about to fall into an exhaustive sleep, a vehicle pulled up outside and ground to a halt with doors slamming. Rising, Zach saw the green camouflage Humvee sitting out front with their guards approaching an officer and two staffers, saluting them briskly and gesturing toward the tent. Grizzly rose from his slumber with a snort and a grunt, and Gina offered Zach her hand. Liza and Craig got up and walked to the opening as the officer strode up and stepped inside, his hard blue eyes scanning the group.

Colonel Leopold turned to the guards. "Are you men going to let that lady haul that giant up herself?"

"No, sir!"

The soldiers grabbed Zach's hands and lifted him off the ground, turning him carefully and sitting him on the bench as the commander stood over him with his arms crossed. Leopold was a big man, standing over six feet tall, but lean. He glanced to the side, noticing the blood on Zach's pants and boots, and he shot an order at a guard.

"Get a medic in here, Rainer. Let's get this man's wounds looked at."

"About time," Liza murmured as she turned and took a few steps away.

Zach glanced at the Russian scientists before smiling apologetically. "You must be Colonel Leopold?"

"Correct. And you're from Colonel Red Hawk in Fairbanks."

CHAPTER SEVENTEEN

"I've got direct orders from him to get these two scientists back to DC as soon as possible."

"But you're not military?"

"I'm not, sir, but I assisted Colonel Red Hawk and the Marine unit on a mission in the Beaufort Sea to shut down the hydrocarbon emissions pouring from the Alaskan Rift site. We were only partially successful."

"So, this weather might end soon?"

Craig stepped in, keeping a respectful distance from the Colonel. "It's possible the gas well could run itself dry, but it doesn't look likely based on the firestorms we're still seeing."

"And you are?"

"Dr. Craig Sutton. I worked personally with President Holland on the solution we executed."

Leopold turned to him with more interest. "Impressive. I've got to give it to the US military for sticking the landing every time."

"As Zach said, the rift wasn't fully closed, and we still have a long way to go to survive this thing. Not to mention the Russians."

"We've been drilling for this scenario for the past few decades. My men and women are more than up to driving the Russians out of the Yukon."

"And I hope that's going well for you, Colonel."

Leopold took a deep breath. "We've got the resources to handle it, but the push from the Russians is heavier than expected, and sometimes they're dropping heavy equipment from planes. The bastards are ballsy. I'll give them that. Speaking of brave, what you did out there was incredible. Thanks for anchoring the line until we could get more troops online."

"Don't mention it, sir. I saw what needed to be done and did my best to fill the hole."

"If they'd broken through, there'd be a lot more dead Canadians around. I owe you one for that."

"We've had run-ins with the Russians before and saw what was happening in Fairbanks firsthand. We're guessing the Russians are going for Alaska's resources and causing havoc along the way, hoping

CHAPTER SEVENTEEN

to gain ground in the confusion." Zach glanced at Craig. "But we're not military specialists, of course."

"That's what a lot of the big brass are saying, too. Right now, we're trying to get our bearings and hope this insane weather tapers off so we can get those American jets in the sky. It won't even be close, then."

"We saw some aerial fights over Fairbanks when we came in," Craig said.

"I'm sure you did, but neither side will commit hundreds of planes into those messy skies. Right now, it's only air skirmishes confined to Alaska and Russians landing on our shores." He gave a firm nod to Liza and Grizzly. "Are these the two Russians you brought down from Fairbanks?"

"That's right, sir," Craig replied. "One is former Russian military but has been our driver. We call him Grizzly. The lady here is Liza Kovaleva, and she's currently..." Craig looked to Liza for an answer.

The diminutive woman stepped up. "Defecting to the United States, though not entirely by my choice. We were betrayed by a Russian military commander, the very one who is eliciting this attack on your two countries."

Leopold grunted and scanned over them again. "You're an interesting group, I'll give you that. And your orders from Colonel Red Hawk check out. Communication has been spotty, but we've got one strong radio connection between Fairbanks and us."

Zach shifted in his seat with interest. "How are they faring?"

"Fairbanks is still standing, though Red Hawk is off directing some of the fighting, and that's all we know. Other than that, we've got United States military equipment columns coming through. You may have seen some pass on your way down here."

"Yes, we did."

As they were talking, a pair of medics entered, faces smudged and uniforms dirty from what must've been their proximity to the fighting. Wordlessly, one placed her kit down, kneeled by Zach, and began looking at his leg wound. The other straddled the bench and examined his shoulder.

"Can you raise your right arm, sir?"

CHAPTER SEVENTEEN

"I think so." Zach winced and pulled his hand toward his chest, raising his elbow so the medic could check him out.

"If you need to do this first, we can talk later," Leopold said.

Zach shook his head. "No, sir. We want to get back on the road as soon as possible. I'm not sure if our Humvee still runs, but we'd like to have it back if it does. Our weapons and supplies, too."

"I'd advise against that. You saw what the Russians are bringing, and they might be anywhere on the road."

"I understand that, sir, but my orders are clear. I need to get Dr. Sutton and Dr. Kovaleva to DC, or at least to a working air force base in the United States, as soon as possible. Red Hawk gave us some waypoints to explore, hoping we can find someone to fly us at least part way there."

The Colonel squinted. "You're willing to risk your life and those with you to run that gauntlet?"

Zach winced as the medic used tweezers to pluck a piece of shrapnel from his leg, setting the grain-sized piece in a cup. Once the pain had passed, he glanced around at his friends. "I can't speak for everyone here, but I want to get to the States as soon as possible, so I'm willing to take that chance. So far, we've faced attacks from Russians and American citizens, and the roads are far from safe. In Fairbanks, we heard reports that things weren't going well in the States, though I don't know if it's still true."

"It's probably worse now." Leopold firmed his stance. "There's rioting in major cities, and the President is fighting a two-front battle between the Russians and taking care of the situation at home. It's not much better in Toronto and other Canadian provinces. Whether it's firestorms or unexpected cold fronts, rains, and mudslides, the weather is beyond tumultuous and is causing major resupply problems, spurring all the panic. The news had people in a frenzy before the power went out, and it's only gotten worse."

"And that's exactly why we need to continue," Zach said with a set jaw. "It won't get any better out there."

The Colonel nodded and glanced around. "The rest of you feel this way, too?"

"I can't speak for the others," Craig replied quietly, "but I'd like to

CHAPTER SEVENTEEN

get back on the road as soon as possible, too. We've all got families to get back to and an obligation to the President to bring the samples we took from the rift site and hard data drives back to Washington. As Zach said, it won't get any easier for us. I would appreciate anything you can do to help us."

The medic working on Zach's leg looked up. "I'm going to numb the area and apply some sutures. You'll feel a little pinch."

"Yeah, go ahead." He glanced up. "Sorry, Colonel."

"That's quite all right. I want to see you get the proper medical attention before you leave if that's what you want to do."

"We do, sir. As soon as possible, please."

Zach leaned forward to emphasize the next point. "And I'm sure that when you get back in touch with Fairbanks, they'd love to know that we arrived here safely and that you helped us on our way with no delays."

Leopold stared at Zack for a moment before breaking into a smile. "Well said, Mr. Christensen. We always want to be helpful to our allies, so I don't see a problem with seeing you on your way. We'll perform a routine check on your vehicle and bring it up with your supplies and weapons. Give us an hour or two to make that happen, and you'll be back on the road before nightfall. On top of that, I'll add my clearance to that of Colonel Red Hawk's, and any future Canadian checkpoints you reach will be amicable to you."

"We appreciate that, Colonel Leopold. Thank you."

"In the meantime, if you need food, make your way over to the mess tent and eat your fill."

"Thanks again, sir."

Leopold gave the group another once over and took his staffers with him. One staffer stayed behind, speaking to the guards before leading one away. The remaining soldier stepped back into the tent. "I'll stay here with you to assist, but it won't be as a guard. You can go to the mess tents and latrines as needed."

"Thanks, Private..." Zach leaned closer to read the man's name.

"Girard, sir. Private Girard." The soldier nodded and stepped inside to sit on Zack's right, on the other side of the medics. "Good to meet you, and thanks for standing by while we wait to

CHAPTER SEVENTEEN

get our gear back. Sorry about the attack on your facility. I was with a Sergeant Coultier when we were attacked, and he didn't make it..."

"Twenty casualties so far," Girard replied. "Fifty wounded. We were all just cadets here when this started, and now we're in the middle of a war."

Craig stepped over with his arms crossed on his chest. "Let's just hope it stays localized and doesn't spread to something more provocative."

"I am hoping there are sane elements left in the Russian government who would not engage in such a war," Liza said, coming up. "That would be idiotic."

"Many would say they're idiotic for what they're doing now," Craig countered.

"Is true."

Grizzly stretched his arms over his head, yawned, and lumbered toward the exit. "I will take the Colonel's advice and eat fill at mess tent. Driving makes Grizzly hungry." He gave his belly several heavy slaps. "And we have long road ahead."

"Eat up my —" Zach winced as the last stitch plunged into his calf and the thread was drawn through. "My friend."

"All done here," the female medic said as she tied off the thread, gave the area a final cleaning, and applied a thick bandage. "Sorry we had to cut your clothes up."

Private Girard stood. "I'll go find something for you in the supply hut... extra tall."

"Thanks," Zach said as the soldier jogged off.

"Good luck getting back to the States." The male medic finished applying the last bandage to Zach's side and gave him a final nod. "I hope you make it home safely."

"And I hope the Russians have seen enough of this facility and won't try attacking it again."

The Canadian smiled wanly. "Let us hope they come to their senses, yes."

"I'm going with Grizzly to get something to eat," Gina added, standing and nodding at Zach. "Do you want anything?"

CHAPTER SEVENTEEN

"I'll have a plate of whatever you're eating," he replied. "And thanks."

Gina gave him a thumbs up and joined Grizzly as they walked off in search of food.

"We're going to grab some grub, too," Craig said. "Will you be okay here by yourself?"

"I'll manage," Zach smiled. "Honestly, I could use a little quiet."

"I understand. We'll be right back."

Left alone in the briefing tent, Zach listened to the sounds of the camp as trucks came and went, soldiers shouted, and news bulletins were piped through loudspeakers. As they often did, the kids popped into his mind; Charlie's golden hair and David's quiet caring, held together by Wendy and her rambunctious spirit. And while it felt good to be given the go ahead to leave by Colonel Leopold, the distance they needed to travel to get to the States was staggering and seemed even more impossible with Russians running around and crazy weather falling on their heads. All that remained true were his feelings for his family and the raw longing to have them in his arms again. Still, until then, he had a responsibility to keep those with him safe, and he vowed to do so as long as he was able.

Zach drew his legs beneath him and applied some weight to his injured leg, feeling a slight tightening of the stitches and bandage wrapped around his calf. Leaning to his left, he shoved himself up and stood on his good leg, putting his right foot down and balancing his weight a little at a time. Taking careful and experimental steps, he limped to the entrance and peered outside. The ever-dark skies and churning clouds shifted in conflicting air currents. Swaths of gray fog moved beneath the primary cloud banks toward the north as the ones in the upper atmosphere continued barreling south, carrying flames and poisonous fumes. After some practice, he realized he could put a good deal of weight on his leg, though he wouldn't be running anywhere anytime soon.

The sounds of laughter drew his gaze toward the exit as Grizzly, Gina, Craig, and Liza approached with food trays. Grizzly said something that Gina took mock offense to and bumped him with her shoulder, almost causing him to lose the meals he was carrying.

CHAPTER SEVENTEEN

Zach grinned as they came up. "I thought you guys would eat in the mess tent."

"We started to," Gina said with a smile, "but we didn't want you to eat alone. Here you go. I'm sure it's as good as American Army food."

Grizzly handed him a tray with what looked like a mush of Salisbury steak or meatloaf, off-color mashed potatoes, limp green beans, and a single square brownie in their separate sections.

"Thanks. Looks great."

"They gave me a small pot of coffee." Craig held up a pot in his other hand with a stack of paper cups on top.

"I don't care how bad it is," Zach replied, "I'll take a cup of coffee any day."

They spread out across the first two bench rows, Zach and Gina straddling one and facing each other with their trays in front of them, while Craig and Liza sat a little way off with their meals resting on their knees. Grizzly sat between them, going off about military slop compared to truck stop food. The giant Russian made it challenging to eat as Gina and Zach couldn't stop laughing. Soon they were finished, wiping up gravy with pieces of soft bread, and washing it down with water. When they were done, Craig came around and poured each a big cup of coffee, and they sat in quiet reflection, wondering what the road ahead would be like.

Craig commented that the weather would be a significant factor, though he couldn't predict what they'd run into, and Zach and Liza were concerned about the Russians. But as the turbulent skies rolled overhead, distant but less frequent booms rang out in the north. Girard returned with some new fatigue pants for Zach and a plethora of undergarments for him to layer up in. He took them to the back of the tent, undressed, washed with a splash of water on a rag, and put on his new clothes which made him look like a poorly dressed soldier.

Evening darkened the skies, making the lights around the encampment stand out, and the ones from town giving the impression of fireflies lighting up the distant forests. Girard brought their Humvee up and turned in a sharp circle, pointed toward the road.

343

CHAPTER SEVENTEEN

Grizzly whistled low as they stepped out of the briefing tent and got a glimpse of their vehicle. The engine seemed to run fine, though the windows and sides were riddled with bullet marks. Popping the hatch, Girard showed them their equipment was back in place with their weapons arrayed on top. Zach shouldered his Sig Spear and was glad to see the CAF had provided him with five hundred more rounds of ammunition for the gun, most of it already pressed into magazines and ready to load. They thanked Private Girard, shaking his hand and wishing him good luck, asking him to give Colonel Leopold their best wishes. As they piled inside, Zach peered to the north where shapes fell from the sky, not debris from the storms but something else. He circled the Humvee to get a closer look, drawing everyone's attention as they formed a line and stared upward.

"Is that what I think it is?" Zach asked.

Grizzly grabbed a pair of binoculars from their supplies. After a moment of scanning, he nodded and handed them to Zach. "It is exactly what you think."

Putting the field glasses to his eyes, Zach swept across the line of airplanes with Russian markings circling low to the west with objects dropping from their rears to float in the turbulent air. Soldiers at the end of parachutes swung like pendulums in the high winds. Armored trucks fell fast and hard, their free fall arrested by three massive parachutes per unit as they plummeted through the sky. As they watched, a half-dozen soldiers were hit with sharp cracks of lightning, their bodies and parachutes blazing in bright flashes before streaking toward the Earth, burned up and trailing soot. One plane was caught in the turbulent winds, the wings gyrating back and forth before electric light struck the fuselage, shocked the engines dead, and brought it down. Despite losing a handful of soldiers and planes, Russians continued to fall until the last plane broke off and swept westward, staying low to the ground and sweeping close to the vast mountain slopes where they disappeared.

"The Russians are here in force now," Zach said, then turned to the others. "Come on, let's mount up and get out of here before things get hairy."

CHAPTER EIGHTEEN

Wendy Christensen, Pearisburg, Pennsylvania

The rain had let up as Wendy and the kids trudged down the crumbling highway toward what they hoped was a new home, a place she couldn't begin to imagine. Thoughts ranged in her mind from an abandoned barn to an old broken-down house not much better than the one they'd just left. Their breaths gusted in the cool early morning air, the pavement showing signs of washing out with gravel slipping off from beneath the concrete layer to either side. Parts of the surface cracked and buckled, riddling it with ridges and sinkholes. It was still drivable but getting worse than when they were making their way south from New York.

Charlie and David slogged behind her with their heads low and their heavy backpacks weighing down their shoulders. Clyde stayed by Charlie's side, the dog had grown in strength over the past weeks and had no problems keeping up, sometimes stopping to drink from the many streams they encountered. They'd been walking all morning, and Wendy's feet were aching as she looked around at the Virginia backwoods, stretches of forest not budding, with no sun to drive the growth. With so much rainfall, the temporary creeks and

CHAPTER EIGHTEEN

streams branching off from every high point had become permanent flows that cut gullies through the landscape, carrying parts of houses and other buildings. Dead farm animals piled up in ditches and rotted, the wet stench coming off the corpses curling the hairs inside Wendy's nose.

"Hey, at least the rain has been slowing down."

"Yeah, but the constant drip from the trees is driving me nuts," Charlie replied breathlessly, frustrated at the long hike and ill-suited weather.

"Hey, you're the one who wanted to leave." Even as Wendy spoke the words, she regretted them because she'd wanted to leave, too. Luckily, Charlie ignored her and kept walking without a retort that might've grown into an argument. "Anyway, are you kids seeing anything good?"

"There were a couple of places off to the left," David replied, "but they were sitting in lakes. There's no way we could live in them."

Wendy clicked her tongue. "I guess we lose either way. If we find something on low ground, it'll be flooded. But if we find a house on a hill, there is a danger we could be washed away."

Charlie nodded. "It won't be as easy as we thought to find a place."

Wendy glimpsed a home resting on low ground but elevated above the road with faint lights glowing from the windows, the doors boarded up and spray-painted with warning signs. *Keep off the property! Looters will be shot on sight!* They'd steered clear of places like that, Wendy rushing the kids ahead and staying low. They sometimes came across lines of people heading west, families marching past the highway at intersections, some riding bikes, motorcycles, or walking. After one look at Wendy and her rifle, they hurried by. Once they spotted a group of a dozen men with shotguns and pistols, and they hastily left the road and hid in the woods until they passed, listening to the men's mean-spirited conversations, reinforcing Wendy's previous lessons that the world was a much different place.

"Oh, great!" David said. "Another mudslide."

They'd been weaving through open fields with ranges of trees and wooden or stone fences, three feet high and stretching for miles.

CHAPTER EIGHTEEN

Over the last bit, the north and south sides rose to form a wedge-shaped valley that rolled ahead at random elevations but grew narrower as they walked. Water filled the ditches off both shoulders, flooding a fence line and bushes, the flow trickling in front of them in tiny streams. Up ahead, a thick batter of brownish muck had slid off the northern hill, bringing trees and swaths of grass and brush with it. A tangle of debris was suspended in the flow where it had stretched to the other side, filled up the ditch, and finally stopped. Wendy and the kids stood in front of it, looking up to ensure there were no secondary washouts to carry them away, but thick woods anchored that part of the slope.

"We're going to have to go through this," David stated flatly, pointing off to the left where the flood wasn't so deep. "There."

Wendy walked over and pushed a lock of wet, blonde curls back beneath her poncho hood, the garments returned to them by Morten to replace the plastic bag ones they'd made. "It's as good a place as any to cross. There're a couple of wood slabs out there, be careful of nails and sharp pieces. Stand back. I'm going to go first."

The kids gave her room, and Wendy stretched her foot out and took a step into the mud, squelching deep, the muck covering her boot as she moved ahead. She fought the suction and climbed up on a slanted piece of plywood, slipping to one knee before balancing and looking back at the kids with a hesitant grin. She stood, refocused, and continued, wincing as she walked off the wood and felt the cold mud seep into her tucked-in jeans, soaking her socks. With a frustrated gasp, she plunged ahead, knocking a kid's ball out of her way, grabbing a branch, turning a piece of deadfall over, and bumping her shin against something hard beneath the surface.

"There's something big in the mud here. Be careful."

Without looking back, she shoved her way through, backpack swinging on her shoulders, raindrops dripping from the branches overhead. Reaching the other side, she stepped onto the road, stopped to get the mud off her feet, and gazed back to wave the kids over. Charlie came next, carrying Clyde and following in the indentions Wendy had made in the mud, the girl not much taller than her mother but far stockier with thicker legs she used to bull

CHAPTER EIGHTEEN

her way through. She stomped hard, bypassing the piece of wood, gasping, and pumping her elbows, swinging Clyde in her arms. In thirty seconds, she'd made her way across and stood beside Wendy with an annoyed expression as she stared at her muddy feet. Setting Clyde on the ground and picking up a stick, she started brushing off caked-on muck from where it was stuck in her shoestrings and around the edges. David was already coming. His long legs were seemingly an advantage, though his slight frame struggled to pull his feet from the suck. He made slower progress with his bony elbows swinging wide like he was jogging in quicksand. When he was three quarters of the way across, a low groan vibrated through the pavement, and the massive mudflow shifted, pushing slowly and inexorably to Wendy's right, shoving the kid's ball and plywood into the ditch to bury it deep. The sudden gush rippled until David was caught up in it and started slipping over the roadside.

Wendy leaped into the mud with a gasp, hands out and grabbing for her son. "David, my hand!"

He was reaching, almost lunging forward as mud rushed up to his knees and gripped his thighs, pushing him ever sideways. "I'm trying!"

Wendy stretched more and glanced left as tons of earthy material loomed above her and shifted down the hillside. Despite being up to her knees in it, she felt its strength and undeniable pressure, forcing her feet apart so she had to reposition herself. Heart leaping into her throat, sure they'd be sucked under in a few short seconds, she extended as far as possible without pitching face-first into the flow. David dove forward and grasped her left hand. Then Wendy was lunging backward, squatting and lifting with her legs, pulling David foot by foot to the edge of the mud, grabbing him in her arms and turning them both toward safety.

"Come on, son! Push!"

Knees pumping, they kicked their way through to where Charlie was waiting, grabbing them both by their jackets and helping them the rest of the way until they landed on the pavement. They ran twenty-five yards up the road, turning to watch as the slow-moving

CHAPTER EIGHTEEN

flow pushed another ten feet toward them and stopped again, the rumbling that had been vibrating through the ground quieting.

David was staring at the mud like he wanted to kill it. "Thanks, guys. The last thing I want is to be buried alive."

"Duly noted." Wendy took the stick from Charlie and swiped some of the caked-on mud coating her boots and jeans.

When she was done, she handed it to David and waited for him to clean up before they moved on. They stomped through puddles and over broken pavement, especially wary of the slopes on either side, her eye growing keener for spotting areas where potential mudslides might happen.

"We need to be more careful where there're not as many trees," she said. "That's where there seems to be more of a chance of a mudslide. Like up ahead here."

They half-jogged over the next quarter mile until they were approaching a small township with a couple of abandoned stores on the left, a gas station on the right, and several local businesses interspersed along the road. Water dripped down their walls, and they were missing parts of their roofs, which had been blown off or otherwise deteriorated by an increasing rate of wind and rain.

"We should go inside one of these buildings to rest and get something to eat," Charlie suggested.

"I was thinking about that, I'd like to find a place to settle first." Wendy looked around, squinting into the mist past the businesses and houses set off to the side of the road. "We can try some of those over there on the left. We can cut through the field there. It doesn't seem too flooded."

Of the four homes they tried, one was already boarded up and had likely been condemned before the chaos, its aging walls rotting from the inside out. Two others were falling apart, their foundations wiped out by the continual deluge of flooding that eroded them around their bases. The last was occupied with more of the same signs written on the front door and across the side of the house facing the road.

"We're never going to find a place to live," Charlie said as they got back on the highway and continued west.

CHAPTER EIGHTEEN

The oppressiveness of the weather and Charlie's complaining finally weighed on her. "I get what you're saying, hon, but your attitude is getting on my nerves. Can you please keep it to yourself until we find a place to stop?"

She accepted a faint nod from the girl and was thankful David seemed to be in a decent state of mind after everything they'd been through, and she patted him on the back as they continued walking in the mess.

A family came around the next bend, and Wendy nudged Charlie and David to draw their attention. The man was average-sized, skinny in his brown ski jacket buttoned tight around his neck and a wet woolen cap with a short bill on his head. The mother had locks of dirty blonde hair that fell over her red, water-resistant puffer coat, and the two kids were nine or ten, wearing dark ponchos that covered their faces and big galoshes on their feet. The little girl spotted them with big brown eyes as she pointed. The parents seemed to have been in a walking daze when they looked up, the father's expression brightening with fear while the mother took the girl by her arm and pulled her behind her.

"Mom?" Charlie whispered, and Clyde picked up on her hesitancy with a low growl that grew in his chest.

"They're on the other side of the road, Charlie," Wendy replied. "No need for us to bother one another. Let's stick to the right-hand side of the road and keep walking."

"Gotcha."

Wendy walked in front of them, forming a line with David and Charlie in that order, stepping to the right with their heads down and Wendy glancing over to see what the family was doing. They'd stopped, and the parents were discussing something heatedly, throwing glances at them and arguing about something. Wendy had an inkling of what they were going to do before they did it, and she made a show of switching her rifle from her right shoulder to her left, rolling her arm to let it settle there, hoping the father saw it and wouldn't bother engaging with them. But when they were just a few yards away, his shuffling feet started across the road to cut them off, waving at them as he called.

CHAPTER EIGHTEEN

"Hey, folks. Hey there! Can you stop for a minute? Hold on!"

Wendy kept moving, but he jogged ahead of her and turned, walking backward with his hands up.

"Please. You've got to stop. Please!"

When he stopped retreating, Wendy drew up and placed her palm on the butt of her weapon, prepared to pull it off her shoulder and use it if she needed to. The man gaped and took one step back, but by then, his family had joined him there. The woman pushed her children behind her and clung to her husband's arm, staring at Wendy and the kids with wide eyes. Up close, they were grimier than they first appeared, the boy and girl with dirt-smudged faces, the parents' expressions fearful yet with a hint of desperation she'd seen on so many faces.

"Thank you for stopping," the man said with a gasp and a smile.

"What do you want?" Wendy asked.

Smile faltering, he gestured to his family, who cowered behind him. "Seems obvious. My name is Tom Connor, and this is my wife Tina and our kids, Mason and Olivia."

Wendy nodded. "Okay, but back to my original question."

The man scoffed and stammered. "We were wondering where you folks are going?"

"We're recently homeless and looking for a permanent place to stay."

"Most of the farmsteads around here aren't worth staying in," he said. "Anything that isn't rotting or washing away is occupied, and the people inside are none too friendly."

"That's what we're finding out, too." Wendy kept her lips pressed together, determined to move on. "Now let us get by, so we can keep looking."

"We were thinking the Amish folks up the road might be friendly," Tom said hopefully. "You know, we always used to buy things from them, so maybe they'll —"

"You won't find any help there. We have relatives there, but they're not friendly to outsiders, even us. They won't let you stay, I guarantee that."

Tom shifted to his wife with a suspicious glance, his eyes

CHAPTER EIGHTEEN

narrowing as some unspoken communication passed between them. Then he turned back to Wendy. "Well, that's a shame now. I guess we'll have to find another place. And you say there's nothing back up the road?"

"Not that we could see," David said. "As you mentioned, places are either flooded out or falling apart."

"That's terrible news." Tom's expression fell. "Real bad news for us."

Wendy glanced back at Charlie and David before moving past the man, just three or four yards between them and the edge of the shoulder, which was deteriorating in crumbles of pavement and dirt. But as Wendy tried to guide the kids by, the man sprang to life and leaped in front of her, backing up a few paces to keep his distance, though not as much as before.

"What would you say to us teaming up together?"

"Teaming up?" Wendy shook her head. "I'm sorry, Tom, but we just got out of a situation that wasn't optimal, and we don't want to team up with anyone."

Tom crept closer, his gaze shifting from Charlie and David to the gun hanging from Wendy's shoulder. "What would be the issue with that? I mean, we're a healthy family, and we can work hard."

"That sounds like a great idea," Tina said. "We've all got kids to feed, and you're a single mother out here on your own. It would be good for us to have a man around."

Wendy bristled but kept her temper under control. "I *have* a man, but he's in Alaska trying to—"

"I'm the man of the family until my dad gets back," David said, standing side-by-side with his mother.

Annoyed, the man turned and raised his finger toward his wife while addressing David. "That's not what she meant, son. I couldn't replace your dad, but we could team up —"

"We've got to go, Mom," Charlie said, nudging her.

The man stepped back again, taking his family with him. Something clicked in his expression, mouth pulling into an angry grimace before his features smoothed. "Now, hold on just a second, folks. You guys have weapons, and we're pretty resourceful people."

CHAPTER EIGHTEEN

"If you were that resourceful, you wouldn't be begging to team up with us," David replied, and when Wendy shot him a scornful glance, he added, "Sorry, Mom, but it's true." He stepped past her and addressed the man firmly. "Look, sir. You've got a great family, but we want to get off the road and rest a bit, and we don't want any company or trouble from anyone. Please, back up and let us pass."

"They don't want us around," Tina said, taking Tom's arm and drawing him away. "Let's just go, honey."

"We can't go!" he growled, tearing from her grip and glaring at David. Then his features softened, and he shook his head as if calming himself. "Look, we haven't had much to eat over the past week, and we're swimming in our clothes." Tom laughed nervously. "You wouldn't believe it, but little Mason there was a chunky kid before all this. The boy's lost a quarter of his weight."

One glance at the boy's hollowed expression, and Wendy knew it was true. His face was gaunt, eyes sunken in their sockets, and his coat hung from his shoulders with sleeves that covered his hands. Water dripped from his poncho to his chin, though he didn't flinch or seem bothered by it.

Wendy pulled David behind her, not angry with him for telling the truth about the situation but not wanting it to turn into a pissing match between the two men. "We're sorry to hear that, folks. But as you can see, we're just as bad off as you."

"But you got those backpacks there, and I know you got some food and supplies in them."

"We've got enough for just us, plus some camping gear that keeps us off the wet ground, but that's it. We don't have much to give, but some stuff might be left in some of these houses around here."

Tom clapped his hands, turning his gaze away before coming back with anger twisting his features. "Don't give me that bull, lady. You know how risky walking up on one of these houses is."

While Clyde had been silent for some time, something clicked in him, and his low growl resonated deep in his chest and rumbled from his throat. Mason and Olivia flinched, the little girl gasping and clinging to her mother, while the boy only stared with wide eyes.

"You better call that dog off," Tom said, pointing at Clyde.

CHAPTER EIGHTEEN

"You don't tell us what to do," Charlie countered.

Tom shifted his anger toward her. "And you better put a lock on that mouth, young lady."

"How about not talking to my sister that way, man?" David stuck his chest out, arms held off from his sides with his palm going for his pistol. "And get out of here like my mom said."

"David!" Wendy warned, "I'll handle this."

In tears, Olivia begged her father. "Daddy let's go! There's that one house we saw. It was a little wet, but it would do fine!"

"A roof over our head won't matter if we're starving to death," Tom snapped back, then bore down on Wendy with a couple of menacing steps.

She retreated two paces, grabbing her M&P 15 from her shoulder and swinging it around to a firing position from her hip, shaking her head with a warning. "Hold it right there, Tom. I swear I'll shoot if you try to hurt us. I've done it before, and I'll have no problem doing it again."

Tom froze, and Mason grabbed his jacket and pulled. "Dad, come on! Let's just go!"

The man knocked the boy's arm away. "I won't let them leave without giving us at least something. Just a couple of mouthfuls of food to get us through the next day is all we need." He glared scornfully at Wendy. "Put your pack down and give us something."

"Don't talk to my mom that way." David shoved Tom hard.

"Hey, that was uncalled for!" Tina cried.

The glint in Tom's eyes caused Wendy to raise her weapon to her shoulder with her finger slipping beneath the trigger guard, bumping David aside with her hip and pointing the gun at the man's face.

"Stop!" The energy in her tone drew barks from Clyde, the dog straining at the ends of his leash where Charlie had choked up to keep him from going very far in any direction. "This stops now!"

Tom had been about to leap forward, but the sight of the weapon froze him in his tracks. A long growl curled from Clyde's throat, ending in a snarl that sent Olivia running back up the road a few yards before turning when she realized she had no place to go.

"Come on!" the girl shrieked. "Let's go before they kill us!"

CHAPTER EIGHTEEN

"Hush, Olivia," Tom told her, his gaze never leaving Wendy. "Let your daddy do the talking here."

"Threatening us won't work," Wendy said, her lip curling at the idea of scaring a little girl and stranding the family out in the wilderness without a single bite to eat. Sweat trickling down her back, she fixed him with a look of calm disdain. "If you think you're going to take ours from us, you better think again." Pausing to let things settle, she deliberately lowered her tone but left her rifle pointed at Tom's face. "You can't come with us, but we'll spare a few snack bars from our packs. It isn't much, but they're high in caloric value —"

Tom lunged for her weapon, grabbing the hand guard and shoving the barrel upward. Wendy squeezed the trigger, one shot cracking in their ears, sending Tom's kids running and Clyde barking his head off. David and Charlie shouted, but all Wendy could do was to keep her hands on her rifle, gripping it, fighting back and forth with Tom for control, stomach twisted with the thought of him getting it and turning it on her and the kids. Tom wrenched it with a desperate grunt, pulling Wendy off her feet, but she clung to it with both hands, swinging her scrawny hips in to knock him away, drawing the gun to her chest and holding it close.

Tom was behind her, wrapping his arms around her, the weight pressing her to the ground as he grabbed for the stock. "Give it here, Wendy, you selfish bitch! I'm not letting our kids starve out here!"

Wendy could only cling to the weapon, teeth clenched and straining to hold on. David swooped in and seized Tom, cursing and jerking him backward, only to have Tina leap on his back. She flew into a wild rage, legs wrapped around his waist, screaming and punching his head. Clyde's growls erupted in a frenzy, and his claws scraped across the ground as he rushed in. Tina's angry hollering escalated into howls of pain as the dog clamped down on something. Wendy barely saw anything, just feet scuffling in her peripheral vision. The only sound breaking through was their kids' cries, Olivia shrieking for them to stop fighting while Mason screamed and punched at Clyde. She sank to her knees, clinging to the gun even as Tom struck her. It was chaos, each blow sending stars ringing in her brain, but she clung to the weapon and wouldn't let him have it no

355

CHAPTER EIGHTEEN

matter how much he cursed, begged, and punched her. And then Charlie was striking and kicking the man, swinging her fists wildly, hat flying off, golden hair whipping around. She landed a solid shot to the side of Tom's head, and he threw an elbow at her, knocking her back. Wendy thrashed, escaping his grip for a second and almost getting away.

Grasping and snarling, Tom coiled to lunge. "Get back here you little—"

A gunshot popped off, and Tom screamed, followed by Charlie shouting at the top of her lungs. "Back off, now! Or I'll kill you! I swear I'll do it."

With no more pressure on her back, Wendy glanced around and shook the dizziness from her head. Tina was on her knees, clinging to David's arm and trying to get at the pistol on his hip. Clyde had Tina's coat locked in his jaws, his powerful neck jerking and ripping the material, the suddenly vicious Gray Lab snarling and foaming at the mouth. Mason held a big stick in his hand, cocked back and ready to strike Clyde. Charlie stood a few yards away in a perfect shooting pose, with her .380 pointed right at Tom, who held his arm with blood pulsing between his fingers and running down his coat.

He glared at Charlie in disbelief. "You shot me!"

"You had it coming! Step back, or I'll do it again, and I'll shoot you in the face next time!"

Wendy swung her rifle around and pointed at Mason. "Get away from the dog, son."

Gasping, the boy dropped the stick and backed up as Clyde continued tearing at Tina's coat.

"Hold him there, Charlie." Wendy sidestepped, staggering around her and moving to Clyde, grabbing his harness and pulling him back. "Down, Clyde. Come on, boy. Down!"

Clyde snapped his head a few more times, tearing off another piece of material before his eyes rolled back to see it was Wendy. He growled low in his chest but quit his thrashing.

"Come on, boy! Let her go."

Clyde released Tina's jacket, and David turned and kicked her arm off him, sending the woman tumbling to the pavement with a

CHAPTER EIGHTEEN

cry. Mason and Olivia rushed in and fell on her, pulling her away from danger even as David drew his Springfield and backed up to stand next to Wendy with his weapon alternating between Tom and Tina. Tom collapsed to his knees, crying and slouching forward with his right arm hanging loose, his jacket becoming more saturated with blood by the second. Olivia threw caution to the wind and ran to her father, sliding to her knees next to him and staring at the blood.

"Get her away from you, Tom!" Wendy growled. "I don't want to hit her when I put a bullet between your eyes."

"Shut up!" Olivia howled, throwing her arms around him. "You shot my dad. Go to hell!"

Wendy tilted her head, heart breaking for the little girl and the anguish written on her face. Before things could devolve further, she glanced at Charlie and David. "Charlie, get Clyde and move around the left side of the road. You, too, David."

The kids did as they were told, and the trio circled the family as Tina and Mason went to Tom, where he knelt wounded and sobbing with long lines of drool and snot dripping from his chin. Once they'd passed, Wendy gestured for her kids to keep moving while she walked backward down the road, the M&P 15 pointed in Tom's direction. Tina and her children stared at her with hate-filled eyes. She wanted to say something, but no words would heal the situation, and she'd only be wasting her breath if she tried.

"Here, Mom. Take this."

Wendy stopped to see Charlie holding Clyde's leash out for her. She took it, and Charlie shrugged off her backpack, dropping it on the road and rummaging through it, placing several snacks aside, three MRE meals, and one of their better first-aid kits. Wendy thought about stopping her but let her go with just one comment.

"Honey, that's the one with the sutures, and we may need it."

"I know, Mom, but they need the sutures now." She stood with the things in her arms. "The guy was being a rat face, but he was just desperate. The situation made him reach for your gun. It could've been bad, but it wasn't, and we can't let those kids go without helping them."

Wendy stared into her daughter's dazzling blue eyes like clear-cut

CHAPTER EIGHTEEN

gems in the dreary weather. Finally, she nodded and smiled. "Go ahead."

Charlie smiled back. "Thanks, Mom."

Trotting over to the family, Charlie kneeled and placed the things on the ground, a decent spread of food for at least one night. Then she said something Wendy couldn't hear, holding up the first-aid kit and probably explaining what was inside and how they could use it. No one knew just how deep the wound was and if it had hit a major artery. If so, Tom wouldn't be long for the world.

Charlie's expression was brighter as she jogged back.

"Everything okay?"

"Tina said thanks, but the kids are too freaked out right now to know what's going on." Charlie shrugged on her backpack and took Clyde's leash, drawing the dog along with her.

David stared at Tom, his jaw working back and forth.

"Put your gun away, son," Wendy said.

David did as he was told, shrugging an apology. "He *hit* you, but he won't do it again."

"I know," Wendy replied, hugging him briefly. "It's all over now, so you can relax."

They turned and walked away, Wendy glancing back to see the kids tearing off the wrappers and devouring the high-calorie protein bars. Tina took the first-aid kit to Tom, who'd fallen on his rear with his legs crossed, still holding his arm in the middle of the road.

"That was my fault," Wendy said, "and it won't happen again. I can't believe I let them get so close to me." She glanced over at Charlie. "Good shooting, honey. You only wounded him."

Charlie scoffed. "What are you talking about? That was a terrible shot. I was aiming for his head and pulled down and to the left."

Eyebrows raised, Wendy glanced at David, who was grinning crookedly. "In any case, let's search even harder for a place to stay," she said. "It's going to be dark in a few hours, so we might need to lower our standards."

"I don't care," Charlie said. "I just want a place to sit for a minute that's *dry*."

While their adrenaline was pumping from the altercation, soon

CHAPTER EIGHTEEN

Wendy's feet began aching again as they searched everywhere for the next farmstead or house, discounting those few with lights in the windows or shadows creeping around the property. Some homes were a hundred years old, just off the roadside and ripped apart by trees and foliage growing up through the floorboards. While Wendy was tempted to find any shelter to keep the rain off their heads, she pressed on for another couple of miles until the buckled highway cut between a pair of hills with the woods crowding in on them. With water dripping in her eyes, Wendy spotted a driveway that turned up on the narrow right-hand shoulder. A mailbox with the name *Goodhew* sat tilted to the side, and water poured into a drainage pipe that ran beneath the road to spray out the other end in a gush. Charlie and David kept walking, but she stopped and stared up the driveway as it wound steeply into the woods.

"Hey, kids."

They turned and looked back.

"What, Mom?" Charlie asked.

"How about up here?"

The kids followed her gaze up the hill where it disappeared into the trees.

Charlie rolled her eyes and took one step back toward Wendy. "Are we really going to try this? That's a huge hill, Mom."

"It *is* a huge hill," Wendy replied, "but we've been walking so long, and you guys are tired."

"We'll go all the way up only to stare down some redneck's shotgun barrel," David said with a frustrated gesture. "Or the house will be half washed out down the hill or something."

"You don't know. Could be a rainbow at the end of the driveway or a pot of gold." Wendy smiled humorlessly, hoping the kids might laugh, though her expression faltered when they didn't. "Let's just try it, huh?"

David sighed and gestured to Charlie. "Let's just get this over with. The faster we get up there and get disappointed, the faster we can get back to walking."

"I'm not liking your attitude very much, David," Wendy said as she led them up the hill, her thighs burning at the elevated angle,

CHAPTER EIGHTEEN

kicking herself and thinking she could handle it on her already tired feet.

"Sorry, Mom. I guess the weather has gotten me down."

The way he spoke with sarcastic ambiguity drew a chuckle from Charlie, and Wendy grinned with a bit of slaphappy pleasure. Through the tangle of wet forest, a house took shape, a single-story structure with clean white siding and a wide bay window in front. The main section had a high-pitched roof, indicating an elevated ceiling inside. Squinting through the trees, Wendy searched for any signs of life, movement behind the curtains or lantern light emanating from within, but there was none, and the driveway was empty of cars.

"So far, so good, kids."

"Doesn't seem like anyone's home," David replied, stepping faster up the hill.

"The driveway is empty," Charlie said, tugging on Clyde's leash and keeping him close, "but there could be cars in the garage."

"That's what I was thinking," Wendy replied.

By the time they reached the top, Wendy's legs were on fire, and she stopped and crossed her arms while she scanned the house and far west side, where trellises and a wooden archway stood covered in vines and brown foliage, leading off to someplace in the backyard she couldn't see.

"And look at that." She pointed past the garage where the driveway turned into a gravel lane and swung up to the right against the hillside where a long red stable sat nestled in the trees.

"You think they have horses here?" Charlie asked, immediately starting in that direction before Wendy stopped her.

"Hang on a second, Charlie. We need to check the house first before we even think about going out there. Everyone got their weapons ready?"

David and Charlie both checked their guns, Charlie charging hers after reloading it earlier. The clack of the .380 as she racked a round sounded small in the thunderstorm.

"You kids stay out here," Wendy said. "Back me up if I get into trouble."

CHAPTER EIGHTEEN

"No problem, Mom." David scoffed. "It's crazy how we were on defense for so long, and now we're on offense."

"If it gets too hairy, we'll run. Okay?"

Wendy marched up the walkway and along the front of the house, the once robust gardens flooded with water that drained off in a steady stream to the road. The blinds were all drawn but for the bay window, which had some open space for her to stare in. With a glance at the sidelights, Wendy stepped past the front door and moved through the mulch to stand before the bay window. Cupping her hands against the glass, she peered inside to see a wide-open great room with a fireplace and television mounted across from her, a neat leather couch stretched in front with an assorted array of furniture pieces. She walked around to the other side and peered toward the kitchen, where she gazed at a kitchen table, a cooking island, and stainless-steel appliances. On a whim, she rapped on the glass.

"Mom, what are you *doing*?" Charlie hissed.

"Don't worry about it. Just keep an eye out."

She waited for someone to pop out of a back room or come around the sides, but no one ever did, and the window didn't shake with the vibrations of footsteps. Retreating from the glass, she held her finger up to the kids to tell them to wait. Wendy peered at the vine-covered trellises and archway on the west side of the home but saw nothing in the backyard except clusters of trees and brush. She went to the front door and tried the doorknob, but it was locked, so she gestured for the kids to follow her to the garage doors, finding those locked as well. Around the back, a regular-sized door was built into the side of the garage, also shut tight, though Wendy noticed a small square black shape screwed into the eaves above.

"Check it out, guys. Cameras."

"Can't tell if they're on or not," David replied, tapping it with his long arms but receiving no blinking lights. The back patio was standard at about twenty square feet, complete with a covered grill, a small table with four chairs and an umbrella. The sliding glass door was locked tight with a security camera mounted to the eave.

"We can break into this pretty easily," David said, walking up to the door and inspecting the entire frame along the bottom edges.

CHAPTER EIGHTEEN

"Yep, there's no door bar holding it shut, so I can do it without breaking the glass."

"Are you serious?" Wendy asked, stepping back.

"Yeah. We have a small toolkit in here." David shrugged off his backpack and placed it on the wet patio, unbuckling the flap and going through the sides and pouches.

"Oh, I think I have that," Charlie said, taking off her pack and rummaging around in it. "That's if Grandpa put the toolkits in here. I had them by the first-aid kits… Oh, here it is. What do you need?"

"The biggest flathead screwdriver you can find." Charlie unzipped a general household tool kit, spread it open, and located a long screwdriver with multiple ends. She picked the flat head end and fixed it in place with a magnetic snap, then handed it to David. "Here you go."

"Thanks."

David kneeled by the door and wedged the screwdriver beneath where it rested on the frame. He reached up with his left hand, counted to three, and leveraged the door upward while pulling. With a soft snap, it slid aside easily, giving them access to the dark kitchen beyond.

"Hey, where'd you learn how to do that?" Wendy asked with a frown.

"Don't worry, Mom," David grinned. "I wasn't breaking into houses or anything. Once, my friend Lenny was locked out of his house, and he showed me how to get in this way. One way to keep that from happening is to get a door bar, which is why I was looking for one."

"Oh, I see," Wendy said.

Swinging her rifle up, she pressed past David and went inside, a faint flowery fragrance touching her nose, filling her head with a thousand memories of their own home and the candles she sometimes lit at night when it was quiet. There were no reeking aromas of death, mud, gun smoke, or horses, and she took a few seconds to breathe it in even as she swept the barrel of her rifle across the room.

She glanced back. "We're going to need to split up and search the house. You guys check the garage, and I'll walk through the back of the house and make sure nobody's here."

CHAPTER EIGHTEEN

"If nobody's here, can we stay?" Charlie asked, pulling Clyde by his leash.

Wendy was shaking her head in anticipation of the question. "I don't know, honey. This seems way too good to be true. Anyway, let's check it out. Meet back here in three minutes, and holler if you need me."

"Holler if you need us, too," Charlie said.

A grin touched the corner of Wendy's mouth, and she started through the great room, walking between the couch and TV and glanced at the tasteful decorations the owners had put up, artsy photography and science-related objects: spaceships, stars, Greek symbols, and abstract pieces on every wall. Some of it was well beyond her liking, and they covered the hallway all the way to the bathroom, which was situated on the right. Two guest rooms stood on the left with neutral colors and décor. A nice master bedroom greeted her at the end of the hall with its own fireplace, a king-size bed, and a pair of dresser drawers on opposite sides of the room. The cherry wood pieces had enough personal flair to give her the impression that an organized couple owned them. The only indications of it being lived in were the tousled covers and comforter folded back on one corner. The bathroom stood empty, though Wendy remarked on the beautiful, marbled tile work on the floor, and the sliding glass shower with built-in shelves and stone-gray walls. The twin sinks only had hygiene products on one side, including lotions, jars of daily renewal moisturizer, and a few makeup kits.

"Nice," she murmured, returning to the kitchen.

"Anything interesting?" Charlie asked.

Wendy shrugged. "There's no one here, for sure, and the place is really nice and well organized. Smells great, too."

Charlie let go of Clyde's leash and let him explore a bit. "I want to stay *so* bad."

"It has three bedrooms." Wendy raised an eyebrow. "What about the garage? Any cars?"

"There's an older black pickup with a good-sized cabin," David said. "Looks spotless and well cared for."

"That would come in handy." Wendy bit her lip and glanced

CHAPTER EIGHTEEN

around the kitchen, walking to the pantry that was just to the right of the refrigerator, popping it open, and staring at the shelves with her mouth watering. The bottom shelves were filled with home-canned stewed tomatoes, onions, pickles, and potatoes, to name a few. Boxed meals stood in neat rows at the very top, with packets of powdered drinks, breakfast cereals, bread, and assorted canned meats in between.

"Bingo," she said.

"Oh please, I hope no one lives here," Charlie said, her face twisted, hands thrown together as she pleaded.

Wendy picked up a loaf of bread and studied the mold across the top, turning and tossing it to Charlie, who caught it with a disgusted look.

"What's this mean?"

"I can't imagine anyone would've kept bread that moldy if they lived here. No matter how bad things might get, eating that will make a person sick."

"Does that mean no one lives here and we can stay?" Charlie bounced on the balls of her feet, her expression brightening.

Stepping to the kitchen table, she drew her finger across the surface and raised it to show a dirty smudge on the tip. "Judging by this undisturbed dust and the moldy bread, it's safe to say no one's been here for a few days, maybe a week. We should probably check the stables and make sure no one's out there. Leave Clyde here for now."

The kids led the way, leaving the sliding glass door partially open and tossing their backpacks inside as they crept along the gravel road out to the faded red stables. Wendy was cautious, walking slowly and quietly until they reached the west corner, where the gravel path split, one part circling to the near entrance while the other continued ahead. Pulling open the double doors, they stepped into pitch darkness and were hit with the smells of old hay and horse manure. Wendy took a flashlight from her pocket and flipped it on, shining it around a storage room to reveal an assortment of bridles, bits, and other horse-riding equipment. A desk with repair tools stood on the right side. Wendy guided the beam straight ahead where the main

CHAPTER EIGHTEEN

stable corridor stretched thirty yards to the far end, though it seemed empty and dark until several equine-shaped heads stepped to their stall doors and stared at the newcomers with light glinting from their black eyes.

Charlie's face instantly brightened, and a squeal tore from her lips. "Horses! They've got horses. I just knew it" Despite her excitement, the girl stayed where she was, looking to her mother for permission.

Wendy turned and looked around at the warm stable surroundings, shaking her head, listening, waiting for her instincts to warn her of some danger. She shouted "Hello!" down the passage a few times to the restless nickering of horses and the silent swirl of dust in her flashlight beam.

"What do you think, mom?" David followed her gaze nervously. "Can we trust it?"

"I can't believe it's true, but it seems we found a new place to stay." Wendy quickly and pointedly added, "At least for the short term. For tonight."

"Can I pet the horses?" Charlie asked in a soft but firm whisper.

"I guess it's okay, and maybe they need food and water, too." Wendy's insides turned nervously, though she shouldered her weapon and nodded. "I don't know the first thing about taking care of horses, but the second we're done checking on them, we're going back inside to get some rest. I'll take the first watch while you two get some sleep. It's been a few weeks since we've laid in actual beds."

"Yes!" Charlie crept carefully yet delightedly up the central passage, muting her excitement to coo softly to the wary beasts.

The rain and storms were heavy, whipping through the trees as Matt Stegman scrambled down the hill, sliding on his hip, slipping, kicking leaf mold and sticks, and leaping rotting logs. He was soaked, and his hands were scraped and bloody. Not even the poncho he'd gotten from the supply shed kept him anywhere near dry. But McCallum had something for him to do, and when the boss gave you an order,

CHAPTER EIGHTEEN

you did it—no questions asked. He'd been scouring Buck Ridge for potential scavenging spots when the call came in that Darla Goodhew was messing with McCallum's people at the local department store. His job was to head straight over to the Goodhew place and hit it while Darla wasn't home.

Matt didn't expect anyone to be there, but he remained cautious, coming off the ridge to get a good view of the grounds before trying to enter the house. He'd check to see if anyone was around or if the lights were on, then radio back to McCallum what he'd found. As Matt edged downward beneath the dripping foliage, the property became visible through the trees. A long backyard filled with massive puddles fronted by a ranch-style home stretching from east to west, and a smudge of greenery on the one side that faded into the perpetual mist. The stables appeared east of the house at the end of a curved lane. Just as he was about to drop the last twenty feet to the yard, he froze at the sound of a heavy door closing and voices floating up the hillside. He angled in that direction, descending a few feet as the hills steepened, slipping on the forest debris, pushing plumes of breath, clutching saplings, swinging from one to the next like an ape until he found a good position to watch the driveway as it curved from the house to the stables.

He scooted to his left, squatted and raised up, inquisitive but careful not to slide any farther and be found out or, worse, break a leg. Three people came into view from the trees, a tall skinny guy and two shorter women, wearing ponchos with hoods pulled up over their faces. They were walking quickly, hands in their pockets, the one woman with a rifle slung on her shoulder and leading the other two.

"Who the heck are you?" he whispered into the rain, scooting closer to get a better view, slipping, diving to grab a thin tree trunk and keep from plunging downward. Matt watched as the three walked to the garage's rear door, stepped inside, and shut it behind them. With a slow head shake, water dripping off his hood and into his face, Matt hauled himself up and climbed a few more feet. Plopping on the wet ground, he put his feet against a couple of tree trunks to stay balanced and picked his radio off his belt.

CHAPTER EIGHTEEN

"HQ, this is Matt. We've got a problem out at the Goodhew place. Over."

"What's the problem?"

"You told me there wasn't supposed to be anyone out here, but I just saw three people go inside the house, and one has a rifle."

"Some relatives of Darla?"

"No clue. What you want me to do?"

READ THE NEXT BOOK IN THE SERIES

Edge of Extinction Book 4

Available Here

books.to/thcoy

Printed in Great Britain
by Amazon